EUDAIMONIA

Meghan Godwin

Published by Inkshares, Inc., Oakland, California
www.inkshares.com

Edited by Avalon Radys & Ryan Jenkins
Cover design by Tim Barber
Interior design by Kevin G. Summers

ISBN 9781950301478
e-ISBN 9781950301485
LCCN: 2022944336

First edition

Printed in the United States of America

To my sister, Heather,
who showed me what it was to be a force of nature

To Jonathan, forever a champion of dreamers

To my future- Eden, Morgan, Avery & Logan

Unfortunately, the evolutionary perspective is an incomplete measure of success. It judges everything by the criteria of survival and reproduction, with no regard for individual suffering and happiness.

—Yuval Noah Harari, *Sapiens*

This is how it makes the use of free will less useful and rarer every day; how it encloses the action of the will within a smaller space and little by little steals from each citizen even the use of himself. . .

After having thus taken each individual one by one into its powerful hands, and having molded him as it pleases, the sovereign power extends its arms over the entire society; it covers the surface of society with a network of small, complicated, minute, and uniform rules, which the most original minds and the most vigorous souls cannot break through to go beyond the crowd; it does not break wills, but it softens them, bends them and directs them; it rarely forces action, but it constantly opposes your acting; it does not destroy, it prevents birth; it does not tyrannize, it hinders, it represses, it enervates, it extinguishes, it stupefies, and finally it reduces each nation to being nothing more than a flock of timid and industrious animals, of which the government is the shepherd.

—Alexis de Tocqueville, *Democracy in America*

1

Bette's eyes opened before the lights scheduled to simulate dawn began to fade on. She often woke before she was supposed to, and always when a man spent the night. Partners were not required to spend the night, which was stated in the Mandate. Overnights were a matter of preference, a choice she could make. She lay still, blinking at grayness, petite fibrous hands folded across her concave stomach. Each time she exhaled, the corner of her rib cage slid under her thumbs.

By design, efficiencies were made for one person to exist comfortably; however, cohabitation was a direct violation of the Mandate. The honeycomb that was her apartment building was just big enough to live a half-life. So, when another human displaced her atmosphere, Bette felt the press of all three hundred and ninety-eight square feet like a too-tight jacket. His breathing, the heat that radiated off him, the random shifting in his sleep . . . these things only exaggerated the tight quarters.

Most nights she preferred to sleep alone but these were not days of preference.

We are beyond the luxury of time and preference.

These were the days of the National Fertility Agenda. These were the days of the Department of Propagation, the DOP. These were the days of the Mandate. Days of fertility monitoring and sex compliance. Days of crushing expectations and obligation. Days of struggle, duty, and sacrifice. These were the days they all hoped would not be called "the end days."

JULY 2060 | NEWS RELEASE | GENEVA

WHO Highlights Worldwide Decline in Fertility

The findings of an exhaustive multinational study were released today by WHO and leading nongovernmental organizations on infertility. "If this epidemic is not reversed in the very near future, the extinction of the human species is imminent."

2

2100

Her mother, ever stoic, said nothing as they checked into the school. She said nothing as they sat in the classroom. A stillness hung heavy between Bette and her mother, the way it always had. Her mother kept her eyes straight forward, veined hands interlaced in her lap, breathing even. They could have been anywhere, the way her mother was behaving: in line at the Department of Agriculture, rocking gently on the train, seated around the island in their kitchen. No matter where they were, her mother was distant and aware all at the same time. It bothered Bette today. Today, Bette craved a reassuring pat on the shoulder or some eye contact. Today was *the* day. This was the day that would decide Bette's future. All the testing over the last few years would culminate today in a status. Her status would set the trajectory for the rest of her life. All she wanted was for her mother to acknowledge it, to make some sort of comment about the importance of this day. Maybe tell her it was going to be all right. Maybe not act as if Bette had already let her down.

The status of fertile was ideal. Bette would be able to procreate. She would have the ability to bring life into the world.

She would be able to do something, contribute to a cause bigger than herself. She could join other fertile women in the birthing centers across America to participate in the highest civic duty, perpetuating the species.

Bette was optimistic because both her grandma and mother had been fertile. Granted, both had only one child late in life, but both had been able to procreate. And, unlike nearly every woman today, both also had regular menstrual cycles up to a certain age. There was some genetic glimmer for Bette. She had inherited other things from her mother, such as her flimsy dark brown hair and a bump on the bridge of her nose. Maybe this time she would luck out and get something useful.

What made her stomach flip and drop was the *other* status, inconclusive. This status meant there were no obvious fertility indicators. Since there were no longer any cycles to monitor, the Department of Propagation cast a wide net. Inconclusive citizens were required to have sex for a specified amount of time with a specified number of partners over a three-month period. Every three months they would be tested at a propagation office. This continued until either they showed signs of fertility or aged out. The Mandate was optional beginning at age forty.

Please, please let me be fertile.

Lots of people were inconclusive. Lots of people were doing their part, in their mandated way, for America. But everyone knew the real dent was being made in the birthing centers. Everyone knew that if they weren't fertile, they were a drain on resources. Self-euthanasia was the leading cause of death among inconclusive women ages seventeen to twenty-two. The average American woman's life expectancy hovered around age twenty-four. To Bette, being inconclusive was as good as being dead.

Please, just let the tests say I am fertile . . .

Bette's light breakfast of insect-based protein powder and water sloshed in her anxious stomach, which made disturbing noises as digestion tried to do its job. Her tender hands were clasped so tight in her lap, her knuckles ached. She sat still, just like her mother, her cautious brown eyes wide and attentive. Just when Bette thought she may come out of her own skin, her teacher entered the room.

"Good afternoon, Ms. Donovan," the woman greeted Bette's mother. "It's good to see you, too, Bette," she said, nodding and smiling at her student. "Thank you for coming in." She sat down at the faux-grained laminate table across from Bette and her mother, propping up a film. After making a few fast motions on the film with her finger, she cleared her throat and the results conference began.

"As you know, we are required by the Department of Propagation to test and track certain hormone levels in adolescent girls to comply with the research efforts of the World Health Organization and the Department of Propagation," Bette's teacher began, speaking as though she had memorized this part of the results conference script.

She shifted in her chair and tapped her film. Her demeanor grew clipped and resolute. Bette glanced up and noticed the young woman had a patch of flaky eczema on the left side of her forehead, just near the hairline. She stared at her teacher intently, wondering for the first time how old she really was.

How long has she been participating in the Mandate?

The only reason a woman needed to work was if she was inconclusive.

"As you also know, infertility is a tricky thing to be completely definitive about. Much research is underway regarding this issue affecting a portion of our population. On behalf of the Department of Propagation, I would like to thank you very much for the information you have provided over the last four years."

Bette's mother adjusted and stiffened in her chair, her face stonelike and emotionless. Her weary, pale-blue eyes stared at the teacher. Bette knew by her mother's body position to be cautious. Bette had disappointed her enough to know she only stiffened like this when she was about to get bad news. An uneasy sensation washed over Bette. Even her teacher seemed to be avoiding eye contact and speaking faster than normal. Bette looked from her teacher to her mother, and then back to her teacher. The teacher cleared her throat, progressing through a series of charts and statistics. A chart appeared with her name at the top: *Donovan, Bette: DOB: 6/3/2083: Age: 17.*

"We have monitored Bette for four years," she said, tapping her device, keeping her gaze on the screen. "As you can see here," she said, pointing to a cluster of numbers, "her case is, uh, inconclusive. She has shown no signs of fertility . . . "

There.

That was the hit they'd steeled themselves for, the result her mother was anxious about. That cluster of numbers was what had caused her teacher to tap-dance for the past few minutes. "Inconclusive" punched Bette in the gut, causing all the air to rush out of her. She brought her hand to her mouth as if to keep it in, so she wouldn't suffocate and fall dead on the floor of her teacher's office.

Inconclusive.

Bette's stomach pitched frantically. The light felt unusually harsh. She blinked slowly, turning her gaze to her thighs. Desperately, she began to claw the recesses of her now slowly moving brain for any shred of evidence to prove her teacher wrong. This was a mistake. It had to be. How could she refute it? How could she show them? Her face hot and her mind cloudy, she slogged through quicksand to form a thought. All she could hear was the blood pounding in her head and the strangled gulps she was making to stave off the inclination to puke.

Inconclusive.

That big, ugly word had sucked all the oxygen and noise from the room. Its syllables bounced off every surface edge, churning and swirling around them like a noxious fog. *How were they still talking?* Bette sagged back in the unforgiving plastic chair. Inconclusive? No, surely that couldn't be right. There must be an explanation. She must have showed them someone else's results. This can't be happening.

I can't be . . .

The implication of the word was enormous and beyond her comprehension. Panic fluttered inside her, like a moth caught in a jar, erratically hitting the sides while trying to find the escape before the lid was sealed. This word would chart the remainder of her education, control where she lived, and even determine her resource allotments. Her life had been decided, right here, with that one word. *And it was going to be a hard, bad life . . .* She knew these inconclusive women; they listed aimlessly in her building, moved sluggishly in line at the Department of Agriculture, and rocked lifelessly on the train. Then, every so often, they would just disappear. She would just stop seeing their drowsy, vacant, lifeless faces altogether.

Bette shook herself slightly, struggling to keep what that word actually meant from forming in her mind, fearful that if she didn't, there would be no way back. If she fought it, maybe there was still a chance that it wasn't her future. All the while, her teacher insisted on repeating *that* word. Now that it was loosed from its dungeon, it wanted to noisily flap all about and be seen. Bette couldn't make out any other word, as if her teacher had switched into a code language. The part of her that could communicate, listen, and process thought was paralyzed, replaced by a low-grade buzz that seemed to drown everything out but *that* word. Bette was cornered by it, and she couldn't escape it or what it said about her. Her teacher kept nodding in Bette's direction, and each time, "inconclusive" would puncture the stasis cocoon that encased Bette. It would jab and poke and stab her. Every utterance was like a heavy gauge needle being shoved in, removed, and shoved in again to a fresh spot. Over and over, the pointed word made its assault.

Inconclusive.

Bette's mother nodded like she was receiving instructions about a prescription. Bette needed for her mother to look at her and tell her that her teacher was mistaken. She needed her to explain what was really going on and to reassure her in some small way that her life wasn't over. However, her mother refused to make eye contact. Desperation tingling inside of her, Bette turned her head away from them and began to feel tears well up. The desperation gave way to a flinty repressed anger. Bette balled her hands up tightly, blinked away the urge to cry, and stared at the floor, her mind gusting with gale-force winds. She squeezed her eyes shut and gritted her teeth until it became evident she could not quell the tears. No matter what, she could not cry in front of them. She would not disappoint her mother any further by being hysterical. She could not bear that look, bordering on revulsion, that her mother would give her if she didn't keep her composure. Bette bit down hard on the inside of her cheek, and she stomped down the storm that raged inside of her. She tasted blood as she tried to breathe evenly through her nose.

"She will need to continue after school with a hormone therapy regimen," her teacher continued.

"What will we need to do next?" her mother asked.

"Bette's results will be sent to the Department of Propagation today. A caseworker will contact you within the next thirty to sixty days to discuss the regimen."

Bette's mother nodded slightly, acknowledging that she understood.

Bette wasn't fertile. She was a waste of resources, a drain on society.

The teacher stood, as did her mother. Bette remained seated, not able to make out what they were saying in the muffled haze of destruction. Her head was swimming, and the floor wobbled when she blinked. She was vaguely aware of the two women standing in her presence. *Should she stand?* Bette wasn't sure she could if she'd wanted to. Her whole body felt like quivering jelly, threatening to ooze onto the floor were it not for the chair.

"Bette, someone is speaking to you," her mother said, her taut voice cutting through Bette's emotional spinout.

Bette looked up into her mother's hard eyes and swallowed hard. *Why did she have to be like this? Why was she always so . . . cold?*

"What?" Bette croaked.

"I wish you luck," the teacher said slowly, as if repeating herself.

Luck? Bette grappled for words. *I don't need luck; I need you to change this status on your little film you have right there in your hand . . .*

"Bette!" her mother prompted.

"Thank you very much," Bette whispered from muscle memory.

The teacher exited the room. Her mother turned to her, riled.

"Are we rude to people now?" her mother asked, obviously annoyed.

"No, Mom, I'm sorry—" Bette began to apologize.

"People get bad news all the time," her mother said, cutting her off, "but that doesn't give you the right to be rude, especially to an agent of the Department!"

Bette looked at the floor, ashamed at her lapse in poise. "I know."

"I taught you manners so you would do the right thing no matter how you felt. Everyone has feelings! Having feelings does not mean you are above manners. Do you understand me? If everyone was ruled by their feelings, it would be chaos."

"Yes, ma'am."

"Now, let's go. And please, don't sob on public transit. You will drench your mouth cover and I didn't bring an extra. You know how that affects your asthma."

Bette had taken human sexuality every year for four years. She could label any diagram of the vagina, probably while blind-folded. She knew, in an academic sense, how the procreation process was supposed to work. What couldn't be explained was why so many people, worldwide, could not procreate. It was the question everyone had been asking since 2060.

When they got home, Bette's grandma was standing by the island in the kitchen. Bette was dreading having the status conversation again with her gram. Bette's mother set her bag on the island opposite her own mother, removed her mouth cover, and methodically took off her coat.

"Well?" Bette's grandma asked impatiently.

"Well, what do you think?" her mother spat. "Inconclusive."

Bette moved listlessly into the living room, stopping at the couch.

"Well, that's not so bad, is it?" Bette's grandma said. "The way you two came in, carrying on, it's like you just found out she didn't have a damn uterus!"

"Mother," Bette's mom started.

"Oh, don't you start, Kit," Bette's grandma said with a note of warning.

"Start? Jesus, mother! She is inconclusive! There is nothing else to say!" Bette's mom shouted.

"No. Inconclusive is exactly that. Inconclusive. It can't be decided based on the current facts."

Bette's grandma moved into the living room and sat next to her shell-shocked granddaughter. She reached over and familiarly tucked a section of Bette's fine hair behind her right ear.

"Button, all this means is they can't see everything you're made of yet. You are only seventeen, for heaven's sake. Just take your time and show them when you are good and ready." She gave Bette's arm a little shake.

Bette looked at her and embarrassingly wiped away a tear.

"Come on, give me a smile. I, for one, have a good idea of what you are made of," her grandma said as she leaned in.

Bette did not feel like smiling. Her grandma playfully pinched her on the back of her left arm.

"Come on! I said give me a smile, button!"

Bette gave her a weak smile.

"For the love of God," Bette's mom sighed from the kitchen. "It's over, Mom."

"Don't listen to her," Bette's grandma whispered. "This status isn't who you are, it isn't your identity. Fertile? Inconclusive? *Pashaw!* So that is how they have decided to divide us now. It won't always be like this. Trust me."

As was the way after most catastrophes, Bette continued to live. She felt timid at first, then gained momentum with each passing season. If you string enough of those days together, it could be considered a life.

4:35 a.m. EST
Reports of a massive earthquake on the West Coast. Unable to confirm with affiliates in California, Oregon, or Washington. The reports coming out of Utah are still unfolding. Waiting on verification before posting.

8:09 a.m.
This morning at approximately 1:15 a.m. PST, a 10.1 earthquake ripped through the West Coast of the United States, causing most of California and large portions of Oregon and Washington to shear off into the Pacific Ocean. It is assumed Hawaii is under water, though no contact has been established at this time. Warnings are in effect as Asia and Australia brace for the ensuing tsunami. The anticipated losses can only be described as catastrophic.

2:16 p.m.
Reports are coming in that the tsunami washed away all major cities in the coastal regions of Australia and Mainland China. It is assumed that islands in the South Pacific have been submerged and destroyed. Japan remains uncommunicative; our worst guess is that it, too, is gone . . .

3

Cabe's lean, scarred back was to her as he sat on the edge of the bed putting on his socks. Bette sat up, pulling the cheap sheet to cover her bare chest. She fit it snugly under her thin arm to hold it in place. With her other hand, she began lightly tracing the outlines of the scars marring Cabe's otherwise blemish-free body. What unbridled rage had caused these scars? What insentient machine hadn't stopped in time? The scars were irregular in shape, as if pieces of him had been torn away haphazardly. She guessed they had healed quite a while ago; they felt lumpy yet smooth and glossy.

She had only asked him once, in the beginning, what had happened. Cabe's usually composed demeanor darkened only slightly. "I'd rather not," was all he had said. *I'd rather not.* It was a dispassionate answer given the number of scars and their scattered pattern. Obviously, something traumatic had happened. *I'd rather not.* He'd said nothing, but that was everything. They were not the normal scars that came from years of eczema, contact dermatitis, or melanoma; she'd seen enough of those to be sure. Her finger paused at the top of a crater near a protruding vertebra. His back abruptly fell away from her touch as he leaned down to buckle his boots.

"Chemical?" Bette asked, not expecting an answer. He never gave her any answers. Her finger, reconnecting, slid down his backbone and lingered around the next savage pockmark.

"Mechanical?"

Cabe straightened, pulled on his shirt, and again disrupted her tracing. She withdrew her hand and propped up the other side of the sheet that had inched down. He stood from the edge of the bed and ran his hand through his black, wavy hair. It contracted and bounced back the way only clean, buoyant hair can.

"Biological?"

Her eyes locked with his brown-velvet eyes, which were unreadable as they flicked over her.

"Maybe . . . " Bette said, with her eyebrow raised and daring him to answer, "Canner?"

A half smile formed on his lips.

"Maybe," he countered, "it is just malnutrition. Sometimes, the right answer is the most obvious."

"Malnutrition," she scoffed. "In a Sub?"

"Scandals abound, Bette." His smile broadened, taking up the bottom half of his face. He had all his teeth and they were relatively straight. Another sign that those scars were not related to malnutrition.

She shook her head, "No, I don't think so."

"Well"—he shrugged—"you don't know everything."

He squatted, picked up his jacket from the floor, and wriggled into it.

"So, I guess you are going," Bette said. She tried to sound as if she didn't care, but she knew she wasn't convincing.

"I guess I am." His mouth cover hung from his neck and brushed against the side of Bette's face as he leaned in. He then kissed her on the crown of her head. Her eyes widened. It seemed like a familiar and intimate gesture, something he had never done until just now. While she minded him less than most of the men invited to her apartment, "affectionate" was not a word she would ever use to describe Cabe. But this action appeared to be affection. It wasn't lust or longing or passion, all of which ignited quickly and fizzled out. No, this seemed to come from a buildup of encounters, some shared history, however brief. This was friendly.

Her shrewd eyes contemplated the odd, beautiful man standing in front of her. That was really the only way to describe him. Compared to the flaky, ashen men in the complex, he was radiant. Men from the Subs were like that, shiny and waxy. They were also boorish and cavalier, burning through women in the prescribed manner, treating them as glitzy, luxurious things, always about to be repossessed by the one who owned them. Cabe should have burned through her weeks ago; he should have moved on without giving her a second thought. But there he was, familiarly kissing the top of her head, beckoning attainability she would never know. Cabe was a liar—they all were—and Bette knew that. *Why* he lied, though, didn't make any sense.

They made for a strange transaction. That was what sex was. It was simply another commodity that was bought, sold, bartered, and inflated. A means to an end. At best, sex was transactional; at worst, sex was a messy emotional ordeal punctuated by some kind of violence. Originally, sex was the transaction between the two of them. But when the mandated activity was finished and the mandated time expired, he stayed. So, there they were, still involved in some kind of transaction, but it had ceased to have anything to do with the Mandate. They'd had sex, but it was no longer about sex. For Bette, these were uncharted waters. *Why did this man choose to stick around?*

The easiest answer was symbiosis, a relationship that worked off the natural give-and-take of each organism. They needed a safe place, for whatever reason, and it happened to be each other. Bette did not know what Cabe needed from her, and she doubted he would ever tell her. In him, she had found a place to catch her breath. He required nearly nothing of her, and his orbital presence gave her the legitimacy of compliance. Literal compliance would come later; she could buy that and fill in names and numbers. At least the constant pressure of having to find an interested partner had slackened. If questioned, he was a body to which her neighbors could testify.

The comfort of being complicit in the lie was that it didn't feel like a lie. Her lie was that she wasn't following the spirit of the Mandate. Cabe's lie was that he was just like every other fertile, elitist prick drafted into Mandate participation. So, if he continued to not act like every other fertile male, soldiered and martyred for the cause, maybe she didn't have to act like every other infertile female under the Mandate. If this was the lie he wanted, then it was a lie she could go along with.

Bette felt a draft and shivered as the ventilation system kicked on. She pulled her knees to her chest, wrapped her arms around them, and began rubbing her bare arms. She looked over the edge of the bed for her clothes.

"I'll probably see you next week. I've got a lot going on to keep me in the Sub this week, so I won't be taking the train through town." Cabe put his finger to his lips, smiled, and half whispered, "I left you an orange and a couple of lemons on the counter."

More familiarity, more affection. No normal Subbite would break the rules and smuggle out citrus. *Maybe* he would do it for a cosmopolitan, influential woman in the city, but not for an inconclusive woman in an apartment complex.

"When you say Sub, do you actually mean a Sub, or do you go other places?" Bette asked as she reached for her long-sleeved shirt. She pushed her head through the neck of her shirt, flyaway strands of her brown hair lifting ever so slightly from static.

"Of course." Cabe shrugged. He leaned into the doorframe fidgeting with his face mask, looking like a bored surgeon. The toe of his shoe scuffed the floor softly as he stood there. "That is not an answer."

"Does it really even matter?" he asked.

His restlessness was tangible. Cabe shoved the gray polyester mouth cover up under his eyes. He seemed hungry for something, but it wasn't her. He moved in a way atypical of the people she was used to, urgent and with a purpose. She was curious about what drove him. Was it being fertile that made him that way? She felt like it was more than just being fertile, but he would never tell her. She only hoped she could figure it out before something compelled him to move on.

"I'll see you later," he said, his voice somewhat muffled behind his face mask.

He was always in a hurry because he was important. He was fertile. Bette barely remembered a time when she had moved like that, but it was definitely before her status sealed her future. A hot zinger singed the edges of her feelings. Even after all these years, the term "inconclusive" still smarted.

Cabe had never called her that. He hadn't spoken down to her, mistreated her, or acted like he was doing her a favor.

They all think it, though.

Being inconclusive was the murky undercurrent that directed all her interactions. She tried, but the rules laid out in the Department of Propagation's National Fertility Agenda felt impossible to maintain these days. When she was younger, it was easier. There was hope; there were stories of inconclusive women in their twenties who managed a status change.

In her early twenties, she was still young enough for plenty of men to believe she, too, could get pregnant. Having just turned twenty-nine, she noticed more and more convincing was involved.

Her stomach constricted as she thought about how much time she'd lost. The older a woman got, the less likely she was to get pregnant; she knew this. She just kept reminding herself, however, that her mother had been classed inconclusive once and had gotten pregnant at thirty. That was something; and Cabe was fertile, which was also something. Maybe, just this once, if she disobeyed the Mandate and only focused on one partner, it would happen for her. Maybe.

Amid the "We aren't livestock" and "No one has the right to choose extinction" signs outside the White House today, President Alvarez signed a bill creating the controversial Department of Propagation. It narrowly passed both the House and Senate. "It had to be done," said North Carolina Governor Kim Wells, who attended the signing. "It is a public health crisis wrapped in an economic Armageddon, and for that, bold action is needed."

Opponents of the new department believe the bill is "government overreach at its most egregious." The Department of Propagation was created specifically to handle fertility in what WHO is characterizing as a "worldwide crisis."

"This is a time of testing not only for America, but the entire world," President Alvarez said in a press conference. "I assure you that the Department of Propagation is up to the task. I am confident that they will work hard to ensure America's future."

4

Bette sighed as she walked from behind the canvas divider between her sleeping area and the rest of the room. She crossed the main living area and entered the bathroom, near the apartment entrance. She stared at the shower unit. Without thinking, she reached up and scratched her neck.

Waterless shower units were the way of life, whether she liked them or not. Coincidentally, with the institution of waterless processes came the rise in dermatitis. The Department of Health maintained, as it had for years, that these units were perfectly safe. Any number or combination of environmental factors could be to blame for the blight of skin conditions. The worst patch for Bette was on her neck, the discomfort of which was only exacerbated by the shower unit. Using it meant that for the next two days, she would scratch it until it was raw.

You are really lucky that it isn't on your face. Bette could almost hear her mother's voice. Bette took off her pajamas and left them in a pile in front of the mirror. She pulled open the door of the cleaning closet adjacent to the shower unit. To avoid getting a face full of residual chemicals, she held her breath and shook out the worn pants and shirt before putting them on.

Standing in front of the full-length mirror, Bette wound her skinny hair into a small bun, low at the base of her skull. She tried to smooth down the short new growth around her hairline. From time to time, she lost hair. Malnutrition was a petty bitch. It was hard enough to get a fertile man's attention, but then she had to work around the hurdles of what nutritional deficiencies took from her. She sighed through her nose as she tried to tame the baby hairs that refused to lie down.

Like anyone meant to have bangs this short.

She secured the bun with a few pins, making sure to loosen enough hair to cover the tops of her ears. *A little bit of hair will save those ears.* Her mom's reminders still rang clear. Bette dabbed generous amounts of sunscreen on her face, neck, and shoulders, taking care to blend it in well.

Cutting out melanoma was easy enough, as evidenced by the small shallow divots on her forehead and left cheek. Bette could have had the *imperfections* fixed; the Department would have paid for it. But all cosmetic surgery was done in the city, and Bette avoided the city as she would a quarantined apartment. What she couldn't blame on malnutrition or melanoma was this *nose*. The prominent hump looked as if someone had pinched the pliable flesh while she was still forming and then forgot to come back and smooth it out.

She stepped out of the bathroom and pulled on her boots, clasping them at the shin. She reached for her scarf and mouth cover on a hook by the door. In the kitchenette, on the island, she saw the orange and two lemons Cabe had left for her. She ran her hand over their plump waxen skins. The citrus rinds reminded her of the vibrant elasticity of Cabe's skin, which was the exact opposite of her dry, ridged fingernails.

Don't want to leave those lying around. She put them in a drawer on the island and took out her sunglasses.

She turned to check the grow lights over her baby lettuces, tapping the wonky hydration panel. She had bought the refurbished unit a couple of years ago, so some days the display worked.

As was her routine when preparing to leave her apartment, Bette picked up her bag from the kitchen island and slung it over her shoulder. She rummaged in it until she found her gloves. Patting her chest and side pockets, she confirmed she had her inhaler and an inner-ear device, ID. She positioned the ID in her right ear and tapped. It once to turn it on. She put on her glasses and waited a moment for the ID to sync with her glasses. It was a cobbled-together yesteryear technology, for sure, but it was the one she could afford. She tapped the ID again to clear the notifications waiting for her since she'd turned it off. She waved her hand to open the door and proceeded out.

Police found the bodies of forty-seven people early Friday morning. All the victims had ingested lethal doses of poison. A manifesto, formatted nearly verbatim from the style guide of a predominant area suicide cult, leads investigators to believe this was a consensual mass suicide. The requisite documents were filled out in advance of the event, so authorities will dispose of the deceased in their desired manner.

There has been an proliferation of suicide cults after recent catastrophic events worldwide.

5

There was always the smell. It permeated everything and seemed to be everywhere all the time. The smell wafted through the recycled air of her too-small apartment and hung like a fog in the dingy hallways. Bette could feel it settle on her skin the moment she left her apartment, becoming heavier and more palpable as the day progressed. She could taste it at the back of her throat as it mixed with every breath. She could not escape it. That moldy, rotting, lurking stench of decay.

Death came and went with militant regularity, especially in the apartment complexes. It was so common that when a body faded off thermal surveillance, the property manager received an alert. The limp, expired body would be pulled from the apartment and left at the end of the hall by the trash chute until the Sanitation Collectors came to pick it up.

Death was a reliable and dependable transaction. Someone was always dying. Whether they knew it or not, Decay did. Decay was that dank corroding assault on all living things; it relished everything that led up to death and everything it left behind. It was always hanging around, tormenting its victims, all the while taking great delight in the process of deterioration.

The smell could overwhelm Bette. Then, almost as if it knew, it would relent just enough to keep her conscious. Decay was not done with her yet; it was not ready to release a hostage that still had something it could take. She knew Death would one day take her, but only after Decay had riddled her useless.

Without thinking, she held her breath through the stale air of the tight, dim hall. Head down, she noticed a wet streak on the cement floor. She grimaced, disgusted.

Ugh, the liquid they secreted.

The Collectors would drag the bodies down the hall and, as if there had been a hole in a trash bag, some would leave a trail of fluid. Bette could almost see Decay over the swollen purplish corpse, feasting slowly, grinning greedily with juices running down the side of its mouth.

Billionaire Brad Sokol has just completed the construction of his flagship "Suburban Bubble," a self-contained, application-only community domed with proprietary glass. Applications to get into the community were numerous and fierce. The board of directors whittled the list to two hundred and fifty residents who are set to move in at the end of the month. Membership was granted on a variety of factors ranging from resources, education, trade skill, fertility, and psychiatric profiles.

"We are really just doing our part to be prepared in the event of another disaster," Sokol said.

Many have remarked that this is the most luxurious of the suicide cults. Sokol denies such comments, remaining adamant about his optimism toward the future. "This is the future of community, not a half-cracked death cult wallowing in despair. The goal is to thrive, not end our lives."

6

"Who was that I saw leaving this morning?"

Bette had just stepped out of the building when she was met with playful chiding. A tall man bundled up from head to toe crunched over the gravel of the yard. People needed to wear so many layers of clothing, it was hard to tell who someone was just by looking at them. But Bette knew by his height and cadence exactly who this was. She paused under the roof's overhang at the apartment's entrance.

"Why were you out so early?" Bette shot back.

Bette took off her sunglasses. There was a little beep in her ear, an alert letting her know the glasses had been disconnected.

"I mean, I could be mistaken, but he looked familiar to me," he said, ignoring her spur and removing his sunglasses. His umber eyes glinted at being able to give her a hard time. His face mask hid his mouth, but Bette could tell he was smiling by the wrinkles around his eyes.

David, her neighbor the entire time she'd lived in the complex, leaned his left side on to the wall. He looked down at her— easy to do at six feet tall—and made a *tsk-tsk* sound.

"It was no one, David."

"Bullshit," David coughed into his gloved fist.

Bette began to pick imaginary lint off the front of her jacket.

"Jesus, Bette!" David sighed loudly. "Why are you still seeing that guy?"

Bette looked around, out of habit, to make sure no one else was around.

"Hey now, keep your voice down!" she hissed at him.

"Please tell me that there is at least someone else," he responded in a whisper yell.

When Bette didn't answer, David's shoulders fell.

"Why, Bette? Why?"

"You *know* why."

David rolled his eyes. "This 'I'm almost thirty' thing again?"

Bette clenched, crossing her arms, and glared at the ground. "I've got to get to work, David. So, if we are going to have this conversation again . . . "

"Is he worth relocation?" David asked.

Bette chewed on the inside of her cheek.

"Bette, you are a smart girl, but this Cabe thing worries me. Any guy who disregards the Mandate the way he does is bad news," David said, concern growing with each word.

"I thought being fertile meant you could bend the rules a little," she said as she shrugged her shoulders, looking up at him.

"Yeah, but if Propagation ever dug into his partner records . . . Christ, Bette, you'd be screwed. He can take those risks, you can't."

"No one checks those records anyway. Half of them are fake. I think it will be okay," Bette tried to reassure her friend. David's eyes were skeptical, but he backed off like always.

"Yeah, fine, whatever. But it is weird. He is weird. Everyone knows what the Mandate says. A couple of days or possibly a week, maybe. Bette, it has been months. He knows better. You know better. I wish you would move on already." David looked down and adjusted his olive-colored jacket as he said, "Or at least see someone else from time to time. I don't want you to get in trouble."

Bette laughed a little. "Trouble? Coming from you?"

David feigned offense. "I will be the first to admit my moral compass is busted. So, it should mean something when *I* say this guy is trouble."

"I will take that into consideration." Bette tipped her head in deference.

"No, you won't." He turned his head away in a fake pout. The light above the building entrance glinted off the gray hair poking out from under his hat. "I just keep thinking about Roc and Julie. I don't want anything like that to happen to you."

Bette's stomach dropped. "It won't. *This* is nothing like that. I promise."

Biologically, Roc was female, but his identity mattered little to The Department of Propagation. The only reason Bette knew this was because she'd run into Roc at the propagation office during a quarterly exam. Roc's girlfriend, Julie, had been relocated after the Department found out about their long-term relationship. Roc should have known better; he never should have let Julie move in.

Shortly after Julie's relocation, Roc got word that she had killed herself. Not in a suicide house, the way civilized people did, but a desperate, ugly home job where she bled out on the floor of her bathroom.

Bette remembered Roc's eyes after Julie was taken, brimmed over with a hungry determination to see her again. She also remembered how the light drained from his eyes while his crushed soul disintegrated in the weeks after Julie's death. These days, he wandered the complex a specter, undead, with no ability to control where his footsteps led.

"Well, as long as you promise." David's sarcasm belied the casual shrug of his shoulders.

"I'll see you later," Bette said with a shake of her head.

DECEMBER, 20 2062 | UNITED STATES
EXECUTIVE OFFICE OF PRESIDENT ALVAREZ

Executive Order: Mandating Compliance with the National Fertility Agenda

The National Fertility Agenda put forth by the Department of Propagation establishes the guidelines all citizens should use for ideal conditions for procreation. Citizens classed fertile and female will report to their assigned birthing centers. Citizens classed fertile and male will follow the procedures set forth in the Agenda. Citizens classed inconclusive will follow the guidelines and procedures set forth in the Agenda. Effective immediately, monitoring of inconclusive procreation activity will be done on a quarterly basis by the Department of Propagation. Any citizen found not in compliance will be fined and/or relocated if necessary.

7

Bette took the few steps down from the apartment entrance, relieved to be away from the press of David's questions. She loved David, but sometimes she just wished he would mind his own business.

Her apartment complex, like most, was scraggly and desolate. Puny, brown, sporadic bushes dotted the scraps of yard, which gave way to cracked and disintegrating walkways. The dozen or so buildings, drab multistoried cement structures, formed a glum semicircle around the Depot House.

She noticed the Collector's camo-green, open-bed truck parked at the base of the Depot House's steps. It was hard not to notice since it was slightly larger than a military tank. From where she stood, dozens of feet away, Bette saw an anemic hand, in full rigor, sticking up over the side of the truck bed. Out of habit, she held in her breath.

The truck must be full today.

Only when multiple corpses were stacked on top of one another could anything ever be seen over the heavy-duty canvas tarps that made up the sides of the truck bed. The heavy-duty plastic revealed just enough to make Bette's skin crawl. A morbid kind of burlesque, she could make out the various bulges shoved against the thick tarp side-guards. There were small bulges on top of medium bulges indicating dead bodies arranged in a haphazard brick-lay pattern. The Collector must have been to a few other complexes before stopping here. There were easily forty bodies already in the truck, and he'd probably pick up another seven here.

That was all inconclusives were anymore: bloated bulges, void of identity, tossed together in a garbage truck awaiting trash pickup day. Like trash, the corpses were sorted and processed into what could be salvaged, reused, and composted. Bette's grandmother had told her more than once that people used to mourn the dead. The idea was as incomprehensible as unrestricted water and true love. People would actually spend months' worth of wages to put one person in the ground? Complete with a service, hugging, and sandwiches? Her grandma had wanted that, a funeral. Bette's mother lied straight to her face and promised her one. When Bette, a little dismayed, asked about it after her grandmother's death, her mom just scoffed. "*That was never going to happen,*" she'd said.

As Bette came closer, she caught sight of a small tear near the bottom of the tarp in between the wheel wells, right where the thick canvas met the metal chassis. Glistening moisture had accumulated around the slit and dripped onto the thirsty soil. The Collector opened and slammed the door of the truck, and Bette looked up from this disturbing by-product of death. The dead hand moved ever so slightly back and forth, almost as if it were waving.

The most macabre of welcome wagons.

The entire complex was surrounded by a tall fence that became electrified near sundown. She quickened toward the Depot House: the common meeting hall located in the middle of the apartment complex. Unlike the apartment buildings, the Depot House was elevated on stilts to protect it from flooding. Depot Houses also served as satellite offices for government services. Department of Agriculture deliveries were dropped off and collected here as well. Residents bought, sold, and bartered goods and services here. A smattering of vendors, like Bette, were set up with stalls.

Bette took shallow sips of air; greenhouse gasses left a state of constant mugginess in the atmosphere, which was hard on the respiratory impaired. Pollutants irritated respiration and spindly vegetation didn't produce enough oxygen. Nearly everyone had some form of asthma. Eroded grit milled under her boots as she walked. Though she tried not to smell it, she could taste the thick slime of death on her tongue. Her neck began to itch. She clamped her teeth to take the edge off her discomfort and hurried along.

APRIL 7, 2062 | S. 1144 DISSOLUTION OF MARRIAGE ACT

The Dissolution of Marriage Act is a bill to officially dissolve the institution of marriage during the infertility epidemic. It incentivizes citizens to participate in the National Fertility Agenda guidelines set forth by the Department of Propagation. Monogamy, during this crisis period, is a barrier to fertility.

8

Bette climbed the composite stairs of the weathered Depot House. Her reflection welcomed her in the dark solar glass door before it slid open. Though impossible to see, the glass panel held a web of circuitry that recognized her ID and allowed her access. Even though most days were overcast, solar glass was powered by the UV rays that found their way to the Earth's surface. Probably the only thing they were good for.

The depleted ozone lost more and more of its protective qualities every year. Good for solar glass technology but not so good for the humans exposed, even just incrementally. The high octane sunscreen only contributed to vitamin D deficiencies, which in turn added to the larger malnutrition issue that plagued the population.

The door closed behind her and she pulled the scarf from her head and the face mask from her mouth. In the main lobby, there was a large screen on the back wall. It contained normal information like the three-day weather forecast and announcements on the next water drop-offs. There were a few places where the pixels were burned out, but Bette could still read the most important item: *LAST CANNER INCIDENT—173 DAYS*.

"Hey, Bette!" Ezra called as he shuffled past, pushing a cart filled with a hodgepodge of broken devices. Bette glanced from the announcement board. A gruff leather-skinned man in his late sixties, ancient this day and age, caught her attention. He was tough, unrelenting, and he ran the property without event. This was *his* Depot House.

"If you got a minute, I got something special for you."

"Yeah? What do you got?" Bette asked, rueful.

The short sinewy man with patchy white hair closed one bloodshot eye and leaned on the handle of his cart, grinning. "Trust me, you won't want to miss this." Two missing teeth on the bottom caused him to hiss his last "s." She had been responsible for pulling one of those teeth.

Bette motioned for him to lead the way. Ezra shuffled ahead of her, his flyaway hair undulating like tiny antennas. She followed him across the open lobby to his office. He fiddled with a large key that hung around his neck.

"What time is your first client?" he asked, twisting the key into a well-oiled lock. He had salvaged the old lock and installed it on his door. Ezra did not trust digital devices. *The fucking lights go out and I can't get anything,* she had heard him rant on more than one occasion. *Fix the grid and I'll think about it!*

"In about an hour. I was going to try and get caught up on some reports."

Pushing the door to the side, he allowed her to go first. "Oh, that will work out just nicely." He pushed the door shut.

It was a five-by-five room, just like the other vendor stalls in the building. A wall of cabinets lined one side, while along the other sat an organized workbench. A black cat with scars on his back gave a chirp and jumped up onto the workbench. He sat next to a lamp clamped to one end of the bench, a pegboard behind it holding various wrenches and tools needed to maintain the property. He observed the two of them sagaciously through its one good eye. Ezra had found Dino outside the complex a few years ago and naturally assumed he'd survived a Canner. Ezra claimed that any bit of fear had been scared right out of him.

She'd been in Ezra's office before and remembered that it normally smelled of lubricant and minty aftershave. Today, Bette recognized the surprise in an instant. This wasn't the smell of metal and repair, or the watered-down, diluted scent of reused tea bags. No, this was the enveloping, robust aroma of something decadent.

She smiled and looked at Ezra in disbelief. "Ezra is that . . . coffee?"

The old man slapped the top of his leg and wheezed out a laugh. "Goddamn is!" he exclaimed, his cracked smile pushing more wrinkles into his withered cheeks. Delight pulsed from him at being able to offer such a gift, and her heart swelled.

"How did you get it?" Bette asked. His fraying shoes scraped past her as he shuffled to his bench.

"Doesn't matter." He waved away her question. "Let's shoot the shit over a nice ol' cup a joe."

He situated himself on a high-backed stool in front of the workbench and nodded to the other stool beside him, grinning. Ezra had two mugs, patinaed by age, sitting on his workbench. Dino hopped down onto the floor and crossed the room, tucking his legs beneath him to comfortably watch them. There was what looked like a tall, skinny teapot with a plunger on the lid. Carefully, he poured the coffee between the mugs. Taking great caution, he handed one to Bette. She received it with equal reverence.

"Ezra, this goes beyond special!"

"Don't it, though?" He winked, pleased with himself.

Bette lifted the mug closer to her face, tendrils of nutty steam wafting up as she regarded the rich brown liquid with the slightest bit of wonder. It didn't matter how Ezra had come across it. He had been around a long time, so someone must have owed him big. Just inhaling caused the tension in her forehead and neck to release. This smell ushered in a fragile peace when she was a child. It was one of the few items her mom and grandmother could agree on. No matter the strain between them, if one of them could manage to bring coffee home, there was the inevitable cease-fire. Moments of civil, indulgent, aromatic peace would linger until the last of the grounds were finally composted. It smelled of everything she'd never be able to have: wood, citrus, and spice, all in one place, one cup, one breath.

Bette brought the edge of the cup to her lips and felt herself smile. The round satiny brew curled over her tongue and down her throat, leaving behind its acidic brightness and warming her insides.

A sacred silence passed as they sipped the piping hot beverage.

"Used to be able to get this stuff all the time," Ezra said as he stared at the door, nostalgic. Then, remembering someone else was in the room, he turned to look at Bette. "You full today?"

Bette held the sip, noticing the ring of tiny bubbles hugging the inside edge of the mug. She took a moment before swallowing. "Mostly, but I think I have a couple of gaps."

Bette cradled the mug in her hands, taking great care not to slosh the precious brew as she shifted in her chair.

"You know Raymond?" Ezra asked, referring to his employee. "He, uh, has been in a lot of pain lately, with this rash on his neck. I told him to go see you, told him it pro'ly wouldn't cost him nothin'. But, well, he hasn't done it yet. You think you could get him in today?"

"Course. Can he come by about eleven?"

"I'll make sure he is there, even if I got to drag him myself," Ezra promised.

Dino yawned, stretched out his paw, and began cleaning between his toes.

"You should really get that cat an eye patch," Bette said.

"Ah, he'd never wear it." Ezra waved his hand. "He ain't ashamed, it's just who he is now."

With your help, we can ensure that adults are protected against one of the most common causes of infertility. Click below to find the nearest STI vaccination center near you. All citizens are to be vaccinated by February 15, 2062. These vaccinations are free to the public, provided by the Department of Propagation . . .

9

Cosmetologists were not much revered before the Big One hit. Afterward, they became a health-care imperative. The trade became a vital stopgap for the explosion of services communities needed, but were not a high priority to the Department of Health. Medical professionals were concentrated in cities to focus on traumatic and pressing needs.

Cosmetologists could examine their clients with more expediency than hospitals. It was easier for citizens to see a stylist located in their apartment complex rather than a hospital. Cosmetologists could treat clients with a variety of ailments within the newly expanded boundaries of their licensure. They could lance boils, prescribe steroids for skin lesions, and pull decaying teeth. Cosmetologists had the authority to treat and quarantine those with communicable conditions like lice and hepatitis A. They served at the front lines, bandaging what they could and referring out what was beyond them: euthanasia, amputation, treating infertility.

Yes, hair was cut. While people still existed on the planet, hair would always need to be cut. It was more function than fashion; waterless processes left hair flat and greasy to the touch. Most of the haircuts Bette performed consisted of combing out large yellow chunks of dandruff and cutting a straight line.

"It's bad, ain't it?"

"Well, Raymond," Bette said, examining the rash, "I mean, it *is* inflamed."

"Ez said you might have somethin' for it."

"Is this the only patch you have like this one?" Bette asked, opening her cabinet and pausing for his answer.

"I got another down under my right arm," Raymond answered.

Bette pulled out six packets the size of her palm. "All right, Raymond. These are supposed to last ten days, but, honestly, they will wimp out at about seven. You know how pharma companies are." She winked at him as she handed him the packets. "You've got six of these, three for each area, ten days each. By law, I can only give you more in thirty days. Now, because you know your tolerance: do you think you can make it thirty days?"

Bette knew Raymond was not a complainer. That he even made it to see her said everything. She could almost hear Ezra's fussing now. *He must have given Raymond a hell of a time.*

Raymond nodded, accepting the packets. He looked at the floor, the muscles in his jaw flexing. She could see his mind try-ing to reconcile the pain to days and could almost hear his teeth clack as he told himself he could make it. He stood to leave, making it three or four steps before Bette called after him.

"Hey, Raymond."

"Yeah?" he replied.

"If, uh, if it gets real bad, you know, before the thirty days, come back. I'll figure something out, okay?"

The corners of Raymond's mouth turned up.

"Then maybe I can do something about that tooth that is giving you trouble."

A proper smile spread across his face. "Yes, ma'am."

Where no cure could be provided, management was relief enough. A lot of the services that Bette performed were covered by the Department of Health, but a few were out-of-pocket costs. Teeth were funny like that. Raymond's decaying molar would cost him something because, presumably, the decay could have been prevented. His contact dermatitis would be fully covered because his job, which benefited the community, involved an array of chemicals. *Hazardous injury/condition due to work-related activities* was what Bette typed into his ticket now.

Bette heard her stall door open. The brittle woman who stood there didn't bother with a greeting or with sitting in one of the three waiting area chairs. She strode past the shelves containing products and brightly colored synthetic wigs and made a beeline for Bette's hydraulic chair before Bette had time to finish up Raymond's transaction notes.

"Hello, Deidra Ann," Bette sighed without looking up from her screen.

"Bette, I am in a bit of a hurry today," Deidra Ann muttered impatiently.

The waif of a woman bristled in the chair in front of the full-length mirror as she began tucking and untucking her unnaturally hued hair. The color was completely Bette's fault. Every time she saw that brassy orange mop, she winced. She performed the service against her better judgment just so Deidra Ann would shut up. Bette had learned the hard way that it was not worth the breath to argue with Deidra Ann.

Bette joined Deidra Ann on the right side of the chair, crossed her right arm in front of her, and simultaneously brought her left hand to her chin. Deidra Ann sat up a little straighter as Bette's inspection began. Bette could see that the skin on her neck was a different shade than her face, a clear sign that the heavy foundation Bette sold her had not been blended well.

"I was reading about this thing the other day on one of those health forums. I'm not sure if you saw the article or not, I can send it to you if you like. It was the one on lip fillers. Did you happen to see that?"

Bette stiffened, pushing out the trained smile she wore when asked something ridiculous.

"No." Bette shook her head. "I don't think I did."

"Well, it said that studies show fertile men are thirty-three percent more likely to choose a partner with fuller lips. That is, like, one out of three, isn't it? Really, Bette, in this line of work, you should keep up with those things. I think your clients would appreciate it," Deidra Ann stated with more than a hint of condescension.

Bette gripped the back of the chair, continuing to smile. "Oh, wow, thirty-three percent, you say?"

"I know, right? That is pretty good if you ask me. So, I need a lip filler."

"Of course, Deidra Ann, I've got a few of those. But it seems like, uh, an aggressive first step. Do you maybe want to start with something a little less *permanent*?"

The little lines around Deidra Ann's thin cracked lips deepened while she considered the suggestion. "What else do you have?" she asked.

Bette backed up toward her cabinet as she spoke. "Well, I have some very reasonably priced plumping balms or a serum that you apply at bedtime . . . "

"No. I want something more immediate."

"Okay, sure. Just so you know, there can be side effects with these fillers. To be on the safe side, I'd like to perform a patch test just to make sure you don't have an adverse reaction . . . "

"I won't have a reaction," came Deidra Ann's curt reply. "I never have reactions. Let's get on with this filler."

Bette kept her mouth shut as she remembered the little red bumps that had broken out all over Deidra Ann's scalp when her hair was colored. She turned toward her cabinet to prepare the injectable. The Mandate required inconclusive women to participate in the National Fertility Agenda until they were forty, so as an incentive, cosmetic enhancements were reimbursed by the Department of Propagation. When (or if) you aged out of the Mandate, cosmetic enhancements became an out-of-pocket expense.

"Now, Deidra Ann, you know that this enhancement is not covered by the Department," Bette said as she laid the syringe on her stainless-steel cart and rolled it over to her impatient client.

"I know that, Bette," Deidra Ann practically spat.

Bette stifled a smile as she pushed the button allowing the chair to recline. She wiped a sterilization pad with a numbing agent over Deidra Ann's lips and waited a moment for it to take effect.

Under the light, at that angle, it was hard for Bette to dislike her. There were certain qualities that reminded her of her mother. Like her mother, Deidra Ann was disagreeable and terse on a good day. Unlike her mother, Deidra Ann was still alive, resentfully clinging on to what, Bette had no idea. After all the pressures of the Mandate and the poking and prodding of the Department of Propagation, she'd endured. Self-euthanasia was the number-one killer of inconclusive women. Women much younger than she had faded out.

For womb and country, I suppose.

"I know I don't have to participate," Deidra Ann continued to huff.

"Okay, you are going to feel slight pressure," Bette warned, as she pushed on the end of the syringe.

"But it's habit, you know?" she mumbled, more to herself than to Bette. "What else am I good for?"

We are beyond the luxury of time and preference.

Police Chief Baffled by the Uptick in Missing Person Reports

In a statement late today, Charlotte Police Chief Howard expressed bewilderment with the recent rise in missing persons. Over the last six weeks, two hundred and fifteen people have gone missing in Charlotte and the surrounding areas. "We are working as hard as we can. If you have any information regarding the victims, please call the law enforcement center. We have set up a dedicated web page and hotline specifically for these cases . . . "

10

2112, PRESENT

Bette was wiping down her station at the end of the day when she heard the door open.

"Hey," she said, looking up.

"Hey, yourself," David exhaled, flopping down in a waiting area chair. "Did you pop any huge zits today?"

Bette threw her towel in the laundry bin. "Surprisingly, no. Not today. But guess who I *did* see."

"Who?"

"Deidra Ann."

David rolled his eyes to the ceiling. "Ugh. What antiquated Internet poultice did she need today? Leeches? Crystals?"

Bette joined him in the adjacent chair. "Worse. A lip filler."

"Shut up. You are not being serious."

"Swear to God. She read about it on a health forum."

"But you tried to talk her out of it, right?"

Bette shrugged. "Tried is probably an overstatement. I used phrases like *side effects* and *patch test*."

David shook his head, blinking. "Christ, I bet there are radioactive fish in toxic waterways that look better than her."

Bette laughed. "Oh, you will see soon enough. She is like a beacon with that orange hair. You just can't look away."

"I mean, honestly"—David shifted in his seat—"someone should be responsible for scrubbing those forums. There are simple people who believe that garbage."

"She was convinced that fertile men are thirty-three percent more likely to choose a partner with fuller lips." Bette tried to keep a straight face as she said it.

David erupted in full belly laughter. He doubled over and put his head between his knees. Sitting back up, he wiped a tear from the corner of his eye, trying to catch his breath. "Oh geez, Bette. That was good. I don't even . . . I mean . . . isn't she, like, fifty? Not only does she not have to participate, she hasn't had to in a decade!" He shook his head, confounded.

Bette felt a tinge of guilt. "I think she is closer to forty-eight. It is kind of impressive seeing as how most women would, you know, self-euthanize by now."

"True." David sobered a moment, then shifted in his seat. "Hey, what are you doing tonight?"

Bette rolled her eyes. "A woman of my age is supposed to be engaged in intercourse, vaginal, three times a week."

"And you didn't get those in this week?" David's brows shot up in mock surprise. "Well, slacker, do you want to help me with an errand?"

Bette shot him a suspicious side glance. "No."

"What if I could guarantee a chicken dinner?"

"Absolutely, no, then."

"Oh, come on, Bette! Let me explain."

"Nope." Bette stood up to retrieve her bag from the stylist chair and headed for the door. David jumped in front of her.

"It's cool. I met this guy in line today at the Ag Department. He said he had access to chickens. All I had to do was get them. I mean, when was the last time you had *chicken*?"

Bette paused to contemplate his offer. "David, it's contraband."

"No! You don't know that!"

Bette motioned for him to move out of the way. He lingered and then moved, sighing.

"Fine, David, it's not contraband. But even if it isn't, I don't want whatever diseased experiment the Ag Department is calling poultry." Bette waved her hand, which caused the door to open. David, now sullen, followed her out into the Depot House. She paused at the solar glass doors and waited for him. The sun had set, or more accurately, began to dim behind the cloud cover. At dusk, the fences turned on. The lights atop the electrified fence began to glow, low at first and brighter as it grew darker.

They took the steps down from the Depot House to the cracked concrete landing. Sidewalks jutted off the patio apron leading to the apartment buildings.

The fence hummed ten to twelve feet to their right. Spiraled razor wire adorned the top of the fence, glinting under the intermittent floodlights. Below, ovals of yellow light illuminated areas of dusty barren earth.

"Can you do me a favor?" Bette asked David. "I need some more of those medium steroid patches."

"Oh, contraband is fine when *you* need something," David quipped.

"It's not for me," Bette said. "It's for Raymond. I think he would wait thirty days if I told him to . . . "

Suddenly, David stopped short. They both heard the sound at the same time. Bette whipped her head in the direction of the crunching. A creature of some size was moving on the other side of the fence.

The hairs on the back of Bette's neck prickled.

"David," she managed to whisper.

"Shhh," he warned.

The movement seemed to emanate from the darkness between two floodlights. As they stood, staring hard into the darkness, the movement ceased. Bette held her breath, paralyzed, straining to hear. Long swaths of silence passed. A breeze picked up, carrying with it the scent of stale ammonia. Then, loud as a firecracker, there was the snap of a stick.

Bette and David flinched. She tried to breathe deeply to calm her beating heart. As she stared, her eyes adjusted to the contrast of the floodlight and the falling night. Along the edge of the spotlight was a tremor. A partial shadow began to slowly form as the black mist swirled out of the haze. As the shadow began to take shape, Bette heard David's quick intake of breath; goose bumps erupted over her arms. It was too tall to be a feral hog, which were known to attack people. They could be big, but not like this.

Tall and lean . . . like a person.

The figure hovered just at the edge of the light. Then it zigged out of the light, sprinting down the length of the fence. Moments after it disappeared, a faraway shriek rang out in the distance.

Bette trembled as she turned to David. Eyes wide, he continued to stare in the direction it had run.

"Is that . . . " Bette struggled to find her words.

"Yeah," David answered, his voice low as he turned toward her. "We should get inside."

Piles of Bones and Human Remains Discovered Outside City Limits

Decomposing human remains were discovered today in two neighboring abandoned homes outside of Charlotte's city center. Piles of bones were found in every room of the two homes. The remains of at least thirty-seven individuals have been confirmed, with the expectation that number will rise. The remains have been collected and sent to forensic specialists for analysis and DNA matching. Officers investigated the homes after a report of a "bad smell" coming from the area.

11

Bette brooded at one of the tables in the Depot House lobby, staring at the announcement board. *LAST CANNER INCIDENT—174 DAYS*. The day had rolled over, putting another day between them and a Canner. How long before those numbers started over?

Even after increasing the security settings on her door, Bette hadn't slept much last night. Behind closed eyes, she kept seeing that silent presence watching David and her. Most people wouldn't have even known it was there. A shiver ran up Bette's spine causing an involuntary jerk. She gripped her thermos of hot, weak tea.

The doors of the Depot House whooshed open. Bette turned to see who it was. Ezra ambled in, pulling off his tattered gray hat and glasses. He paused when he saw her.

"You're here awfully early," he said as he made his way over to where she was seated. "What's wrong?"

Bette looked around to make sure they were still the only ones in the lobby. She nodded for him to sit down. She probed the old man's worn face, still unsure if she should say anything. What if she was wrong? What if there was a perfectly good explanation for what happened last night? Worse still, what if she didn't tell him and something happened?

"Well, spit it out," Ezra huffed.

Bette took a shallow breath and shifted in the chair. "Last night, when David and I were walking home we, um, saw something."

Ezra sat up straighter, the crease deepening between his eyebrows. "I don't suppose it was a feral hog, was it?" he asked skeptically.

Bette shook her head no.

"And you are sure?"

Bette paused, chewing on her bottom lip. Ezra nodded, sighing.

"Well, shit." He glanced at the announcement board. The security protocol for a Canner sighting was full lockdown of the complex until cleared by the Justice Department.

"Ez, I've got to be at my propagation office by ten today." Bette cringed at adding another wrinkle to Ezra's day.

"Yeah, I'll wait to call it in so you can get out. But Bette, the only secure transport I have before noon today is the Collection truck," Ezra said.

Bette made a face at the idea of having to hitch a ride with death.

"Sorry, kid. I can't let you take anything else. Not if what you say is true."

Bette pursed her lips and brought her palm to the irritated skin on her neck as she thought about this. "Thanks, Ez."

He groaned a little as he got up. "Well, I guess I'll get the electricity going in these fences."

There were three reasons no one wanted to be outside: air quality, violent weather, and Canners. The thin air made a walk uncomfortable; the smog and UV made it arduous. Acute and powerful storms popped up all the time, washing people away and knocking out power. Canners would kill you and eat you, and not necessarily in that order. No one who was ever attacked by a Canner lived to tell about it.

The working theory was that they were some type of fringe Repatriate group. These types of attacks normally happened on the outskirts of town. The Repatriates maintained territory outside the most recently redrawn territory lines. Some said it was a political statement driven by revenge after the Water Wars and Citrus Deal of the late fifties. Others insisted it was some type of cult, lots of which had popped up over the last twenty-five years. The end pushes people to crazy things.

Bette sipped her tea as the Depot House began to wake up. Vendors staggered in, opened their doors, and chatted politely. As far as they knew, there was no reason to worry. Once Ezra called in the sighting, that would all change.

Justice Department trucks would post up outside the fence and take command of the Depot House as their temporary headquarters. Helicopters and drones would make numerous passes overhead during the next five to six days. Giant search-lights would be brought in and set up around the fences, shining all night out into the forsaken scrub. Getting in and out would be at the discretion of whoever was in charge. It would be easier for Bette to beg to get back in than to ask for permission to get out.

The Collector entered the Depot House and headed for Ezra's office. Bette knew his occupation by his dark denim jumpsuit and elbow-length black plastic work gloves. He stood in Ezra's doorway, looking over once and making eye contact with Bette. When he was finished with Ez, he approached her.

"You the one who needs the ride?"

"I am," Bette replied.

"Just to the train station, right?" The Collector pulled a navy blue bandanna from his pocket and tied it around his forehead, constricting his wavy, mid-length, black hair.

"Yes, please."

Bette capped her thermos. He gave the bandanna a second tug to make sure it would stay put. "That shouldn't be a problem. Give me about thirty minutes. I got a couple of, uh, pickups to make before we go."

When he returned, Bette could see up close that the Collection truck was bigger and higher off the ground than she imagined. The Collector had to help her get up into the cab, which was immaculate and smelled of lubricant and wintergreen.

"Mint?" the Collector asked after he slammed his door shut, pointing to a plastic container in a cupholder. This revealed the source of the heavy wintergreen smell Bette encountered upon entering the cab.

"No, thank you," Bette replied, as she smiled and tried to hide her apprehension at riding in the Collection truck.

"My name is Gus," the middle-aged man said, purposefully not extending his gloved hand to complete the introduction.

"Mine's Bette. Thanks again for doing this."

Gus cranked up the engine, which caused the whole seat to rumble beneath her.

"So, were you the one who saw it?" he asked. He shifted the gear down and the truck began to move.

Bette nodded. "Pretty sure."

The man crunched on his mint like it was hard candy. As they passed through the automated fence entrance, her stomach flipped nervously. It looked like Mars outside the complex, dusty and barren. This area had once been a suburb or small town surrounding Charlotte. The only thing that remained the same after the upheaval of the Big One was the name of the largest nearby city.

"Pretty freaky, isn't it?" Gus asked as he watched Bette survey the landscape just outside the massive windows of the Collection truck.

Bette jerked her head to look at him, surprised. "You've *seen* one?"

"Two, actually. Well, the first was dead, out along the side of the road. I don't think that counts. I mean, it had been picked apart real good. I *assumed* it was one. Who else would be out there? But I wasn't about to get out of the truck and investigate." Gus reached forward and scooped up a couple of more mints, popping them in his mouth.

"The other one"—he chomped—"ran out in front of my truck one evening, near dusk. 'Bout made me wet my pants. I got a better look at him since, you know, he was in my head-lights. I looked out my window here," he said, pointing to the driver-side window, "and there he was, staring up at me. He looked like a castaway, with long mangy hair, nearly starved, and dirty. I'll never forget it; he opened that mouth of his and shrieked something awful."

Gus shivered but continued, "I gunned it away as fast as I could."

"How long ago was that?" Bette asked.

"Oh, long time ago," he answered. "But you got nothing to worry about in this truck. No, ma'am. We've got defense grade steel, bulletproof windows, reserve gas tanks. You could almost live in a Collection truck if you wanted to," he added after not-ing the fear in Bette's face.

Riding in a Collection truck was bad enough. She couldn't see the corpses, but she knew they were back there, bouncing around in the bed of the truck. Bette turned her head to look out the passenger-side window. The only indication that there was life out this far were the few other battered apartment com-plexes along the cracked and bumpy road.

Luxora, Arkansas 11:41 p.m.

Firefights along the Mississippi River in northeastern Arkansas escalated into a full-scale battle today between Repatriates and the United States military. Troops were brought in at the end of October to stabilize the region. Groups fleeing the United States Proper have unlawfully annexed these areas, claiming sanctuary from what they believe to be an overreaching and amoral government. The government contends that squatting on federal lands is trespassing. Negotiations have been going on for months, the most contentious point being area water rights. Over three hundred people have been killed on both sides since the skirmishes erupted into intermittent gunfire and shelling at the end of September.

12

There was a stark change of scenery as Bette and Gus approached the station, evoking a feeling in Bette much like what ancient sailors must have felt upon seeing trees after months on the open sea. Bette hopped down from the Collection truck's cab, thanking Gus. Posted around the manicured lawn of hardscape and green succulents were three guards, known to Bette as Sub enforcement. The government couldn't afford to maintain the train stations, so the Subs did. It worked out better for everyone; the stations were the epitome of modernity and efficiency.

The building was a glossy new mirage in the crumbling, oxidized desert that surrounded it. Bette did not see a lot of new things. Brand new, scuff free, and right-out-the-packaging was not part of her reality, but she did feel that way about the train station. Every time she arrived was like opening something new, a gift carefully wrapped just for her. It hadn't been ravaged by the years of others wearing it down, handling it callously, grating off all the shine. It hadn't yet been mistreated by interlopers trying to punish it for not already being broken, like they were jealous it started out without deficiencies.

The guard nodded to Bette as she walked past him. She nodded back. While the gesture seemed amicable, Bette knew he was scanning her. His technology was well beyond the antiquated tech that regular citizens had.

Bette took the low, wide, smooth concrete steps to the ticketing kiosks. They had been swept clean of the mustard-colored dust buffeted by daily winds. No rust corroded the metal surfaces; the plastic was seamless. The absentee sun glinted with veneration on the sleek building that dared to be painted white. There were no nicks in the facade, no peeling paint, not even those flecks of clay and dirt that splash up onto the building after a hard rain. It was the definition of pristine, as if buffed daily with intention and a soft cloth.

She placed both her hands on the dark screen. There was a short delay before the introduction screen lit up. Access to the main menu was only granted after a quick background check. An outstanding warrant or another flag would be cause for detention. Sub enforcement was known for being paranoid, so it was best to keep your head down and follow the rules.

Bette typed her destination into the screen, which listed a series of departure times. She tapped the time she needed.

Accept? the screen queried.

Accepted.

Charged to your metro account?

Confirmed.

Thank you! the screen announced.

The ID buzzed, indicating that it had acquired Bette's ticket information. The station had two entrances, one for Subbites and one for everyone else. She went over to the citizens' station doors. The solar glass slid open, revealing a hallway paneled in steel bars on either side, cut up into vestibules by three glass doors.

As with most things in life, heaven can't be experienced without a little bit of hell. It was something Bette's grandma used to say, and the train station was a prime example.

The first vestibule had a set of yellow footprints painted on the floor. Bette moved to the spot, her feet about six inches apart. She raised her arms and interlocked her fingers, resting them on the top of her head. Staring straight ahead, she focused on the reinforced glass window in the door in front of her, searching for a pattern in the crisscross of thin wires. The X-ray finished and the door slid open on its own.

The next compartment of the barred hallway contained a large metal table along the right side of the wall. Underneath the cold table was a stack of plastic bins. Bette squatted to grab a scuffed black bin, placed it on the table, removed her glasses, bag, and scarf, and put them in it. Conditions didn't allow for advance preparation for this step of the boarding process, so it always felt like a production to Bette. The harsh unflattering lights beat down on her and made her feel as though she were under a magnifying glass focusing the sun's rays onto her pale skin. She slid her belt off, unclasped and removed her boots, and placed them into the bin as well. Lastly, she peeled off her long-sleeved shirt and added it to the top of the pile.

The humidity made the room unbearably sticky. Some Subbite in charge of a budget somewhere refused to run the air-conditioning in this staging area. Bette stood under the unforgiving lights, covered in a clammy sheen, clad only in her threadbare camisole and pants. The door opened of its own accord, signaling Bette to pick up her bin and walk through.

Barefoot, she crossed the gritty floor and handed her bin to the enforcement officer waiting over the threshold. The stern uniformed woman with closely cropped black hair took the bin and let it clatter on the floor behind her. Bette moved over to the right side of the wall, her back against the cold bars and her hands on her head.

The enforcement officer surveyed Bette from head to toe before approaching her. The lines between her eyes wrinkled in concentration as she tried to divine if Bette was a threat. She took three heavy steps forward before gruffly patting her hands up and down Bette's body. Satisfied, the woman grunted, "Turn around."

Bette did as she was told. Turning her head to the right, she pressed her body into the metal bars. Bette fixated on a hairline fracture in the cement in her sight line, willing her mind to be elsewhere. The bars smelled of perspiration and iron. Steel looked flawless until you were right up on it; the smooth foreboding glint was predicated on rust spots and minor imperfections.

As the enforcement officer pushed and patted, the cold bars dug into Bette's shoulders, forehead, and cheekbones, causing her to wince a little. The jostling pressure finally subsided, and Bette waited for further instruction.

"All right. Turn around," the officer finally said.

Bette was cautious as she turned around and cast her gaze to the grimy floor.

"What is your purpose for taking the train today?" the woman barked, hands on her hips.

"Quarterly," Bette said, mindful to enunciate clearly and get right to the point.

"And when do you anticipate you will be back?"

"This evening."

The woman gave a curt nod and Bette heard the last door open. She scurried over to pick up her bin and exited through the open door. She had noticed the pressure building in her chest and a slight wheeze as the officer grilled her. If she could just sit down, calm her breathing, she could avoid having an episode here. On the other side was a row of benches; Bette set the bin on the bench and put herself back together.

DECEMBER 8, 2062 | ASSOCIATED PRESS

Electrified Fences Erected; Curfew Put in Place

Apartment complexes surrounding metropolitan city centers are getting a face-lift, but maybe not the kind residents were hoping for. All over the southeast, tall electrified fences are going up to protect citizens from a shadowy terrorist group commonly referred to as "Canners." The name comes from the alleged cannibalistic nature of their attacks. The Department of Justice has been working since the summer to identify and locate members of this organization. No arrests have been made at this time. As an additional precaution, curfews will go into effect in the coming weeks.

13

The bright lobby was just beyond the benches where Bette left the empty scuffed bin. To the left was the train platform; in the middle sat a small green space with shrubs and better-looking benches. A myriad of flowering plants bloomed in beds. Decay had no dominion in this space.

Bette tucked her scarf in her bag and allowed her mouth cover to hang around her neck. She turned and approached the side of the lobby with the drinking fountain. Subbites were geniuses with their water condensation and recycling. The fact that they could offer a public water fountain was evidence enough of this. Apartment complexes were dependent on the Department of Agriculture to deliver public water once a week. Only Agriculture could reclaim and process rainwater, which they fortified with moisture control. The additive enabled a person to retain moisture better so they could consume less water overall, making respiration and perspiration more efficient.

Bette bent over and let the water wash over her teeth and tongue, hydrating her dry throat. She lingered longer than was polite, but for the price of a one-way ticket to the other side of town, she felt entitled. Sub water didn't contain moisture control. It was cold and crisp and lacked the heavy smell and metallic aftertaste of public water.

Her train wasn't set to arrive for another forty-five minutes. It was anyone's guess how long it might take to get to the station and through security. When there was time, like today, Bette liked to sit on a bench in the green space with her eyes closed, taking deep and cleansing breaths.

The amount of time and resources that had been put into this garden was impressive, and it was just in a train station. These trees and plants were only for beautification. No one even relied on it for food. If her Depot House had a garden even half this size, the residents could have fresh supplemental produce every day—not just what they could grow in their apartments. Her kitchen garden left a lot to be desired. The little grow lights did the best they could with the seeds she could get. Department of Agriculture seeds were mostly trash after all the modifications, but their inventory was cheap and convenient. She could get better quality plants from independent sellers. This was tricky, though, because too much of that and she'd risk being flagged. The problem was origination. Much of what was sold by independent sellers was smuggled in from Repatriate farms. Possession of Repatriate produce was illegal. The Department of Agriculture would test a plant's genetic makeup at the slightest suspicion. They had an ever-growing list of known Repatriate produce, so if found in possession of Repatriate organic matter, one would be subject to fines, plant confiscation, and probation.

Bette opened her eyes. Soft light from the ceiling panels gave the whole station a glow. Preoccupied, she reached for a firm yet pliable leaf and caressed it between her fingers. The shrub rustled as if a breeze were blowing. She peered between the maze of branches to find a little brown bird, its head twitching to the left and then quickly to the right. Bette held her breath and remained perfectly still to not startle it. He looked like a sparrow, with darker shafts of brown dotting his back. *Maybe it's a* he, she thought to herself. Something about his playful yet vigilant manner reminded her of David. It hopped to another branch and kept Bette in his sight line. His head twitched again to the left and then to the right, like a crude, jerky animation. Then he spread his wings and flew to another shrub. She didn't take it personally that he sought another shrub; they always did. She was an unknown, a hesitant, gangly stranger. She could not blame him for not knowing if she was friend or foe. In all honesty, it really just depended on the day.

This bird was lucky to have sneaked in here; from what she'd heard, being in the train station was much like being in a Sub. This was as close as an inconclusive person would ever get without the brutal application process, of course. The best part of sub living without the biometric implants, separate trains, and no council to monitor your every move. Bette knew that this train station was as close as she, too, was ever going to get; it was the best part of going to her quarterly.

Her mother had applied to a Sub while Bette was still in utero. She had about a dozen interviews where she provided all kinds of medical, physiological, and genealogical documentation. She took blood tests, urine tests, and personality tests. Her entry was contingent upon a successful birth and a quick subsequent conception. Bette was one and a half when they officially denied her mother. Bette's Gram railed against the idea, even years after the fact.

"You were going to join humanity's country club!" Bette's grandma had said, throwing her hands up, exasperated. "Give up your freedom to a panel of strangers for what? Citrus? Recycled water?"

"Yeah," her exhausted mother had countered. "Maybe I was. Like that is so crazy."

Bette's eyes were closed, and in her relaxed state, she felt drowsy. A mellow-sounding bell let her know it was time to depart. Her ID buzzed in her ear to second that. She had just enough time to circle back to the drinking fountain. Two men were in line ahead of her; Bette waited with anticipation, drinking deep when it was her turn before heading over to the platform.

She fiddled with her mouth cover while she stood. The gleaming bullet-shaped train glided into the station. Stopping with almost no sound, the train sat a moment before the doors slid open. A handful of layered and crumpled people got off. She chose a bench seat by the window. She knew that she would see nothing but darkness as the train traveled underground, but this darkness didn't scare her. This darkness felt liberating.

Memo to Directors of Birthing Centers

Offspring of consistently producing mothers in birthing centers will officially become wards of the Department of Propagation upon birth. It is the Department's belief that mothers can't effectively care for children and focus on the rigors of pregnancy at the same time. The needs of the infant pull an inordinate amount of energy from mothers, which in turn reduces production efficiencies within the centers. We have reached a deal with the Sub Guild to outsource the care of these children. The Subs are to care for the wards of the Department of Propagation until the adolescents can be classed. Once the adolescents are classed, the Sub will relinquish the fertile females to the Department of Propagation birthing centers. The Sub will retain all fertile males and have the right to first choice of the inconclusive candidates. All other inconclusive candidates will be sent to Sub-monitored dormitories for a two-and-a-half-year training program based on community job needs at the time.

In the event of "one-off" births—meaning a woman who has given birth to one child but is unable to produce any more—it is the prerogative of the Department and a cost reduction to the State to leave those children with their mothers for raising. Genetically, it is not worth the Department's investment at this time. Such children shall be monitored through Sub-sponsored schools but will continue to be the responsibility of the mothers.

14

The train approached Bette's stop. Bette rose from her seat and held on to the handrail above her until the train came to a complete stop. The doors whooshed open as she and one other traveler exited the car. It was like her side of town; there were tall razor-wire fences surrounding clusters of buildings, except no one lived in the industrial park. It was just a series of buildings intended for business. The way it was set up reminded Bette of old-timey movie sets built for Westerns, where a dirt-packed main street was flanked by buildings along either side.

A four-story building, long ago painted gray, stood out against the backdrop of the tall fence. Neighboring buildings of various heights were flush with it. A little one-story deli sat next to a two-story building that housed several tech firms, while scraggly weeds forced their way up between the cracks in the cement sidewalk. The few people out were walking fast and with a purpose. The ground-level windows were covered with rusted, corrugated sheet metal. The entrances lacked solar glass doors like the station. Instead, they featured a small rectangle to the right side that granted entrance when IDs synced.

Bette approached the propagation office, a nondescript, single-level cement building at the end of the street. The only thing that set it apart was the additional layer of fence that surrounded it. The entire industrial park was already surrounded by an electrified fence topped with barbed wire, but there was another wrought iron fence around the propagation office.

Decay had managed to find a foothold even here, a place devoted to birth. It was a little more constricted due to the lack of flesh and bone, but Decay was not deterred. It still did its best to erode progress. Oxidation found its way along every nonorganic and corrosion-worthy surface. Weeds pushed out of the seemingly impenetrable spaces where the building met the concrete sidewalk.

The wind picked up as Bette stood staring at the C-shaped building that housed the office. Her scarf flapped loose from her head, and she lunged to catch it before it blew into oblivion. Beyond the fences, she caught sight of a dust devil dancing nimbly in the anhydrous Carolina scrub.

The dark solar glass slid open for Bette. She entered a medium-sized lobby filled with beige kiosks and cheap plastic waiting room chairs, like the ones in her vendor stall. The six freestanding kiosks were in a row at the back of the lobby. Each contained a small touchscreen with flimsy privacy dividers on either side. Two of the kiosks' screens were dark, indicating they were out of order. Bette was pretty sure they still hadn't been fixed since the last time she'd been in. A dozen chairs were arranged in a couple of rows in front of the kiosks, their backs facing the machines.

Bette moved to a working DOP kiosk. She entered her DOP number and waited for her ID to buzz. When it did, she looked at the screen. *Twelve.*

Bette slumped in a worn, off-white plastic chair and regarded the giant screen on the wall with reluctance. She'd disengaged the audio stream that automatically synced with her ID upon entering the building.

Drivel. She got enough propagation protocol reminders, advertisements, and general propaganda on a regular day. The last thing she could stomach was another advertisement for a pill that would enliven her love life. Bette was familiar with their claims and price points; she was one of the few licensed sellers in her complex. So far, no one had come back to thank her for curing their infertility.

A light above her flickered. Four other women were seated in the lobby, immersed in whatever they were looking at behind their glasses. Faint, ambient background music took the edge off the boring silence.

She was obligated to put herself through this examination on a quarterly basis. Every quarter, she was reminded she was not yet good enough. Part of her wondered if she ever would be. Bette's results had been the same since she was seventeen. She had done everything she'd known how to do with their prescriptions, pills, and creams. She meditated, exercised, and thought positive thoughts. She tried different positions for prescribed amounts of time with young men, older men, and men the exact same age as her. Still, after all these years, the Department only told her to try harder.

If I could just shake being inconclusive . . .

If only she could get off this monotonous infertility regimen. For once, it would be nice for someone to look at her and see more than what she wasn't. All she needed were a few events to align, and she could get out from under these mind-numbing protocols. It had happened to her mother once. And Cabe was fertile. She had looked him up, too, not just taken his word for it. It could work if she hit at the right time. The problem was, she really didn't know *when* that was. The biggest unknown was her. Had she done enough to boost her fertility? There were no guarantees she'd end up like her mother.

A beautiful pregnant woman appeared on the screen in front of her. She was draped ever so carefully in red satin. Her flawless porcelain skin was rosy; her dark hair flowed behind her as if she were standing in a gentle breeze. Her hand was on her exposed pregnant belly and she gazed longingly at her enlarged midsection. Above her, text appeared: *Fertility . . . It's a growing trend.*

Bette brought her elbows to her knees and rested her face in her hands, sighing.

Jesus. Nothing like the Department missing the point.

There was a ding overhead; a voice in her ear said, "Twelve." Bette stood up, adjusted her bag, and walked to the double doors. She took off her gloves, placed her thumb and finger on the keypad, and waited for them to open. The double doors swung open into a hallway. There were two doors on each side as Bette walked to the standalone desk at the end of the hallway.

"Twelve," Bette said to the inattentive man behind the desk.

"Over here, please." He gestured to his left, not bothering to look at her. He tapped the screen embedded in the desk. There was another little waiting area adjacent to him with six more hard plastic chairs. No monitors or screens or kiosks awaited Bette back here.

The doors Bette had passed were the interview rooms for the history panel. This interview took anywhere from thirty to forty-five minutes. DOP staffers always said that there were no wrong answers and that everything was confidential, but only a fool believed that.

Bette leaned back in her chair, closed her eyes, and rested her head against the wall.

"Room number four, please," the man instructed her, shaking her from her attempt to relax in the uncomfortable perfection of this place. She opened her eyes and stood, quickly noticing one other woman had joined her in the waiting area.

Bette walked to the room labeled four. She sat down on a tan love seat facing an oversized chair. These interview rooms were designed to make people feel comfortable, like they were in a friend's living room and could relax. No one Bette knew had this much furniture, let alone a separate living room. A small, round plastic table sat to the right of the love seat. A couple of faded abstract paintings hung on the wall, one drooping slightly to the left as if it had been bumped. The wall had numerous gray scuffs. She could make out the faint background music she had heard before.

The visit, comprised of a sexual health interview and a physical examination, brought the same questions quarter after quarter. Bette had learned that the right answers would get her out of the interview faster. With each visit, she was more determined to get out of there as fast as possible.

The sexual health interview consisted of questions about all the intimate details of Bette's sex life, from how often she had intercourse, the number of partners, and the positions used. It had also come to include questions that seemed to be written by the Department of Agriculture, such as how much she ate and where she bought supplements, seedlings, and produce. While these were conducted under the guise of monitoring public health, they had little to do with procreation. The physical exam was more straightforward, with a scan and some blood and urine samples.

After a few minutes, a bright and bubbly woman came in. She was overly enthusiastic in true Department of Propagation style. "Hello! Good morning! How are you today, Ms. Donovan?"

"I'm well. Thank you," Bette replied, aiming for spirited but not at all trying to mirror the staffer's intensity.

"Great! I am very glad to hear it! It looks like you are here for your quarterly assessment." She was wearing the thin translucent glasses that employees of the Department wore. They had the newest UV tinting and were not dark like Bette's. Instead of an earpiece that had to be paired every time you put on the glasses, there was a little pad adhered to the wearer's temple. If you didn't know to look for it, you'd never see it. The woman focused on Bette and consulted her display. Bette found it unsettling to be stared at and not be seen all at the same time.

"All righty," the staffer said when she was all set up. "How do you feel?"

"Good," Bette answered as she crossed her legs and rested on her left elbow.

"Oh, one hundred and five, that is great! You've added a little weight since the last visit," the agent said to herself as she grazed through Bette's information. Her dark hair was smoothed back into a shiny bun. Her skin was noticeably dry and only magnified by the flaked foundation across her forehead, cheeks, and chin. Shifting in her seat, she crossed her legs. The stiff fabric of her standard-issued white uniform scratched as it rubbed together. She bobbed her head a little, while maintaining what looked like eye contact.

"Have you had any dark thoughts lately? Despair or melancholy? Thoughts of self-euthanasia?"

"No," Bette replied.

"Good! What about any signs of depression? Sleeping too long? Suppressed appetite? Or any behavior that seems out of place?"

"No."

"Great. Are you getting adequate nutrition?"

"I try."

"How so?" the staffer asked with a genuine look of concern.

"I've got a garden and I take supplements. You know, the normal stuff." Bette smiled and shrugged her shoulders, adding, "Do what you can, right?"

"And this garden, do you trade or sell products from it?"

"Oh, no, not really. If there is anything extra, I'll barter with my neighbor."

"And that neighbor is still—" She paused, looking up information on her glasses. "Mr. David Rey?"

She glanced at Bette to confirm.

"Uh, yes."

"Where do you purchase your gardening materials? Your seed, soil, implements . . . those types of items?"

Oh, the Department of Agriculture was always trying to track Repatriate activity.

"When I need something, I go to the Pantry," Bette answered.

Bette had become accustomed to lying about gardening, just as everyone else had. Not everyone liked to be used as unwilling, unknowing test subjects. If they could confirm she'd been to the Department of Agriculture's Pantry a couple of times a year, they couldn't give her a hard time.

"Are you able to get enough vitamin C in that way?"

"Uh . . . not really. Citrus is hard to get out where I live." This was true, but it was also a trap. Everyone knew that citrus could be connected to the Repatriates; saying yes to a vitamin C question would only lead to more questions. Subs also had citrus, but it was against their laws for any produce or agricultural product to leave their perimeters. The consequences were steep for being in possession of citrus. No matter how they asked it, "no" was always the answer to a citrus question.

"And you said you were taking your supplements?" the staffer asked, her eyes scanning back and forth across the lenses of her glasses.

"Yes, I am taking them," Bette replied.

"Including your fertility citrates?"

"Yes, ma'am."

"Where do you purchase your supplements?" She smiled suddenly as if someone had just reminded her to perk up.

"I get them when the Ag agent comes to our complex." Bette's tailbone was starting to ache from all the uncomfortable chairs. She uncrossed and recrossed her legs to the opposite side this time to lean on her right elbow.

The agent nodded and proceeded. "And how often do they come?"

"My complex is on a six-week rotation."

The agent asked more questions about Bette's gardening. She asked again about her access to citrus. Then she started asking questions about water, a serious set of questions and not a normal part of the interview.

"Are you getting enough water, Ms. Donovan?" The staffer grinned, her eyes unblinking.

Bette sat up a little straighter and forced herself to be more alert. Water was heavily regulated; a wrong answer could lead to detainment. She was cautious not to think too long about this because her answer needed to sound natural. "Our water carrier comes every two weeks. That seems to be perfect timing. Yes, I'd say I am well hydrated."

"Have you or anyone in your building noticed any leaks or dripping near the water reserve?"

Bette cocked her head to the side, to make it look like she was thinking. She was trying to keep her breathing even, to help calm her racing heart. *Something must have happened out at the complex recently.* She racked her brain to see if she remembered hearing anything. "I'm trying to think if I've heard . . . No, I don't think anyone has mentioned anything like that."

"All right, then," the woman said in her sweet, perky voice. "Let's switch gears a minute, what do you say?" Her bun bobbed as she nodded.

Bette smiled and exhaled at the same time. "Great," she said, happy to move on from the water discussion.

"I'm going to get a glass of water. Would you like one?" she asked, her dry flaky skin taut across her cheeks.

She must need a moment to confer with someone. "Yes, I would love some water," Bette said.

The staffer smiled and stood up. "I'll be right back!"

Bette took the reprieve to stand and stretch out her tight back. She crossed her arms across her chest and reached to grasp her protruding shoulder blades. Even though the DOP staffer had stepped out of the room, she did not for one second think that she was alone. Bette looked up at the ceiling. There were no obvious surveillance devices, but it was safe to assume there was some sort of monitoring. She released her arms and rolled her shoulders a few times before retaking her seat. The perky DOP agent came back into the room with two small cups of water.

"Here you go!" she said perkily.

"Thank you."

She settled back into her chair, once again staring blankly at Bette before she began. "So, let's change subjects now. Are you currently seeing anyone?"

"Yeah, I am," Bette answered.

"Wonderful! And how long have you been seeing him?"

"Maybe two and a half weeks."

"All right. And what is his status?"

"He is fertile."

"Very good!" the staffer replied with an upbeat tone. Bette couldn't help but smile as a tiny bit of accomplishment warmed her. She had sat in this very room before, unable to find a fertile partner and had been subjected to the agent's reproach. Of course, inconclusive women were encouraged to have sex with all men, but fertile men were to receive preference.

"How many relationships have you had in the last twelve weeks?"

"Four, five counting him," Bette lied. She couldn't actually remember the last time she'd been able to hit the DOP's suggested number of relationships.

"That is very good. And you have entered their DOP ID numbers in your profile?"

"Of course." Bette was twenty-nine and inconclusive, so no one was digging into her prospect history to see if she was telling the truth. She had bought records in the past to pad her prospect history. It was technically fraud, but everyone did it from time to time.

"On average, how many times per week are you having intercourse?" The propagation agent's questions made Bette realize her mind had wandered.

"Uh, I guess about three."

The staffer's juiceless brow furrowed. "You are aware three is the *minimum*? Department standards suggest three to five."

Bette's face felt hot. "Well . . . he lives in a Sub and only takes the train in this area a few times a week."

The staffer clasped her hands in her lap and pursed her lips while her dry skin exaggerated every crease in her face.

I should have known better.

"Now, Bette, I don't need to state the obvious here. I think we both know that you could have a lot more, well, *influence* over the number of times that you see him each week. Let's try to be more proactive, what do you say?"

"Sure. I will work on that," Bette said as she pushed down her indignation.

"I know that it is common to become complacent about your age. You are getting older and haven't had much luck. But you still have a commitment to your country for the next few years. So, let's not get lazy, okay? A lot is at stake here."

Bette set her jaw and adopted her work smile. She balled her hands up in her lap and her lined, brittle nails dug uncomfortably into the palms of her hands. "I am fully aware of that fact."

"Just to clarify, when I say intercourse, you do know that I am referring to vaginal intercourse?" the staffer asked.

"Yes, I do," Bette replied woodenly.

"While oral and anal sexual activity are considered sex, those are not the kind of encounters the Department of Propagation considers intercourse for the purposes of procreation."

"I understand."

"So, just to confirm, these, uh, three-times-a-week encounters you referred to previously, they are vaginal intercourse, correct?"

"Correct."

"With full and complete ejaculation?"

"Yes," Bette answered, shifting a bit in her chair.

"And you are sure?" the staffer asked, one eyebrow raised.

"I am." Bette was hoping to spare herself from the "erect penis and seminal fluid" diatribe most agents were apt to launch into at this stage of the interview. The agent paused and considered her, weighing the need to have such a discussion. She seemed to think better of it and moved on to her next question.

"And how long do you wait after each transmission?"

"About fifteen minutes," Bette said.

"Well, that is adequate, I suppose." The agent clicked her tongue, thinking. "But ten more minutes wouldn't hurt, would it, Ms. Donovan?"

"Of course, it wouldn't." Bette's cheeks ached from the strained unnatural position for so long.

"And, remind me, what position do you use during transmission?"

"Missionary."

"Every time?" This agent was thorough.

"Every time," Bette said without batting an eye.

The agent circled back around to ask the same questions again with slightly different wording. Once her questioning was complete, she lectured Bette at some length on the benefits of various sexual positions, how vaginal intercourse was the only way to get pregnant, and something about how long sperm can live in a woman's body. Bette tried to look engaged as she tuned out the tired Department of Propagation rhetoric that she knew by heart.

"And finally," the agent said, "it looks like this relationship will soon run its course. Do you have any prospective relationships lined up?"

"Yes."

"Wonderful. Well, that about wraps up what I need here. If you want to head back to the waiting area, Miguel will alert the next station that you are ready."

Bette stood up to leave. As she opened the door, the DOP staffer stopped her. "And Bette?"

Bette paused, mindful not to roll her eyes or drop her shoulders.

"Don't lose heart. You *are* pretty, considering your age and status. Don't give up hope." The agent smiled as if she really meant it.

Bette nodded, all too familiar with the hot thoughtless insult that singed the edges of her confidence.

"Thanks," she responded, cringing on the inside.

JUNE 13, 2062 | MEDICAL EXAMINER'S OFFICE |
PRESS RELEASE

As of June 13, the Charlotte Medical Examiner's Office has
completed the identification and autopsies on all remains
found at the crime scene. Of those who could not be positively
identified, there were either not enough remains or the remains
were too degraded for testing. Due to the Justice Department's
injunction, the Medical Examiner's Office is unable to comment any further on these autopsies.

15

Back in the little lobby, Bette stretched her arms toward the ceiling, trying to break up the tension that had settled in her shoulders. Bette reached and reached until it felt like the skin on her ribs was about to tear. Then, she leaned forward until her fingers were under her boots. Face-to-face with the reason she was there, she let out a sigh. She closed her eyes and held the position, despite the complaint from her hamstrings.

"Ma'am?" The man at the desk raised his voice to get Bette's attention. She exhaled and stood up to face him.

"They are ready for you."

She skulked past his post and stopped in front of the metallic double doors. It slid open. Again, there was the music Bette kept hearing. The physical exam area was a sterilized white, a nice change from the dingy beige that monopolized the rest of the facility. The reception kiosk was immediately inside the door, made of a smooth light stone and a seamless extension from the wall.

A well-groomed man stood behind the kiosk. Directly behind him, along the wall on the left, were six doors. Across from the doors on the right side of the room were six smooth, white stone benches extending from the wall, serving as the exam tables. They could make the exam areas more private by using curtains, but they never did. The curtains stayed bunched up against the wall behind the patient. The entire area was under camera surveillance; Bette could plainly see them mounted on the ceilings, their black a stark contrast to the sterile white.

It was busy today; Bette was the third patient waiting to be examined.

"Exam one," the man behind the kiosk said. Bette walked past him and sat on the first white stone bench. She let her legs swing a little, bouncing off the stone beneath her.

One of the first priorities of the newly formed Department of Propagation had been to vaccinate citizens against sexually transmitted diseases, which was the logical culprit for an infertility epidemic. People were now free to have sex with little consequence. The Department viewed this as a victory, but in this era of mandated consequence-free sex, the vaccinations hadn't stopped the rise of infertility.

A woman dressed in gray approached Bette. She had on her DOP-issued glasses and stooped a little to look into Bette's eyes. "Please state your name and DOP identification number, please."

"Bette Donovan. 208366-4."

"Thank you. You will notice a red dot on one of the lenses of my glasses. Blink once, and then stare at the dot. Please try not to move or shift." Bette blinked and did as she was told.

"Thank you. Now, please give me your left hand." Bette stretched her left hand to the woman. The exam tech took a flat silver square out of the pocket of her gray tunic.

"Hold this between your thumb and forefinger. Make sure the pad of your finger is as flat as possible." A click signaled her fingerprint had been taken. The tech waited for her display.

"All right, Ms. Donovan, identity verified."

An assistant rolled over a small steel tray with various implements on it. She picked up a two-inch-wide strip of paper and handed it to Bette. "Please go over to the restroom and place this strip in your urine stream." Bette took the strip and walked across the room to the line of doors with the assistant in tow. Bette opened the door, allowing the assistant to enter the restroom first. She smiled at Bette as the door shut.

"How are you today?"

"Great," Bette said as she unzipped her pants and sat on the toilet. Once complete, Bette handed the strip to the assistant. She placed it in the clear container she was holding. Bette put her hands under the waterless sanitizer unit to the right of the toilet. She stood up, rubbed it into her hands, and fastened her pants. The exam tech had already imprinted a barcode on the urine sample. Upon opening the bathroom door, Bette found another tech and Mandate participant waiting in a stiff awkward silence for their turn. Bette followed her tech, glancing at a woman who seemed to be about her age. The woman gave her a half smile and shrugged as if to say, *What are you gonna do, right?*

Bette hopped back up on the bench.

"Please hold out your right arm."

Bette stuck out her right arm. The examiner drew one vial of blood and handed it to the assistant who now held a stylus-like device. Bette watched as she held the vial in front of the stylus, saw a tiny flash, and a barcode appeared on the vial. Meanwhile, the tech placed a gray plastic sheath with a small clear window over Bette's forefinger. She felt a little prick and watched as the blood oozed into the window. Then the tech removed it and handed it to the assistant to be barcoded. The assistant rolled away with the filled containers.

"If you will go over to the reproductive imaging room, please," the exam tech said, continuing to both look and not look at Bette.

Bette hopped back down and walked across the room to the fourth shiny metal door on the wall. In the middle of the room, a white circle had been painted on the floor to indicate where to stand. The assistant came in, standing up against the wall by the door to observe. "Please spread your legs and arms apart, like you are making a human X." The disembodied voice of the tech came over the speakers and echoed in the empty room.

Bette did as she was told.

The assistant pressed a button on the wall and a chirp followed. "All right," the assistant said, "you can follow me back to the exam table."

The tech was waiting near the exam table. Bette walked over and leaned back on the table.

"Well, Ms. Donovan, everything looks normal. There was just the slightest uptick in your hormone levels, but we get that from time to time if a device's calibration is off. Well within the department's margin of error." This had happened to Bette before. Just because it never registered on reports didn't mean that it wasn't important.

The assistant handed Bette a bottle, smiling as she gave it a little shake. "Don't forget these."

Bette accepted the bottle, putting it in her bag.

Bette left the propagation office and trudged into the balmy overcast that was every day. She plopped down on the busted curb just outside the wrought iron fence and exhaled into her mouth cover. She closed her eyes and ran her fingers up the sides of her temple and into her hairline. Her stomach growled loudly. She took a small sip of humid air and held it a moment before breathing out through her nose. She opened her eyes.

This place is ugly.

Dust swept across her boots; loose bits of concrete jiggled under the heels of her hands as she stared at the desolate abandoned movie-set town. She lived in an era of crisis. They were taking it in the teeth these days. The infertility epidemic had not gotten better. Canners still stalked neighborhoods. She barely scraped by on supplements and a small indoor garden. She slept with a man she shouldn't sleep with who brought her illegal oranges.

Planet Earth had been thrust onto jagged rocks, its hull pierced, groaning and cracking under the weight of everything done to eek a little more from it. Humanity watched from the bow of this sinking ship, panicked and scrambling to avoid drowning when it finally went down. It seemed almost counterintuitive to bring children into the world.

Would things be better or worse in ten years? Twenty? Do we even have that long? But to not at least try? No one could say they were okay with the extinction of humanity. Everyone understood; that was why they subjected themselves to the demands of the DOP.

A flutter of movement at the edge of Bette's vision caused her to look over. Across the dirt street, a tiny patch of dandelions was jittering in an unintelligible breeze. They had grown up between the gaps in the concrete next to an ancient bus stop. A rusting metal frame curved over a cracked plastic bench, part of its back torn off to reveal the tarnished support. The tops of the dandelions were white and fuzzy, ready to release their seed into the world.

Funny, I bet you didn't even have to think about it. Bette gave a disgusted huff. It was the natural propagation process a plant went through. The damn thing was it worked. There was no dandelion decline. They didn't need to be monitored, prodded, or doused with fertility medication. They were weeds in the world, largely ignored and under no crushing obligation to perform. No one looked to them as a vehicle for the salvation of the species.

What would that be like?

She wasn't alone. Inconclusive women went in and out of the propagation office every day. They received the same sexual admonishments and weak results Bette did. There was a time, not all that long ago, when the procreation process hadn't needed an intervention. The United States had been facing an *over*population problem before the Big One.

We are beyond the luxury of time and preference.

Bette sighed and shook her head as she gazed at the dandelions across the way. What were humans missing? The weeds seemed to have it figured out. They had managed to keep their place on this Earth.

Gravel crunched behind her. Startled, Bette began to turn.

Her nostrils were assaulted with the stench of urine before she could see anything. There was a muffled grunt right before something hard connected with the back of her head. Pitching forward, her brain rattled in her skull with an explosion of pain. Her hands skidded out from under her as she tried to stop herself from falling. Grit scoured her cheek as she face-planted in the street. A shooting, stabbing pain filled her chest and caused electric white rays to blur her vision. She arched up a little but felt pressure. She couldn't catch her breath. She couldn't scream. Something was wrong. Something heavy was holding her in place.

A deafening shriek roared over her panicked thoughts; she felt it all through her. Bette tried to move her head to see where the terrible screeching was coming from. Suddenly, an intense penetrating pain shot through her neck. She opened her mouth but couldn't get a scream out. Hot moist breath was behind the multiple tearing cuts on her neck. Body odor and urine enveloped her. In the distance, she heard alarmed yelling and felt the pressure on the side of her neck slacken. The earsplitting scream started again, higher now, floating above her, jarring her to the core.

She lay there, unable to move, and everything fell out of focus. Then there was nothing at all.

FEBRUARY 11, 2063

"If we hope to survive, they must realize that we are beyond the luxury of time and preference."
   —President Alvarez, in response to protests

16

2112, PRESENT

Bette blinked her eyes open slowly as they adjusted to the bright light. She stared at the unfamiliar light fixture on the ceiling, confused. She shivered and blinked again.

"Well, well, look who has decided to come around." A disembodied woman's voice came from Bette's right. A face soon followed and peeked into Bette's periphery. A pile of short wavy red hair, obviously color treated, seemed to sit on top of her head. Her skin had a yellowish hue, and dark circles ringed under her eyes. She was older than most women working these days, in her fifties maybe.

Bette's eyes hurt. Come to think of it, all of her felt achy and stiff. She looked down. She was covered with a light blue blanket, a single tube in her right arm.

"Mmm, it hurt my heart when I saw them wheel you out of surgery. I mean, I've seen it before, plenty of times. But there was just something about you, the way you were lying there, it just hurt me, in a physical way." The woman continued to speak as she attended to whatever she was doing.

Bette tried to speak, but nothing came out. She tried to sit up and move around, somewhat agitated. The older woman pushed Bette's shoulders back ever so slightly. "Nope. Not right now. I just need you to lie back."

Bette didn't really stop struggling; she just ran out of energy.

"Yep, yep. They weren't quite sure about you," the woman said, clucking a little. "But me? I was pulling for you. I've seen a lot of girls not make it. But you? There was something real sturdy about you."

She could see that the room was tight and narrow, with a large closet complete with modular cabinets and drawers to the side opposite the door. Bare sterile walls surrounded her on all sides. The tile floor squeaked under the woman's rubber-soled shoes as she walked around Bette's bed. The older woman put her hand behind Bette's head, gently pushing it forward.

"You ever had that feeling?" the woman asked. "That compulsion to root for a stranger?" In her other hand, she offered a straw. Bette shivered as she took a sip of the freezing water. The woman guided Bette back down to the pillow and started pressing buttons on a machine.

"That was a nasty scrape you got yourself into." The red-haired woman pressed her tepid hands on the left side of Bette's neck, checking for something. It was then that Bette noticed the stiffness on the right side of her neck. She clumsily brought her hand to the bandage on her neck.

Scrape?

Bette remembered sitting outside the propagation office. She had fallen.

Wait, no, I was pushed. I couldn't breathe. What the hell happened?

"Most people, especially your age, wouldn't have made it." The nurse winked and continued. "I guess you had something worth sticking around for, eh?" The woman squeaked toward the doorway. She paused, turning as if remembering something.

"I think your friend will be by today."

David. Good, maybe he can tell me what is going on.

SEPTEMBER 3, 2062 | INTERNAL DEPARTMENT
OF JUSTICE MEMO

RE: Missing Persons / Possible Terrorist Faction
(Unknown)

A dozen more crime scenes like the one in Charlotte have been
identified across the southeast. It appears victims are alone and
in sparsely inhabited areas at the time of the kidnapping. There
is no obvious link between any of the victims. All victims have
numerous lacerations to soft flesh and visible teeth marks have
been identified on bone fragments. Of the bodies found mostly
intact, organs are missing, namely eyes, but there doesn't seem
to be a consistency of pattern for which organs are taken.

17

2112, PRESENT

"It's so good to see you awake," David said, visibly relieved, standing next to the bed. His mostly pepper hair was damp, and his jacket was dotted with water droplets. He reached for Bette's hand. "You had me really worried."

Bette smiled weakly, grateful to see him, too. David was devoid of his usual joking banter. An awkward moment passed between the two of them, strongly reinforcing the fact that something bad had happened. It was unnerving to have him speechless.

"David, what happened?" Bette croaked, not recognizing the voice that came out of her.

"You don't remember?"

Bette shook her head.

"Oh, Jesus, I am so sorry! I thought you knew. I haven't been able to get here for a few days, so I wasn't sure how long you'd been awake."

"I've been here for a few days?" Bette said as she blinked rapidly, amazed.

"Oh, darling girl, you have been here for a couple of weeks."

Bette felt her mouth drop open.

"Yeah, your attack made the news streams. But you know how vague they are with attack details. No images, and they didn't release your name." He went on to explain that she had been attacked by an unknown assailant who had stabbed her in the back, causing her lung to collapse.

Bette's mind swirled slowly. It painfully gained the momentum necessary to wrap itself around the words that were coming out of David's mouth. He pulled up a chair and sat down by the bed. She noticed that his height made the chair look freakishly small. "Man, it is so good to see you awake. I just can't tell you. He must have bonked you pretty hard on your head. The staff has been so cautious about the status of your coma, they wouldn't tell me anything definitive. If you hadn't still been in this place, I was liable to burn it to the ground. They made me *crazy*, a bunch of bureaucratic soulless bastards. And when you wouldn't wake up, Jesus . . . " David trailed off and the room grew quiet.

Bette was still foggy, but there was something she didn't understand. "David, do they know who did this?"

His hands on his knees, David shrugged. "They haven't identified him."

"But it was the middle of the day. I was at a propagation office. There are cameras everywhere. Someone had to see something. I . . . I don't understand why someone would do this." Bette coughed, trying to clear the grogginess from her throat. The right side of her neck ached with the vibration.

"And what happened to my neck?" Bette asked.

David averted her gaze, staring at the floor. "I don't know."

"What do you mean, you don't know? They didn't tell you?" Bette asked as she gingerly touched the bandage, patting around its edges.

"They just kept referring to lacerations." David looked up. His eyes hinted a warning and connected with her questioning stare. The guarded way her friend spoke had not gone unnoticed.

"Well, that is weird," she said, pulling back from her line of questioning.

"I know, right?"

Bette probed his eyes for an explanation while she tamped down her surging curiosity. While he wouldn't come straight out and tell her, he was warning her something was off. He had lived a decade longer than she had under the ubiquitous reach of the Department of Propagation. If he was cautioning her, it would be stupid not to trust him.

JUNE 15, 2100 | SUB GREENWOOD

RE: Prospective Candidate—CONFIDENTIAL
Donovan, B #208366-4

Inconclusive. *Note: Her biological mother was inconclusive
but became pregnant at age thirty, carrying one child to term.
This candidate may be a one-off, or the fertility genes of this
line may have run their course. TBD. Continue to request data
for three years. If the status remains unchanged, purge from the
candidate pool.

18

2112, PRESENT

I nearly died.

She blinked and tried again to focus. Bette puffed out her cheeks, letting the air escape slowly through her barely parted lips.

But I didn't.

How she didn't die wasn't even a question. It was logistics. EMS had been able to save her before she lost too much blood. They were able to repair all the wounds. How she hadn't died was due to medicine and science. Why she hadn't died? That was a question her grandma might have asked. Maybe it was a stupid question, but it was the way David had said it that still bothered her.

And when you wouldn't wake up . . .

That nurse had said something like that, too. *I guess you wanted it,* that's what she had said, right?

I do want to live, don't I?

Bette fingered the bandage on the right side of her neck. A sense of calamity swirled in the air along with the greenhouse gasses that pressed toward the Earth and sealed in the pervasive doom that could be felt every day. If given the opportunity of an out, why not take it? The flare of anger, the cooling of numbness and the weariness . . . God, she was just so tired. She was tired of the days of falling into bed, unable to get her own shoes off. She was weary of waking up at three in the morning to wonder, *What is the point?* No one would miss her if she was gone. Well, maybe David, and possibly Ezra, but they were used to death. She wouldn't have been the first inconclusive woman they'd known to pass into the haze. Staring down the void of desperate, wasteful uselessness while worrying about being "lust-worthy enough" was just too much. Trying to maintain glowing skin and a wanton shape on cut rations and no electricity was a maddening seesaw. Wearing gooey lip gloss and some lacy getup made of stiff wires for the boys only to eat protein chews and clover for dinner was a harsh existence. Don't make them feel bad, but also exist exquisitely on nothing.

If death deemed her attractive enough, then maybe it was worth considering.

But she had promised. Emphatically and to a dying woman, she had promised. She was stung with guilt realizing that she'd wavered.

I promised her.

Her mother chose to self-euthanize seven years ago. She had been an unhappy and harsh woman, and she bordered on brooding most days. This was why Bette had never thought twice about her decision. Time had eroded the superficial details of that day, but Bette did remember the message. It hadn't come from her mother, but from the suicide house after she was gone. It was professional and succinct, the most man-agerial way to find out that Bette was now alone in the world. Her final DNA tether was unmoored, and she was left listing in a sea of strangers. Even now, she could envision her mom's wiry frame sitting on a worn stool in their kitchen, sipping hot water, going over the pros and cons of her decision. She'd never been a rash woman, and Bette thought she'd have spent weeks thinking about it. There she would ponder and tidy up all the loose ends in her mind, while her pale, tired blue eyes stared off into space. It was preferable for Kit Donovan to end her life on her own terms than to wait and see what happened.

I am not like my mother.

It frightened Bette that somewhere inside of her, she, too, would consider it. With all of her heart, she had pledged herself to a promise, but that was a long time ago. Bette didn't know anything then. It was unfair for someone to ask for such a promise from a naive child who couldn't yet truly understand the world in which she lived. Bette hadn't yet endured, close-fisted and hungry, the life that was coming for her. Very few were holding on these days. Decay had wrapped itself around Bette's species and was squeezing the life right out, little by little. Death wouldn't be outrun; it wouldn't be beaten. It was only a matter of time before Death came to collect and put an end to Decay's sport.

Now it made sense why her grandma had demanded such a promise from Bette. Her grandma could see the darkness that lay ahead. Still she begged Bette, made her promise, as she lay dying. Bette understood now why her mother chose self-euthanasia. She was a pragmatic woman. Sentimentality is meaningless when you are so tired and out of options.

Maybe she and her mother were more alike than Bette realized.

But she had promised.

MAY 28, 2055 | ASSOCIATED PRESS

A tentative trade deal was reached today between Repatriates and the United States to ensure produce grown outside of the United States Proper will not be impeded. The scarcity of produce in densely populated cities has led to price gouging, hoarding, and in some cases, murder. To monitor the fair distribution of produce, especially citrus, all imports will go directly to the Dept. of Agriculture depots.

19

The footsteps were heavier than normal, reverberating like drums through eggshell-thin walls. Hospital staff passing by her room that day had been much lighter on their feet than these clunky footsteps. They fell in a disjointed rhythm, which made it sound like more than one person was walking down the hall. Bette turned her head toward the open door and waited for them to pass. The steps stopped within inches of the doorframe. She sat up straighter and held her breath as she strained to hear.

"This is the room," a man's voice said, pulsing from the hall.

"And you are sure?" a woman challenged him. "Let me see that."

Advancing from the hall, three strangers became visible. Two uniformed men from the Propagation Department's Enforcement Unit and a well-dressed woman with silver hair ceremoniously walked into Bette's hospital room. Quite an odd trio, she thought to herself, and out of place in this cramped space designed for a single inhabitant.

"Get her up," the silver-haired woman ordered, her words cutting through the air like a fast-moving whip. Stern, yet poised, the older woman was clearly in charge. She wore a white tailored pantsuit with royal blue piping along the lapel and around the sleeve cuffs. The blue in the piping matched her clear eyes and the blue suede flats she wore. Her shiny hair was short in the back but became progressively longer as it framed her oval face. Her peach skin was flawless, not a freckle, not a scar, not a patch of eczema. A walking testimonial for the benefits of access to resources.

The bald enforcement officer immediately complied and approached Bette's bedside. His dark blue uniform looked like it had just been removed from the package, complete with the creases and corners of a garment that has yet to be laundered for the first time. He paused, expectantly. The creases from his forehead rippled up and over his hairless scalp.

The woman gave a curt nod to the other officer with medium-length black hair slicked back out of his face. The bald man at Bette's side grabbed one of her spindly arms while the second man threw back the thin bedsheet, pushing her legs over the edge of the bed. He took Bette's other arm. She could feel their fingers poking into her underarms as they began to crudely hoist her out of her bed.

"Hey, wait a minute!" Bette yelped. "What are you doing?"

Her back lit up the moment the longer-haired man touched it, pain incinerating up and down the entire length of her body. They tugged her from the bed and her feet hit the floor. The abrupt contact with the cold hard floor caused a jarring shock to every bone in her lower half. Pain and fire blazed up her dormant legs to her brain. She gasped as her knees crumpled and left her suspended between the two enforcement officers.

"Put your feet flat on the floor," the woman instructed, indifferent to Bette's obvious pain.

"I can't," Bette wheezed, surprised and breathless.

"Yes, you can. Put your feet flat on the floor." The woman enunciated her command with a merciless staccato.

"It hurts," Bette said, tears forming in her eyes.

"What is going on here? Who the hell are you?" David yelled, rushing into the room.

"Get him out of here," the woman said with a flick of her wrist to the longer-haired officer. He passed Bette's weight off to the bald officer.

"Why are you moving her? She has only been awake for twenty-four hours!" David cried.

"Sir," the officer sternly said as he motioned toward the door, putting his hand on David's arm. David swatted at his hand.

"Don't touch me! You people aren't doctors! What are you doing here?"

"Sir," the man repeated a little louder.

"No, I demand to speak to someone who is in charge!" David yelled.

"I'm Dorothea Tyler, director of the Birthing Center HQ." As she said this, the woman pulled herself up to her full height while her lips formed a condescending smile. Her teeth were perfect, as if expertly mitered from shiny white quartz.

A stunned silence filled the room. Bette gulped in dismay. David glanced at Bette, his eyes asking the question his mouth couldn't quite form.

Birthing Center?

"Unless you would like to be arrested," Ms. Tyler continued, "I suggest you listen to the enforcement officer."

There was a tense pause as David thought about his next move. The Birthing Center comment had thrown him for a loop. Bette could almost hear the questions whirring through his brain because they were the same ones running through hers.

Why would anyone from the Birthing Center Headquarters be *here*? Let alone the *director*?

He could yell at the hospital staff, but he was not stupid enough to engage head-on with the Department of Propagation's Enforcement Unit. Bette knew he carried two healed breaks from the last time he had done that; she remembered when Enforcement had broken his nose and cracked his collarbone over far less.

David held the director's stare a moment or two more. The gravity of the situation pressed down on everyone in the room, except the director. Then, surrendering under the weight, he glanced down at the floor; his shoulders drooped, and he turned toward the doorway.

Bette sniffed and watched helplessly as her only advocate left the room.

What is happening? It didn't make any sense. There were no matters of propagation that needed to be enforced here. Bette had been attacked, so if anything, this was a Department of Justice (DOJ) matter and not something for which the Department of Propagation should waste its time. This eerily composed woman did not seem to be in any hurry to give any sort of explanation.

"Ms. Donovan, get dressed," Ms. Tyler snapped.

The bald officer released his hold on Bette. She willed her weak legs to move as she hobbled over to a folded stack of clothes on the counter. Her shirt was missing, probably because they had to cut it from her. She tucked the gown, best she could, into her pants. She balanced on the edge of the bed and leaned forward to put on her socks and boots, wincing as the bandage on her back pulled on her tender skin.

The stab wound that had punctured and filled my lung with blood.

The longer-haired officer returned from the hall after seeing David out, signaling the end of that tense episode.

"Let's go." Ms. Tyler trotted out the door. The enforcement officers, each with a hand on Bette's arms, led her out of the hospital room. Bette looked behind her, hoping in vain David would appear and stop whatever was happening from happening. But he was not there, only a rumpled unmade cot in a tight hospital room. The hospital staff took great pains to pretend they didn't see Ms. Tyler or whatever she was there to attend to.

As suddenly as Bette had found herself in the hospital, and with even less explanation, she was being taken from it by enforcement officers at the behest of the director of the Birthing Center.

We are beyond the luxury of time and preference.

NOVEMBER 5, 2062 | CDC RESEARCH FACILITY—RESEARCH DICTATION NOTES

Subjects will never be able to be reintegrated into society. The cognitive regression, lack of impulse control, and tendency to cannibalize those without the mutation all seem to be hallmarks of the mutation. The females are much less violent than males. Interestingly, they seem to be highly adept at behavior modification with reinforcement. The subjects could have military implications but more testing would be required. Of the ones tested in this facility, all are fertile. This information has been passed on to the undersecretary at the Department of Propagation.

20

The wind snapped Bette's hair outside the hospital as she looked up into the cluster of high-rise buildings made of steel and solar glass. Like its inhabitants, the city was beautiful, cold, and distant. Electric transport vans and cars plodded along noiselessly on the street in front of her. Individual citizens brushed past, bundled up in stylish protective UV gear. Being in the city had always made her feel claustrophobic. She didn't belong there, as evinced by her out-of-season thrift fashion or clunky eyewear.

Important places like hospitals, police stations, and seats of government were located in the city. Road and rail radiated out of it like spokes on a wheel. Farther down each spoke, past the sharp clean architectural lines, lay the fenced-in pockets of complexes walled by cracked clay wasteland.

In the car, seated across from Ms. Tyler, Bette noticed one of the woman's eyes was a lighter shade of blue than the other. The disparity was not caused by genetics, as if she had two different colored eyes, but looked as if a thin film covered the lighter eye, causing the slight discoloration. Not eager to further irritate the director by staring, Bette looked down at her folded hands. Her heart hammered in her chest as sweat damp-ened her underarms and spread down her sides. Bette tried to reposition the oversized square gown to absorb the wetness. Even as she sat there sticky with sweat, chills ran through her.

What is this even about? The fact that Enforcement was involved filled Bette with dread because they had a reputation of cracking skulls first and asking questions later. *Had they found out about Cabe? Had they audited her partner records? But would they do that without a reason? Did they have a reason? Had someone tipped them off? Shit. Am I being relocated?*

There was a tightening in Bette's chest as her mouth dried out. The tightness moved up her throat, making it hard to swallow. The car seemed to contract to a third of its size; Bette was suddenly aware of the closeness, the motion, and the intense herbaceous aroma of whatever Ms. Tyler was wearing. David had been right. Why hadn't she just listened to him? She should have been more careful. She felt her activity was incon-sequential, so why would they even bother with her?

Maybe they thought she had something to do with the attack at the propagation office? Surely not. She had been the victim. But the way they had pulled her out of the hospital . . . *Do they think I know something? Did something else, something worse, happen that day? Jesus, they don't think I'm involved, do they?*

Bette tried to catch a few ragged breaths under the ava-lanche of uneasy thoughts. The car seemed insulated from all noise on the outside, and for a moment, Bette wondered if she had lost her hearing. All she could hear were her quivering breaths and blood pulsing in the sides of her head. The scent of the car, a mixture of upholstery cleaner and stringent lavender, was overbearing. Bette closed her eyes and clenched her fists. The wound beneath the bandage on her neck tightened every time she swallowed.

"Can I ask what this is about?" Bette asked unsteadily and quieter than intended.

Ms. Tyler leaned back, draping her arm over the top of her seat. Her icy eyes drilled into Bette, cataloging every facet. Bette's arms and legs began to tingle, and she faltered under the consuming stare. She cut her eyes from Ms. Tyler's glare as her stomach churned, and she bit down to keep her teeth from chattering. The director seemed pleased to feast on her fear while not saying a word.

Bette swallowed, fighting in vain to right her tumultuous thoughts and get above the undertow of her rolling, splashing emotions. *What are they going to do to me?* That was really what she needed to be afraid of. It didn't really matter *why* she was in this car. Once Enforcement was involved, that was the only question that mattered: What were they going to do?

The thought made Bette's stomach drop and a wave of nausea swept over her. She thought back to when Julie had been relocated. The Department of Propagation enforcement officers had come, but there were only two of them. Bette had been leaving the Depot House that day as the scene unfolded before her at the bottom of the steps. Julie had not gone quietly, but she had never done anything quietly. She squawked and spat, dropping to her knees every few steps causing the enforcement officers to yank her back to her feet. At one point, she refused to stand, so they dragged her while she shrieked obscenities. Her partner, Roc, trailed fretfully behind the scene, with David just a few steps behind him. As the officers and a caterwauling Julie reached the cement apron at the bottom of the stairs, she began kicking. One of the officers tripped forward and fell hard, forearms first, on the roughly graded cement. He stood and proceeded to kick and punch Julie until she stopped moving. Roc cried out, trying unsuccessfully to run to her as David held him back. The furious officer spit on Julie's inert body. Blood was smeared under her nose and purplish-red lumps swelled on her face. The officer then grabbed her by the ankle and yelled for his partner. Her long dark hair mingled with the dust and gravel as they pulled her to their vehicle. The only sound was Roc, howling from his knees mere yards behind her, his arms outstretched. David stood with his hand on Roc's shoulder . . .

"As you know," Ms. Tyler began, her frigid words slicing through Bette's hot pulsing flashback, "all reports pertaining to fertility must be investigated in accordance with the law."

Bette blinked, remembering where she was. Her brow furrowed and she blinked a few more times as her mind replayed what the director had just said. *All reports pertaining to fertility . . .*

Bette's eyebrows shot up as her eyes widened. "Excuse me?" she asked, not sure she had heard correctly.

"I believe you heard what I said," came the woman's curt reply.

A report pertaining to fertility? My fertility? Did the director of the Birthing Center believe there was a fertility report about her?

"Um, why would there be any of these, uh, reports concerning me?" Bette stammered.

The woman raised a meticulously shaped eyebrow. Bette willed herself to maintain eye contact. She focused on the barely perceivable discolored eye while pressing her cold fingers into her neck to relieve the sudden itching. Bette was more confused than ever. *So, this isn't about Cabe or relocation; it is about a fertility report? That might explain why the director is involved, but who would have reason to file a fertility report?*

Bette had been inconclusive her entire life. There were years' worth of data to prove that. Bette's last exam had been the same as all the ones before it. There had been no change, except now there was this whole attack incident. *Did the hospital doctors find something? Are they the ones who reported this?* She was nearly thirty. *Her mother had been thirty . . .*

Bette brought one hand to her lips and began to nervously chew the nail on her right index finger as she looked out the tinted car window. *So, they believe there is a fertility report to investigate, which must mean . . .*

"Where-where are we going?" Bette asked.

The director smoothed her jacket and crossed her legs, the fabric of her white suit whispering as it brushed together. The manicured fingers of her left hand lingered on the royal blue edge of her lapel; her attention focused outside the window. "It is protocol to place you in the Birthing Center to begin the brokering process."

Bette's eyes bulged as she leaned in a little closer, her tongue slogged like sandpaper across her teeth. "The what?"

The casual way in which the director said it left Bette grasping for words. These kinds of car rides weren't normal. No one was just *placed* in the Birthing Center. *Placed?* Vases are placed. Wigs are placed. This was a place one trained for, tested for, was observed and recruited for. The Birthing Center was earned. Women were not placed in the Birthing Center; they pleaded and bled for the opportunity to be turned away.

Ms. Tyler shifted in her seat, impatiently exhaling through her nose. "Some things have changed, Ms. Donovan."

NOVEMBER 10, 2050 | *THE NEW YORK TIMES*

Groups of domestic refugees have fled the United States Proper for areas abandoned after the Big One. Repatriates, as they have come to be known, cite fundamental and irreconcilable differences with the United States surrounding the use of alleged genetic modifications to produce, livestock, and humans. These agricultural settlements have sprung up in what used to be viable farmland before mono-cropping and fertilizer depleted the soil and leached into the river.

After the economic crash following the Big One, in an emergency effort to conserve resources, the United States voted to redraw its official borders to consolidate federal funds. Areas outside of the redrawn borders are still considered territory, albeit uninhabited, and are not entitled to federal monies.

21

2112, PRESENT

The Department of Propagation lay in the heart of the city, apropos since the Department of Propagation gave the city life. This was the hive to which the drones flocked; this was where some of the fertile women were housed. The entire city served the Department of Propagation and its National Fertility Agenda. It was a towering, impressive building covered in state-of-the-art solar glass and rising at least twenty floors above the thick concrete walls that surrounded its base. She'd never been there, but Bette recognized the building from the news and commercials.

The officers parked the mobile unit in a semicircle drive in front of the massive building. The stone and glass structure sat back off the street a ways. A cement plaza was laid out artfully before a row of yellow crash barriers at the base of the steps leading up to the Department. Its large emblem, a baby surrounded by laurel leaves, was etched in the stone facade above three sets of double solar glass doors. A police officer was posted at each set of doors, resolute and placid in a dark blue uniform and dark glasses. Bette's group moved through the slate-gray concrete walls and a detector; blinking lights signaled they had nothing to hide. They made their way through another set of glass doors that opened into an airy lobby. A few preoccupied people zigged across the travertine floors like black ants in search of their colony. The officers, the director, and Bette approached a tall, smooth counter in the middle of the lobby. A bored-looking man merely glanced at them and asked, "Admitting?"

Ms. Tyler nodded.

"Go ahead."

They walked past the counter, down a set of stairs, and exited through a set of glass doors into a courtyard behind the building. Bette paused once they were outside, looking around. Across the field, by a domed building, were a handful of Propagation staff stationed about a machine that resembled a cherry picker. On the side of the dome, light reflected off a four-legged robot. The robot was advancing up the side of the building. The staff clustered in twos and threes, shielding their eyes as they monitored the robot's progress. The bald enforcement officer tugged at her elbow as they strode through the parklike yard.

"You can go," Ms. Tyler instructed the dark-haired officer. He nodded and peeled off on a tangential sidewalk toward the cluster of uniformed agents.

Ms. Tyler strode ahead of Bette and the other officer. Behind them stood the looming high-rise, monopolizing what Bette could still see of the sullen sky. *We just walked through,* she thought, as if the Department of Propagation was just some kind of shortcut. They had breezed past security, moved unimpeded through the lobby of the most influential body of government, and then walked out. How they must have looked, Bette in her crumpled paper gown and matted hair with two burly enforcement officers, and Ms. Tyler looking ready to give a televised speech. They were not questioned and there were no other pat downs, as if this was a regular sight.

To her left and right, other buildings, not quite as tall, formed a protective cluster around a stone cupola in the middle of the Department of Propagation campus. This was Birthing Center HQ. There were three other satellite birthing centers throughout the United States, but they all got their direction from HQ. The windows, if you could call them that, were mere slits narrowed by suspicious panes, which seemed to squint as they checked and rechecked its protective barriers. It was not stately like the Department of Propagation or visionary like the train station. Bette was rather surprised at how *functional* it was. *This is the revered, ultraexclusive Birthing Center?* "Stone" was the wrong word to describe it; "stone" implied a polished finish, which this building did not have. Its composition reminded Bette of something akin to stucco's natural, more resilient cousin. It looked like a bunker, hunched over and squat in the midst of lean skyward buildings, a practical stronghold amid opulence.

Bette counted three above-ground levels as she walked, more crag and less solar glass than the Department of Propagation. A cement half-wall buttressed the perimeter of the Birthing Center. Bette could see over the top of the half-wall as they approached another verdant courtyard. Large, leafy trees lined the walkway of a bright green lawn to the front double doors. On its face, the entrance looked vibrant and welcoming, but there was a blue-blooded stillness to the scene Bette could suss out anywhere; catching a whiff of demure condescension intermingled with the scent of freshly cut grass.

What the fuck is happening? The phrase echoed over and over in Bette's mind. Who was she? Nobody. Useless. Inconclusive. Worthless. How was she being escorted to the Birthing Center by the director herself? *What the fuck is happening?* It was the only question to ask. She'd woken up this morning in a hospital bed. Now, still woozy and achy, she was standing in front of the Birthing Center. *The Birthing Center.* This was the premier facility for fertility, available exclusively for those able to procreate. How had it come to include her? *What the fuck is happening?* Was this her life? Had they been mistaken and taken the wrong person? That would make more sense. Any minute she expected Ms. Tyler to rear up like a meerkat, sensing an intruder, and explain to Bette that she was free to go. Of course they picked up the wrong person; there was a much younger and fecund individual who had a similar name or DOP number as Bette. Maybe they had transposed a number or just read their orders wrong. Maybe it was a Betty or a Benji, or someone with the last name Bonovan who was supposed to be here.

Bette's head buzzed as she stopped a few feet from the door of the Birthing Center. It was beautiful but seemingly void of the living. There was no breeze, no drones overhead, and no noise from passersby. There were no other people out here besides them. There were no birds or rabbits or humming insects. *Surely, birds and bugs would be attracted to this place. Why aren't there any?* Bette looked again at all the buildings that surrounded them like an impenetrable fence. She could see no spaces of sky or grass between any of them. Bette blinked, wondering if this was a real place or just some kind of giant illusion meant to disguise something else.

Ms. Tyler stopped at the glass door of the roughly textured mound of a building, waiting for her ID sync. The tinted solar glass door yawned open silently, in no real hurry to receive them. "Quickly now!" she ordered, gesturing toward the open door.

The lobby they entered was plush with warm cream-colored walls, lacking scuffs or signs of wear and tear. Perky fresh-cut flowers seemed to cover every surface and perfumed the air. A massive aquarium rose behind the reception area doubling as a wall. It made sense that creatures would be drawn to this place, but fish Bette had not expected. They moved by so slowly that it took a moment to grasp they were real. The floors were covered in thick dark-blue carpet, absorbing Bette's and her entourage's footsteps. Bette did a double take, confused by the hard plaster look of the outside and the high-caliber furnishings on the inside. At one end of the empty reception desk sat a large glass vessel containing water and citrus fruit with a valve on the end.

What the fuck is happening? Oranges in the water? Bette had entered another dimension. That could be the only explanation. Had the doctors accidentally given her some experimental drug that physically transported her to a parallel universe? Had they snipped a brain wire and now she was involved in a vivid hallucination. *What the fuck is happening?*

"You can go," Ms. Tyler dismissed the officer. "I can handle it from here." The bald officer nodded, let go of Bette's arm, and took three large steps back, not unlike an underpaid courier grateful to be rid of a toxic package. He remained in place while Ms. Tyler a crossed the room to open another door. Bette eyeballed the empty room with its pooling damask drapes and new lustrous couches. Peonies, lilies, and aster of all colors filled the vases on a handful of end tables, their stems straight and petals velvety, notable signs of being recently cut. It appeared to be decorated for some type of posh reception that no one had attended.

"Keep up, Bette," Ms. Tyler snapped. Bette shook her head, dazed by her surroundings, and followed the director into the hallway, which was a departure from the luxe lobby. This was more in line with what Bette had expected, a windowless, nondescript gray with utilitarian overhead lighting. Ms. Tyler's heels clacked on the sealed concrete floor as they came to a fork in the hall and continued down the left corridor. Ms. Tyler halted at an unremarkable metal door in a hall filled with other unremarkable doors. As she placed her hand on the door, she stared straight ahead without blinking. A few seconds passed, and the door opened.

This room was bright in relation to the dimness of the hall, with recessed lighting overhead and domed lights on the wall. Sparse, it only contained a round table with three metal chairs. Bette noticed the tabletop was lit up.

"Have a seat." Ms. Tyler sat down, placing both palms on the illuminated table. The table screen came to life and she made a series of swipes and taps. Bette pulled out a chair.

"Um, actually there please," Ms. Tyler instructed Bette, indicating the chair directly across from her.

A document appeared on the table, facing Bette's direction so she wouldn't have to read upside down. "Ms. Donovan, this is the orientation for the Birthing Center. I will go over what is expected of you. I can't permit entry into my birthing center until you have agreed to all terms and conditions. Understand?"

Bette's stunned silence seemed answer enough for Ms. Tyler, so she began swiping through the documents. She'd obviously recited this speech a thousand times based on the disinterested way she rushed through boilerplate, jargon-filled agreements concerning the privacy and procedure of the Center. There was an extensive and tedious description of the duties expected of the candidate and what the candidate could expect from the Center in return. Bette tried to keep up but the language, completely foreign to her, passed over her head like whistling bullets. Terms like "gestational surrogacy" and phrases such as "if the trimester overlaps a calendar year" and "in the event lactation is not an option" were so out of context, it made no sense to Bette.

But then, everything here was out of context.

"You are not sponsored so we can skip this," Ms. Tyler murmured to herself. Her forehead tilted down at the screen causing a lock of her silver hair to fall in her face. She brushed it back, tapping the screen twice with finality. Looking up, her emotionless eyes rested on Bette. Ms. Tyler did not strike her as a maternal woman with any penchant toward mentoring. This look felt more like she was appraising an item for purchase, but not a personal purchase. This would be a business purchase, an acquisition. Would it work the way it was supposed to? Would it generate some return or value? Or, was this going to be a loss leader, money hole, dud? Then she blinked and gave a slight nod as if making the decision.

"Well, I guess it is time to go in." The weight of the last two words landed heavy on Bette's shoulders.

Go in.

"Initial here and sign your name here," Ms. Tyler ordered. Bette's finger hovered over the document. *What the fuck is happening?* She didn't know what she was signing. She did not even know if signing mattered since it was clear this was not voluntary. She had the distinct feeling that she was going where the director wanted her, with or without her consent. At least this way it seemed like it was her choice.

"Here and here." Ms. Tyler's tone grew sharper as she poked her nude polished fingertip at the screen. The acerbic lavender cologne this woman wore hung in a cloying brume around them. In small diffused amounts, it might have been quite pleasant, but here it only acted like a scented closer, coercing Bette to sign.

Bette swallowed, scrawling her name.

2110 | INTERNAL BIRTHING CENTER HQ MEMO

Birthing Centers' Security Levels Raised to Moderate

It is our conclusion that there was a breach at Birthing Center South. Security was alerted to a pile of crumpled-up uniforms in the delivery bay. Upon further search, a security officer was found dead in a maintenance closet. Burn marks on the body indicate he was pulsed. Nothing was taken, information systems were not compromised, but no surveillance could be collected of the intruder(s).

22

Ms. Tyler sprang up and purposefully made her way to the door. Bette stood to follow, glancing one last time at her name on the table behind her. Ms. Tyler continued briskly down the gray hall. At the end, she opened another door. The light caused Bette to squint as they walked through the doorway. "I'll show you to your suite. From there, your suite mate will give you a tour of the facility, going over the schedule and rules. And Bette—" The director paused.

Bette was overtaken by the splendor of what lay beyond the doorway. The center was oval with a giant garden in its middle. The large dome ceiling above mimicked a blue sky and white fluffy clouds. They had entered a large hallway that made its way around the garden in an elliptical shape. It was the most beautiful place she had ever visited. Large pillars framed the hallway on the right and left. Just beyond these pillars were cutouts for doors and other smaller hallways. Bette blinked, abruptly realizing that the prim woman had stopped talking. She turned to make eye contact.

"I would strongly suggest that you listen to your suite mate. She is one of our top producers," Ms. Tyler finished.

Bette only nodded.

"This is the main common area," Ms. Tyler narrated in her dry, matter-of-fact way.

Two girls, not even twenty, passed Bette, engrossed in conversation. Dressed in dark leggings and pastel-colored, three-quarter-sleeve tunics, the girls ambled down the hallway, taking a moment to evaluate Bette. Bette noticed the slight tightening of their shirts around each of their middles. As she looked a moment longer, she was able to make out a bulbous outline under the shirts.

They are pregnant! Both of them! Bette gawked around, noticing more pairs and trios of young women in the hallway. They were everywhere, all of them pregnant! Some of them had more pronounced bumps and fuller faces, but nearly every one of them had a protruding belly. Pregnancy was everywhere.

"Ms. Donovan?" The pointed voice drew her back. "Are you coming?" Ms. Tyler was a dozen steps in front of Bette.

"Yes, yes. Sorry," she apologized, hurrying to catch up.

"As I was saying, after your tour, you will be escorted to the medical wing where I will assess you."

They turned right off the large main hallway into a smaller but equally grand corridor. Bette glanced over her shoulder to catch another glimpse of the pregnant women behind her. She collided with something. She turned to find a waist-high robot rolling down the corridor. She jumped out of its path and watched, curious, as it sped silently away.

"Seriously, Bette!" Ms. Tyler admonished.

"Yes, I'm coming!"

It was apparent that the Birthing Center did not have to abide by the rules everyone else was required to live by. The use of robots shouldn't have surprised her, but it did. With scarce resources and a population needing to work to survive, outsourcing jobs to robots was anathema. Companies and the government capitulated to only use them when there was no human alternative. It helped to be seen as sympathetic to the economic hardship their fellow man lived under. But robots were used, just not publicly flaunted.

The halls were carpeted with similar decadent carpet from the lobby, only with muted color swirls. The sconces from the wall threw off gold ambient light. Every so often, they passed a wooden door with a bronze triangle placard. The doors were spaced far apart, meaning the rooms must be sizable. Beside each door was a square of solar glass. They stopped at a door with the number four on the triangle placard.

Ms. Tyler tapped the square of solar glass a few times. "Place your palm here," she said as she pointed to the solar glass.

Bette did, and after a moment it beeped.

"Now, take it off and do it again." Bette took her hand away and pressed it back into the square. It beeped a second time. The door swung open.

"This is your suite." She gestured to the open door. Bette stretched her neck to get a peek.

"Well, go on then," Ms. Tyler said, indifferent to Bette and her newly capsized life.

Bette swallowed nervously. Ms. Tyler rolled her eyes and turned on her heel, heading back the way she came.

SEPTEMBER 17, 2064 | DOJ RESPONSE TO DOP PROPOSAL

Due to the dire trend of your projections, we agree with your suggestion to deploy more units to assist in the location of potential fertile candidates. The data/evidence is compelling. While somewhat unconventional, these are unprecedented times, and another tool in our arsenal is simply that: a tool. It is our determination that the gains of this proposal far outweigh the liabilities. A hybrid of tactics must be used to meet the National Fertility Agenda.

23

Bette stepped through the doorway and into the suite. The room was invitingly lit and spacious. Skylights simulated a perfect day, and the bamboo floors shone under them. A young woman sat on a rich, neutral-colored couch, pregnant, her head tilting a little to the left. It looked as if she were in some kind of trance.

Bette stood a moment before clearing her throat. The girl blinked, finally taking notice of her. Bette locked in on a slight discoloration in her large expressive eyes, like the one she noticed in Ms. Tyler's. Heavy black bangs rested above her large dark eyes, framing the minor color difference. Her face so clear and bright, she was the picture of vitality and health.

"Oh, so you are, like . . . old." The woman straightened, unimpressed. As she sat up taller, Bette noticed her round midsection.

A little taken aback, Bette didn't know how to respond. The woman went on to explain, "They said the new girl would be a little older. You are, like, what? Thirty?"

"Yes. Well, twenty-nine, actually," Bette answered with a nervous smile as she surveyed the new living quarters.

"Yeah, so, like, old." The dark-haired woman sighed. "I don't know why they bring you guys in. Two good years, maybe."

Bette floundered, waiting for this to turn into a real conversation. When it didn't, she attempted small talk. "So, how old are you?" Bette asked, shifting on her feet.

"Twenty-three," the woman answered snappily.

"Oh, so not so much younger than me," Bette concluded, trying to feel less insecure.

"I'm *six* years younger than you," she said defensively, "which is an eternity when it comes to fertility."

It suddenly occurred to Bette that most of these women had been there since their late teens. That was when her own status had been determined. This was the only way of life they had ever known.

"Oh, I didn't mean . . . " Bette stammered, worried she had already offended her new roommate. "Forgive me; this is kind of, uh, strange for me. Let me start over. Hi, my name is Bette."

One of the woman's eyebrows went up and she took another look at Bette. "What happened to your neck?"

"Oh, uh . . . " Bette put her hand to the stiff dressing on the right side of her neck. "I'm not really sure." Bette felt like a bug in a jar the way the young woman examined her; she conducted herself like an uncouth child that hadn't quite yet learned to respect all life-forms.

"I guess you want to know where you'll sleep," she said, changing the subject and sidestepping any attempt at civility. "In there." Her head tipped to her left.

"Thank you." Bette breathed a sigh of relief as she darted from the living room into the other room, grateful to remove herself from the uncomfortable conversation with her terse suite mate.

Her room was the size of her apartment. There was a large modern platform bed covered in white and yellow linens and framed with a gray upholstered headboard. Bette sat on the edge and began to sink down in the comforter. Her shoulders relaxed and fell from their position around her ears as a throbbing ache radiated through her body. She had barely rejoined the living when Ms. Tyler had pulled her from the hospital. Her experience had not been that of a complete recovery by any means.

Looking around, she saw a tall open door off the right side of the bed. Through the doorway, she noticed the white tile floor. It was the bathroom, but it was unlike any bathroom she'd ever seen. There was a hefty white ceramic basin in the middle of the room, resembling a sink large enough for a person to get in.

So, it's true. Pregnant women do take water baths here.

"Fern." A voice from behind startled Bette. She turned to see the indifferent woman standing in the doorway, one hand on her belly, the other on her hip.

"Where?" Bette asked, not seeing any plants in the stark white bathroom.

"That's my name, Fern."

"Oh, well, it's nice to meet you, Fern."

"Yeah, okay." Fern shrugged off the greeting. "Schedule is a big deal around here. We get up every day at seven. Weigh in, get ready, and go to breakfast."

"Weigh in?" Bette asked.

"Yep, you will notice there's a scale here, by the door," she said in the worst tour guide impersonation Bette had ever heard. She pointed to the only silver tile in the whole room. "You will stand there after you get up. I mean, not right when you get up; you can go to the bathroom and whatever, but before you leave the room, stand on that. It will beep, letting you know when it has captured its data."

"What data is it collecting?"

"I don't know. Like, weight and temperature and metric stuff. They are monitoring your condition."

"Hmm." Bette's sober brown eyes fixed on the lone silver tile.

"You know, for, like, prevention and stuff," Fern said as if trying to anticipate Bette's next question. She continued talking as she walked out of the room. Bette, still wondering about the metrics the Center was collecting, interrupted her.

"Prevention of what?"

Fern stopped out in the living area, watching Bette in a way that indicated she was really seeing her for the first time. "You sure do ask a lot of questions, don't you?"

"Well, I was just curious . . . "

"Try not to make a habit out of it, okay? The rules are the rules for a reason. Don't try to think for the Center; you are not smarter than them." The two women stared at each other, uncertain of what to think of the other. Fern blinked twice and continued her orientation.

"After breakfast, we head to the gym. A doctor checks your vitals and gives you a workout regimen. At nine, we have individual scheduled time. Mostly, that is sponsor work but I don't think you'll be doing that. Then to lunch. After lunch, we rest for an hour. Whatever you didn't get done before lunch you do until dinner. After dinner, we meditate. Then back to our suites. Lights out by nine-thirty. Got it?"

Bette's eyes kept drifting to her belly as she spoke. "How pregnant are you?"

"Five months. It's a boy," Fern replied, disenchanted.

"Wow," Bette said. "How many children have you had?"

"Live births or transfers?"

Bette's brow furrowed in confusion.

"Live births are when we carry the baby to term for a live birth. Those only happen on a lactation rotation, which is about every fourth or fifth conception."

"Oh, uh, I guess live births then?"

"This is my third live birth. That is why they put you with me. I'm a consistent producer. I'm, like, your trainer or mentor or something," Fern offered.

"Fitting," Bette remarked. "You sort of propagate like a fern."

Bette was amused by her joke, but Fern stared at her blankly. "I don't get it."

"You know, ferns create lots of spores . . . "

Fern froze a moment, distracted, like she was trying to overhear another conversation. "Anyway," she said, looking up when the distraction passed, "that is the suite. We share a living area and a kitchenette. We have separate sleeping quarters and bathrooms. So, I don't go in yours and you don't go in mine. Got it?"

Bette nodded.

Fern made a half-hearted sweep with one of her hands. "Now, for the rest." She walked to the entryway.

"You will notice a symbol and a number on each door. Our hallway is Triangle Hall. There are two girls in a suite, five suites to a hall. Only four of ours are full, so there are six other members of Triangle Hall. We eat together, work out together, get medical checks around the same time. You get the idea; we see a lot of each other."

She pressed her hand on the solar glass pad by the door and paused. "You and I have access to our room as does the staff and their bots. So, nothing is really ever private around here. We are friendly, not friends. If you remember that, you will be able to hack it."

She held up her hand as if she knew what Bette was about to say. "Having babies is the easy part," Fern said as if that explained anything.

She stepped out into the hall, ready to continue the guided tour. "Are you coming?" she asked impatiently, as if she had other pressing matters to attend to.

"Uh, yes." Bette was caught a little off guard. She quickened her pace to keep up with Fern.

In the hall, Fern made a motion to one of the other doors. "See? Triangle."

Bette was unfamiliar with the way pregnant women moved. She had assumed that being burdened with the ability to give life was a weighty thing, requiring a slower pace. Fern moved like she was participating in a fire drill. Before she knew it, they were back in the common area where Fern stopped abruptly. "Common area. Self-explanatory. There are hallways all around the perimeter of this main walkway. Sphere Hall." She began pointing as she spoke. "Dining room. Square Hall. Gym. Triangle Hall. Meditation room."

She stopped, training her aloof black eyes squarely at Bette. "Obviously, this is the garden, here, in the middle of everything. I suppose you are sort of into that with your spores and all."

The corners of Bette's mouth turned up at Fern's reference to her earlier spore joke. Keeping to the outer edge, they walked to the farthest point in the elliptically shaped hallway before it started to curve back around. Every other door in the hallway was recessed, but in the middle of this wall was a larger door that stuck out. It was covered in what looked like sheet metal. Fern stopped in front of it and placed her hand on it.

"Elevator." A moment passed and the door slid open. Once in, they turned to face the closing door. Inside was the same sheet-metal look. Fern pointed at the sparse keypad with only three buttons on it.

"Not a lot of options, right? That is because this is the resident elevator. We don't get to go wherever we want. We are restricted to the main floor, floor one, and floor two. See M, for main. Floor one is the floor directly below us where all the medical facilities are. Floor two is directly above us and everything related to sponsor work is located there."

She raised her eyebrow as she appraised Bette. "I assume, based on the looks of you, that you are unsponsored." It was more of a statement than a question.

Why did everyone keep saying it like that? "Yes," Bette said.

She nodded and pushed the button. They waited in silence until the door opened without a noise. "Floor one, or med floor," Fern said as she began her quick pace. An empty white quartz reception desk sat directly in front of the open elevator doors in an empty, white, egg-shaped lobby. It was polished to a high shine and gleamed a pearly shade of white under the light. This appeared to be the only feature in the whole room, Bette noticed as she looked out of the elevator. As she looked to her left and right upon exiting the elevator, she noticed hallways on either side of the elevator. Fern motored right up to the desk, her shiny black hair swinging back and forth across her shoulders.

"Wait here. Someone will be back to take care of you. When you are done, go back to the main floor. Can you handle that?" She crossed her arms, her unsentimental, unblinking eyes hungry for acknowledgment.

"Pretty sure I can," Bette said.

"It's the *M* button," Fern reminded her.

"I got it," Bette reassured her.

Fern scrutinized her as if she wasn't fully sure Bette could follow such simple instructions. She blinked twice in rapid succession as if making up her mind. "Good. Dorothea is expecting you so don't wander off." Fern turned to leave but then thought better of it, adding, "And don't ask a bunch of stupid questions, okay?"

"Okay," Bette said.

"Wait here. Don't wander off. Press M for Main. Okay?"

"Will do."

Satisfied, Fern sped back to the elevator. She stared dully through Bette as the doors closed and whisked her away.

Bette wondered what responsibilities awaited this self-important twenty-three-year-old pregnant woman who was limited to three floors of living.

24

Nervous about the next phase of her orientation, Bette drummed her fingers on the counter, smooth and cool under the pads of her fingertips. From here, she could see the long hallway behind the desk with closed doors along both sides. It reminded her of the propagation office she visited each quarter, only about twenty years newer. She stretched her tight neck a little to look over the counter, hoping to see an open screen, some sort of a report lying around, or maybe a collection vial that had been labeled to give her some indication of what was going to happen here. But it was as stark and sterile as it had initially appeared. All information was sanitized from this area. She turned around and rolled her shoulders to help with the stiff tension, the bandage crinkling with movement.

It was quiet in the way all medical offices were. She thought she could make out footsteps, but they were soon swallowed up by the faraway hissing sound of the ventilation pushing around disinfected air. Bette started to wonder if this was a prank, but the smug way that Fern carried herself and the succinct way she dispensed rules left no question.

Suddenly, a sharp, pained cry pierced the silence, causing the hair to stand up on Bette's forearms. She spun around. The thin, miserable sound had come from somewhere down that hallway. She stiffened, holding her breath, waiting.

There! Bette heard it again, like a stifled yip. She sprung up on her tiptoes to see over the counter, spotting another rolling robot. Its lens paused and adjusted as Bette came into its sight line. It was like the one she'd seen earlier in the hall, white and gray, boxy looking with two arms, one much bigger than the other. It backed up, turned, and went back down the hall disappearing into a door that had recently opened. A moment later, Bette heard footsteps coming from the hallway. A medium woman, round in both height and features, emerged through the doorway. Her brown eyes alighted on Bette.

"Ms. Donovan?"

Bette hesitated as she tried to reconcile the distressed sound she'd heard and the ambivalent woman who had just come from the same direction. "I am."

The woman pointed to her chest, smiling. Her round glasses matched the roundness of her cheeks. "My name is Maria. I'm Dorothea's assistant. We will be guiding you through the medical evaluations. Lord, you are a skinny-minnie, aren't you? Have you ever broken your nose? Well, never mind, we can fix all of that. Come with me and we will get started." She motioned for Bette to come around the side of the desk and follow her back.

Maria spent a considerable amount of time asking Bette about her mother and grandmother; she inquired about their habits, height, known sexual partners, drug use, and menstrual cycles, all things for which Bette really didn't have answers. That didn't seem to deter Maria, though. When she was satisfied, she proceeded to ask all the same questions about Bette, often asking the same question multiple times, just phrased differently.

"Okay," Maria began as she stood from her chair, "now we will do the physical sampling over here in the next room." Bette stood just inside the physical sampling room where she could see a table in the center of the room. Above it was what looked like a large metal claw with four apendages. To the left, she could see Ms. Tyler positioned behind a console. "There is nothing to be afraid of," Maria whispered next to Bette. "She looks scarier than she really is." Bette was not sure if she was referring to the four-legged machine or Ms. Tyler.

"Take off your clothes and lay down on the table," Ms. Tyler instructed from behind her console. "Face up to start."

"What exactly does this thing, uh, sample?" Bette asked, careful not to take her eyes off it as she undressed. Naked, Bette faltered at the edge of the hulking multi-legged machine. She looked down at the floor. David had said she had been in the hospital a couple of weeks and her prickly bottom half corroborated this. Body lice was less of a problem when there was no hair. Angry, coiled ingrown hairs were interspersed among the itchy pubic hair growing in. The stubby quills on her legs stuck out defensively, lost and unsure of how they should lay on her flaky skin. Her veiny and jaundiced casing clung to her skeleton like packing tape wrapped tightly around a package, highlighting her corners and edges. Her hip bones jutted out from her body, like the knobby protrusions on a tree trunk. Her less exposed and more supple skin dipped in at her rib cage and around nearly deflated breasts. Her knees and ankle bones looked like parts borrowed from someone two sizes bigger. Standing under these lights made her feel even uglier than she thought she was.

"The exam table is heated, so you won't get chilly!" Maria said, trying to calm Bette's obvious nervousness.

Bette climbed, exposed and defenseless, onto the table. The glaring lights made her squint. Maria was right; it was warm to the touch, but it wasn't warm enough to melt away the wave of uncertainty rising inside of Bette's stomach.

"Maria, take that bandage off her neck," Ms. Tyler's annoyed voice echoed throughout the room. Maria sheepishly ambled over to Bette.

"Oops," Maria said as she carefully pulled the bandage off Bette's neck. Fresh air rushed to the sequestered patch of skin and Bette stretched her neck from side to side.

The ominous metallic hands began to move above her, causing Bette's stomach to flutter. Anxious shivers oscillated unbidden through the web of her nerves. She held her breath as the arms neared her skin. Bette winced in anticipation of pain. The machine looked as though it could tear her limbs from her trunk. But as the robotic pincers landed, they began to simply press, poke, and pinch nearly every square inch of her body. Bette opened her eyes and tilted her chin down for a better look. Then a prick came from a pincer down by her left thigh. Bette jerked. The other pincers did the same in a volley of succession, stomach, right arm, and left calf.

"Ow!" Bette exclaimed. The arms shifted and repeated the process of pressing and poking before the little stabs of pain. Bette did not exclaim the second, third, or fourth time. The exam finally completed, the robotic arms stopped and retreated to the center of the machine.

"Okay, face down," Ms. Tyler methodically ordered.

Bette gritted her teeth and exhaled through her nose as she flipped over. She closed her eyes and tried not to jerk when the quick stinging punctures came.

It had been unpleasant when Bette began participating in the Mandate. Her grandma would hold her in the kitchen, smoothing her hair while Bette tried not to cry. Her mother, from her perch on her hard metal stool at the kitchen island, would say, "It is just a process, Bette. Like every process, you will get used to it. It won't be long until this is just as routine as everything else." Her mother had been right. Eventually, you could take whatever they did to you. Squeeze your eyes shut and disassociate with the present moment. Nod your head and tune out the words; their faces always told the story better than words ever could. It was better not to hear those words most of the time. The occurrence always ended and then repeated itself with exacting regularity. It wasn't personal, but it was necessary for survival. Hard things had to be endured to ensure the future. Bette's mind wandered back to that pitiful cry she'd heard earlier, and she found herself wondering if it had come from someone new to this process. She felt a pang as she remembered what it had been like to be seventeen. *What would it have been like here?*

A gentle tap on Bette's shoulder startled her. "You can sit up," Maria said, offering Bette a starchy white paper gown. Bette accepted it gratefully and pulled it over her head to cover her grisly, trembling body.

Maria returned to the console where Ms. Tyler controlled the probing arms. Sitting in the crinkly gown on the warm exam table under the four-armed robot, Bette's eyes drifted to a set of thin white lines on her inner right forearm. She felt a pang of sorrow for the girl who had put them there with a straight razor over a decade ago. It was all she could do then to exist and feel something. Being left-handed she had more control of the blade and could slowly apply pressure and drag it along the delicate skin on the right inner arm. Watching the orbs of crimson seep out of the self inflicted cut had been calming. The exhaustion of being newly available to the Mandate often left her listless, staring at the ceiling as tears shimmered in her eyes.

Bette shivered in the cool, clinical air under the unrelenting fluorescent lights, rubbing her chilled hands up and down her marbled red-and-purple arms. *Was this the place that cry had come from? Or was it a different room?* Bette hadn't seen any other residents in the med floor.

Maria nodded as she conferred with Ms. Tyler and then made her way back to the exam table. She pressed a button on the end of the exam table by Bette's feet, and levers slid out on either side. They looked like stirrups. "This is the part a human does," Maria said, winking as she pulled on a glove. "Ladies don't tense up as much with a friendly face. So, if you could scoot on down and place your feet here." Maria's glove snapped on her wrist and she patted the end of the exam table. "Yep, just like that . . . "

No one relished seeing those stirrups, but a few deep breaths and it was over, not unlike most of Bette's sexual encounters. "Okay, that'll do it!" Maria chirped.

Bette slid off the exam table, wiped away the excess lubricant, and wriggled on new clothes Maria gave her. A familiar wave of waking up washed over Bette as she left the room. A sense that she had dreamed something but couldn't quite remember all the details. It was a trick she'd learned early on. What was a body anyway? Or feelings? A Propagation examination was just another event easier to endure if detached and not completely present.

As she walked out of the exam room and down the hall, Bette noticed one of the few doors with a window. The word *Lactation* was etched into the glass. She stopped to look into the room, sensing movement somewhere within. Two male staffers dressed in teal knee-length, long-sleeved smocks walked past the door in conversation. One laughed at something the other had said. They moved to reveal an enormous contraption in the center of the room. It looked like a circular couch with dividers between each seat. Clear tubing ran from each seat to a pipe rising ominously from the space behind the seats. In each seat sat a half-naked girl. Bette's eyes widened, her hand shooting to her mouth to stifle a gasp.

One girl, maybe sixteen, sat in one of the seats facing the door with her eyes closed. Her head leaned against a divider, and her dark hair was in a ponytail, its static-charged strands stuck to the divider. She was naked from the waist up and a clear cup covered each of her breasts. The cups were attached to the tubing that fed an opaque substance back to the pipe. Like a target, Bette was drawn to the dark leathery areoles, which highlighted a striking contrast to the girl's pasty skin. Her ribs were painfully obvious under the domed, clear plastic. One of the blue-robed staffers tapped the girl on the chin. She opened her eyes and straightened up, looking as disoriented as Bette felt.

"Bette?" Maria's faraway voice came from the reception area.

Bette glanced toward the lobby and back into the lactation room. The two men's backs were to the door, blocking Bette's view. The staffer on the left turned to his coworker, laughing. But there was something in the lines of his mean face that made Bette uneasy. The sneering staffer walked out of sight, revealing the ponytailed girl. The skin over her collarbone dipped and hugged the natural depressions, accentuating the bones in her neck. She grimaced and wiped an errant tear from her face as the man moved to the control panel situated on the divider. Suddenly the girl jolted, her eyes wide with shocked pain. Bette's hand went to the door as she felt and looked for a way in. The man started shouting at the whole room. Even with Bette's ear pressed to the door, he still sounded far away.

"Wakey-wakey, ladies! Let's grit up and do our jobs! This production schedule ain't going to meet itself!"

The girl in the ponytail had slumped over. The other staffer returned with a bucket, which he swung back and forth to release a barrage of water onto the girl. The other staffer pulled her up by her ponytail. Blue-lipped and shivering, water dripping from the clumped-together tendrils and only supported by the staffer's rough hand, she didn't open her eyes. He slapped her face, barking something unintelligible. The girl did not respond. The two men exchanged words Bette could no longer hear. They roughly removed her from the couch contraption, yanked off the clear cups, and dumped her on the floor in front of it. She lay on her right side, facing the door. Blood droplets from her nipples mixing in with a thin milky substance formed a sick pink mixture that slid to a drain on the floor. This time both men exited from view. The girl's eyes were still closed.

"Bette, did you get lost?" Bette heard Maria's singsong voice again and then the sound of motorized wheels. Bette spied the robot at the end of the hall, now rolling toward her. She glanced from the petite girl lying motionless on the floor to the advancing robot. Bette guiltily tore her feet from her spot in front of the door marked *Lactation* and made her way to the lobby.

What are they doing?

"Everything okay?" Maria asked as Bette emerged from the hallway, the robot at her heels. Her head was cocked to one side like a curious animal, completely unaware of the barbarity down the hall. For a split second, Bette considered asking Maria about the girl in the lactation room, but something kept it from spilling out. Bette only nodded.

"You did great today, Bette. Enjoy your dinner. I'll see you tomorrow!"

Bette felt like she had been punched in the stomach. *Tomorrow? There would be more?*

Her shoulders sagged. *More of what? Round after round of painful sticks? Humiliation and nakedness?* The vision of that girl on the wet concrete and the others hooked up to those tubes made her shudder as she got into the elevator. Bette pressed the M button, just as Fern had told her, trying to put as much distance between her and *this* floor as possible.

25

Bette arrived on the main floor, shaken by what she had seen. Pregnant women milled about everywhere, funneling toward what Bette assumed must be the dining room. A few were talking to each other, the mood in the room muted and calm. No one seemed to be in distress. Bette slowed as she walked past the garden, spotting a leaf leaning out into the hallway as if trying to escape its paradise. She stopped to examine it, eager to think about anything other than what had just happened.

Dropping back in line behind everyone else, Bette moved into the dining room. There were a dozen or so round tables but none of them were completely full. The girls were fresh-faced and young. While she was dressed like them, Bette was keenly aware that she didn't look like them. Nearly all of them were sitting as if in a trance, awake but not engaged.

It took Bette a moment to find Fern, sitting with two other women in the middle of the room. Seated next to Fern was a brunette, and across from her was a younger woman with striking blond hair. It was an uncommon hair color; as America had become more beige, blond hair had become increasingly rare.

Her hair looked like it could be gathered and braided into a beautiful rope.

As Bette sat down, she noticed the brunette was sitting with her eyes closed, while Fern and the blond sat staring into space. The blond had the same discolored eye as Fern.

So, the hypnotic state and the discolored eye seem to be related, Bette thought to herself.

The brunette with the closed eyes sensed Bette's arrival and opened them. They were nearly black, yet the right eye was more matte, indicating that she, too, had the pallid eye. She smiled, the energy animating her. "You must be Bette!" she said with a lilt of excitement as if she had been waiting for her.

Bette nodded.

"My name is Roya. It's nice to meet you." Roya had long, dark, wavy hair pulled back off her face and trailing down her back.

"It is very nice to meet you, too," Bette replied, relieved to be greeted with something other than boredom and distaste.

Bette scooted in her chair while Fern and the blond girl still seemed wholly uninterested in her arrival. At the other tables, a few of the girls were beginning to engage in muffled conversation, but most of them were transfixed by something unseen. Bette was itching to know what was in everyone's eyes and why it seemed to immobilize them. Ms. Tyler also had it, but she didn't behave like these girls. She just needed to find the right opportunity to ask about it.

Bette felt Roya's eyes on her. However, her eyes were actively roving and not held in the trancelike suspension of the girls around them. She was studying her; Bette could feel her fascination. Roya sat with her hands folded in her lap, her posture both erect and relaxed. As the silence at the table became more and more pronounced, Roya spoke. "They will serve dinner soon. I think it's fish tonight."

Bette nodded her acknowledgment.

"Ugh," Fern sighed, finally perking up and looking around impatiently. "Fish again? Didn't we just, like, have that?"

Bette raised her eyebrows, a little taken aback. She couldn't remember the last time she'd had fish for dinner. Her dinners normally consisted of baby lettuces she'd grown herself and insect relish to help keep her sated.

"It might be a different kind of fish tonight, Fern," Roya offered.

"Whatever. I just wish they'd get on with it already," Fern said, shaking her glossy bangs out of her eyes.

"You got somewhere to be?" the entranced blond girl said, still not looking at anyone directly. Her honey-colored eyes shifted from side to side as she spoke. The corner of her mouth twitched, ever so slightly, in an unconscious sneer.

"Yeah, Melody, my room," Fern spat.

"Bette," Roya said, sidestepping the bickering, "I heard you came from the city. Is that where you are from?"

"Well, sort of," Bette stammered.

Fern glanced in Bette's direction and her eyes widened. "Oh, that is why you were wearing a bandage." Bette put her hand up to her neck, suddenly self-conscious at Fern's tone. She could feel half a dozen bumpy scabs. Melody disengaged what she was watching.

"Uh, it looks like someone bit you," Melody said, grinning. "Is that what happened? Did someone *bite* you?"

"No, I don't think anyone bit me," Bette said incredulously.

The smell of food overpowered Bette before she could continue. She internalized the aroma of cooked food, which awakened dusty memories from her childhood. Smells, sounds, and feelings she hadn't thought about in years wafted over her. There was movement in her periphery. At the tables around them, plates were being delivered by robots similar to those in the med floor. Bette stared at the plate in disbelief. Her astonished eyes saw a whole cooked white fish fillet with seasoning, a pile of multicolored rice, raw broccoli, and a dish with mango slices. It was so much food! The other girls began to eat as if this was an ordinary event.

Surely, this was some type of special occasion. This couldn't be every dinner. That would be impossible. Fish farming was highly regulated due to the amount of water used. The costs for such a delicacy were marked up and passed on to consumers, making the price of fish outrageous. Most of the greens Bette could afford were cheap cover crops; broccoli was a luxury. She didn't even know where a person could still get mangoes, legally or illegally.

Bette picked up her fork and cut a small bite of the fish. It was too hot. She rolled the bite around in her mouth to avoid the inevitable burn to her tongue. Once it had cooled a bit, she focused on the saltiness. It caused the sides of her tongue to tingle a little. The fish broke apart with ease as she chewed. She poked a mango slice and watched it glisten on her fork. The tangy-sweet flavor burst on the tip of her tongue. It was softer than she had anticipated and nearly melted as she chewed. She ate each morsel in amused delight. Picking her plate clean before any of the others had finished, she sat back, content and full for the first time in a long time. The other girls paused to gawk at her.

"So, what? Were you like poor or something?" Melody asked skeptically, her crystal-clear amber eyes squinting.

"She wasn't poor, you idiot," Fern said, rolling her eyes.

Melody shot Fern an insolent glance.

"Melody," Roya intervened quickly, "things are harder on the outside."

"I don't think they are *that* hard. Are they?" Melody looked to Bette to confirm this, her dewy skin aglow beneath the overhead lights.

"Uh . . . I mean, if you can get it, quality protein like this fish is very expensive," Bette said, dumbfounded by Melody's ignorance.

"What are you? Like, a scientist?" Melody scoffed at her answer. "Quality protein is very expensive," she said, mimicking Bette. "Blah, blah, blah."

"Melody, you are being rude," Roya chided, raising her voice only slightly.

Fern continued to eat, ignoring Melody's childishness. Melody resumed eating, stopping every so often to snicker at her fish. "Quality protein."

Bette sipped her water while they finished. It tasted like the water from the train station and not the water delivered to her complex. She wondered if the Birthing Center had a similar condensation system as the Subs.

They had aquariums and citrus, why not?

A robot rolled silently up to the edge of the table. The girls stacked their plates on its outstretched tray and began to file out the door. Bette couldn't tell anything about the size of their bellies. Even if she could, it wasn't like she would be able to accurately gauge how soon their impending births would be. All she could tell from walking with them was that they were all some degree of pregnant. She tried not to stare at their alien middles. Bette was a few steps behind Fern when a couple of girls came alongside and joined her. Roya, a half step behind Bette, watched as the girls cut in front of Bette.

"Is that the skinny?" Bette overheard one of the girls say to Fern. She cast a sidelong glance over her shoulder, toward Bette.

"Yeah," Fern said flatly.

Both girls turned their heads this time, eyeing Bette up and down. "Hey," they both mumbled, nearly inaudible.

Competing emotions surged inside Bette as she felt their eyes flit over her. Grateful as she'd just had the most delicious and filling meal of her life; uneasy the way their eyes judged her.

"Hey, Bette," Roya said, "why don't you walk with me to the meditation room? I hate being the last one in there."

Bette gladly slowed to walk with her.

26

Bette followed the subdued girls as they marched single file into the meditation room. Round linen globes hung suspended from the ceiling in a three-by-three pattern, bathing the room in pale, pink light. The bamboo floor was soft underfoot, cushioning the pads of feet. Neutral-colored blankets were folded into thick rectangles on the floor like children's nap mats, anticipating the arrival of the attendees. Bette didn't notice the low music until she had arranged her sit bones on the blanket. Music was the wrong word for the all-encompassing sound. It was more like one low note held indefinitely, reverberating all the way through her. She felt it in her stomach, her spine, and deep within her ears.

The walls were painted a blue-gray. On each side of the room were three brass urns, each with a delicate patina and large plants. Bette could pick out a snake plant, split-leaf philodendrons, and, of course, ferns. These all drew one's eye to the front of the room where the Department of Propagation emblem had been painted in dark gray, contrasting starkly with the wall color. On either side of the laurel leaves encircling the baby were tall, skinny water features, adding another layer of soothing sound to the insulated room. The ceiling was abnormally low as if to squeeze out any unnecessary air. A lantern hung from a gold wire just in front of Bette, and with a longer look, she discerned the honeycomb skeleton that supported its parchment shade. Its faint little cells glowing in the hushed, rosy light.

Twenty-five to thirty women sat on their blankets, each cross-legged awaiting the meditation to begin. The single note chant grew louder and then abruptly stopped. There was a long silence, and Bette could hear the undulating ocean sound of the women's around her breathing. She turned to look at Roya on her left. Her eyes were closed, her tiny wrists sitting atop her knees. Her slight chest rising and falling in a deliberate rhythm.

A low intermittent chiming began, causing Bette to look around the room for some explanation. The chiming went on for many minutes before it gradually faded out. The ensuing silence lingered before a calm, regal voice broke in from behind them. Bette recognized it almost immediately. Her eyes still open, she turned around. She was at the back of the room in her tailored, white pantsuit with blue piping, weaving back and forth between the rows of pregnant women relaxed and seated with their eyes closed.

"I understand that there is violence all around me," Ms. Tyler cooed in a soothing voice. Her voice filled the still room. There was no chiming, no other sound beside the faint trickle of the water at the front of the room.

So, maybe she did have another mode beside drill instructor.

"I am aware of the violence inside myself." Bette noticed that Ms. Tyler would touch each woman on the head or shoulder as she walked past them.

"I breathe in awareness and expel violence."

The entire room inhaled and exhaled loudly a few times.

"Breathe in awareness. Breathe out enmity."

Bette had never really been one for meditation, even though every study on the planet recommended it. She had a hard time sitting still and trying not to think. She felt herself yawn.

"I am special. I am important. I contain a gift," Ms. Tyler said.

"I am special. I am important. I contain a gift."

Bette started when the entire room repeated the phrase back in one voice.

"Propagation is my purpose. Pregnancy is my duty." Ms. Tyler stopped beside two girls and bowed her head. She put her hands on either of their shoulders, remaining an extended moment before moving on. "Breathe in purpose, breathe out selfishness."

The unified breathing sounded like a slow, controlled wind.

"I invite health and vitality to flood my being."

Ms. Tyler laid her hand on the top of Bette's head as she intoned this. The edge had returned to Ms. Tyler's voice as she pressed her hand into the crown of Bette's head. It was less a mantra and more like an order. Bette tried to shrink from the pressure of the director's hand. *You are not going to jam it into me.* Bette heard Ms. Tyler breathe out slowly before she continued to the front of the room.

When Ms. Tyler reached the front of the room, she positioned herself in front of the emblem. She stood right between the laurels, obscuring the baby, and faced the room. Eyes open, her hands folded in front of her, she raised her voice a notch. "We are the hope of our nation."

"We are the hope of our nation," the women repeated in unison.

"Our nation is the hope of the world."

"Our nation is the hope of the world."

"We shall be successful in our purpose."

"We shall be successful in our purpose."

Then the room became perfectly still. No one shifted or coughed; it was like all their switches had been turned off simultaneously. The only breathing Bette could hear was Roya's right next to her. Ms. Tyler remained at the front of the room, unmoving, her eyes now closed. The silence went on for what seemed like forever. Bette finally closed her eyes, hoping something would happen.

Maybe she is just waiting for me to close my eyes.

All the chanting and breathing seemed a bit over the top. Then again, everyone in this room besides Bette and Ms. Tyler was pregnant. Maybe there was something to it. But it was going to take more than sitting in the dark, repeating mantras with expectant mothers for Bette to believe she was ever going to be a part of this. She felt completely out of place here. This was something sacred, something she wasn't supposed to see, a place she didn't belong. Bette felt like a fraud sitting next to these expectant girls. If asked, she would not be able to repeat even one mantra to Ms. Tyler. They might be the hope of the nation, but Bette was doubtful she was.

Finally, Ms. Tyler's voice broke her mind buzz. "May peace reside with you this evening. Rest well, ladies."

The room began to stir as the women stretched and stood up. They dispersed quietly to their respective hallways. Bette walked with Roya back to their hall. "So, you guys have to do that every night?" Bette whispered.

"Yeah." She smiled.

"That talk about violence, that's normal?"

"Um . . . it can be, uh, a little chippy around here sometimes," Roya deliberated as she found her words.

Bette's forehead wrinkled as she processed the comment. For clarification she asked, "This is a metaphorical violence we are talking about, right?"

Roya shrugged her shoulders as she answered, "You know, hormones and stuff." She stopped at suite two and wished Bette good night.

No, Bette did not know. Their only purpose in life was to give birth, so what could be violent about that? They lived in a facility dedicated to that sole purpose. Why would one of the safest places in the world even mention violence, be it in the heart or elsewhere?

These women were weird, though. Maybe that was just what pregnancy did to a person.

27

Back at suite four, Bette placed her hand on the panel. It beeped and the door swung open. Fern was already there, seated in a stupor on the couch. She must have run from the evening meditation, not that Bette could blame her.

"So, what exactly are you looking at?" Bette asked Fern.

"A show," Fern said absentmindedly.

"What are you watching it on?" Bette inquired further.

"My lens."

"And this lens, is it in your eye?"

Fern blinked, shooting Bette an annoyed scowl. "Where else would it be?" she huffed impatiently.

Bette had heard of corneal lens replacements; they were the future of glasses. She didn't know that it was being done, however. She was actually looking at one in real life. She stepped cautiously toward the couch.

"What?" Fern snapped, somewhat self-conscious.

Bette carefully sat down next to Fern so as not to spook her. "I've never seen that before." She leaned in to get a better look. "How does it work?"

Fern's defensiveness melted, replaced with a sprinkle of pride. "It is grafted onto my eye. All I have to do is blink, focus, or think, and I can watch shows, play games, or send messages."

"Send messages to the girls you see all day long?" Bette asked with a single raised eyebrow.

"Yeah. They *are* the only people I can talk to," Fern said. "The Center has a closed network, just so you know."

"No kidding?" Bette said sardonically.

"They don't want us talking to creepers."

"But what about the news?" Bette asked, a bit dismayed.

"News about what?" Fern smirked. "Vampire attacks?"

Bette ignored her jibe. "The world. The weather. Rice prices."

Fern contemplated Bette, her eyes dark ambivalent pools. "You really want to know about the price of rice?"

"Sure, I do. I like to be aware of the things that impact my life," Bette said.

"It looks like that bite impacted your life."

Bette sat silent. She needed to get a look at her neck to see what all these comments were about. First, she needed to get out of this ridiculous conversation.

"Are you a rice farmer?" Fern asked seriously.

"No. Jesus," Bette sighed. "So, can the Center, like, read your mind?"

"Sort of." Fern shrugged. "They follow brain-wave and chemical activity—it's kind of like reading my mind."

Bette had been envious of Fern's technology until she heard the last part. Something about the way she said it didn't sit right with her. The Center was in Fern's head; well, in her eye to be exact. They could read her heart rate, monitor what she watched, and analyze her brain activity. Without warning, chills rippled up Bette's arms, making the tiny hairs stand at attention.

"Are you just going to sit there and stare at me?" Fern asked, annoyed, interrupting Bette's thoughts and reminding her that she was staring.

"No, sorry," Bette said embarrassed. "I'm really tired. I'm going to my room now. Good night, Fern."

"Later," Fern said, as she gave a quick blink, pleased to get back to her show.

Bette shut the door and pressed her forehead against it, closing her eyes.

So, this is the Birthing Center.

It felt as if she had lived a week in one day. The scene from the hospital room seemed to have happened so long ago, but it had only been this morning. This morning, she had been an inconclusive woman in a hospital room. By the evening, she'd been admitted to the Birthing Center. What was she even doing here?

She turned, opening her eyes to scan the scarcely furnished room with white walls. She walked over to the bed, let out a sigh, and sank down into the mattress. She pulled her knees up to her chest, wrapped her arms around them, and exhaustedly rested her head on her knees. For not being much of a conversationalist, Fern had given Bette quite a bit to think about. Bette marveled at how oblivious she and that other girl were. What was her name? Melody. The only one who seemed to have any idea of how the world worked outside of this place was Roya.

Why should they know? This was their work; this was what they had been groomed for. Pregnant women were contained in a resource-rich bubble, not expected to scratch out a living in a toxic environment. That kind of survival was reserved for the day-to-day grind of people who had nothing to offer. These girls were too precious, too important. Too much was at stake to treat them like everyone else. Why compromise the future of the species? Bette rested her hand on her neck, her fingers touching the bumps. Reminded that she had not seen what the others were ogling at, Bette stood, making her way to the bathroom.

It was cavernous compared to hers at home. All bathrooms contained only a toilet and a cleaning closet. But here, this bathroom contained a sink, a toilet, *and* a bathtub. *A bathtub.* Bette laughed quietly to herself. *Of course there would be a bathtub.*

She went straight to the vanity. The ugliness of her healing wound caused her to step back. The bruising had faded away, leaving behind vague jaundiced blotches surrounding dark red scabs. One cut was wide enough to have been cauterized back together, so it was much smoother and further along than the others. Melody was right. *They do look like bite marks.*

Bette stretched her neck to get a better look and ran her fingers over each wound, counting seven little mounds. Did the man who attacked her bite her neck? *Why would someone do that?* Puzzled, Bette stared at her reflection. When she did not find the answer in the mirror, she turned her attention to the rest of the room.

She settled on the edge of the tub and ran her hand back and forth along the smooth, sloped side. It had a faucet, which meant that it must be tied directly to a water line. In theory, Bette could turn it on, and water should fill the tub. She looked up at the sink to confirm her assumption. *Yep, the sink has a faucet, too. Can I turn on the water whenever I want?*

There had to be some type of restriction. No one had this kind of access to water. Bette scooted closer to the bathtub faucet and cautiously rested her hand on the lever. In her nervousness, she turned it slightly. Water dripped out of the tap, reflecting the light in a way that made it look like diamonds. It was far more valuable to her than diamonds, however.

No way! Placing her hand under the stream, she was delighted to sense its warmth. Then, a sense of guilt swept over her. She turned the water off and headed back into the common room.

"Hey, Fern, what is the story with these tubs?" Bette asked, trying to sound casual.

Fern raised her eyebrows but kept her attention locked on whatever she was watching. "You mean, like, where they were made and how that could impact your life?"

Bette had to give it to her; she remembered everything and had no trouble needling her with it. "No, what are the rules with them?" Bette said, trying to make plain what she meant. "I can't imagine that they give us unlimited use of water."

This caused Fern to look up. Confused, she stared at Bette as if she had five heads. "Ooohhh," she said as a sudden flash of understanding changed her face. "That's right, you guys don't take baths on the outside."

This situation was far more amusing than what she'd been watching. Fern blinked a couple of times, coming back to the present, and stood. "Follow me," she said, breezing past Bette. Following Fern into the bathroom, Bette watched with anticipation as Fern stood next to the bathtub and began the demonstration.

"This is the hot water. This is cold. Make sure to flip the stopper switch, or all the water will run down the drain," she instructed as she pointed to the faucet in the bathtub. "They only let us run water at night after meditation. It will shut off at a certain point, so you can't let it run indefinitely. The sink faucet is enabled throughout the day."

Fern walked to the sink and pointed to the cabinet beneath it. "In here are washcloths, towels for drying off, soap, and tooth-wash. You do know what those are for, right?"

Bette shifted on her feet, feeling like an idiot. She had always used waterless processes; they were all she'd ever known.

"I'll take that as a no," she sighed. "All right, then . . . " She opened the cabinet and took out a small cloth along with a bigger cloth. She walked them over and set them on the side of the tub. She went back to the cabinet and brought out a plastic bottle and a bar, then placed them on the cloths.

"This is shampoo," she said, pointing to the plastic bottle. "Get your hair wet, put a small amount in your hands, and scrub it into your hair. And Bette, like *really* scrub, okay? You sort of need it." She imitated quick movements on herself. "Then, rinse it out."

Wouldn't it contaminate the water?

"This is soap," Fern said, picking up the white bar. "Get your washcloth wet, rub this soap on it, and then scrub your body. Rinse the soap off. And, of course there is tooth-wash. I assume you are familiar with that?" Fern asked as she shook the little bottle of tablets. "Remember, let them dissolve on your tongue and then start brushing."

"I know how to use tooth-wash," Bette said.

"All right, I'll leave you to figure this out." Fern shrugged. She left the bathroom, closing the door on her way out. Bette returned to the edge of the tub, running through the process in her head. It sounded like she was to fill this bathtub and make a soup of herself. She leaned forward and turned the tap. Water began to flow out slowly. She watched for a moment before realizing it wasn't collecting in the basin but running straight down the drain.

"Oh, yeah," she said to herself as she flipped the little silver switch under the tap. *Fern said to remember to do that.*

Soon, the tub began to fill. She turned the tap, so the water would come out faster. She was interested to see how much water she could get for a bath. *Couldn't be more than a few inches in this tub. Anything more than that would be careless. And when I'm done? Then what? I'm just supposed to let it all go down the drain? Is it reused, even with soap and shampoo residue?* Her mind ran with questions as the water continued to run. Steam rose from the tiny torrent. She reached her hand under the stream again to test the temperature.

Yow! Bette turned the other tap to add cooler water. She gave it a moment before testing it again.

Much better.

It filled and filled until the water trickled to a stop. Bette turned the taps to the off position. *God, it must be at least five inches deep!*

Excited, Bette stripped off her borrowed clothes and left them next to the tub. She stepped her left foot in. It was still a touch on the hot side. She quickly removed her foot, waited a little bit, and tried again. It was still hot, but she willed her other foot in and eased herself down. The water rose as her body displaced it. It came up over her pale thighs, covering them. It was hypnotic to watch the height of the water move up and down ever so slightly. It was even stranger to feel that boundary whisper and move against her skin. She was enveloped in something warm, but she did not feel confined.

She wiggled her toes and watched the movement cause the water to ripple around her. She bent her knees slightly so more water would cover her torso. It mostly did, all except for her belly and breasts. As she inhaled, her belly expanded causing the water line to cover less of her. As she exhaled, her belly collapsed and the water line covered more of her. Finally, she bent her knees completely to submerge her head.

Her face still remained above the water, her ears just under the surface. The only thing she could hear was her breathing. Every time she breathed in, her back met the bottom of the tub. Then, when she exhaled, her back would rise. It was subtle, but she was floating. Her fingers hung suspended in the water at the surface, weightless. She could feel every muscle in her back releasing. The tension from her shoulders, neck, and back melted away as if it were bleeding out of her.

She lay there, relaxed, until the water grew cold.

Bette pulled back the soft comforter and wriggled down into the even softer sheets, feeling a sweet sense of drowsiness overtake her. Everything smelled brand new. She pulled the comforter snugly up around her neck and looked at the ceiling. The lighting in the room began to fade of its own scheduled accord.

Maybe this won't be so bad. I had more food in one day than I normally get in three. The lights never flickered. I took a bath.

Bette couldn't believe the sheer wealth of the Birthing Center. It was as if she had been transported back in time to a year when there were plenty of resources and the extinction of humans was still unimaginable. Bette rolled to her side, faced the door, and adjusted the rounded pillows under her head. She brought her knees up to her chest, making herself as compact as possible.

Three live births. That was what Fern had said earlier. At twenty-three, Fern had already given birth to three children. Having a child a year, to make the math easy and since Bette still didn't understand what a transfer was, Bette guessed Fern must have been about seventeen when she started. It was impressive. When Bette was seventeen, she'd been classed inconclusive; when Bette was twenty-three, her mom had already self-euthanized, leaving her completely alone.

The girls Bette met today were odd, that was for sure. They had the bodies of women but acted like adolescent girls. She couldn't tell if it was their personalities or a by-product of institutionalization. They did not exude the kind of excitement depicted by the Department's propaganda. Maybe their behavior was perfectly normal. Maybe Fern's temperament had nothing to do with happiness. Maybe it had more to do with her genes or personality. She might be perfectly happy, what did Bette know? These girls moved in an easy manner from one place to the next, as if the weight of human extinction didn't depend solely on them.

Besides, it was their civic duty; part of the Mandate. They were able to, so they had to.

Bette's eyes felt heavy. The room had transitioned to indigo dusk. *If she listened to Fern, maybe she could have three live births someday.*

28

Bette entered the common living area dressed in clothes that were provided to her yesterday, rubbing her arm. It was the outfit of the Center, consisting of dark compression leggings to help with swelling and varicose veins and a lighter cotton tunic. The tunic, unlike the leggings, was loose around the middle, leaving room for growth. The clothes were soft and supple, making Bette fleetingly wonder how laundry was done around here. No clothes she owned had felt like this right out of the cleaning closet. She also wondered if she was allergic to something they used to clean her clothing and linens; she'd woken up feeling congested, her eyes watery and her upper arms itching.

Fern stood, elbows at her side, distracted by something in her field of vision. Sensing Bette enter the room, she asked, "Did you weigh in?"

Bette had not remembered to do that. She wiped her eye and tried clearing her throat. Breaking up the congestion made her aware of the ache behind her eyes and above her ears.

"You need to go do that," Fern said, enunciating each word to make her point.

"But, I'm not . . . you know . . . There isn't anything to monitor right now," Bette crabbed.

Fern cut a warning glare Bette's way. "Oh, so now you are a Center doctor?" she asked, verbally checking Bette's moody disposition.

"I just don't see what the point is," Bette snapped. This entire conversation dug its bony elbow into Bette's last frayed nerve. How hard was it to tell someone they were fertile? Why no communication? What was the reason for keeping it under wraps? Did she just not need to know? *Well, then,* Bette thought as a flame burned up her throat, *if they don't feel the need to say anything, then I don't feel the need to follow stupid rules.*

"It doesn't matter if you see the point. The rule is you weigh in first thing in the morning. So . . . go weigh in."

"No," Bette said, rooted in place as a sweat broke out all over her. The sudden sweat bothered her, as this was not a fight-or-flight situation; she was merely annoyed with this girl who seemed to think she had some ounce of authority. *What a dumb time to press a dumb issue.* Bette had not even been there twenty-four hours.

Fern blinked out of her screen, turning to face Bette, her attention completely undivided. She opened her mouth to say something and then stopped. A mix of confusion and indignation tugged on the flawless planes of her face, almost as if she was surprised. A slight crease formed between her eyes. "What do you mean, no? We weigh in every morning."

"Fern, I am not pregnant," Bette said as she pushed up her sleeve, scratching her arm. "I just got here. I think it will be fine."

"You really aren't going to weigh in?" Fern asked astonished.

Jesus, she really isn't going to let this go. "I'll do it tomorrow, okay?"

Fern crossed her arms, visibly uncomfortable. How easily the balance of power had shifted. Fern normally occupied the moral high ground that came with the emphatic adherence to rules. It hadn't occurred to her that someone could say no *and* get away with it.

"Let's go already, Fern. I think I am hungry; I have a bit of a headache."

They walked out into the hall. "Why are you itching so much?" Fern murmured as she noticed Bette's constant scratching.

"I don't know. My arms started to itch when I got up this morning."

"Uh, you should have someone look at that," Fern said, wrinkling her nose at Bette's arm. "Just don't get near anyone else. We don't want what you have."

"Your sympathy is touching," Bette said dryly.

"You, obviously, haven't spent much time around a sick pregnant woman," she snipped back.

The same group from dinner was seated in the same spots for breakfast. Melody and Fern sat staring into space; Roya buoyant and eager with an easy smile on her lips.

"So, how was your first day?" Roya asked, leaning forward.

Bette gritted her teeth and tried to sit still; both her arms felt like they had been burned. "It was, uh, it was something."

"I bet it was." She winked. "They will only get weirder, I promise."

Puzzled, Bette started to ask what she meant but Fern interjected. "Eh, you get used to it. Sort of loses something once you've done it five or six times." Fern craned her neck to see the double doors where the robots came from.

"Fern is all business, all the time," Roya said, glancing at Bette with an amused glint in her eye. "A very serious propagator."

Fern rolled her eyes. "Roya, it's what I am here to do. You would do better if you took this more seriously."

"Oh, Fern, you really are no fun, are you?" Roya admonished playfully. This seemed a well-worn trek. Either Fern was passionately defensive of the subject or did not realize that Roya was baiting her into an argument.

"What?" Fern began, exasperated. "What do I care what the baby looks like? What do I care about his father's marketable features? The Center won't let me make a bad baby. Why should I waste my time thinking about it?"

"It's more than that, and you know it," Roya replied, shaking her head.

"No, Roya, it really isn't. They only do it to make you feel involved in the process."

"And you can honestly tell me you aren't even the least bit curious how the baby turns out?" Roya asked with a knowing look on her face.

"Again, it's not my problem. A baby is a baby, I have done my job. The rest of it is for the Center to worry about," Fern answered resolutely.

Roya noticed the lost look on Bette's face and mercifully clued her in. "Fern and I have differing opinions on the brokering process. It is where you spend a few hours going through profiles of ideal DNA candidates. They have photos and accomplishments and interests of the father. I think it is a nice distraction." She shrugged her shoulders, adding, "She believes it is a waste of our time."

"Is it like marriage brokering?" Bette asked.

Fern and Melody burst out laughing. "Marriage broker-ing?" Melody said. "God, what year are you from? Marriage brokering, ha!"

Fern was still smiling. The smile looked out of place on her face. This was something, Bette gathered, she almost never did.

"They don't really do that anymore," Roya said, trying to spare Bette's feelings.

"Oh," Bette said, feeling stupid.

"Traditional marriage brokering limited the production pool and wasn't as fast as they needed it to be, too much nego-tiating back and forth," Fern explained. "They phased that out decades ago."

Bette rolled that information over in her mind. To be hon-est, she really didn't know what happened after girls went to the Birthing Center. That part was never really covered. The most important thing was your status—you were either fer-tile or infertile. Fertile was good, but that was about where it ended. Fertile girls went to the Center to get pregnant and have babies, and that was that. But reproduction did require DNA from both sides . . .

"That's just what my mom told me she did . . . " Bette trailed off as everyone at the table stopped laughing and stared at her.

"What?" Bette asked, self-conscious that she'd said some-thing stupid again.

"What do you mean, your *mom*? Did you . . . like, meet her?" Melody asked, rapt. The twitch in her face made it look like she was winking at Bette.

"Uh, yeah," Bette said. "We lived with my grandma after my mom left her birthing center."

"She left?" Roya asked, perplexed. "How?"

"She couldn't have any more children." Bette shrugged, not really sure what else to tell them.

"But, why did you go with her?" Fern asked, confused. "Why didn't you go to a Sub?"

"I don't know," Bette said. It wasn't anything that Bette had ever really thought about. That was the way the story had been told to her; she had no reason to second-guess it.

"I guess that makes you sort of special, Bette," Roya said, nodding at her and smiling.

Steaming bowls of oatmeal with a side of bananas and oranges interrupted the exchange. Out of habit, Bette looked to see if anyone else was startled by the oranges. The girls didn't skip a beat eating them as if it was normal. The conversation picked up again involving stories about growing up in a Sub.

"God, my Sub matron beat me every chance she got," Melody said, laughing.

"That explains a lot," Fern quipped.

Melody glared at her, sneering, "Well, you know, only the strongest survive."

"I don't know why they kept you then," Fern taunted.

"Because my genes are better, Fern. How many twins have you had? Oh, right. I remember. None," Melody shot back. Then, turning to Bette, she said, "So, you got to have the real fun, then."

Bette cocked her head unsure what Melody was talking about.

"You know," she said, looking around and then lowering her voice. "Lots of sex? Is that why you got bit?"

Bette almost laughed. "Uh no, and I didn't get bit. Also, I don't know that *fun* is the word I'd use. It's the Mandate. So, you know, civic duty," Bette said.

"But you've done *it*, lots of times, right? That has to be fun?" Melody asked, leaning in even closer with each question.

"Don't you do that here?" Bette asked, a little confused. It was her understanding that sex was *the* way to procreate.

"No. They say it takes too long," Melody sighed as she sat back.

"Having sex takes too long?" Bette tried to suppress her amusement.

"Getting pregnant *that way* takes too long," Fern said as if to clarify. "It's not an efficient use of our time."

"Right," Bette said, nodding her head slowly. *It wasn't an efficient use of my time, either.*

"God, I'd sure like to waste time doing that," Melody said wistfully, resting her head in her hand and sighing.

"I just don't understand the allure of a dangling scrot," Fern said, shrugging her shoulders.

Melody let loose a brash, irreverent laugh.

"Melody, people like what they like. There is nothing wrong with that. Fern, no woman is actually attracted to the look of a . . . dangling scrotum." Roya's lowered voice filled with mock reproach. "It's passion and desire, things you can't produce in a lab."

"I'm attracted!" Melody chimed in enthusiastically. "Bring on the scrot!"

A few furtive glances came from the other tables. "Jesus, Melody, keep your voice down." Fern shushed.

Roya laughed a little.

"Dangling scrots," Melody whispered, grinning wide eyed.

29

The gym was noticeably cooler than the other rooms Bette had been in, which felt pretty good. She was hot but her skin was clammy to the touch. To the left were a couple of rows of treadmills, and on the right, a couple of rows of chairs. A few women ambled, unmotivated, on the moving belts. The rest sat in the chairs, being evaluated before they were released to the treadmills. Each chair had a divider on one side coming up from the armrest.

Bette watched as Fern, Roya, and Melody took a seat in the chairs on the right side of the room. A robot rolled over to Fern. She extended her arm to the silent mechanical assistant. Bette took a seat in the nearest empty plastic chair, the divider to her left blocking her view of who was seated next to her. She let out a relieved sigh as she sank into the chair, closed her eyes, and began to massage her temples. Her brain felt like it was trying to rip a hole through her skull. Even after breakfast, the headache persisted. Her neck and shoulders felt like old sinewy fish jerky. Her congestion caused her to breathe with her mouth half open. As if telepathically summoned, Bette heard a robot roll up beside her. Bette opened her eyes and stretched out her arm the way she had seen the other residents do.

A doctor in a white uniform paced nearby to monitor all those having their blood pressure taken by the three roving robots. Her head perked up as she received some kind of alert. She came over and stopped in front of Bette. "Do you have any food allergies?" she asked as she examined Bette's arms.

"I don't think so. Do you think that is what this is?" Bette asked, hopeful for some relief.

With gloved hands, she drew Bette's arm toward her. She examined the developing rash and then tapped the screen on the side of the robot. A frown formed on her face when she couldn't find what she was looking for. She concentrated on the screen as she typed and retyped, finally lifting her head.

"Ah," she said triumphantly. "Did your water contain moisture control?"

"Uh . . . yeah."

She nodded. "The Birthing Center doesn't use this additive. This must be a little side effect as you acclimate."

"What do you mean?" Bette was shocked. "Like, withdrawal? From moisture control?"

"It would appear so. It seems to be pretty common, from what I understand."

Withdrawal from moisture control? But the government added it to the water. Everyone drank water with moisture control in it. "So . . . is that why I feel so bad? How long will that last?"

"Well," she said as she consulted her robot, "symptoms do include an acute to full-body rash lasting anywhere from three to seven days."

"Three to seven days!" Bette nearly choked on her phlegm.

"Let's hope you're closer to the three-day mark," the doctor said, picking up one of Bette's arms for closer scrutiny.

"Well, is there something you can give me for this itching, in the meantime?"

The doctor smiled as she released Bette's arm. "We have to be careful about what we prescribe our pregnant girls. It looks like we will need another day to analyze your results from yesterday. So, until I get those, I'm kind of in a holding pattern."

"But I'm not pregnant." Bette's voice was louder than she had intended. The doctor's eyebrow raised as her lips tightened.

"Not yet," she scolded.

Irritation exploded within Bette. She glared hard at the floor while biting the inside of her cheek. *What is wrong with this woman!* Bette wanted to rip the skin from her forearms but would settle on being able to lie down and roll around on a stiff carpet. She swallowed the thin mucus draining in the back of her throat. The throbbing in her head seemed to be exacerbated by the quickening of her angry pulse. "Is there nothing you can do to help me *now?*"

"Policy states that no medications are to be administered to residents without prior approval of the supervising doctor."

"And that's not you?" Bette asked, resting her hot face in her hands.

"No."

Bette sighed. The pressure around her ears aimed to make her deaf to this useless woman. "How soon can you get some type of approval?" Bette asked, sitting up to look the woman in the face.

Department of Propagation employees were excellent liars, mostly because they wholeheartedly believed what they were telling you. The earnestness with which they supplied an answer was the best indicator of its truth; the more earnest the answer, the bigger the whopper. "Hopefully by this afternoon." Confident, but not overly earnest. The woman pulled a pair of slim, clear glasses out of her lab coat pocket and tapped them to hers. "There you go." She handed them to Bette.

"What is this?" Bette asked, turning the lightweight glasses over in her hands.

"The Center issues these until you can get your corneal replacement lens. It'll push your daily schedule and other pertinent information to you. You'll have access to everything you'll need for right now."

Bette slipped them on. The date and time were at the top of the left lens. Down the right side were neatly sectioned blocks in different colors. The current time block was highlighted *exercise*.

Bette approached the basic-looking treadmill while scratching her forearms. She guardedly stepped up on the belt. Nothing happened. She waited a moment or two and noticed two metallic cradles on the support bar. She placed her wrists in them to see what would happen. Sensing the pressure, they cinched around her wrists and locked her in place. The belt began to move under her. Bette clasped her fingers around the bar in front as she walked, but it wasn't likely that she'd slide off. A countdown timer showed up in the lower right-hand corner of her glasses where the schedule blocks had been previously.

As she studied the rest of the room, she noticed that the other treadmills were full of users clamped to the machines. The slow-moving behind of a girl swayed ahead of her. Beside her, slack-jawed women gazed forward, absorbed in what was on their lens. The only sound in the room was the soft brush of shoes against the treadmill belts. They moved with the indifferent gait of an undead battalion. The entire room plodded the same steps over and over again, going nowhere.

Bette blinked and closed out of the timer screen. The home screen only had four colored bars on the side. There was the schedule, which she'd just closed. The next was a yellow triangle with an exclamation point in it. She stared at this one. Text popped up: *Calling emergency staff.* Bette blinked quickly to turn it off. The third was a dialog box icon, but it seemed to be disabled. *Must be for the messaging that everyone around here is doing.*

The last had a gold star in it. Bette trained her gaze on the star icon and a dashboard opened. An unhappy face greeted her, informing her that she *hadn't earned any stars yet.* Out of options, she brought the timer back up. There wasn't anything that looked like a distraction on these loaner glasses. What were these girls even watching that kept them so entranced? Maybe entertainment wasn't something she had access to until she had earned some gold stars.

Jesus. I am back in high school. What a time that had been. Long days of instruction and testing. Long nights of studying. The cold, friendless competition of peers and constant one-upping. The looming fear of being classed inconclusive. The humiliation of being left behind to participate in the trade program. Being licensed to cut hair and identify the tell-tale signs of bedbugs. It had been a long time since Bette had thought about that place. Now, here she was in a shinier, newer version of that old torment.

Only this time there was a report of fertility.

What exactly had Ms. Tyler meant by that? No one had explained it to her yet. They had just thrown her in with all these pregnant women as if vicinity would make it so, as if they were hoping for pregnancy by association. Were they hoping that it was circulated in the air and she could somehow catch it? Bette scoured her memory, trying to think of where this alleged report could have come from. Apart from the attack, nothing was out of the ordinary.

As she walked on the treadmill in this facility, she wondered if this was how it had been for her mother. For a short time, she, too, had been in a birthing center; maybe it had been this very one. Had she been pulled in off the street due to a fertility report? Were there no clues ahead of Bette's conception? Bette churned to remember any detail her mother might have given and came up empty. It was in keeping with her mother's personality, though; she was aloof and kept everyone at arm's length.

Her mother was thirty when she became pregnant. Bette had clung to this single fact her entire life but failed to give it any context. Now, she kicked herself for never prying harder. Bette had hoped and begged and willed and schemed for a status change. And then what? *I sure didn't think it would go like this.*

"Hey." Someone startled Bette from her reverie.

"Hey. Roya, how do you get out of these things?" Bette asked, tugging at the cuffs around her wrists.

"Oh, I've got a shorter exercise time. Doctor's orders."

Bette stopped struggling and just scowled at the confines.

"Are you okay, Bette?" The sprite-like gleam in Roya's eye morphed into concern. "You don't look so good."

"Not really, no. I'm itchy, I'm sweaty, and I have this strangling headache."

"Yuck, I'm really sorry about that."

"Yeah, and that do-nothing staffer won't give me anything." Bette gave a groan of frustration. "I mean, did you feel this bad when you came here?"

A muzzled smile fluttered on Roya's face before she was able to smother it. "Yeah, I felt real bad when I got here," she replied.

"What did you do?"

"I gave birth." Roya shrugged. "And then I felt even worse." She winked at Bette.

Bette felt the way she had as a child when she'd complained. Her mother had that backhanded reproach that could make a trivial issue evaporate with the scorch of something consequential.

"I overheard that they are putting you on lab maintenance," Roya said, glancing around the room. Residents began to stir and wake from their stupor to step down off the treadmills and drift toward the door.

"Oh? What is that?" Bette asked.

"Check your schedule," Roya said, nodding to Bette's glasses.

Bette reopened the schedule screen. Underneath the highlighted block was the next hour block. She stared at it. *Lab Maintenance. Report to Hector.*

"Yeah, that is what it says here," Bette confirmed.

"I'm headed there, too. I'll show you where to go."

"That'd be great. Thanks." Bette felt the pressure slacken and the cuffs slowly released her wrists. Bette rubbed them and brought her hands to her neck. She pressed her cold fingers against her neck to relieve the itching, hopeful she would feel better as the day wore on.

30

Residents filtered down the hallway in groups of twos and threes. Bette and Roya walked side by side toward the elevator. Ahead of them, a group of girls waited for the door to open. When the elevator arrived, Bette began to move with the group of girls. Roya reached and put her hand on Bette's arm to stop her.

"We will get the next one."

Bette stepped back and watched the elevator door close.

"They are going to the sponsor floor," Roya explained.

"What exactly is that?" Bette asked, hearing the term for the third time in two days.

"It's a kind of marketing division." Roya's intense black eyes glimmered with amusement. With her arms crossed over her belly, Bette could see her midsection was less pronounced than Fern's. She began to move slowly up and down on the balls of her feet as she studied the metal door. Roya and Bette found themselves alone at the elevator as the traffic in the hall trickled down to just a few darting girls.

"You know," she whispered, "I knew my mother, too."

Bette swiveled her head, but Roya continued to focus straight ahead as if she had said nothing. Bette thought about asking her to repeat what she'd just said once inside the elevator. Roya pressed the button for the med floor and Bette silently groaned. "A word to the wise," Roya said, her voice barely audible as the elevator moved them to their destination. "They see everything."

She turned to face Bette and tapped her right temple two quick times. The right temple was the side with the corneal lens replacement. The door opened and Roya exited, moving into the hall and continuing to murmur. "They can't technically hear you, but they do monitor electronic signals in the brain and other vital signs that give you away," Roya said as she glanced at Bette. "Nod if you understand."

Bette nodded, picking up her pace to hear the rest of what Roya was saying. "Needless to say," Roya continued as an exaggerated smile spread across her face, "it is important to remain composed at all times."

Bette looked at her quizzically. Roya pointed to her smile. Bette felt this was a hint to do the same, so she complied. Roya nodded, pleased.

Instead of stopping at the desk like Bette had done the day before, Roya led her down one of the hallways adjacent to the elevator. In front of the third steel door on the right, Roya pressed her hand on the panel beside it. A moment passed. Unconsciously, Bette reached down to scratch her thigh through her leggings, finding that the thick compression material made it hard to get at the itch.

The door slid open. The first thing Bette noticed was a huge machine in the middle of the room, a hulking steel vat with stairs leading up to the top. To the left of this great machine was a long table containing about a half dozen smaller appliance-like machines, each with protruding curved tubes and digital displays. Black electrical cords snaked from prongs in the ceilings to the machines; tubes flowed with red, yellow, and blue liquids to destinations unseen. Metal columns lacquered in white enamel broke up the wide room. There were two closed doors at the back of the room. On the other side of the room sat an elevated metal box with a glass face. The front contained sockets, which were attached to gloves that reached inside the front glass of the metal box. Scattered throughout the room were gray octagonal workstations, each containing something different: a microscope, a robotic arm, racks of test tubes, and spray bottles.

Bette had only ever been in a facility like this once when her complex had won a lottery for a refurbished antibody machine. The catch was she had to lug the old machine into town and trade it in at the manufacturing plant. Even though she'd just glimpsed the automation floor then, it was an intimidating sight; the machines moving unbidden with purpose, the mechanic hum and whir, and the smells of warm metal and lubricant all unnerved her. There was not a human on the floor. It was an unsettling sight as Bette realized that their time was terminable. That was the thing about machines; you could teach them to do a task and they could do it, correctly and perpetually, as long as they were maintained. They never got any smarter unless you updated them. They never got any faster unless you altered them. They were at the complete mercy of an engineer. They never wondered why they were doing this same thing, over and over, for eternity. Their task didn't mean anything to them. Time didn't matter, survival didn't matter; they just worked until they were obsolete. What happened when the engineer stopped optimizing them? What happened when the engineer became obsolete? Machines, too, would fall victim to rust and decay. One day, even this gleaming, state-of-the-art lab would be just another forgotten dilapidated structure.

A bald man stood at the foot of the stairs of the bulky vat, which was covered in various warning decals. As the door closed behind them, he turned expectantly. He wore a white coat over dark green overalls. A genial smile curved across his middle-aged face.

"Hey, Roya!" He stepped away from the machine, swinging his strong arms, and met them in the middle of the white-and-silver room with an energetic step. Black-and-yellow-striped tape designated the walking paths along the floor.

"Hello, Hector!" Roya greeted the man.

"I see you brought a friend today." He nodded toward Bette.

"I did! This is Bette. She just arrived. Bette, this is Hector."

"Hello," Bette said politely.

Hector was a short man, shorter than Roya but nearly the same height as Bette. His skin was glistening and showed no scarring or visible skin conditions. Other than his eyebrows, he had no other facial hair. All his teeth seemed well maintained.

"Welcome to fertility central!" Hector lifted his hands full of vigor. "Here is where we prepare all the genetic material for the Department of Propagation."

"Oh, for *all* the birthing centers?" Bette asked while she glanced around the room again.

"Yes, to maintain product continuity, the Department produces everything here at HQ and then pushes the product out to the satellite centers."

"And what are they producing?" Bette eyed the stainless-steel cabinets topped with screens illuminating important-looking charts and graphs, wondering if she was smart enough for any of this.

"Good question! Bette, your timing couldn't be any better. You two will be preparing sterile dishes today. We just got the monthly quotas," he announced enthusiastically, walking as he talked. "The trays are on the tables and the dishes are in the storage closet. Make sure you grab a couple of pairs of gloves, too." He pointed in the direction of the closed doors along the back of the room. "Roya will show you everything, okay?"

Roya started off toward the back of the room. Bette began to follow, but Hector stopped her and put his hand on her shoulder.

"And Bette." Hector paused until she made eye contact. "It's nice to have you here." Bette flushed with a touch of embarrassment.

Roya led the way and opened the door on the right side, which was flanked on either side by blinking lights and sensors. Inside were rows and rows of white plastic shelves with bags, boxes, and other implements. Her back was to Bette as she spoke while reaching for a bag on one of the shelves. The smell was hard to place, like a mixture of bleach and yeast. The room was some kind of ultraclean industrial lab area. The bleach smell made sense, but the weird yeasty undertone stumped Bette. *The smell of new plastic?*

"As you can probably imagine, the Center uses a lot of petri dishes. Our task is to prepare them for storage in the cold room. We'll start by mixing the agar. That's the jellylike substance that the cultures grow on." Roya handed two densely packed bags to Bette, then she reached for two more as she continued. "These bags go into that giant machine out there. They will be mixed with hot sterilized water. Once the solution cools, it will dispense the warm agar in the dishes that we'll lay out."

Roya turned to scan the supply closet, ticking items off a mental checklist. "Ah. Bette? Can you get that bag behind you? Yeah, the one with those clear, round containers. Yep. Thanks."

They exited the supply closet with their hands full and placed everything on a long empty worktable behind the vat. Bette followed Roya for a second trip to the supply closet to gather more petri dishes, multiple pairs of blue latex gloves, face masks, safety goggles, and thick, stiff-fitting plastic aprons.

"You probably won't need those safety goggles," Roya said as she motioned to Bette's face. "You already got a pair." She fastened her apron behind her and slipped a face mask over her mouth. The loud ventilation system kicked on overhead. Startled by how loud it was, Bette looked up at the ceiling to see shiny platinum ducts that ran the length of the room. Bette looked to Roya but couldn't tell if her mouth was moving. The loud push of air drowned out whatever words Roya might be saying. Roya pointed to her eye, then Bette's glasses.

Realizing that Roya was trying to tell her to use the messaging feature, Bette shook her head and pulled down her face mask.

"I can't!" Bette yelled over the noise, "It's disabled!"

Bette climbed the patterned steel stairs with two bags from the supply room. She cautiously steadied herself on the yellow handrail opposite the large chrome basin. Her heavy dark blue apron stopped just below her knees and limited her movement somewhat. Once at the top, she waited for Roya's instruction. Roya was on the ground next to a panel with buttons, gauges, and lights. The ventilation roared overhead as Roya mimed the motions of opening a door and dumping in the bag.

Bette stood on her tiptoes and peered over the top ridge of the basin. As Roya had indicated, there was a one-foot-by-one-foot black square with a handle. Bette adjusted her slightly oversized gloves before lifting the handle. Once the lid was open, Bette pulled the tabs on the bags to find them filled with fine silt-like powder. The smell permeated her nostrils through her face mask and answered her earlier question. *This* was the origin of the yeastlike, meaty smell lurking under the tidy smell of disinfectant. She poured it in the opening of the large vat. When the bag was emptied, she moved across the grated metal platform and looked down for further instruction. Roya pushed a large button and then motioned for her to come back down. Bette lumbered down the stairs as the ventilation shut off.

"Okay, while that heats up and mixes, let's load these plates."

Roya spritzed six large metal trays and wiped them off. She pointed to the petri dishes in the bag at the end of the table, requesting that Bette retrieve the bag. Roya reached in and took out a stack, then set them in front of her. She began to systematically pull them apart, placing the shallow lids to one side and the slightly deeper bases to the other. Bette took the cue and copied what Roya was doing. Once all the dishes were apart, Roya took the deeper bases and started lining a tray with them.

The two girls had just finished lining all the metal trays when the machine beeped. Roya picked up her tray and walked to the backside of the machine. Bette followed with her own tray of empty petri dishes. There was a rectangular cutout at the base of the vat that revealed a moving conveyor belt. Roya placed her tray on the belt and then nodded to Bette, indicating she should do the same. The belt advanced under the vat and through the cutout, appearing on the other side where it stopped under five sterling cylinders. A pipe connected all of the cylinders to the base of the vat. The cylinders dispensed a steaming, murky, yellow liquid onto the waiting plates. Once all the plates of one tray were filled, they took turns carefully and slowly walking them back over to the workspace.

At the table, Roya's eyes roved over the dishes. Every now and then she would pick one up, tilt it to the left and right, and then set it back down. "Now, the lids," she mumbled from behind her face mask.

Bette and Roya worked quickly, putting the shallow lids on top of the dishes. Bette noticed that each lid fogged slightly once in place.

"Bette, there is a rolling cart in the supply closet. Can you get it? We will move these dishes in there to let them cool so we can reuse these trays for the next round."

Bette turned, unsure, toward the supply closet. "Do I need any kind of clearance?" she asked, nervous about the red lights on the side panel of each door.

"No, it remains open during work hours."

"Just a rolling cart, right?"

"Oh, and can you get four bags of that powder, please?" Roya asked.

"Sure." Bette stared at the racks and rows of supplies in the closet. As she pulled down four more bags of powder, she saw multiple bins filled with bags of petri dishes. *Of course, the Center uses lots of petri dishes.* Bette located a rolling cart over in the corner and laid her bags on it. This was the centralized distribution hub for all the birthing centers. All the genetic material for the centers originated *here*? Bette's eyes wandered around the warehouse-like facility. *Why must it go through here?* she wondered, pushing the cart back out into the lab area.

At the top of the vat, Bette poured in the powder again and Roya pushed the button. They moved the filled dishes into careful stacks on the cart, disinfected the trays, and lined them again with new empty plates. When they had lidded the last of the dishes, Hector approached their workbench. Bette reached up to scratch her neck. Her back was beginning to catch fire. Hector assessed all the cooling dishes on the cart and the table. "This looks good for today. Nice work, ladies."

Roya led Bette over to an alcove with a perimeter boxed off in black-and-yellow tape. Within the tape was a green incinerator, a squat, wide machine with a chute. Along the wall and directly across from the incinerator was a row of four trash cans, each with a white decal and black block letters. Roya discarded her gloves, face mask, and safety goggles in the various bins.

"We can sanitize the goggles and aprons," she said while pointing to one bin. "The rest is trash," she said while pointing to another. Bette peeled off her gloves and tossed them in the bin designated for trash. Next to the trash cans was a wheel-shaped blade encased in Plexiglas with buttons on a panel beneath it. This area of the lab seemed less about production and more about elimination.

"Do you guys ever use any of this stuff?" Bette asked as she eyed the cutting tool. The glinting blades and incinerator adding a layer of incongruity to the same room with cold storage for the preservation of stacks and stacks of petri dishes.

"More than you'd think," Roya said, glancing toward the incinerator. "More than we should. What do you have after this?" Roya asked as the door to the lab closed behind them and they made their way down the hall.

"Looks like I have to stay here," Bette said with a sigh and a hint of dejection in her voice. "What about you?" Roya paused in the round lobby of the med floor and looked up. Bette followed her gaze. There was nothing on the ceiling except lighting and small black orbs, which she recognized as cameras.

"Look, Bette," she said, her tone hushed, "you are going to get a lens soon. Might even be today." Roya was still craning her neck back to survey the ceiling. Bette swallowed hard at the idea of having a lens like all the rest of the women in the Birthing Center, with their empty stares and distracted manner.

"Just remember," Roya continued, looking to her left and then to her right as they approached the elevator, "be mindful of what you do, and what you look at. I know you are used to a lack of privacy, but this is a whole new level of invasion. It will be uncomfortable but it will not kill you."

As she waited for the elevator, she glanced at Bette, and Bette held her gaze until the door opened. Roya smiled and shrugged as she got into the elevator. The door closed and left Bette to figure out what had just happened. This girl had a habit of shape-shifting from bright and chipper to enigmatic and back again as easily as if she were fluent in multiple languages.

31

Bette scratched her stomach as she walked toward the med floor desk. Her stomach flipped when she noticed the formidable director marching up the corridor. Her frosty blue eyes landed on Bette.

"Right on time, Bette. This way," she said, motioning back down the corridor.

Ms. Tyler opened one of the first doors along the corridor and Bette breathed a sigh of relief for not having to pass the lactation room. This room was barely lit and contained a row of what looked like five dental chairs.

"Sit," Ms. Tyler said, pointing to one of the middle chairs. The white leather straps with gleaming brass buckles on each of the armrests heightened Bette's unease.

"Open your mouth, stick out your tongue," Ms. Tyler instructed Bette. She placed a pill the size of a small bearing on Bette's tongue. "Let this dissolve. Once it has taken full effect, we can begin."

"What are we doing?" Bette asked thickly around the pill in the middle of her tongue.

"Corneal replacement," Ms. Tyler chirped as she exited.

Bette sat alone in the dim room for thirty or forty minutes. As her eyes adjusted, she could make out the outlines of instruments and machines at the fringes of the room. Her leggings slid as she shifted on the chair's padded synthetic surface. The names of surgical procedures had a way of imparting little to no idea of what to expect. For example, corneal lens replacement. It sounded generic enough to not immediately warrant any concern. But the more Bette sat there, meditating on the idea of a corneal lens replacement, the more concern began to creep in. The cornea was the outermost part of the eye. It was "corrected" if one had a vision issue. Bette didn't have any vision issues, but they were going to replace hers today. Replace, meaning what? Upgrade? Enhance? Remove? Bette shifted uncomfortably at the idea of a surgeon peeling off the transparent cover of her eye. Is that why she was given a sedative? Doctors were notorious for saying something wouldn't hurt and it always did. Maybe that was because it didn't directly hurt them.

With astounding clarity, Bette heard the whir of the mechanism in the door before the door opened. A bright rectangular patch grew quickly along the dark wall containing the silhouette of a slender man. The door closed and the stark contrast left Bette momentarily blinded. She only heard his footsteps on the tile. The tall, lean man appeared again under the small spotlight above her chair, his crisp white uniform indicating he was a doctor. His short tight hair was parted exactly and slicked to one side.

"Hey there, Miss Bette," his voice sickeningly sweet. "How are we feeling?"

"Fine." The word was harder to say than she'd expected.

The unctuousness of his tone put Bette on alert. She had heard this tone before. Lots of men were vulgar and insensitive, and more than a few liked to hit; but the ones who talked like this were really the ones to be afraid of. They could make you hurt in ways you didn't even know were possible, leaving you trembling long after they'd gone. These were the ones who had self-actualized their dark urges and grown completely comfortable and patient in directing it at their victims.

"Oh, I hope we are feeling a little better than fine after that medicine Ms. Tyler gave you." He smiled as he gently put his hands on either side of Bette's neck, groping around her ears and the base of her head. Bette sucked in a startled breath. She blinked, and the doctor blurred briefly, splitting into two.

He stooped, using long thin fingers to push open one eye and then the other. His piercing black eyes stared into hers. They were the eyes of a stuffed museum animal, glassy, new, and inorganic. "Oh, yes, I think you are feeling really good right now," he said in his soft leering way.

He took her wrist and buckled one of the white straps around it. Fear crept up her spine. She tried to move, withdraw her hand, but she couldn't make her arm move. She watched, alarmed, as he did the same to the other wrist. It was as if her body had turned to lead. With ease, he maneuvered her head into the headrest of the chair. There was pressure on her temples and a click as he restrained her head. The sedative had knocked out the kick of adrenaline that flashed through her, so all Bette could feel was a warming sensation.

"There," he purred, "that ought to hold you." He moved in over Bette, so close she could smell the earthy scent of his soap. He stretched the eyelids of her right eye apart. He stared, keenly focused on whatever it was he was looking for, undeterred by the angst in her wide eyes. With her right eye propped open, Bette blinked her left eye rapidly as if to make up for it. The air on her eyeball made it tacky from lack of moisture. She tried to speak, but her tongue was immobilized; the only sound that came out was a strained grunt.

"It's okay. There is nothing to be afraid of," the doctor cooed. "We have a bit of work to do on this eye, but we also need you awake for it. This is an excellent sedative for keeping you cognizant, but you won't feel a thing."

He cocked his head as he studied her face, a specimen under observation. No tenderness softened his aquiline features; no empathy sprang to those glossy manufactured eyes. Instead, he lifted his hand to her face and ran his left index finger down the side of her left cheek. Bette could see it, but she could not feel it. There was no sensation whatsoever as he touched her. Cold primal terror welled up inside of her.

"See, not a thing."

Out of the periphery of her left eye, she watched as he traced his finger all the way down her arm. Her breathing became swift and shallow as her heart thundered in her chest. Every impulse inside of her screamed to move, to shake loose. It was that paralyzed place between sleep and wake where the mind ran wild, but the body could not be roused.

"You are older than the others, which I find interesting. I bet you have done lots of things they haven't."

Bette could no longer see where his hands were. Only the side of his face remained in view. A thoughtful smile caused the corner of his mouth to turn up. "I mean you had to. It is basically government-backed prostitution. A kind of sexual slavery, really."

He moved back toward Bette's face, appraising her inert body with his fulsome survey. He paused inches from her face, his buttery voice solidifying. "I bet you are very good at taking direction."

His waxy face blurred again when she blinked. The doctor moved from Bette's field of vision and a robotic arm materialized out of the rayless edges of the room. It whirred down toward Bette's propped-open right eye. It came down toward her, its thin metal pin glinting off the spotlight as it hovered closer and closer. Defensively, her left eye squeezed shut. The arm paused just above her right eye, adjusting, clicking, and whirring as it anticipated its landing. Bette held her breath and braced for excruciating pain as it met the outermost layer of her cornea. But no pain came as the metal pin traced the surface of Bette's eye.

It is just tracing.

A trembly sigh of anxious relief left her. But as she drew in her next breath, she noticed the burning smell. It wafted into her nostrils and reminded her of the scent of singed hair. It took her only a few seconds to realize it was her; she must be the one who was being burned, but she could not feel it. Panic jolted through her and demanded action. Again, she tried frantically to move her arms or her legs. She could not make any noise louder than a belabored groan.

Suddenly everything in her right eye went blurry as if over-exposed. Nothing came into view. Bette's breathing was heavy, and her blood rushed in her ears. She lay there, strapped down, her right eye clamped open but not seeing. Each agonizing minute felt like an eternity.

Something is wrong! I'm going to be permanently blinded!

The clicking noise started again to her right, but louder this time, and pulsed through her swirling anxiety. She could tell nothing from the shadowland of her right eye. She opened her left eye in a last-ditch effort to see what was going on. Above her, she saw the arm of the machine stretched toward her right. It twitched back and forth as if adjusting. With each movement, the clicking to Bette's right intensified; when it paused, the clicking stopped.

A warmth right above her ear began spreading forward toward her right eye. She was aware of the warmth like she was aware of the sun. She knew it was out there, but dense humid clouds kept her from seeing it. She was conscious of its effect without knowing what it felt like. The warmth intensified as a thin hot line radiated along her right temple. A succession of three tiny pops sounded and the clicking of the machine started back up.

When the clicking died down, a shadow moved over her exposed right eye. It moved back and forth in an up-and-down motion. With every repetition of the movement, the eye began to come more and more into focus. Bette felt the knot in her stomach release gradually as she was able to make out what looked to be a small paintbrush over her right eye. The vision in her right eye was still misty, but she could see almost as clearly as she had before this began.

The smirking doctor came back into view. "All right, better than new," he said calmly as if detached from the terror of the ordeal. "Just one last thing. I like to seal my work when I'm done. It's like the bow on top of a present."

The machine was lowered out of Bette's sight on her right side. She heard the clicking and the whirring of the machine recalibrating for its next procedure. She watched as the doctor pulled up her shirt and rested it at the top of her breasts. He then maneuvered her so that he could view her back.

"We will just unhook this and get that out of the way . . . " he sleazily whispered in her ear.

Bette gulped and steeled herself for the worst, her mind trying desperately to console her. *It might not be that bad, you might not even feel anything, maybe that won't happen . . .* The doctor moved away, and the machine repositioned itself, close, at the base of her right breast.

What the hell is he doing?!

Bette was soon aware of sustained warm pressure. The doctor stood to the other side of the machine, so that he could watch. A satisfied smile spread slowly across his thin lips as

Bette began to smell her flesh burning. Fine wisps of smoke drifted into her periphery. The scorched fatty smell of her skin filled her nostrils, while the image of her skin bubbling and turning to charcoal filled her thoughts.

"There we go," the doctor said as the machine became quiet. Moving it out of the way, he stooped so that he could inspect his work. "Ah, yes. Perfect. Just a little good luck charm on your way to multiplication."

Straightening, he came in closer to Bette. He brought his left hand to caress her cheek before smoothing her hair. "Remember, now, be a good girl and take care of this eye." He winked. "Hopefully, I'll see you around."

32

"Bette. Bette."

Whoever was saying her name sounded faraway. The more they said it, the closer they got. Bette opened her eyes with a start and saw Roya next to her. Wild-eyed Bette glanced around the room, suspicious and confused.

"Bette," Roya said, raising her voice slightly to get her attention. "You are safe. Calm down." Roya's tone had the intended grounding effect. Relief washed over Bette when she saw that she was back in her bed. Still, she looked around to make sure that the doctor wasn't lurking anywhere. In her right eye, she saw the time, but only as a hazy luminance. She blinked. It was still there. She turned her head to the left and the right, but the time was still there like it was a part of her.

The corneal lens replacement.

Bette reached up to touch her right eye. "Don't touch it!" Roya warned. Startled, Bette withdrew her hand quickly from her face.

"Trust me," Roya's voice said as it returned to its normal tone. "That is the last thing you want to do. Whatever you do, don't touch it until the lens has had a chance to fully graft in."

Bette's right temple throbbed each time she blinked. She gingerly brought the tip of her finger to examine it. "Yeah, that will hurt, too. The incision usually heals perfectly. That guy is a creep, but he is good at his job. In a few days, you won't even know it's there," Roya assured her.

Bette gaped at Roya. "What did he do to me?"

As her remembrance of the day's procedure rushed back, Bette yanked up her shirt and saw she was not wearing her bra. She pushed up the skin to see the base of her breast, where the laser had been. She gritted her teeth as hot stabbing pain pulsed from the area. She blinked in disbelief and stared at the red irritated X.

Roya seated herself on the bed next to Bette, empathetic. "It's a symbol for multiplication. He does that to everyone."

"I thought this was an eye surgery!" Bette raged.

"It was. He did replace your corneal lens," Roya said as she tried to calm her friend.

"But why is . . . " Bette's voice shook with barely contained anger. "He branded me!" Her altered temple pounded the more she spoke. Little bursts of light popped in her right eye as the skin stretched and contracted. Lightly, she stroked her fingertips over the temple and made out a raised line.

"Is this an incision in my temple?"

Roya gently took Bette's chin and turned it so she could inspect the incision. "The way I understand it, they have to tap into the brain for the lens work," Roya explained.

The brain. *My brain?* It was one thing when it was Fern; she was used to this life. It was another thing completely for Bette. She thought that she knew the invasive procedures of the Department better than anyone, but this? Her eye? Her brain? This stupid X? Why? This had nothing to do with procreation. This had nothing to do with fertility. This had only to do with control. She was theirs now, burned and branded, property of the Birthing Center.

We are beyond the luxury of time and preference.

"It's unnecessary, I know." Roya spoke softly as she watched indignation settle on Bette's face. "There is really no way to prepare for it. I thought if I warned you, I don't know, maybe it would be easier for you than it was for me."

"Uh, no. Nothing would've prepared me for this," Bette said, jerking her chin back from Roya, who let her hands drop into her lap. Her eyes slowly followed them.

"I won't say that you get used to it. But you'll figure out how to work around it," Roya said.

"Work around it?" Bette scoffed. How could Roya say something like that? Like this wasn't the end of what little agency she had to begin with. Work around it? It was in her eye! There was no working around it. Bette glared angrily at the willowy girl sitting on her bedside staring at her hands. Why would she say something so insensitive, unless . . .

Unless . . .

"Is that why you look around randomly all the time and never make eye contact?" Bette asked.

Roya shrugged her shoulders and handed Bette a small rectangular package. "I brought you this sandwich. You missed dinner."

Bette accepted the sandwich, unwrapped the paper, and took a tentative bite, not quite sure if she was hungry. "What time is it?" Bette asked with her mouth full. She did notice that the lights had transitioned into dusk. As she looked down, the tiny glowing numbers in the lower-right corner of her eye answered her. Bette swallowed. "Oh, never mind."

She paused before taking another bite. "How long have you been here?"

"I asked one of the techs if I could duck out of meditation to check on you," Roya answered.

"No, I mean, here, in the Birthing Center. How long have you had this"—Bette swallowed the bite she just took and pointed to her right eye—"this thing?"

Roya turned her eyes toward the sheets and ran her fingers back and forth in a line along the fabric before answering. "About three years," Roya uttered, almost as if she couldn't believe it. "Another lifetime ago."

Roya rose from the side of the bed as if she weighed nothing. She continued to stare at Bette's comforter as if in a daze. Then she blinked as if remembering where she was. "Sorry," Roya said as she tapped her temple, "for whatever reason, it makes memories extra vivid. I think it has something to do with the temporal lobe. So, when you have one, it'll knock you on your heels. It, uh, also affects your dreams. So, that is something to look forward to. I'll see you in the morning, okay?"

Bette nodded and said, "Thank you, Roya."

"Sure thing." Roya tottered out of the room, shell shocked and uneasy.

33

Bette dreamed of her grandma's fall.

She'd been in school shortly after her results conference. The message came and she was excused early. She'd met her mother in the hospital waiting room. Her mother told her that her grandmother had fallen and shattered her hip.

"What happened?" Bette demanded.

"I don't know, I wasn't there. I came home from the market, and she was lying on the kitchen floor. I called for an ambulance."

"But she is all right?" Bette asked.

"They were able to stabilize her," her mother said, contemplating what to say next.

"What does that mean?" Bette asked, accusingly.

"Bette, your Gram is eighty years old."

"But she is stable. You just said so. She is going to be fine, right?"

"I don't want you to get your hopes up. This is a hard thing to come back from at eighty. The osteoporosis has made her bones so brittle . . . " her mother explained.

"Where is she? I want to see her."

"She is resting right now."

"Take me to her. I want to see her."

"She just came out of surgery. I can't. They haven't even let me see her yet."

A hard lump had formed in Bette's throat. She sat down in a waiting room chair, leaning forward and putting her elbows on her knees. Her mother sat down next to her, saying nothing. When the doctor finally arrived, he didn't have anything good to say except that they could go back one at a time, to not overwhelm her.

Bette had a hard time believing it was her. Her Gram was always standing. She was always talking, so commanding in her presence. As she lay there in that hospital bed, so still, so quiet, fear swept over Bette. She sat gingerly next to her, afraid to touch her. "Hey, Gram," Bette whispered.

"Hey, button," she murmured. "Sorry about this whole mess."

"Don't worry about it." Bette put her hand on her bony shoulder. The machines beeped. Staff footsteps echoed outside. The fluorescent lighting magnified every line and shadow to create a craggy backdrop. Her grandma was an odd shade of gray. Bette had never noticed how old she looked.

"Bette, I am a little worried about it," she said, breaking the din.

Bette couldn't say anything. She would not. *If I don't say anything, maybe nothing bad will happen.* She stared at the cheap, thin blanket her Gram was lying under, too anxious to look at her face.

"Button, I need you to listen to me. I need you to hear what I am saying. Can you do that?"

"Yes," Bette said, her voice cracking. She wiped her eyes.

"Hang on to those tears a minute, please. Will you promise me something?"

"Anything, just tell me . . . "

"Don't be like your mother," she said abruptly.

Bette sat back, surprised. "What?"

"I swear to God, button, I did the best I could. Maybe she got it from her father, I don't know. But she has given up. She quit a long time ago. Promise me that you won't do that."

"I promise."

Her Gram smiled. "Good."

Her grandmother lay there, breathing heavy. "Life is not easy," she started, "but it is always worth it. No matter what anyone tells you. No matter how bad it looks. There has always been purpose in the struggle, even if you can't see it. I want you to remember that."

"I will," Bette said.

She closed her eyes. "I need you to remember that," she whispered. Her brow furrowed like it did when she was thinking through something. "I'm an old lady, so that probably doesn't make much sense to you. What I'm trying to say is that I have seen some really amazing things in my lifetime, but I've also seen some pretty horrible things, too. So, you will just have to trust me when I say that no matter what happens, you can overcome it."

"I do," Bette said, hoping that if she just agreed with everything she said, her Gram would stop this silly charade and get up.

"Aww. You don't. Not yet anyway. But I do appreciate that you will tell a dying woman what she wants to hear." A little smile appeared on her chapped lips.

"You aren't dying," Bette said defensively.

Tears began to stream down the old woman's face. Bette reached up to wipe them away. Her cold fingers wrapped around Bette's hand. A long moment went by, then another. "I'm so sorry, Bette."

"Please, Gram, stop. There is nothing to be sorry about. It was an accident . . . " There was something to the sound of her voice that made Bette feel helpless.

"No, button, not that." She was trembling. "I know once I'm gone, your mother . . . I know that once I'm gone, you will be alone. That is why I held on as long as I did. And it . . . " She trailed off unintelligibly.

Bette leaned in and laid her head on her grandma's frail chest. Gaunt arms covered in papery skin enveloped Bette's neck as tears flowed freely from her eyes. Bette's insides quaked. Her Gram's tremors subsided, and she gently stroked Bette's hair. "Look at us, what a sight we must be." She chuckled a little. "Bette, look at me."

Bette sniffed and sat up. She wiped her eyes and nose with the back of her hand before looking into her grandma's face.

Her Gram smiled. "I wish you knew how perfect you are," she sighed. "But you will have to figure that out as you move through life. And it will be a wonderful life, although you may not feel that way until the very end. It's not a weakness to survive, Bette. It is not undignified to do whatever you have to do to make it to the next day. Life is worth it."

She stared at Bette for a minute. "Bette, would you go get me your mother?"

Bette was standing in the hall when the hospital staff came running. She was pushed to the side as they swarmed the room. The door was left ajar. Bette stood outside and watched as people shouted and passed instruments over her grandmother's body. Bette stood, right outside the fray, invisible in a curtain of tears, already feeling very much alone.

Unsure of how long she'd been awake, Bette found herself sitting up in bed. A cold sweat had broken out over her body.

Her teeth were clenched and her face was wet with tears. Her heart thumped as she tried to regulate her uneven breathing. It was hard for her to catch her breath. The burn on her right side pulsated.

Roya had not been exaggerating. This dream was as intense as the day it had happened.

And if *this* was how she felt right now, what had Roya seen earlier that had caused her to stop mid-sentence? If it had been anything like seeing her beloved dead grandma, well, Bette got it now.

The day it had happened.

The years had blunted the heartache of the day Bette's grandmother had died. So, to relive it now with such force and clarity was jolting. Bette sat in uneasy anticipation of what else she might have to relive when she closed her eyes. Bette's mind was drawn back to that frail woman in the hospital bed. To when she had promised not to give up on her own life.

34

Bette spotted Roya in the hall the following day on her way to dinner. She quickened her pace and tried to close the gap to catch up with her. Just then, from a tributary hallway, Melody appeared and fell in behind Roya. She did not seem interested in coming alongside Roya. Instead, she moved in slightly, directly behind as if trying to avoid Roya's periphery. Melody's controlled, adroit pursuit caused Bette's skin to prick with adrenaline.

What is she doing?

Melody's gait was reminiscent of an old nature documentary where the lion prowled and trailed behind its unsuspecting prey. Every muscle in Melody's body tensed as her footsteps quickened. Bette watched as Melody stalked up behind Roya, pounced, and wrapped her tightly in her arms, the crook of her right arm pinching Roya's neck. Roya let out a surprised yelp.

"Hey!" Bette shouted from behind.

Melody spun around, dragging Roya with her, her head to the right side of Roya's face. A sneer twitched on her face. Bette's eyes darted from Roya to Melody as she carefully stepped closer. Roya's hands dug at Melody's forearms, the veins bulging in her wrists as she strained to break the grip. Roya's eyes ignited, but it was not with fear as Bette might have expected. The look on her face was of equally subdued strain and resolve. Bette stopped a few yards from them.

"What are you doing, Melody?" Bette asked, mindful to keep her tone calm and even.

"What do you think would happen if Roya stopped breathing?" Melody's left hand abruptly jerked and grabbed Roya's throat, eliciting a gurgle. The knuckles in Melody's fingers pulled the skin around them taut, exposing sinewy lines that contracted on the top of her hand. Roya clenched her jaw in an attempt to twist her head out of Melody's clutch. Melody shifted on her feet, bracing against Roya's resistance, squeezing Roya's larynx harder.

"Melody, you aren't going to hurt Roya," Bette said, inching forward.

"She will flutter a little bit," Melody continued, as if in a daze, "but it's not as long as you think. They never fight as long as you think they will . . . "

"Melody," Bette said, raising her voice.

Melody blinked, as if awakened. She looked around the empty hallway and then back to Bette. Her eyes narrowed and she smirked. "What are you going to do, Bette?"

Bette sucked in a breath.

"Ha. That is what I thought: nothing."

Roya brought up her knee and stamped down on Melody's foot. Shock registered on Melody's face and her hold on Roya loosened. Roya gasped as she ripped the hands from her neck and broke free, stumbling toward Bette. Melody took two swift steps forward and kicked Roya in the back of the knee, sending her sprawling to the floor. Roya turned over, defiant. Melody, her chest puffed and pupils wide, stood over Roya, glowering.

A tense boundary separated them. The air circulated around the two of them like weather fronts; each mass billowed in a line of threatening rolling clouds.

"You'd be too easy," Melody growled before stepping back and turning toward the dining hall. The pressure between them equalized and then dissipated. As she walked away, she shook out her hackles, stretched her arms above her head, and started to skip.

Bette knelt beside Roya to help her up. "Are you all right?" Bette asked.

"Yeah," Roya said.

"What the hell is wrong with her?" Bette exclaimed.

"Oh, Bette, it's not that big a deal. I'm fine."

"Not that big a deal?" Bette glanced back to the grown woman skipping. "Roya, did you see her face? She is fucking crazy!"

"Not so metaphorical now, is it? I told you, these hormones and stuff."

"She could have really hurt you, Roya"—Bette eyed her midsection—"or your baby."

"It's fine," Roya said as she tried to reassure Bette. "She wouldn't have hurt me."

"Uh, no, I'm pretty sure she meant to." Bette considered Melody's targeted follow once she saw Roya in the hallway and the zoned-out way she spoke, only to shake it off and *skip* down the hall.

"Bette, you've interacted with her. I don't need to tell you that she's not, mmm, working with the same capacity you and I have," Roya said, cautiously choosing her words.

It was true. Bette had observed it in the limited time she'd spent in Melody's company. The girl couldn't sit still, and she couldn't focus. She talked and hummed to herself incessantly. It was obvious by Melody's comebacks that she wasn't quick witted. She seemed at odds with everyone, often rebuffed or ignored outright by nearly all the other residents. But this? This was not the action of someone mentally deficient. This was more disturbing than just a learning disability. This had been done with intent. Melody hadn't shown a morsel of empathy or even guilt.

"Bette, don't make a big deal out of this, okay?" Roya said, adjusting her tunic.

"Has this happened before?" Bette whispered. Bette thought about the steely look on Roya's face as Melody held her. She had rolled in a practiced way after she'd been kicked and had immediately flipped over. Like she would've fought Melody, if needed. Roya caught her gaze, smiling. Bringing her pointer finger to her expression: "I said, it's fine."

At the table, Fern was enthralled in her display while Melody grinned with a secret that would erupt if she didn't tell someone soon. Her mouth twitched in anticipation. "Did you have a good fall, Roya?" Melody blurted out the moment Roya was in earshot.

Roya smiled graciously. "Quite the joke, Melody."

Melody began to rock ever so slightly in her chair. "Fern, don't you want to know what happened?" Melody asked.

"Nope," Fern said, refusing to engage. She finished what she was viewing, blinking to reorient with her surroundings. "Does anyone know what we are having for dinner tonight?"

Melody's face clouded over.

"Isn't the menu posted somewhere?" Bette asked, finding herself somewhat pleased that the subject change irritated Melody.

Fern scanned the room, looking for the robots.

"I thought it was going to be a chowder," Roya said.

"Chowder," Melody said in a low voice to herself, "chowder, chowder, chowder." She emphasized different syllables each time she said the word, as if tasting it for the first time and not sure what she thought of it. She continued to rock back and forth and repeat the word "chowder" as she surveyed the dining room, no longer interested in the people at her table.

Melody was off, way off. The only real interaction she seemed to have with anyone was at mealtime. All she seemed to do then was get on everyone's last nerve. Melody remained inside her own head until she saw an opportunity to be mean or one-up someone. If someone had only described Melody to Bette, she might have felt sorry for her. But, having met her and looked into those soulless amber eyes, Bette just wanted to stay out of her way. Melody had this way of looking through a person and snickering; she'd found their weakness and was delighted at the idea of exploiting it. There was a percolating volatility to Melody that didn't make Bette feel safe.

I understand that there is violence all around me.
I am aware of the violence inside myself.
I breathe in awareness and expel violence.

35

That evening in their suite, Fern assumed her usual position on the couch. Bette lay on the cool floor and desperately tried to distract herself from the itching. It had gotten worse, but no medical person could or would do anything to help her. The only time she hadn't itched was during the corneal replacement surgery, but she'd rather have this over *that* any day. Eager to train her mind on something other than her unbearable condition, she tried talking to Fern.

"Melody . . . she is a, uh, quite interested in this sex thing, isn't she?" This seemed a surefire way to get more than a mono-syllabic answer since Fern had an evident distaste for Melody.

"Ugh. She is disgusting," Fern huffed, taking the bait. "It is so gross. It's like she has an *appetite* for it or something. She is so primitive. This is a birthing center, not a sex center."

"Well, you can get pregnant by having sex," Bette reminded her.

"How did that work out for you?" came Fern's scathing retort.

Bette let the barb pass without comment. Waiting a beat or two, she tried a different avenue of questions. "What can you tell me about Roya?"

"Bette, don't itch your eyes," Fern scolded.

Bette removed her hand from the corner of the right eye. She'd been receiving fuzzy notifications throughout the day. Fern told her the text would clear up once the graft fully integrated with her eye. Its features were comparable to her glasses, only updated, and now much closer.

"But it itches." Bette exhaled. "Everything itches, but my eye is the itchiest at this exact moment."

"Well, stop touching your eye. The first few days after the implant are crucial to the grafting. If you mess with it, it might not adhere properly. And then you will have to go back for a correction surgery."

Bette shuddered as she remembered the fingers of the lecherous doctor. She shoved her hands under her behind and blinked rapidly to quell the discomfort.

"I can see what you are doing," Fern reprimanded.

"I can't blink now?"

"Not like that."

Bette gritted her teeth, determined to never see that doctor again.

"So, uh, what about Roya?"

"I don't know much about her. None of the girls recognize her from their Subs. She just showed up one day at breakfast a few years ago, pregnant. It was weird, because they normally come as skinnies, in groups, from the Subs. But Roya came by herself, already pretty far along," Fern said.

"Girls don't get pregnant in Subs?"

"They are not supposed to. The Subs and the Department have detailed arrangements regarding candidates, residents, and fetuses. Maybe she was part of a Sub crackdown. All I know is whatever happened to her before didn't do her any favors here."

"Why do you say that?" Bette asked, sitting up.

"Residents have to follow the rules, Bette. If you don't, there are consequences. Even being associated with someone who doesn't follow the rules can get you in trouble. The way she came in, no one wants to be friends with her." Fern shifted on the couch, her voice cautious and her tone wary. "Roya has spent a lot of time on probation. If I were you, I would steer clear of her and worry about your own problems. How long is this itching going to last, anyway?"

Bette looked at the rash on the back of her left hand.

Good freaking question.

Bette began vomiting in the middle of the night.

She woke to the cold sweat that breaks out right before it happens. Her stomach was making distressed gurgling noises. Her toes just touched the floor as the first wave hit, splashing around her feet. It spattered up the front of her legs as she bolted toward the bathroom.

The soft ambient night-lighting came on as she staggered in. She collapsed in front of the toilet bowl, her shoulders tightening around her neck as the second violent wave rolled up. The pain flared with every involuntary spasm. Tears streamed down her face.

At a break in the motion, she sat back, holding her mouth open to avoid the taste on her tongue. She pulled her knees up to her chest and put her head in her hands. Cold sweat started at the base of her spine and seemed to shoot up and out her fingertips, causing her to pitch forward and retch again. After the third cycle, she sagged down on the tile floor, grateful for its coolness. The vomiting had subsided, but the itching seemed to just be getting started. The floor was both her best friend and worst enemy as chills came and went.

A headache had been gradually building when Bette noticed Fern's bare feet in front of her. "Fuck," was all Bette heard before they fled from view.

It was quiet a moment longer before a flurry of shoes and murmuring scuffled in. Someone helped Bette to her feet and guided her back to bed. "Sorry," Bette whispered, "The floor. I didn't mean to . . . I tried . . . " Bette swallowed hard. Her head was pounding, and she was so thirsty. She collapsed on the bed.

"Here," the staffer said, "drink this." She pressed a glass to Bette's lips. Bette gulped it loudly before handing the empty glass back.

"Lie down," the staffer instructed.

Bette felt a little prick in her right arm. "Hey," Bette yelped, scolding her, "what are you doing?"

"Shh . . . this will help."

Bette's eyes throbbed. She cupped her palms over them and pressed just like her mom taught her to do when she was younger. The intensity of the pain began to lessen, the voices became less pronounced, and her racing heart began to slow.

36

You look like hell.

Bette stared in the mirror above the sink in her bathroom. Her sunken cheeks only made her nose appear bigger and bonier. Even in the pinkish dawn light of the panels, her skin was sallow and waxy looking. Scabs and brown-red scratch marks peppered her arms and neck. The previous marks on her neck were just beginning to fade. At least she knew how she got these new marks. One of the side effects of moisture control withdrawal was uncontrollable itching, and she would've clawed the skin right off her muscles if they hadn't restrained and sedated her. It had been one bad day and three horrendous days. The whole episode seemed like a bad hallucination. That doctor who had first examined the rash said it could last anywhere from three to seven days. Thankfully, it had only been four; she was not sure she would've have lasted a full seven days.

She combed her fingers through her dull, lifeless hair, pulling it up off her neck to form a rudimentary bun. She bit the inside of her cheek as she considered the dark circles and chapped lips. Bette didn't feel great, but she felt better. And she was hungry; all she'd been able to keep down over the last thirty-six hours were nutrient broth and protein chews.

Blinking, she felt something catch against the back of her right eyelid. She rubbed her eyes and blinked again. She could still feel it, like a bit of grit on the front of her eye. She leaned in, opening her eyes wide and tilting her head ever so slightly to see if she could spy what it was. She took her right ring finger and touched a glistening spot on the bottom of the lens. It was not noticeable looking straight at it, but there was a little tag sticking out, right at the edge of the new lens. As the pad of her finger touched it, the time in the corner blurred and went out. Curious, she pushed the tip of her nail to see if she could get underneath it, but there was just enough to be annoying and too little to latch on to.

It didn't graft properly.

Bette remembered that the first few days were important for the grafting of the replacement lens. During those crucial days, Bette had been violently ill and barely conscious. She must have rubbed it with all the vomiting and itching. She frowned, blinking a few more times. "Perfect," she grumbled to her reflection.

Bette slowly plodded down the hallway while the warm hall sconces created halos in her newly modified eye. She closed her eye, pressed the tips of her fingers to the deformed edge, and massaged in light circles. The time fizzled and blacked out. She blinked it back open. The halo was still more or less there. Giggles erupted up ahead of her to her left. There was no one in the hallway. She paused, listening. They rippled again. It sounded like they were coming from inside the garden in the middle of the concourse. Curious, Bette made her way toward the laughter.

A group of about five or six girls huddled in a semicircle around Melody, her unique blond mane giving her away. They giggled and gasped, turning every now and then to look at their neighbor and point, enthusiastically. Bette pushed her way into the group of twittering girls to get a better view of what was so funny. Melody flashed them a grin and then concentrated her focus at her shoe. Bette stretched her neck to see what Melody was staring at.

"Can you hear it?" a girl with dark hair parted down the middle murmured.

"I know, right?" Another dark-haired girl with a small upturned nose responded, "I thought it would for sure be louder."

Bette didn't see anything but grew uneasy as the grin on Melody's face tightened. Then Bette saw a little movement under the shoe as a feathered wing fluttered out from the side. Bette's eyes widened as she became aware of the smothered, panicked chirping. Bette felt sick as Melody turned once again to her onlookers, her grinning lip twitching. She leaned forward, purposely transferring all her weight to the foot with the bird trapped beneath it. She lifted the other foot slightly to give the murderous foot more of her weight. There was the revolting sound of tiny twigs crunching and the desperate tweeting stopped.

There was a pause as the girls waited, expectantly, for something else to happen. When it was clear this exhibition was over, animated chatter sprang up with a few hand claps. Melody clenched her jaw and made a show of slowly grinding her foot into the bird, smug satisfaction on her face, the little tip of the exposed wing undulating with her movement.

"What is going on here?" A man's sharp voice drew everyone's attention. Hector approached the circle, scolding them. "Where are you all supposed to be?"

His questioning eyes landed on Bette with confusion, as if to ask why she would be hanging out with this rabble. The look on her face must've conveyed how sorry she was to have stumbled onto these hooligans. Hector pursed his lips and said, "Move your foot, Melody."

Her golden eyes narrowed as she contemplated his command.

"Now!" he barked.

A half smile formed on her lips as she lifted her foot to reveal a broken, lifeless sparrow. A flash of irritation streaked across Hector's face when he saw the tiny innocent bird.

"All of you, get out of here." He glanced around at the girls, who stood gawking and ogling the revealed little body with fascination. Melody shrugged, making a point to grate her foot over the bird as she left.

"Go!" Hector raised his voice. Like lemmings, they looked to him and turned to leave, only steps behind Melody, whispering as they went.

"Do birds not have blood?"

"I thought there would be at least a bone or two sticking out."

"It just looked like it was asleep."

"I mean, smushed, yeah, but just asleep."

Hector knelt beside the murdered bird and shook his head solemnly.

"She . . . she just crushed it," Bette stammered. "For no reason. She just . . . "

He gently picked up the bird in his gloved hands, lowered his head, and closed his eyes briefly. "To bear witness," he said quietly, then he opened his eyes. Stoic calm returned to his face as he glanced over at Bette. "Why don't you get going, Bette. I'll take care of burying this little guy."

37

Bette crossed her arms over her chest as she and Roya entered the lactation room. They were there to clean, so no one else was there, but still, Bette's whole body tensed. The room was similar to the bottom of a basin; smooth stainless-steel walls with no windows to see out and no handholds to grasp on to. It was as if, by design, whatever happened in there could just be sprayed away at the end of the day. Violate, rinse, repeat.

Slotted drains were situated on the floor underneath the stalls. Sets of two clear plastic cups rested on each station. The tubing that ran from each set of cups snaked its way up and back, like tributaries that fed the larger steel duct stemming from the center of the circular couch. They then bent and disappeared into a wall. "Couch" was a generous description; on closer inspection, it was a sturdy industrial bench devoid of cushioning. Bette could now see with more clarity the dividers that split the bench into seats, details she could not see on that first day. The plastic dividers did contain panels to monitor diagnostic information of the girls posted in these stalls.

"What exactly do they *do* in here?" Bette asked, creeped out at the thought of the topless girl hooked up to the tubing. In the empty room, their voices echoed, amplifying the desolation of the space.

"Milk production," Roya said, somewhat distracted as she lugged a wheeled machine out into the middle of the room.

Bette's stomach fluttered at the term. "Production" sounded like a positive thing. In stark contrast, the vision of that tearful, exhausted girl with those plastic cups on her breasts was more traumatic than a neutral-sounding industrial process. Breast milk from residents? Who needed such a product?

"What do they do with the milk when they are done? There aren't any babies here. Do they give it to the Subs?"

"They *sell* it to the Subs," Roya corrected as she shook out the hose connected to the machine she was still fiddling with. "This is the only place with access to breast milk, so they pretty much have the market."

Bette surveyed the room again, unconsciously rubbing her upper arms.

Satisfied that all the kinks had been removed, Roya laid the hose in a straight line. There was a large utility sink in the back corner of the room. Stacked underneath were buckets and brushes. Roya motioned for Bette to follow her to the sink. Roya pumped a clear solution into two buckets and proceeded to fill them with steaming hot water. She handed the first bucket to Bette. "Grab a couple of those brushes."

Roya led the way back to the white circular bench with its dividers. She set her bucket on one of the seats, resting her brush on her hip. "Let's each do half. Scrub everything, except the diagnostic panels."

Bette got to work on the other side, carefully navigating the scalding water. "So, if it takes nine months to have a baby, how much breast milk is actually needed?" Bette asked, starting at the top of one seat and scrubbing in a circular motion. "How long does an infant need breast milk? It seems like there would only be enough for each baby. Why do they need all of this?"

Bette stood and looked around the metal pipe in the middle of the seating area. Roya was scrubbing away at a station.

"Bette, we produce more than one fetus every nine months. And you can keep a mother pumping, if you want to."

Bette stopped scrubbing. "What? How is that even possible?"

Roya crouched and disappeared. Her words volleyed over the bench. "Live births take nine months. But transfers happen at eighteen weeks. We get two transfers in for every live birth. It is possible to end up with more babies than mothers to breastfeed them. So, the Center gives them production hormones to keep them lactating."

Water dripped from Bette's brush as she listened. Fern had said something about transfers, but since Bette hadn't known what she was talking about, it hadn't stuck. "What exactly is a transfer?" Bette asked.

"They *transfer* a fetus at eighteen weeks to a bio bag where it completes gestation. This frees up a womb so they can start another fetus. Two to three times more fetuses in roughly the same amount of time it would take to bring one fetus to term." Roya stood as she said this, gauging Bette's reaction.

"Where do the, uh, bio bags go?" Bette asked.

"To the Subs."

"What do they do with them?" Bette felt her nose wrinkle as she said it.

"Well, it depends. Subs do a lot of research and development. I imagine they use the fetuses for parts or experimentation. And I have heard that for a hefty fee, Subs will finish growing the fetus to full term so a wealthy citizen can come in and pick out a live baby to adopt."

Hmm, diversification of revenue streams.

"Where are the bags now?" Bette asked.

"Oh, you will never see them. The womb room is off-limits. It is not even on the med floor. We couldn't get to it if we tried," Roya explained as she scrubbed.

The thought was only mildly reassuring to Bette. "How many transfers have you had, Roya?"

"I don't really keep track, probably five or six by now," Roya said, tightening her ponytail.

Bette resumed scrubbing the dried flecks of blood and patches of off-white crusty residue as she mulled this information over. She followed a spurt line of crusty residue that had landed on the panel. Carefully, Bette tried to smudge out the fleck with her thumb. Suddenly, a sucking sound filled the air. She looked up and around, trying to figure out where it was coming from. She jostled the plastic tubing lying on the seat as she staggered back. The cup flipped over, adhering itself violently to the side of her left leg. The whooshing noise intensified as the cup tried to extract anything from her thigh. Bette tugged and tugged, trying to remove the mini dome.

The whooshing noise stopped, and the cup fell away from Bette's thigh. She looked to her right. Roya stood next to the panel. "I told you to not clean the panels," she admonished.

Bette rubbed the spot where the cup had gripped her thigh. "Jesus, you put these on your boobs?"

Roya wrapped the cups and tubing and set them back on their seat. "Not because we want to," she groused.

When they had finished scrubbing down the entire lactation station, Roya turned on the machine she'd spent so much time uncoiling earlier to pressure wash the seats. She positioned the hose on the floor, nudging the suds toward their respective drains. Bette rinsed out the buckets and brushes, propping them up so they could air-dry. *And just like that, the inescapable stainless-steel room is ready for its next round of extraction*, Bette thought grimly.

38

Roya leaned against a clean edge of the worktable. "Bette, would you get another rolling cart from the supply closet?" she asked. "Hector has a bunch of plates in the cold room that need to be cleaned."

This was the first full day Bette had been cleared to return to a normal schedule. While nothing about the Birthing Center was normal, working was better than being laid up in the med bay going through withdrawal. Bette nodded, setting off for the supply closet.

"Just roll it over to Hector, he'll help you." Bette couldn't see Roya's face, since the face mask swallowed up most of it, but she could still detect her subdued energy.

A brisk draft greeted Bette as she rolled the cart into the cold room. The room was bigger than the supply closet, with a walkway down the middle lined by glass doors. Behind those doors, she saw nickel-colored shelves containing stacks of petri dishes. Hector was on the left side of the room behind one of the glass doors. Bette rolled her cart to where he was and tapped on the glass. He turned around and opened the door for Bette.

"Hey, Bette, we'll move this entire section."

With her gloved hand, Bette picked up a stack from the shelf. The tops of each dish were labeled. In black lettering, she saw the words *For Disposal.* Hector and Bette packed the cart with as many "for disposal" plates as they could. Once the cart was full, Hector instructed Bette to take them back to the worktable, unload them, and return.

As Bette rolled the heavier cart back across the room to the workbench, she saw a large black plastic trash can at one end. Bette noticed a few spatulas on the table; two were of regular size, and one a miniature version. Roya helped Bette transfer the containers from the cart so Bette could make a second trip to retrieve the rest.

Roya had already begun lining up the disposal dishes in two straight lines, leading down the length of the table toward the trash can, when Bette returned with the final load. She stood on the other side of the table near the trash can with her spatula. "Leave the cart at the other end. It can sit while we work through these," Roya said.

Bette rolled the cart to the vacant end and positioned it at the end of the table opposite the garbage. Imitating Roya, Bette picked up a spatula.

"Now, you will want to twist off the lid," Roya said, demonstrating, "and then place the lid in this container." Bette had not noticed a smaller black bin divided into small plastic cubbies next to the trash can.

"Take your spatula and scrape out the, uh, contents." Roya ran her spatula around the edge of the container. Then, in a quick movement, she shoved the tip of the spatula under the agar. A soft sucking sound indicated that the jellied medium was released from the side. Roya shook it over the large, lined trash can. Bette heard a soft *splat.*

"What is in there?" she asked.

"It's just a trash can with a liner," Roya explained. "Lastly, you put this in the bin." She nestled the newly emptied petri dish next to its companion lid in a bin slot.

The loud ventilation system kicked on and filled the room with its roaring blast, echoing off the sterile walls and shiny metal machines. Roya and Bette worked in silence as it circulated loud, cool air.

Bette detected shadows and spots in the dishes as she worked and wondered what they were. Every now and then, her jelly would break and crumble into gooey, jiggling blobs. She was careful to scrape every quivering bit into the can, just as she'd been shown. The ventilation system quieted down, leaving only the *tink* of spatulas against the glass, the slimy sound of the glutinous medium being freed from the edge, and the wet *plunk* of the discarded blob on the floor of the garbage bin.

"Try the mini one," Roya offered from across the table when Bette had a particularly hard time freeing a firm sticky disk. Bette reached for the mini spatula and was able to wedge it between the side of the glass and the agar. She continued to wrench and slide the spatula around the entirety of the plate. When she tipped it over the can, it slid out in one piece. She smiled behind her face mask, pleased at her accomplishment. She looked over the edge of the bin lined with a clear plastic liner. It was hard to make out the translucent goops against the dark side.

Roya's conversation had trickled to one-word answers. She moved slower and slower with her spatula as if every jab pained her.

They finished the first batch, and then set the second batch in rows leading to the garbage. Bette picked up a dish. She'd found that most of the semisolid discs came out without a problem but, every now and then, she encountered one that she'd have to score and chip at, breaking it into globules. It slowed her down and simultaneously made her more determined.

"What do they do with all these dishes?" Bette asked Roya as a glob of agar dangled from the end of her spatula and fell into the bin with a nearly imperceptible *plop*.

At first, Roya didn't say anything, and Bette wondered if she'd heard the question. Bette tried again. "Hey, Roya? What do they do with these?"

Roya did not look up from what she was doing.

"Embryonic cultures," came her heavy reply.

A chill ran through Bette and froze her in place. She looked at the empty dish in her right hand, the spatula in her left, and the row of containers on the table awaiting disposal. The overhead lighting seemed harsher as she realized what she had been so vigorously scraping into the garbage bin.

"You don't mean . . . " Bette hesitated, not sure how to ask her question.

Roya nodded, placing an emptied dish in the compartmentalized container. She pushed back some loose hair with the top of her forearm.

"Why?" Bette asked.

"They aren't viable."

"But"—Bette shook her head in amazement at the line of dishes—"there are so many." Bette turned to the trash can, finally understanding its true purpose.

"What happens to this?" she asked Roya, pointing to the trash bin. Roya's shoulders dropped as she sighed.

"Biohazardous waste has to be incinerated."

The infernal ventilation system kicked on again, leaving Bette to the white noise of her own thoughts. Roya continued to plod along in her work. Bette conscientiously placed her empty dish in the bin. She swallowed hard and reached for another dish. She read and reread the phrase *for disposal* on the top before twisting off the lid. This time, with a little more reverence, she took to her task with a slightly gentler hand.

We are beyond the luxury of time and preference.

When all the dishes were empty, Bette eyed Roya nervously as she walked to the trash can. Slipping her hand inside one of the side handles, she motioned for Bette to take the other. Together, they carried the trash can over to the incinerator. Roya tied the top of the liner and secured it with a knot.

"If you would," Roya said as she exerted effort to pull out the liner. Bette carefully grabbed a handful of the heavy clear plastic. As they lifted the bag, she could feel the motion of the jiggly semisolids slosh back and forth. Bette made the mistake of looking down at the blobs of agar, which reminded her of chunks of dirty ice, cracked and trembling. Roya opened the door of the incinerator with one hand. Together, they heaved the bag in, and it tumbled into the belly of the machine. Roya stretched forward to turn on the machine. The flames whooshed to life within and, in seconds, Bette could feel the heat coming off the machine.

Roya removed her face mask, closed her eyes, and lowered her head briefly. "To bear witness," she whispered before opening her eyes. She stared at the machine a moment or two longer.

"Come on, Bette, there is nothing else to do here."

39

Bette awoke with a start when she heard the door open. The window simulation had progressed to dawn. The pert silhouette of a woman in a white pantsuit stood in the doorway. The last time the director had shown up in her doorway, Bette's life had been completely upended. Something about the purposefulness of her walk made Bette think today would be no different. Ms. Tyler's shoes clicked as she strode across the room, stopping to stand at the foot of Bette's bed. Her white hair glowed in the simulated light and made her seem almost angelic. She cupped a small juice glass in her hands.

"Ms. Tyler," Bette said and nodded warily in her direction.

"Now that the moisture control has been purged from your system, we can begin our work."

Bette studied Ms. Tyler's face. It was impossible to determine her age, which was an inherent benefit of resources and position. The only real indicator was her gleaming white hair that carried just the slightest streak of gray. The haircut was precise; each strand was trained into place by the highly skilled hand of a city cosmetologist.

"Our girls have been at this since they were fifteen or sixteen, educated in a specific way. You, on the other hand, are a touch feral. I appreciate this rags-to-riches cliché that you seem to be living out. But there is one thing you must never forget." Ms. Tyler leaned in, steady in tone. "I expect compliance with every direction given. Do you understand?"

Heat rose to Bette's face. She hadn't done anything wrong, so why was she so nervous? "I do."

"Good," Ms. Tyler said as she offered the glass. "I'm going to need you to drink this."

Bette accepted it and examined the contents. The dull orange liquid, not more than six ounces, smelled like dirt.

"What is it?" Bette asked.

"What did I just say?" Ms. Tyler chirped, her left eyebrow jumping up.

Bette scrutinized the orange substance.

"Today begins an aggressive nutrition regimen. These juices are freshly pressed for you as part of a carefully calibrated meal plan."

"Oh, okay," Bette said, peering inside the glass hesitantly.

"I would suggest that you not smell it," Ms. Tyler advised. "Drink it up, nice and fast."

Bette put the glass to her lips and quickly dumped it all into her mouth. The smell was pungent, almost like mold, and it was pulpier than Bette expected. She chewed and then swallowed the lumpy goop.

"Now you'll wait thirty minutes before you eat breakfast. You might feel a little queasy, but trust me, that's normal."

"How queasy?" Bette asked, having flashbacks to the last few days.

"Your body is adjusting to hyper nourishment. The concentration of nutrients should help alleviate the various deficiencies you have. Pregnancy exacts a lot from a body. This will help to shore up your foundation so the body can repair and strengthen itself."

The juice left a bitter aftertaste in Bette's mouth.

"And correcting my nutrition will help me get . . . pregnant?"

Bette stumbled on the last word. It wasn't because she didn't know how to say it; she had said it thousands, if not millions, of times. *Pregnant.* In tears, with intention, the object of wishful thinking, the smolder of determination. She was intimately familiar with the word. But there was something about the way it was being used now, as if it was attainable. A commonplace occurrence as opposed to what it was, a miracle. Like it was an inevitable event, not something that she had pined for nearly her whole adult life. It wasn't even contingent on anything. There were no words like "maybe" or "hopefully," and there were no warnings to manage Bette's expectations.

"Nutrition is where we start. We will work on several aspects to prepare you for pregnancy. This cumulative approach helps to create a stronger resident."

A stronger resident.

"It is very important that you adhere to the schedule for the quickest maximum benefit," Ms. Tyler said, one eyebrow arching higher than the other. "I know what I am doing. Do you believe I know what I am doing?"

Ms. Tyler's jaw tensed as if she expected Bette to challenge her. Bette nodded. "Yes, I do," Bette said, her throat constricting slightly to make herself heard.

Ms. Tyler's steely eyes roved over Bette, pulling her apart and putting her back together in a matter of seconds. Her lens cycled through every byte of information about Bette; it searched every corner to see if Bette was brazen enough to defy her.

"Now, why don't you go ahead and get ready for the day? I will see you on the med floor after your exercise."

Bette's stomach gurgled.

We are beyond the luxury of time and preference.
I understand that there is violence all around me.
To create a stronger resident.

40

Bette's breakfast arrived before anyone else's. Bette knew it was intended for her because as the robot rolled up behind her, an alert flashed across her vision. She turned and removed the bowl of oatmeal from its serving surface.

"Oh, Dorothea stopped by this morning, didn't she?" Roya asked, casting a knowing glance at Bette's oatmeal.

"Yeah, she came in with some juice."

"Yum." Roya grinned.

"Not really," Bette said as she set the bowl down in front of her.

Minutes later, the rest of the table was served.

"Well, that juice is nothing compared to the coffee enemas and hormone shots," Roya spoke into her food.

"The what?" Bette asked as if she'd had misunderstood her.

Melody began to snicker.

"Coffee enemas," Roya said. "When a body in distress starts receiving an abundance of nutrients like you will be getting through your juices, it starts to flush toxins out of the body."

Fern picked up where Roya left off. "The purging can be hard on the liver. Coffee enemas are used to assist the liver, so it's not overburdened during the process."

Bette blinked twice. "And this is a real thing?"

"Quite real," Roya said. "You will probably be downright miserable for the next week or so."

"Oh," Bette said, suddenly worried. She had just recovered from the moisture control withdrawal.

"Don't worry, it won't be anything like that moisture-control thing." Roya winked. Bette couldn't shake the apprehension of yet another Birthing Center procedure. She did not want to ever be that sick again.

Fern zipped out of the dining room as soon as breakfast was over. Normally, Melody was not far behind her, humming to herself, but today she hung close to Bette as they made their way out of the dining room. Bette, not wanting to dignify her presence with any kind of response, ignored her and talked with Roya. Melody pressed in closer to Bette's left side and whispered loudly, "It is going to happen soon."

Bette stopped and took a couple of steps away from her, returning space between them. "What are you talking about, Melody?"

Melody took a defiant step back into Bette's personal space. "You know." She grinned from ear to ear, her lip twitching. "I can almost smell it. Don't you feel it?"

Melody was only a few inches taller than Bette. This close, Bette could make out faint freckles she hadn't noticed before and the blue veins underneath Melody's cream-colored skin. This time, her eyes were not squinted or narrowed in their normal contentious way. For a fleeting moment, Melody seemed to be telling the truth. *But about what?* Bette eyed her guardedly and decided that this was some kind of game she did not want to get caught up in.

"Melody, I don't know what you are talking about; you are being ridiculous," Bette said dismissively as she continued toward the doorway.

"No, I'm not," she sang. "It is going to happen soon." She skipped out of the dining room.

Bette turned to Roya. "What the hell was that about?"

Roya shrugged as she feigned bewilderment. "No idea."

Bette was unconvinced; there was something in Roya's astute eyes that flickered when she wasn't telling the whole truth. Maybe Melody thought she knew something, but Roya *did* know something.

Bette teetered on the edge of the exam table. Every time she heard footsteps from the med floor hall, she stiffened and waited to see who would appear to administer the scalding doom. What a terrible thing to do to coffee. A rare and beautiful elixir was being used like a commonplace laxative. The thought made Bette's insides pang with regret. The fish, the citrus, the coolers of water sitting in empty rooms . . . it boggled Bette's mind that the Birthing Center had enough resources to just waste. And now, coffee? Impossible-to-buy coffee?

"If you will lie facedown on the table, we will get started." Maria's perky voice interrupted the irritation coalescing in Bette's thoughts.

After snapping on her gloves, the pint-sized woman with dark hair and bright eyes noticed the spooked look on Bette's face. "It is not as bad as it sounds," she said. She motioned her gloved hand at the table. Bette leaned all the way back in resignation before flipping over onto her front. The flaps of the medical gown settled beside her and left her behind exposed. Maria's back was to Bette as she busied herself at the counter with unspooling some tubing. As Bette watched,

Maria removed a quart-sized bucket and a yellowish solution in a sealed jar from the two-doored cabinet above the counter. *It doesn't look like coffee. I can't smell any coffee.* Maria opened a long rectangular package and removed a bright orange catheter tip. Bette's face puckered in disgust.

"Is it . . . hot?" Bette asked sheepishly.

"No!" Maria began to laugh. "And actually, it isn't real coffee. Since coffee is so hard to come by, we make a solution that imitates the desired chemicals and effects. I promise, nothing about it will remind you of real coffee."

Bette's trepidation subsided, but only a little. Maria moved a square rolling tray holding a container of lubricant to Bette's left side. She attached the tubing to the bucket, the catheter tip to the tubing, and brought it over to the metal tray. Lastly, she uncapped the solution and brought it with her to Bette's hind end. Bette gulped as she heard the liquid being poured into the bucket.

"Shall we begin?" Maria asked in her brainless, giddy way.

Bette squeezed her eyes shut and cringed.

41

Bette had just changed into pajamas and pulled back the covers in her room when she heard the thumping sound. At first, she thought she'd imagined it. It started out low and distant, then slowly increased its patter before stopping abruptly and beginning again after a few minutes.

Bette climbed into bed and pulled the covers over her. She stared at the ceiling as the thumping began another refrain. Again, and again, the thumping would start off slow, steadily crescendo, and then stop. It sounded as though it came from another room on the hall.

Bette began to count how long the thumping verses lasted from start to finish. Then she switched to counting the time between the ends of the fastest patters to the beginning of the next slower thuds. They were close, but not consistent. Each strain differed from the last, as if each new verse were being improvised by its creator.

What would be timed like this?

It seemed too erratic and unpredictable to have been programmed in such a way. Suddenly, there was a high piercing shriek. Bette shot straight up as goose bumps erupted all over her skin. There was another shriek and another. It didn't sound like an alarm or a siren. She sat, paralyzed, and quietly listened.

It sounds like a woman screaming.

Bette swung her legs out of bed. Small motion-detecting lights along the floor lit up as her feet hit the floor. She walked quickly to the door. There was no handle on the inside. She waved her hands in front of the door, quickly at first and then a little slower. It would not open.

Bette stepped closer to the door and put her ear up to it. She took a deep breath because all she could hear was the sound of her heart in her ears.

It was definitely coming from nearby. The shrieking seemed strange and without reason. This woman was not yelling for help, she wasn't calling out to anyone, she wasn't even using words. It was just shrieking in loud staccato bursts.

As Bette stood there listening, it reminded her of something. A chill ran down the length of her entire body, and her stomach lurched as the memory fully materialized.

She could feel the breeze as she sat on the concrete curb. Bette tried to blink the image away, but it was bright and forceful. She could see those little dandelions across the street, as they danced and mocked her infertility. She could smell the urine and filth as it wafted over her. Her stomach flipped, and a cold sweat broke out over her whole body. Paralyzed at the door, she was helpless to stop the memory as it played out before her. The pain, the stench, the unrelenting pressure on her neck. And *that* sound.

Then, as suddenly as it had started, it stopped. Silence waved away the curling wisps that outlined the memory. Bette blinked; she found herself drenched in sweat and breathing fast as the adrenaline dispensed throughout her body. She blinked twice and looked around to confirm her surroundings. In the darkness, all that remained was the uneven rattle of her own breathing.

42

Bette woke before the lighting signaled daylight. She rolled onto her side and faced the room. She pulled the blanket closer to her neck as if hanging on a little tighter would change how poorly she'd slept. Her rest had been plagued by nightmares of lurking, smothering shadows and disembodied shrieking. More than once she sat up because the pressure on her chest made her feel as though she were suffocating. *Why would anything in this place make that noise?* Canners were an outside problem. *But this had been a woman . . .*

The door opened and Bette was startled upright.

"Good morning, Bette," Ms. Tyler greeted as she swept through the door, offering Bette a small glass. "I trust you slept well?"

"Uh, yeah," Bette said, taking the juice glass. It was a rhetorical question; Ms. Tyler was not concerned about her sleep. If she was, she had access to Bette's vital signs. A quick blink and that information could be pulled up for Ms. Tyler to make her own conclusions on Bette's sleep. She probably already knew how Bette had slept and was just testing her to see if she would complain.

"Stand up," Ms. Tyler instructed.

This is new. Bette pulled back the covers with one hand while she held the juice glass with the other, quickly chugging the remainder of its contents. Ms. Tyler produced a small needle, leaned in, and lifted Bette's T-shirt.

"Hold still."

Bette held her breath and stood motionless. Ms. Tyler rapidly administered the injection just below Bette's belly button. A tingling sensation spread at the injection site. Letting go of the edge of Bette's shirt, Ms. Tyler took the empty glass. "You can breathe now."

Bette exhaled and stared quizzically down at her stomach, lifting her shirt to inspect the injection site.

"Are you going to do this every morning?" Bette asked.

"For the next couple of weeks, yes." The director's face tightened, no doubt preparing to censure Bette about challenging her authority. The corners of Bette's mouth turned up as she chose another avenue.

"I guess we will become friends, then."

Ms. Tyler's eyes narrowed. "I highly doubt it," she said icily as she turned to leave the room.

43

The elevator ride made Bette nauseous. She closed her eyes and leaned against the wall.

"Is your eye still bothering you?" Roya asked.

"Yeah, a little bit. I have this weird tag," Bette said as she rubbed her eye. "I don't think the lens grafted correctly."

Roya took Bette's chin in her hand. Bette opened her eyes wider.

"Can you see it?" Bette asked.

"I can," Roya said.

"It is sort of driving me crazy. Do you think they can fix it? Maybe smooth it back over?"

"No," Roya said before the last couple of words left Bette's mouth. "No, you don't want to do that."

"I don't?"

"No," Roya said thoughtfully. "Does it go fuzzy when you touch that tag?"

"Yes."

"But fully functioning otherwise?"

"Yeah."

"And no one has said anything to you about it yet?"

Bette shook her head.

"Interesting," Roya said.

The elevator opened onto the sponsor floor. The thick, dark-blue carpet that covered the floors absorbed Bette's and Roya's footsteps. On the left side of the reception desk was a large glass container that held water and citrus fruit.

Bette still couldn't get over it. For as highly as citrus was regulated, the only people who had regular access to it were the ones who grew it. The everyday, regular people outside these walls suffered from scurvy but in this building, oranges were just floating in unattended water. Her mind wandered back to the fish she saw swimming in the aquarium when she first arrived. The ocean was a watery desert after years of warming and acidification had killed off most marine life. With the water-rationing restrictions, only approved fish farms could get permission to use water in this way. But Bette didn't see any of the aquaponic trappings that normally went along with fish-farming.

Are those fish intended for consumption?

"It's ostentatious, isn't it?" Roya whispered as they padded through the deserted luxe lobby.

"What are they sponsoring?" Bette whispered back, careful to keep her eyes down.

The display of wealth in this lobby was no accident. It was gilded, sumptuous, and oozing with decadence; Bette felt as if she were about to partake in something degrading.

"Just your run-of-the-mill filming for advertising and voyeur porn," Roya said. As she did so, she opened an intricately engraved and ornate metal door.

Bette's eyebrows went up. She was familiar with the concept of voyeur porn, having been a subscriber herself for many years. Traditional porn was everywhere; anyone could make it and, in the process, make a little bit of money. Her mind drifted to David. But there was something about the exclusivity of pregnancy in this infertile world that drew people, especially young women, to the voyeur porn streams like insects. You could watch pregnant women doing just about anything for hours, if your budget permitted. They were terrible actors but the fascination with their condition was compelling and quite lucrative. Bette had not known that the Department was in league with the makers of such content. She had always assumed that she was being fleeced while watching actors pretend to be pregnant and yet, she still had a hard time looking away. It was strange now, being on the other side of it, being on the side where it happened. The very girls who roamed these halls, those who had gotten on the elevator ahead of her the other day, were the ones being filmed. They were the ones practicing lines and putting on costumes and starring in these streams. They were being pimped out in content made for any kind of kink who would pay for it. Did they have any idea the droves that lusted and obsessed over them? Did they have any idea the amount of financial ruin these streams caused? It had come down to survival for her when she canceled her subscriptions. Either she paid the rent and ate or kept her subscriptions. Were they even aware of the addicts these streams created, the hopelessness and longing it fueled in desperate, empty people? Still, they charged them, raised the prices every few weeks, recommended other channels, and bombarded them with the possibility that if they just spent enough money, they could attain something similar to these stars. Maybe, just maybe their good genes would osmose through the screen and grant them what they were searching for.

The room they'd entered had a half dozen sets built to resemble kitchens, dining rooms, and markets. Cameras and lighting equipment framed each stage like electronic sentries guarding the sets against the disarray of the world around them. Cluttered tables and disorderly chairs were strewn between each tableau. It looked as if a dust devil had swirled through this place, leaving in its wake cellophane wrapping, hair wefts, and used towels. Makeup brushes and containers were strewn all over the tables along with brushes and bobby pins. Tumbleweeds of hair quivered on the floor as they walked past.

"Geez," Bette exclaimed, "someone was in a hurry."

"The sponsors only get the girls for a few hours," Roya explained, as she began to sort out the mess on a table near a stage set up to resemble a bathroom. "So, they work fast and messy."

Bette picked up a piece of lacy black fabric, watching reflective confetti spill from it.

"Oh, that goes to another sound stage," Roya said as she took the stringy costume and tossed it in a bin at the end of a table.

"Do they make them do, like, regular porn, too?"

"Not much." Roya shrugged. "I don't think people want to pay a premium when they use body doubles for the activity. They'll do a little bondage stuff, pregnant dominatrix mostly. That seems to be popular. And they must beat the shit out of people for those. I normally have *a lot* of dried blood to clean up."

"I bet Melody loves doing those," Bette mused.

"But do you want to know the ones that make the most money? The ones where girls eat. They just eat and talk about what they are eating. That is why we have almost an entire sound stage of kitchens and dining rooms. Can you imagine? Hours of watching someone slurping and chewing?"

Bette grabbed a push broom that was leaning against a nearby chair and began to direct debris on the floor into a pile.

"I guess I don't feel so bad not having a sponsor now," Bette said.

Roya laughed. "Right?"

There was not a lot of laughter in this place. Not even a sense of pleasant sociability. It was a facility filled with muted young women. The only one who laughed with any regularity was Melody, but it was mean spirited. She was never laughing jovially; she was always laughing at someone. Was it their age? Bette easily had a decade on most of them. These were not emotionally mature women with any kind of life experience, except for Roya. She wasn't as socially awkward as the rest of them.

"Hey, Roya, how old are you?" Bette asked.

"Twenty-one," she said.

So, she was younger than Fern, which surprised Bette.

"When did you know you were fertile?" Bette asked. She shuffled behind the broom in short bursts of motion, playing keep-away with a tiny white, downy feather.

Roya paused, her towel frozen above the table where she was wiping up powdered bronzer. "I knew for sure when I was fifteen."

"And was it something you looked forward to? You know, wanting to get pregnant and procreate?" Bette asked.

"Jesus, Bette. You really *are* a product of the Mandate." Roya stopped spritzing disinfectant and looked up. A long moment passed, which made Bette wonder if she had offended her. Roya rested her hands on her hips and finally answered. "To be honest, I'd never thought about it like that. *Want* to get pregnant? Those weren't the kind of questions I was asking, not then. Everyone just kept saying how lucky I was. And I was. Just the ability, right?"

Roya continued as she wiped the beaded spray from the table with a towel. "I was sixteen when I first got pregnant.

God, trying so hard to be an adult. That was all I ever wanted, to grow up and do what the grown-ups did." She shook her head and chuckled softly. "I think, well . . . I guess, to answer your question, Bette, yes, I did look forward to it. I'd been conditioned to. That is the way we are raised, you know? But after he was born, I don't know what I thought. It was harder than I expected. Maybe if I'd had more time, you know, before everything . . . " She trailed off.

Roya's vulnerability caught Bette off guard. She'd just assumed that everyone who was fertile was filled with never-ending joy. Now, as she observed Roya, she felt stupid for thinking that. Bette had seen that sorrowful softening in Roya's eyes before, but in women much older than her. This was a look she caught on her mother's or grandmother's faces when they didn't think Bette was paying attention. It was a faraway look that came from having to revisit past heartache.

"But," Roya said, gulping back her memory and glancing at the ceiling, "sometimes that is just how life goes."

The transaction side of procreation had been touted repetitively and in detail. The entire reason the Department of Procreation existed was to see to that. The urgency of their message focused on the ability to get pregnant. But here, human beings—women—were the ones processing the transaction. Fragile teenage girls were held in this menacing concrete fortress, surrounded by sophisticated platinum machines, and everything they could possibly need.

"I'm sorry . . . I . . . " Bette stammered.

"Don't worry about it," Roya said, her eyes fixed to the table. Her right hand came to rest on her temple. "I told you, it makes them worse."

Though only yards from each other, a chasm of knowledge separated them. Bette shifted her eyes from Roya's profile to the floor as she watched Roya wipe tears from her cheek. Roya sniffed and straightened, going after the trash on the table with a new resolve. "Like you, my life was different before I came here. What about you? When did you know?"

Bette shook her head. "I'm still not sure."

Roya turned to face Bette, a slight crinkle on her forehead and a renewed curiosity shimmering in her eyes as she tilted her head to the side. "What do you mean you aren't sure?"

Bette paused, her broom momentarily hovering above the shellacked floor before tapping it down. "Ms. Tyler came to the hospital with two enforcement officers. All she told me was that she was following up on a fertility report."

Roya nodded slowly and turned her right side to Bette as she began combing out hair from a hairbrush. "Why were you in the hospital?" she asked, condensing the discarded hair from the brush into a ball and dropping it into a trash bin.

"I'd been attacked." As Bette spoke, her hand went to her neck, as though guided by its own mind. All that remained were pinpricks of the earlier gouges.

"What were you attacked by, Bette?" Roya's voice was barely above a murmur and there was a delay as the question registered with Bette.

"They haven't caught him yet, last I knew."

"Do you remember anything about this man?" Roya asked, her volume still reduced. "Anything that stood out? A sound, maybe?"

Bette stopped sweeping and held her breath as a shudder went through her arms. Roya turned to meet her gaze with steady, tranquil eyes.

She knows.

"How do you . . . " Bette couldn't get the question out for the lump that now resided in her throat. How could she have known? Roya was a stranger to her. There were no news streams in the Birthing Center. David wouldn't have even known that.

How could this cloistered resident know that detail from Bette's attack?

Roya squatted and picked up plastic wrappers from the floor. "You've heard it again since you've been here?" She directed the question away from Bette, to the underside of the table.

Bette's stomach dropped. "How . . . how did you know?" Bette managed a strangled whisper.

Roya stood with her back to Bette. She tilted her chin up and wiped a stray piece of black hair from her forehead as she directed her gaze to the ceiling. "It's weird the things you come across in life, Bette," she said, then hesitated slightly before continuing. "I'm not your average Center resident. But, then, neither are you."

It's all related. The attack, her admission into the Birthing Center. They were related, but how? Why? What about any of this made sense? Where was the connection? Ms. Tyler knew, of course, but why would Roya know?

Footsteps echoed on the floor. Roya's head snapped toward the doorway as every fiber in her body became alert. "Shhh," she hissed. Alarmed, Bette turned toward the shadow moving within the shadows.

"Hey, girls," Hector said as he entered the light. "Time to wrap it up."

44

Four days into the coffee enemas and mystery injections, Bette was lying on the exam table on the med floor. She would rest there until Ms. Tyler or Maria kicked her out. Her insides wobbled after the enema; her abdomen was tender from the repeated sticks. Her stomach refused to settle at mealtime and the smell of food made her nauseous. Her breasts were so sore, she winced each time she put on her shirt. A dull headache waxed and waned its way through her brain most of each day. The muscles in her shoulders couldn't seem to relax even when she was lying down.

A sudden rapid motion outside the cracked door caused her to look over. Someone darted past the doorway, someone with long, blond hair. It happened so fast that Bette thought her eyes must be playing tricks on her.

Great, hallucinations now. She propped herself up on one arm. Then two Center staffers ran past the doorway, yelling, "Stop, get back here!"

Bette was not hallucinating. Curious, she pushed herself up and hobbled over to the doorway. She poked her head out in time to see the staffers' backsides as they sped in the direction of the med floor atrium. Ever so gently, Bette crept down the hall after them. She stopped just inside the hallway that opened into the round space behind the gleaming desk.

The blond girl's back was to all of them as she scanned her head back and forth and looked for a way out. The Center staffers clambered to either side of her, one of them with a fresh cut above his eye. She darted around the lobby like a fruit gnat while her medical gown flapped behind her.

Bette leaned into the doorframe for support; she was tired, but not too tired to see what would happen. Abruptly, the blond girl stopped and turned to her left. She tilted up her nose and began sniffing the air. Her profile looked familiar to Bette and, as the blond figure turned around fully, Bette knew why. Something about the light washed the age from her face and made her appear a little younger. But that catlike stalk she had was unmistakable and so was that hair.

Melody's eyes narrowed as they locked on Bette with an expression Bette had seen before. Bette waved weakly and smiled. Ignoring the staffers, Melody prowled toward Bette. Her face was like stone, revealing no recognition that she'd ever seen Bette before. Alarm leaped up Bette's spine. Halfway across the lobby, Melody broke into a run, never taking her eyes off her prey. Bette began to look around and felt panic build inside her; she hoped the staffers would do something. They ran just inches behind Melody. She opened her mouth and let out a bone-rattling shriek as she prepared to crash into Bette. Unable to move as her body froze at hearing the familiar scream, Bette braced for the impact.

Bette's breath whooshed as her feet flew from underneath her and she connected with the floor. Disoriented, she felt hands on her throat. Melody was squeezing Bette's neck with a machinelike grip. The staffers pulled Melody off in a matter of moments. Bette sat up slowly, but remained rooted to the floor.

"Jesus Christ, Melody, what the hell is wrong with you!" Bette sputtered.

Ms. Tyler appeared on Bette's left side. She rushed over to the staffers who were frenetically trying to restrain Melody. She was thrashing and screaming like a feral animal. Ms. Tyler produced a menacing syringe and plunged it into Melody's thigh. Melody screeched in pain.

"What is going on out here?" Ms. Tyler yelled at the pair of staffers who had finally gotten control over Melody. Her thrashing subsided and she began to droop. "Why is she out of her room? Get her back to her quarters, you idiots!"

The staffers murmured apologetically as they carried Melody back down the hall. Melody must have been stronger than she appeared if it took two grown men to restrain the twenty-something pregnant woman. Bette's hand went to her neck as she recalled Melody's vise grip choking off her oxygen supply. Even though she had only choked Bette for a few short moments, it was plenty of time to show what Melody was capable of.

Ms. Tyler trained an irritated glare on Bette. "Well? What are you still doing here?"

Bette scrambled to stand up. "What is wrong with Melody?" she asked.

"What did I tell you about questions?" Ms. Tyler snapped.

"I'm just wondering if she's okay." Bette said as she looked down the hall where Melody had been taken.

"She is fine. I suggest you move to your next activity block."

Bette lingered, taking in Ms. Tyler's uncharacteristic lapse of cool control.

"Now!" Ms. Tyler roared as she angrily aimed her arm toward the elevator.

Bette jumped and skittered over to the elevator. As she waited for the door to open, Bette tried to quell a building sense of unease. She heard the distant clipped footsteps of the director moving angrily down the med floor hall.

So, the shrieking the other night was Melody?

As the elevator door shut, a notification blinked in the message section. Bette willed it open. The message read: *Schedule Change*. Bette opened the schedule to find that she was to spend the rest of her day in her suite. There was a note indicating that dinner would be served in her room and she would only be released for meditation.

45

He was long gone. It was raining . . . again. The somber ashen clouds hung overhead and pushed all life and hope down. Bette rocked back and forth alone in the waves. She couldn't move forward; she couldn't move backward. She was stuck . . . again. She wasn't scared anymore. She was annoyed at being blocked and hindered.

She wildly kicked and thrashed her hands about. The cold rain splashed so fast and so hard on the watery surface all around her she wasn't sure if the drops were falling down or erupting up. Her foot bumped something solid. Then her knee knocked on the hard object. She reached her hands out in front of her. They, too, touched the solid slippery surface. Her cold, stiff fingers groped to find a hold. She grappled in the rain and finally managed to pull herself out of the water.

Bette sat up abruptly to find herself alone in her room. Her hair clung to her sticky neck. She kicked her legs out from the blanket and planted her feet on the floor. She gulped in air as the water from the dream faded.

It was just a dream.

It had been a dream, but it wasn't a new dream. She'd had it on and off for years, ever since her Gram had passed. The only thing different about this version was the intensity.

She had seen his eye, heard his breath. Never had those details stayed with her. Normally she woke with only a vague sense of déjà vu, but nothing like this. Bette leaned over and rested her face in her hands, mindful to take deep and even breaths.

Her grandma always had a way of making bad situations tenable. During the difficult times following her death, as if on cue, memories of her Gram triggered in Bette like a vaccine or an antibody. It felt as if her psyche knew exactly what it needed to heal itself; it needed to tap into the comfort of a woman who had truly loved her.

Her grandma used to take her to the natural history museum when she was a child. They'd gone as often as they could, just the two of them. Those visits were a welcome respite from the daily tension that rolled off Bette's mother and crashed into every immutable surface. There had been one mural that mesmerized Bette. To this day, she couldn't figure out why. There was nothing fancy about it, nor did it have dramatic lighting or an interactive touchscreen to accompany it. It wasn't even an excellent artistic rendering, but its bronze plaque told the story: This piece of the painting had survived the quake of '49, the Big One.

It had been excavated near what had been California's border, after the Golden State fell into the sea, and brought back east to serve as a memorial of things fallen, a reminder that life will always rise. The edges of the mural were ragged, proof that they had broken off something bigger. The cracked plaster produced tiny lines along the painting like haphazard spiderwebs. A shoreline filled the left side of the recovered mural and hugged an expanse of water that encompassed the remainder of the painting. On the right side, half-submerged like a massive green egg with flippers, a dinosaur floated on the water. Bette would scan her gaze from right to left, and sometimes if she did it quickly enough, she could have sworn he'd moved. Toward the middle of the mural, his flippers began to morph, and by the time he'd arrived at the shore, his flippers were shaped into crude, heavy feet. At best, it was a clunky interpretation of everything involved in his evolutionary trek from sea to land.

Bette's grandma often fell asleep while Bette stared at him. "Gram? Gram, how did he know he wanted to change? How did he know he wanted to live on land?" Bette asked, giving her arm a gentle shake.

Her Gram's eyes would blink open as she reoriented herself before responding. "Well, why do you suppose he wanted to get to land?"

Many scenarios were discussed over the years ranging from "the water is hot lava" to "he missed his family" to "maybe his food supply is dwindling." Bette's grandma never answered outright. She'd answer a question with a question because, she said, it encouraged original thought.

"What about this, button?" Bette's grandma would lean over. "Maybe the land wants him to be there?"

Bette would look at her, skeptical. "Gram, land can't do that."

Her grandma would sit back and feign offense, but her mahogany eyes glittered at the chance to rebut Bette's school-yard logic. "Remember," Bette's Gram would whisper, "evolution is a relationship. The one evolving senses the need to change but so does the environment. On some vibrating atomic plane, there is an understanding between the two of what needs to happen next."

Even then, Bette's hare-like eyes saw everything, constantly roving and ever vigilant. She'd rest her pointy elbow on the armrest of the bench, her keen chin in her palm, as she mulled her grandma's hypothesis. A serious divot would appear between her brows as she pursed her lips and dared the painting to give up what it knew.

"How did you know when to change?" Bette would whisper.

The dream always started out with the two of them in the water, the dinosaur from the mural and Bette. He would swim. She would try to keep up with him, all the while wondering where they were going. The sky would cloud over and the water would grow choppy; then the rain would start. Eventually, her arms got tired. She would bob up and down, then fall below the surface and gasp for air. So focused on her survival, she would always lose track of him. Anger, disappointment, and irritation would sweep over her. Then she would hit land and wake up, her heart aching for her Gram.

Only this time it was much worse. Bette sobbed and shook as she melted into the matress. Pulling her knees up to her chest, she tried frantically to hold together the pieces of her heart that were rending and calving.

46

"Come, come," Maria said, already walking down the hallway. "We have a lot to do today. Yes, yes, quite a bit. Making up for lost time."

She was talking more to herself than to Bette. Maria opened one of the first few doors on the right and motioned for Bette to go in first. The white room was just big enough for two chairs and a circular metal side table between them. They faced the back wall, which was predominantly a dark screen.

"All right, you have a seat," Maria said, pushing her glasses up the bridge of her nose.

Wary, Bette sat down and clasped her hands in her lap.

"Today, you get to do your initial brokering selection!" Maria's excited sentence hung suspended in the air.

Bette smiled politely but was not entirely sure what Maria was talking about. Not deterred by Bette's lackluster response, Maria went on to explain. "The geneticists have finished working through your DNA map. From that, we have compiled compatible matches for you to choose from. Compatible, in that, there are no anticipated genetic marker issues," she finished sheepishly. "True compatibility is for you to decide."

Bette waited expectantly and stared at her. Maria's smile fell. "You don't seem very excited, Bette," Maria said, a little disappointed.

"What? No, I'm excited. I'm just not familiar with *how* brokering works. Like, the process," Bette said, trying to clear things up.

"Oh." Maria started to nod. "Okay. I see. There is nothing to it, really. We are just going to look at some men and you are going to pick a few you like."

Bette considered this as she shifted in her chair and crossed her legs. "So, I'm just going to scroll through a series of men's profiles?"

"Yes!"

"And then what?"

"Well, you will decide which one you want, and we will arrange the brokering."

"And brokering is basically what? Insemination?"

"Oh, Bette. I suppose, if you want to be *scientific* about it, yes." Maria rolled her eyes as if Bette had just explained how a magic trick was done, ruining the illusion.

True compatibility.

"Do I have to actually meet this person?"

"No!" Maria scoffed.

"I *don't* have to have sex with him?" Bette asked.

"Exactly!" Maria said enthusiastically, walking over to the screen. "Who even has time for that?"

She tapped the screen and then made a couple of swipes. She pulled a little silver disc out of her pocket and handed it to Bette. It was comprised of only one button. "Now, there will be a short informational spot at the beginning, which will probably be helpful since this is your first time. But all you need to really remember is to press the button for each profile you are interested in. Don't worry if you click the wrong one; we can edit your selections at the end."

The presentation began as soon as Maria shut the door. The Department of Propagation's circular silver seal flashed on the screen, proudly displaying its laurel leaves surrounding a baby. After a second or two, a well-dressed woman in a dark suit appeared. She held her hands the way a politician would, her fingers steepled in front of her.

"Evolution has always been the master designer when it comes to creating and maintaining the trajectory of any species. Though superior to our neighbors in the animal kingdom, we are still a species of this planet, still subject to evolution's prerogative."

Bette shifted in her seat, already bored. While she hadn't seen this exact video before, she was well versed in the Department of Propagation's rhetoric. Propaganda seemed to be all that Propagation propagated with any consistency.

"It is an honor for you to sit in this place today. Evolution has chosen you to help move us forward. We here at the Department of Propagation hold your gift in high regard and are grateful for your contribution. It is our commitment to assist you in all you need to achieve that goal."

We are beyond the luxury of time and preference.

The woman in the recording smiled. Bette yawned and stretched her arms above her head, listening to the stiff sinews creak in the tops of her shoulders.

"We have come a long way from the primordial soup, but we still rely heavily on evolution for what it does best . . . choosing winners. Shortly, you will see a presentation of these winners. We have already gone the extra mile to ensure you are completely compatible. There are no 'wrong' answers for the following selections."

She pointed to a picture of the silver disc Bette was holding.

"In your hand, you have a decision remote. We have found that applicants who click based on an initial feeling have better

results than those who *overanalyze* during the selection process. As you move through the presentation, please press the
remote within the first few seconds of a selection profile. Do
not worry; you will be able to edit your selections at the end of
the presentation."

Bette turned the remote over in her hands.

"Good luck. May your brokering be effective and your
future prolific."

The nondescript woman from the Department of
Propagation faded from view. A short video followed next. It
was a profile for a handsome young man. His smiling face was
on the left and a list of bullet points appeared on the right.
Half of them Bette didn't even understand—volume, liquefac-
tion time, motility, pH level, fructose level. The things she did
understand were those that he spoke about—interests, education, accomplishments, and occupation.

At the bottom of the screen were instructions: *Press twice to
select, press once to pass.* A quick video, some data, and a choice.

Bette stared at his frozen face when the video stopped. His
name was Mike. No last name. Mike was eighteen years old.
He liked to exercise and read. His job was classified. There were
a series of metrics, such as his grade point average, his weight,
his body-fat-to-muscle ratio, his vision scores, genetic marker
information (which she didn't understand). Finally, there were
his testosterone and serotonin levels. His brokering percentage
was 91.

Outside the Center, Mike might not have been all that
interested in a twenty-nine-year-old woman. But, if she
had shown a little interest, it was Mike's civic obligation to at
least try. A bit of awkward small talk, laughter, and in no time,
he would have been on his way home. But here, Mike was
just a short video. There was no feigned interest, no tentative
pawing, and no strangely formal goodbye when they finished.

Based on this information, do you want to make a baby with Mike? Bette pressed the remote once. It made a soft clicking noise.

Javier was sixteen. *Gross.* One click.

Barton. Twenty-one. Really interested in astronomy. *No one has seen a star without a high-powered telescope in forty years due to the constant greenhouse cloud cover.* One click.

Amos. Nineteen. Majored in philosophy. *Completely useless.* The brokering percentage is 99. *I bet that means something to someone.* One click.

Mark had scary eyes. *Nope.* One click.

Phil, Bryan, Juan, Ian, Andrew, Cooper . . . on and on.

Bette sighed and leaned her head back in the chair, rolling her eyes to the ceiling.

Fern was right about this part.

These profiles had plenty of information, way more than Bette usually had about men she'd actually been with. She just couldn't tell if she *liked* them or not. She advanced to the next one. The voice in the next video startled her.

I know him . . .

The information next to his video said his name was Alex. Bette had known him as Christopher. She blinked, finding herself back in her apartment. He had shown up with some beer. Being undernourished, she didn't need much to soon feel its effects. Even now, she felt the warmth in her cheeks as her capillaries widened. They laughed and flirted. His smile was easy and his confidence was intoxicating. He leaned in to kiss Bette. As they moved to her bedroom, he became rougher. Once again, she could feel the pressure as he yanked her arm and shoved her just a little too hard.

"Hey, be careful," she said, half joking.

In one quick movement, he grabbed her arm and twisted it behind her. His hot breath was in her ear. In an instant, the mood had shifted. Panic leaped in her stomach.

No. no. no.

"I don't like this," Bette had said, trying to shake her arm free.

He'd pressed himself closer into her back. She could feel he was turned on and it made her stomach turn. "Oh, come on, Bette, can't you feel what you have done to me? It's not fair to leave me like this."

She broke free and ran back to the doorway, only stopping to turn around.

"You need to leave," she'd said loudly, her voice shaking.

He sighed, obviously annoyed.

"Jesus, just give me a minute." His hands reached down to his zipper.

"No! I mean it!" she yelled at him. "Get the fuck out!"

He made no move to leave but instead turned his back to her. She noticed he started to sway as his knees bumped the edge of the mattress. Revolted, she backed out of the room.

He emerged, sporting a smug smile on his face. He walked over, leaned on the kitchen island opposite of where she was standing, and sarcastically said, "You don't, like, want to cuddle or something, do you?"

"Get out," she spat.

"Gladly." He rolled his eyes and made for the door. "I don't know what your problem is . . . this is sort of what you are here for. You guys are, like, made for speed, you know? Plus, it's, like, the law, you know."

"Take your stuff," she'd said between clenched teeth, motioning to the leftover beers on the counter.

He turned around and glanced first at the counter and then her. "You know what, keep them. You need to loosen the fuck up."

The door whooshed open and he was gone. Bette reached for a bottle of the abandoned beer and hurled it at the closed door. It shattered into pieces, liquid splashing up the door and wall and pooling on the floor. Her vision blurred as she started crying. Trembling, she put her hands over her face and took a couple of deep breaths to calm herself.

As she returned to the bedroom, she saw the dark, wet streaks of semen splattered across the bedspread. They culminated into a large wet spot right where he had been standing.

What an asshole.

She sniffed, angrily flinging away the tears. She tore all the bedding off, right down to the mattress, and slammed it into a nearby laundry basket. She picked up the basket and walked out into the hall. At the end of the hall, she opened the hatch to the incinerator chute and crammed everything in there. Clutching the handle of the closed chute, she rested her head on the wall above it, relieved. It had been a bad evening, but it wasn't the worst that had ever happened.

Bette trembled in her chair as the memory faded. She blinked back to reality and scrutinized the video that stood paused in front of her. His conceited smile caused her to wince. She crossed her arms in front of her and drew her knees up in front of her arms. Was any of this true? Did *Alex* really have a GPA of 3.8? Was he really interested in food futures and mixed martial arts? Where were the stats indicating he was a selfish asshole who treated infertile women like trash? Because *those* were genes she did not want to see repeated.

One click.

There was no reason to trust anything after that. Bette defiantly single-clicked until there were no more videos to watch, no more faces to look at.

Tabulating selections, the screen read. The little cursor spun. Another message popped up on the screen: *Error: Please see selection proctor.*

Less than a minute after she read the error message, the door swung open. "Oh, hey, Maria . . . I think something is wrong," Bette said, pointing to the screen.

Maria breezed past her. "Yes, I got the alert. Let's see what is going on here." She went up and tapped the screen. A series of reports and graphs appeared. As Maria scrutinized the data, her face wrinkled in confusion.

"Well, this doesn't make any sense." She put her hand over her mouth and tapped her cheek, deep in thought.

"Hey, Bette, can I see your decision remote?"

Bette handed it to her. She pointed it at the screen and clicked it once, then twice. Once again and twice again.

"It seems to be working . . . Did you have any error messages during the selections?" Maria asked.

"No."

She put her hands on her hips and turned back to the screen. "That just can't be possible. This silly computer seems to think that you didn't even make one selection."

Bette looked at the floor. Maria pushed and swiped at the screen a few more times. "Nope, nothing. No data saved anywhere," she said to herself, amazed. "You did select a few, didn't you?" she asked.

The look on Bette's face told her everything she needed to know.

"You didn't make one selection?" Maria asked, amazed.

Bette shook her head.

"Well." Maria's eyes widened. "What was the problem?"

"I . . . I . . . I just didn't like any of them."

Speechless, Maria's mouth gaped open. Bette knew how it sounded the moment it left her lips; it sounded as lame as Bette felt. This was not something that was said; she knew better. If her mother had said it once, she had said it a thousand times: Feelings aren't reality. Bette had spent years listening to propagation center employees. It didn't matter how she felt, it was her responsibility.

We are beyond the luxury of time and preference.

"No, Bette, that is not how it works," Maria chided as she shook her head.

Embarrassed, Bette glanced to the floor to save herself the brunt of Maria's bewildered watch. "Honey, you are about five days and fifteen years behind. Dorothea will not tolerate this. She is already perturbed by the delay from the moisture control incident. No, this will not do." Maria sighed. "Bette, this is the National Agenda. This is a part of the Mandate. Your job is to choose. It's *serious* when residents don't perform." She turned her back to Bette to reset the presentation while Bette wallowed in hot shame.

You know better. You shouldn't have done that. You've dealt with jackasses before, why did you let him get to you? What is wrong with you? Get it together, Jesus.

"Now, I am going to restart the selection process. You are going to pick no less than eight selections. I am giving you twenty minutes." She tapped the screen. The first video came up again and began to play.

"How many do you need to have?" Maria asked sternly, pausing at the door.

"Eight."

"Good girl. Don't dally. You've already wasted too much time today."

The door shut behind Maria. Indiscriminately, Bette clicked twice on eleven profiles, not even letting the videos play as they came up. But she did take special care to avoid Alex or whatever his name was.

47

"Hey, where is Melody?"

Bette tried to sound casual. She'd been a little antsy when mealtime rolled around after what had happened on the med floor. Bette had not seen Melody anywhere since that episode over twenty-four hours ago, not skipping in the halls on her way to the gym, and not in line as they entered the cafeteria. Roya idled as she loosely braided and then combed out a braid in her long, black hair. Her sagacious eyes shifted to Bette, interest piqued. She continued playing with her hair but now her full attention was engaged.

"Who cares?" Fern murmured as she stared intently at her lens.

"I thought she was on the med floor," Roya said, shrugging as if this were common knowledge.

"Is she sick?" Bette asked. Based on the way Melody looked and behaved yesterday, it probably wasn't a cold.

"You don't have to be sick to go to the med floor, Bette. Residents go there all the time."

Roya was being purposely vague. Her right eyebrow rose ever so slightly as if asking what this was really about. *Why all of the sudden interest in Melody, Bette?* She couldn't just blab what had happened. Ms. Tyler would definitely hear about that, and then what would she do to Bette? No, there had to be another way to figure out what was going on with Melody. Stuck, Bette drummed her fingers on her chin, locking stares with Roya.

Roya could already tell that something was up.

Maybe, Roya could answer without Bette actually asking the question. Bette rested her chin in her hand, looking down and tracing on the tabletop with her other hand.

"I just haven't seen her since yesterday on the med floor."

And then I wasn't here last night because of it.

Roya nodded. Her mind worked fast, probably because she was not interested in any of the distractions that the Center offered its residents. She paid close attention to everything and seemed to have a sense about a situation before it happened. She was finely tuned to detect any ripple, no matter how slight. Her practiced forehead didn't even crinkle as she contemplated how to proceed. "And what you saw, when you saw her, caused concern?"

"Yes." Bette brightened as she saw they were on the same wavelength.

"Fern," Roya asked, turning her head, "do you remember how far along Melody is?"

"No."

"Fern," Roya prodded deftly, "you remember this happened the last time, right?"

Fern blinked away what she was watching with an irritated scowl. "What?"

"You know how she gets in that second trimester, kind of mean, and they sometimes quarantine her?"

Roya shot Bette a quick side-glance, as if to confirm this was the question Bette was asking.

"Oh, that. Yeah. I don't know where she is. I find it best to ignore her until she has her transfer or gives birth, whatever rotation she is on. Basically, I ignore her all the time."

"So, like, what does she do?" Bette asked, leaning in.

Fern blew her bangs out of her eyes, looking for the robots.

"You know, throws fits over nothing. Screams a lot. Picks fights for no reason. The stuff crazy people do. I guess we got lucky today, we didn't have to deal with her tantrums."

"Has she ever, you know," Bette asked, her voice dropping a little, "hurt anyone?"

Roya leaned back in her chair crossing her arms, her lips pursed as she listened.

"Yeah," Fern said, disinterested.

"Yeah?" Bette said, brow wrinkled. "What do you mean, yeah?"

"I said, yeah, she has hurt somebody."

"Well, like, what did she do? How badly were they hurt?" Bette began to fire off questions in rapid succession but stopped as Roya's eyes widened slightly in warning.

Fern smirked at her. "Is this another one of those things you care about because you think it affects your life?"

Bette stared at her, too much like those dead-eyed fish in the aquarium, befuddled at the alien creature in front of her with whom she shared the same environment. *Does she think this is funny?*

"She has the crazy hormones." Fern shrugged. "She's not the only one, just the one we have to deal with."

Bette's brain spun as she gravitated weakly toward the meditation room. *Does Fern think this behavior is normal? Is it normal here?*

She felt a tug on her right arm changing her trajectory. Looking over, she saw Roya's hands clasped with hers. She was pulling Bette, trying to slow her down. Bette allowed herself to fall in step with her. Roya's head somewhat bent down as they walked at the back of the pack. "Melody is naturally quite aggressive," Roya began to whisper, "but she is probably not a topic you want to continue with Fern. Fern only sees things in black and white because she has only been taught things in black and white."

Roya paused, hesitating as if maybe she wanted to say something else. She glanced around to make sure no one was behind them.

"I saw Melody tear the skin off a girl's cheek with her teeth. A girl over in Circle Hall. It was a little over a year ago. Pretty girl—well, was a pretty girl. It took them months of cosmetic procedures to get her skin smooth enough for sponsor work again. Still, she needs a fair amount of makeup . . . "

Bette stopped mid-stride. "You saw what?"

Roya glanced up and down the hallway, refusing to look at Bette. "If you think Melody wants to hurt you," she whispered, "then Melody will hurt you."

48

Bette stared at her reflection in the mirror as she brushed her teeth that night before bed. Between the juice, coffee enemas, and injections over the last week, Bette had spent a good deal of time in and out of the bathroom. At present, it seemed, she'd ceased to be a human being and existed now only as a sieve for rehabilitative purposes. She glanced down at her belly and recalled where she'd been stuck earlier. Though it was fast, like a pinch, the shots had grown more painful. Bette had asked how much longer they were going to need to do them, only to get a vague, "Not that much longer."

Her skin didn't itch the way it had before she arrived; the problem spot on her neck was almost gone. She'd not had one coughing fit. In fact, her cheeks had filled in a little and the overall texture of her skin was smoother and brighter. Not quite as dewy as Fern's, but those years were long gone for Bette. The darkness under her eyes had faded and her ribs were less visible. She couldn't see the numbers on the scale but was certain she was putting on weight. She only hoped her hair would see these lustrous healthy effects soon. She ran her hands over the baby hairs around her hairline, trying in vain to smooth them down.

While things seemed to be turning up physically, she couldn't shake the foreboding. The gaping impersonal void that absorbed all warmth from every room; the calculating exactness that waited expectantly around each corner, analyzing and optimizing; the machine-like indifference to the pulsing heat of skin; the gleaming shiny surfaces designed to wipe away the indignities. The Birthing Center ran on a predetermined schedule under Ms. Tyler's watchful eye. The lights never flickered; the food was more than enough. Since Bette was a little girl, there was always a reason to worry about the volatile weather and lack of food. Most of the solitary days in her apartment orbited around those two issues. Would she have enough power to do her work? Would there be enough food to buy? Of course, there was never enough money, but that wasn't the problem. She could have money, but when food ran out at the market, that was that. Money could never fix the shortages. Money couldn't make food appear. Money couldn't stop the violent storms. Money couldn't keep her safe.

Vast sums of money seemed to do the trick here, however. The Birthing Center had quantified, exploited, and parceled off every part of the procreation experience into separate revenue streams. They had managed to take the one thing people couldn't do and turn it into a successful empire. There was something about the preciseness of the facility that left her with a shiver, though. Every object had a purpose, every purpose had a place, every place had a time.

Also, Melody didn't help. She could believe what Roya had told her about that girl's cheek given the way she'd come after her, gripping her hands around Bette's neck while not registering any recognition or emotion.

Those cold, flat eyes.

They were strangers, never having met until predator cornered prey. Then there was that shriek . . . nearly identical to the sound she'd heard when she had been attacked outside the propagation office, and nearly identical to the sound in the hall from the other night. But Bette had been attacked by a man then, at least that's what David had said. *How could Roya know any of that?* It didn't make sense. But, Ms. Tyler had showed up after the attack and isolated her after the med floor incident. It was related, even if none of it seemed to go together. *What am I missing? What the hell is going on in this place?*

I understand that there is violence all around me.
I breathe in awareness and expel violence.
We are beyond the luxury of time and preference.
We shall be successful in our purpose.

49

Her lens alerted her to go to the med floor after gym time. That was how it worked; no one ever needed to say a word to each other. Girls would just move wherever their lens directed them. Bette had seen girls in mid-conversation stop, as if unplugged and restarted, and then move wraithlike in a completely different direction. The room Bette entered was bright, and she could tell she wouldn't be alone. Around the perimeter of the room were what appeared to be stalls. Not permanent structures, just rectangular spaces separated by poles and greenish curtains that had been erected for a temporary event. Each contained a collapsible gurney. A few more girls trickled in, each shown to a cordoned-off area by a wrinkled and pucker-faced man darting back and forth. Bette could overhear everything on the gurney next to her through the sheet.

"Yes, very good. Just like that. Perfect. The doctor will be here soon," the sour-faced tech instructed an anonymous and silent patient. Once the tech was satisfied that the girl was ready, the curtain to Bette's right parted.

"Well? Why are you still dressed and standing? Come on now, you know the drill," he clucked at her.

"I, uh, actually, this is my first time."

Surprise registered on his lined face as he looked her up and down.

"Oh, you are one of those. Here, put on this gown. Quickly now. Oh, lord, you act as though I've never seen it before. Come on now, quickly. The doctor doesn't like delays."

Bette struggled out of her clothes in front of the demanding, hurried tech and anyone else who happened to be walking by.

"There we go. Now up, up." He patted the gurney. In the center lay a square with light blue plastic around the edges. "Yep, there you go. Good, now don't move."

The plastic-backed absorbent square crinkled under Bette as she shifted. She sat perfectly still as he zipped on and scolded the girl one cot over.

"Oh my, no! Stop messing around, the doctor does not like delays."

Bette was surrounded on three sides by the sheets, but in front of her, across the room, she could see young women sitting patiently on their gurneys. They had the bored expectant face of someone waiting for a train. Nowhere did Bette see any sign of nervousness or excitement from this room of women about to undergo brokering.

Bette's stomach fluttered as she tried to prepare herself for what to expect. Fern had said there was nothing to it. Fern had said it was easy.

Yeah, but she has also done this a half dozen times.

Next to her, Bette heard a rustle of the curtain and the sound of motorized wheels. A woman's authoritative voice cut through the background noise.

"Confirm patient ID."

There was a momentary pause, and then a man answered, "Confirmed."

"Confirm patient sample," the woman said.

Another pause, another, "Confirmed."

"All right," the woman said, "knees up and let them fall to the side."

Bette heard the distinct crinkling from the shifting of the woman on the gurney. She listened hard to make out the sounds of what came next, but they were indistinguishable. Before she knew it, her own curtain parted and two masked doctors in glasses appeared; one pushed a bulky cart.

The female doctor looked at the male doctor and stated, "Confirm patient ID."

The man glanced over Bette's face and then to the top of his display, "Confirmed."

"Confirm patient sample," the woman said as she wriggled on a new pair of gloves.

The man opened a drawer on the cart and pulled out a thin tube. His glasses scanned the tube. "Patient sample confirmed."

"Knees up and let them fall to the side," the woman instructed Bette. Bette's knee grazed the sheet partition as she complied.

Fern said to just relax and think pregnant thoughts during this part, which was much easier said than done. The intrauterine procedure felt like being abducted by aliens. Maybe it had something to do with the lighting or that these strangers were wearing masks, gloves, and shapeless medical garments. The room smelled of new latex and cleaning solution. Or maybe it was that as Bette lay there, she could feel something was happening, a slight pressure, but couldn't really tell exactly what was happening.

"Do they have the next room prepped? I think we will be done early here," the woman said, making small talk with the man. She haphazardly pulled Bette's gown back into place and tapped her left knee, indicating that she was finished, and that Bette no longer had to remain spread-eagle.

"Yep, it is," the man replied.

"Good deal," the woman said, pleased, as she snapped off her gloves and threw them to the floor. They exited to the next makeshift procedure room.

Are we done? Is that it?

The irony of this moment was not wasted on Bette as she lay there looking up at the lights in the ceiling. The glow from the bulbs spread outward the longer she stared and spots began to appear when she blinked. She had spent her entire life convinced that this moment, when sperm meets egg, was the purpose of her existence. And, like every other procedure by the Department of Propagation, it was performed with the gravity of changing a filter in an appliance. Nobody cared that only a short while ago the idea of fertility for Bette was a long shot. No one seemed to revel in the significance of sparking life. No one took a breath to consider the momentousness of conception. No one's heart swelled with patriotic pride as they realized the service being done for their country, their future. This was not a first for them; they had done this so many times that it was just a job. She was simply another container to be filled and put into circulation with the rest of them.

50

Fern was making herself some tea in the kitchenette when Bette entered the suite after the procedure.

"Hey," Bette said, acknowledging her.

"Hey," she answered back, "how'd it go?"

"Um, good, I think." Bette's voice was unsure, which was a precise description for how she felt. She'd lain on that table for what seemed like an hour before the harried tech told her move along. *That was it?* That was what everyone made such a big deal about? Those doctors could have been sorting packages for all the inattention they showed their patients today.

Bette gingerly sat down on the couch. Fern had a tea bag on the counter next to her mug. Holding a spoon to her lips, she waited for the kettle to boil. Her right hand rested on her protruding stomach. Fern rocked back and forth staring intently at the kettle, her expression masked by the spoon over her lips. From behind, she didn't even look pregnant.

How many times has she done this? She seems so calm. So . . . natural. It's like nothing fazes her. How does she do that?

Pregnancy, on her, seemed to work. It didn't look uncomfortable. It didn't look alien. It didn't look forced. She was pregnant like it was the most natural thing in the world.

"Fern, how does it work?" Bette asked.

"I think," she said, her back still to Bette, "you have to let the water get to a near boil, instead of a full boil—"

"No, Fern, how does getting pregnant work?"

She turned around with a half smile on her face. "Well, when a daddy loves a mommy—"

"Jesus, Fern, I'm being serious," Bette sighed.

"What do you want to know?"

Bette shifted on the couch. "I, uh, I went through the brokering process today . . . "

The kettle began to make a low whistle. Fern removed it from the eye.

"Well, um, how do I know if it worked?"

"What was your top selection's brokering percentage?" Fern asked.

"What?"

"You know, on the profile, there are a bunch of numbers and graphs and stuff? What was his percentage?"

"I . . . I don't remember," Bette said.

Fern poured the water into her mug, placed the tea bag in, and jostled it a little with her spoon. She took the spoon out and set it in the sink. Picking up the mug, she turned and leaned against the counter to face Bette. Her expression was thoughtful, not something that Bette had seen before. It almost reminded Bette of an instructor or tour guide.

"That is a good one to remember. Sure, you want your baby to be good looking and smart and all that, but how fast that baby is conceived is more important. Always go with efficiency metrics over cosmetic ones."

"Okay . . . " Bette shrugged, puzzled.

"Yeah," she said as she shook her head, "that attraction crap, they always tell the skinnies that in the beginning. I don't know why. Attraction is useless here. Like, you are just going to *know*? Dumb. Another good one to look at is the fructose level. Fructose provides the energy for the sperm to swim."

"Right . . . because you want them to swim fast?" Bette asked, feeling stupid. Her brain was trying to remember everything that she had once learned about conception.

"Exactly." Fern tested the temperature of her tea by taking a little sip. The temperature suited her, so she took another sip.

"So how do you know if it worked? How do you know if you are pregnant?"

"Oh, someone will tell you."

"When?"

"Maybe a couple of weeks."

Fern made her way over to the couch, hesitating slightly before sitting down next to Bette. "Are you going to sit here awhile?"

"Uh, no," Bette answered, somewhat annoyed that Fern had claimed the only place to sit in their common area. Heading toward her room, she paused and turned back to the glossy-haired girl sipping tea and staring off into space.

"Hey, Fern, have you ever seen any of your children?"

Fern looked at her as if this was the stupidest question ever asked. "No. This is a *birthing center*," she said stretching out all the syllables. "We give birth here."

51

Bette was startled to see Melody seated at the table for dinner that evening. As Bette took her seat, Melody tilted her nose up, ever so slightly, as if she had gotten an unpleasant whiff. Melody's tawny eyes rested unblinking on Bette, following her every move.

"I'm glad to see that you are feeling better, Melody."

"I feel fine," she said, defensively.

Gone was Melody's humming and incoherent prattle. A shift had taken place, and everyone felt it. Fern and Roya exchanged furtive knowing glances.

"So," Bette transitioned, "does anyone know what we are having for dinner tonight?"

Melody's face contorted as she slammed her fists on the table, causing the silverware in the basket at the center to jangle. "It is bad enough that I can smell it on you. Could you not make it unbearable with your talking?" The words came out of Melody's gritted teeth as a low growl.

Everyone at the table froze, eyes glued on Melody and the barely bridled anger that seethed from her. "Shut up," Melody grumbled.

Bette swallowed, watching what Melody might do next.

Later, out of Melody's earshot, Bette turned to Roya and asked, "What the hell?"

"Yeah," Roya said, her eyes bulging.

"What was she even talking about, a smell?"

Roya bit the inside of her cheek as if there was something she didn't quite want to admit. "You know, I wouldn't be surprised if you are pregnant, Bette."

"Huh?"

"Melody kind of has a way of sussing these things out before anyone else does," Roya said with a pained expression.

"That is impossible."

"Is it?" Roya countered. "I've been here a lot longer than you have. You may just want to steer clear of her, if you can."

Over the next week, Bette kept her head down, tried not to engage, and gave Melody a wide berth. She was so easily agitated. One afternoon, at lunch, she hit the tray containing her food so hard from the underside that the food and tray went flying, splatting and clattering all over the floor. The force of her rebuff knocked over the delivery robot. It lay on its side, wheels still spinning, trying to grip the floor to right itself. Everyone at the table kept their heads down while the Center staff cleaned up the mess and removed Melody from the dining hall screaming and yelling. Bette looked to Fern who only shrugged, as if to say, *See? I told you she was crazy.?*

52

Bette and Roya were filling buckets with water from a hose inside the garden. They had to fill quite a few all at once since the water was only turned on for a few hours during the day. The water was loud as it hit the bottom of the empty five-gallon buckets. Roya stood holding the hose while Bette crouched and steadied the bucket, spray misting her face.

"I, uh, put out a feeler for you."

Bette turned to look at her. Roya did not make eye contact, instead keeping her eyes trained at the bottom of the bucket. Confusion spread over Bette's face. Of course, now Roya chose to tell Bette; the background noise helped them disguise exactly what they were saying, making it more difficult on the listening ears.

"A feeler? About what?"

"About your status change. And, uh, I think we found something."

"We? Who is we?"

"Hector has been working with Dorothea a long time. He can sometimes manage to find things that others can't."

"What did he find out?" Bette asked.

"I'm not quite sure," Roya answered.

"What do you mean, you're not quite sure? You just said you thought you found something," Bette said.

"Your information was, well, classified."

Seeing that her statement wasn't having the desired effect, Roya moved closer with the hose and knelt down. Roya's words came fast, and Bette strained to make them out over the sloshing, gurgling task. "There isn't really a need to classify a resident's records within the Birthing Center. It's when they get moved around, say from one department to another, that they might take extra precaution."

Bette looked back to the water rushing into the bucket.

"Well, I'm not from here. I guess they would have to transfer my information from one department to another," Bette said, shrugging.

"Hector said the information looked like it had originated from the Department of Justice," Roya whispered at the ground.

"Justice?" Bette whispered loudly over the water. "Why would it have come from the Department of Justice?"

Roya chewed on her lip while they switched out the full bucket for an empty bucket.

"I think it has to do with those bite marks you had when you first arrived," Roya said.

"Those weren't . . . " Bette paused as she thought about what Roya had just said. Roya seemed to have a theory but the surveillance of the Birthing Center made it impractical to have a single conversation to get all the pieces of the puzzle in one place so they could begin piecing them together. The slow drip with which all information had to be assembled was infuriating. As the water came closer to the top, Roya pressed the nozzle to slow the flow of water while Bette readied the next bucket.

"Well, Roya, that makes no sense."

"It might make more sense than you think. But I think there is a way we could find out for sure."

Bette wiped some spray from her cheek. "And what would that involve?" she asked skeptically.

"We'd need to break into the director's office," Roya said, matter of fact.

Bette nearly spilled the bucket she was steadying. "Are you crazy?"

Roya reached for the wobbling bucket, getting very close to Bette's ear. "Shh," Roya soothed, glancing around quickly to make sure no one was around. "I wouldn't say it if I didn't think we could do it."

Bette stared at the pools of water glistening on the concrete floor. What Roya was suggesting was out of the question. How could they even pull that off? What if they got caught? What would Ms. Tyler do to them?

The water sputtered from the end of the hose, the stream lessening until only drips came out. Roya squeezed the nozzle handle to push out the last little bit of water.

"I guess we are cut off," Roya said as she turned, gathering up the hose.

Bette lugged the bucket, careful not to spill it over the side, to the rest of the full buckets lined along the gravel pathway. Hector would have his work cut out for him this afternoon.

"Hey," Bette said as she met Roya coming back from the hose hang up, "why do you think those marks have anything to do with the Department of Justice?"

"I think whatever did that to you is under the purview of the Justice Department."

While a simple statement, the implication was as thunderous as water roaring into a plastic bucket.

53

Ms. Tyler stood in front of Bette, carefully observing her reaction as she spoke the words. Bette heard them, but it took an extra five seconds for them to fully register.

"Wait, what?" Bette asked, squinting.

"You are pregnant," Ms. Tyler said nonchalantly.

"Are you sure?"

It had been weeks since that open-air procedure had taken place. Bette had almost forgotten that it had happened. She thought today was just another routine med floor visit to check her urine sample and blood work.

"You are pregnant," Ms. Tyler repeated.

"You mean," Bette whispered in disbelief, "it worked?"

Ms. Tyler nodded. "Now, don't get all atwitter. It is still pretty early, just over five weeks, but I thought you'd like to know."

It worked. It actually worked.

They had done it. Years of inconclusive stigma and guilt slid off Bette's shoulders. She felt her cheeks lift as she smiled. She, Bette Donovan, was *pregnant*. Just like her mother. It had happened. *Lord, what would she think about this? And her Gram? Would they have really believed this was possible?* Bette had been right to believe it was. There were so many times when she thought she was being stupid, but she could never shake the thought. Not completely anyway. It existed inside her as the thinnest shard of hope. She wished she could tell David. Half from the glee garnered from telling him, "I told you so," half because he knew her the best; he would've understood what this moment meant. Her heart dropped as she wondered if she would ever see him again.

Ms. Tyler's mouth was moving. Her stern eyes glinting like granite.

"What?" Bette asked, once again aware of the exam room around her.

"I've seen this before in situations like yours. There is a chance it might fizzle out. But that is not uncommon. The fact that we got it to take this first time is encouraging."

Fear jabbed the gauzy joy enveloping Bette's head. "What is the chance it might fizzle out?" she asked, alarm rising in her throat.

"Hard to say. Could be everything goes off without a hitch. I only tell you to manage your expectations," Ms. Tyler said as she moved in closer, locking eyes. "It is schedule as usual. Pregnancy is not an excuse to shirk any of your duties, understand?"

Bette nodded emphatically to convince the director she would never do that.

"And while we are pleased you are pregnant, it doesn't make you special. You are just like everyone else here in the Center."

Just like everyone else . . .

Ms. Tyler lingered gravely before breaking the stare. "All right, then let's move along," she ordered, motioning toward the exam room door.

Bette slid off the table, then paused when her feet landed on the floor. "Is there anything I'm supposed to do?" Bette asked.

Ms. Tyler's eyebrow raised. "The same thing you have been doing."

"But, I mean, is there anything, you know, *special* I need to do now that I'm, well . . . "

"No."

"Oh."

"Bette, this is our job. There is nothing for you to worry about."

Bette remained in her spot, feeling somewhat dazed.

This isn't happening. This can't be real. I can't really be pregnant, can I? I don't feel pregnant. But Ms. Tyler said it, so it must be true. I guess I wouldn't know what being pregnant feels like. Oh my God, pregnant.

"Bette!"

"Yes, sorry! I'm leaving. Thank you."

Bette couldn't stop the grin spreading across her face on the way to the elevator. Once inside, she leaned up against the stainless-steel wall and exhaled a sigh of relief. Wiping a few tears from the brim of her eye, she leaned forward and pressed the button.

Finally.

54

Bette leaned on an armchair on one of the staged sets. They were cleaning the sponsor area when Roya asked, "Any updates from your procedure? They should know something by now."

It took Bette a minute to respond, just like it had taken her a minute to respond when Ms. Tyler told her a couple of days ago. She had yet to say the words to anyone else. They sounded strange coming out of her mouth. She knew from saying the phrase over and over in front of her bathroom mirror. "I am pregnant. I *am* pregnant? Me, yes, oh, because I'm pregnant."

For some reason, Bette thought there would be more of a delineation between being pregnant and not being pregnant, but she felt the same. Ms. Tyler told her brain, but Bette's feelings hadn't gotten the message. For all the Department of Propagation's urging, solicitations, and entreaties, she felt almost guilty she didn't feel more pregnant.

"Well, yeah. It is funny you ask . . . "

Roya studied Bette's face from across the table she was cleaning up. Bette smiled, a blush creeping across her cheeks.

"You are pregnant," Roya said, reading Bette's mind. "Melody was right."

"I mean, sort of," Bette stammered, "but only like a little pregnant. They are still watching me pretty close."

"No such thing as a little pregnant, Bette," Roya said as she looked to her left and kept wiping the table. "You either are or you aren't."

Bette shifted on her feet. Ms. Tyler said she'd start to feel symptoms in the coming weeks. She said that Bette would gain weight, but she had steadily gained weight since she'd gotten there. She couldn't tell any difference right now between eating-well weight and pregnancy weight.

"Congratulations are in order, then," Roya said stiffly. To Bette, her statement didn't carry any congratulatory heft at all.

"It is weird. I'm pregnant just like everyone else."

"You are one of them now. Part of the procreating class. A breeder." The sourness of the last word smarted as if Roya had physically slapped her. A moment of silence followed.

"I'm sorry, Bette. That was ugly. Honestly, I'd hoped the procedure would fail so they might send you home. You don't belong here. I knew that from the moment I met you. But now, well, I just . . . I don't like the thought of you leaving," she said quietly. "But I want you to be okay, does that make sense?"

Bette's heart melted. "Yeah, of course."

Roya nodded. "I'm sure you will be fine. This is your first time and there is going to be a lot that goes through your mind. But remember, Bette, this is just a process. Sure, it is great and all, being able to conceive but . . . just be careful."

"Careful of what?" Bette asked.

"Of getting attached." Roya lowered herself to the stage behind her, scooted back, and folded her legs into a lotus position. Absentmindedly, she placed her hand on her belly and stared off over Bette's shoulder. "This is not your child. It will never belong to you. It will never know you. You must remember that. This pregnancy will happen *to* you but will have nothing to do *with* you. And you can't take it personally. If you do, it will tear you up. I know it is crazy to say, especially to you, now, because you always remember the first . . . " Her voice trailed off.

Bette walked around from her side of the table and took a seat next to Roya. She glanced at the sets. Being able to see all the production equipment ruined the sense of drama that must've been evoked when filming. What the sponsors created and perpetuated was the caricature of pregnancy. Fake hair and rolls of padding lay scattered on the table in front of them.

"*We* are breeders," Roya mumbled as she looked at the floor. "It's such an ugly word and an even uglier process. God, the things they'll do . . . " She sighed heavily.

Up close, left to clean up the mess from the illusion, Bette felt depressed. It was a ploy that took advantage of a barren society. They profited from the hopeless, teasing them with fiction while trying to finance the reality.

"Bette, I hate this place." Roya's voice rose barely above a whisper. "I despair of it most days. But what keeps me going is that one day, I'll go home. I'm just trying to get back home."

It was strange, Bette thought, that Roya wanted to get out of the Birthing Center. From as far back as Bette could remember, *getting in* was the goal. She'd been conditioned to believe that this was the finish line, this was the prize.

"Where is home?" Bette asked tentatively. "Fern said that you came here, alone and pregnant, a few years ago," Bette said, gaining more confidence.

Roya pushed her arms into the stage, stretching her back. "Well, Fern is not wrong," Roya said. "What else did she tell you?"

"That girls don't normally come in pregnant and that you might have been part of a Sub crackdown."

Roya smiled as if she were learning this about herself for the first time and it amused her. "I'm going to tell you something, but I need you not to react. Nod if you understand."

Bette nodded.

"They raided my family's farm and took me. That is how I got here."

Bette took care not to react. There were no farms around these parts, and there hadn't been for some time. The only people that had farms were Repatriates.

But that would mean . . . that would mean that Roya was a criminal.

There was no mistaking what Roya had just said; the look on her face and the tone of her voice was reinforcement enough. Repatriates stole the United States' crops, resources, and intellectual property. They were no better than pirates; they lived and scavenged on the fringes of society. They had overtaken the citrus groves and farmland and had extorted the government to make a fortune off an impoverished population. If anyone was worthy of a raid, it would be the Repatriates. They were greedy and ruthless, thinking nothing of sacrificing people for resources.

But Roya was not like that, was she?

"So, you didn't grow up in a Sub? You aren't even from here?" Bette whispered loudly, hoping that Roya wasn't actually admitting to being a Repatriate.

Roya stood and moved back to the table, busying herself with winding up bolts of padding used to mimic pregnant bellies. "I grew up on a citrus grove with my father, mother, and brother. Every so often, your government raids Repatriate farms. They come for produce, fertile individuals, and children. I was eighteen and pregnant with my second child when I was taken."

Bette blinked in slow motion as her thoughts convulsed and boiled over.

"But, I thought . . . isn't that why they signed the Citrus Deal? To stop the bloodshed and stabilize the flow of food?"

"Oh, Bette," Roya said with a good-natured smirk, "you don't really believe everything they tell you, do you?"

That is why she is different. It made sense now why Roya wasn't anything like Fern and Melody. If what she was saying was true, Roya wasn't anything like them.

Suddenly, the loud *ca-chung* of a heavy door opening shattered the silence of the sound stage. Roya glanced worriedly in the direction of the noise. Motioning to Bette, she pointed to the other door, the one through which they had come in.

"What if it's Hector?" Bette asked.

"That isn't Hector, not from that door." She reached out, yanked Bette's wrist, and dragged her toward the door.

"Who is it?" Bette whispered.

Roya shook her head, her lips pressed into a tight line. The alarm in her eyes caused Bette's skin to prick. Whoever it was, Roya was not about to chance it. Roya pressed herself into the door and cautiously opened it. Bette glanced over her shoulder to see the eye surgeon carrying an inert girl over his shoulder. He was whistling. Bette's heartbeat quickened and she propelled through the crack in the door, stepping on the back of Roya's heels. They stumbled into the hall, Roya still hanging on to the door so that it wouldn't slam. She allowed the door to shut gently, then hurried toward the elevator. It was not until the elevator door shut that she let out a breath.

"What was he . . . " Bette started to ask.

Roya shook her head and closed her eyes. "Just be glad we didn't get caught in there with him."

55

Hector was waiting for them by the door when Roya and Bette entered the lab for work detail. His eyes darted back and forth furtively as he waved them over.

"We need to move quickly," Hector uttered, placing a palm on each of their shoulders and propelling them toward the incineration alcove. A black toolbox sat next to an extension ladder on the floor of the alcove.

"Roya, if you will carry the toolbox, I'll have Bette help me carry this ladder."

"Where are we going?" Roya asked as Hector handed the box to her.

"Dorothea has a meeting off-property today and she took Maria. We have maybe twenty to thirty minutes before the lactation cycle starts."

He picked up the leg end of the extension ladder, nodding at Bette to get the other end. Hector led the way, his hands behind his back as he held his end of the ladder. He paused at the door and adjusted his grip so he could wave one hand over the panel next to the door. Pausing in the open doorway, he looked both ways before entering the hallway. They reached the round of the med floor lobby and hurried past the desk, all the way down the hall. They moved past the empty gleaming lactation room, the brokering selection rooms, the door where Bette had her corneal lens replacement, and, finally, the insemination gymnasium. They stopped at the very last door at the end of the hallway. Hector looked up, rested his hands on his hips, and examined the black orbs in the ceiling.

"For whatever reason, these cameras seem to be experiencing a kind of momentary glitch," Hector said in an exaggerated volume.

Hector took the ladder from Bette and stood it upright. Roya set the toolbox at the base of the ladder. As Hector bent to unclasp the box, he whispered, "But I still need you two to mind your lenses."

Mind her lens? Bette looked up at the ceiling. Roya flicked her arm, causing Bette to turn. Roya put her hand to her lensed eye and began rubbing it before casting her glance to the floor. *Oh, mind the lens . . .*

Bette rubbed her eye and then turned her eyes to the hallway floor.

Hector took something from the box and moved to the door closest to where the ladder now stood. Bette listened as he fiddled with the door for excruciating minutes before finally gaining access. "Wait here," he whispered as he slipped in the room.

"What are we doing?" Bette whispered out the side of her mouth to Roya, careful to keep her eyes on the floor.

"Figuring out why your status is classified," she whispered back.

Surprise turned to fear as Bette realized where they were. "Is this the director's office?"

Hector's shoes reappeared in front of them. "Okay, I've pulled up what I found," he said, his voice changing direction as he looked back up the hallway. "In and out, you got it? And, watch those lenses."

Bette nodded at the shiny floor, bewildered.

"You were never here," Hector whispered as Roya and Bette moved through the crack in the door.

The office was white. White walls, white chairs, white desk. Nothing adorned the walls, and there were no personal effects on her desk. Just a cold, white, functional room. A perfect representation of the individual who occupied it.

"Huh. It doesn't say much but it looks like there are a couple of video files," Roya said. She carefully held her right hand over her right eye as she peered at the large screen on the wall of the director's office. Cognizant of Hector's reminder, Bette used her right ring finger to press the little flap on her lens, turning it dark. Once Bette was certain the lens had gone out, she looked up to see what Roya was referring to.

Roya tapped the screen and backed away to stand next to Bette. A silent black-and-white surveillance video began playing, bringing the dusty entrance of a building into view. A building with two fences. Bette recognized it as the outside of her propagation office. She watched as a figure plopped down on the curb.

That's me sitting on the curb outside the propagation office . . .

She was struck by how dejected and small she looked as she slouched on the curb. Then, seemingly out of nowhere, a sinewy, dirty, wild-haired man raced up behind her and hit her head with a piece of wood. Bette sucked in an alarmed breath but remained mindful of her right eye.

"This is a video of the attack!" Bette breathed, unable to take her eye off the screen. Even though it was a recording, Bette flinched. Even though she already had an idea of what was going to happen, she was riveted. She continued to watch herself hit the ground, face-first. Unconsciously, she touched her healed left cheek with her free hand, her fingers absent-mindedly searching for the scrape.

The crazed man raised and lowered his hand in the video. It looked almost like he was patting her on the back, but he was stabbing her. It was hard to make out the implement in the grainy replay, but the shirt she was wearing bloomed with blood. That motion, right there, was what had caused her lung to collapse. She inhaled as she remembered that awful moment when she couldn't breathe . . . when she was under him, the suffocating pressure in her chest, the rancid smell of old urine all around her. Her mind went to the mark that would forever scar her back.

Finally, as she lay prone and unmoving on the ground, he reared back and opened his grimy mouth. There was no sound to the video, but it looked like he was yelling. He then bent back down to the area between her head and shoulder and buried his face in her neck.

My God, he really did bite me!

Bette's left hand now went to her neck and she was aware of tears on her face. The whole attack had been captured on surveillance streams, once from the front of the propagation office and again from across the street near the abandoned bus stop. She lay there for maybe ten or twelve seconds, the wild and obviously insane man above her. Just as he was poised to touch her again, Bette and Roya saw someone from the propagation office come into the frame. Bette's attacker lifted his nose as if he was smelling the air. He spotted the person dressed in Propagation scrubs, momentarily distracted from his ghastly task. With no warning, he jumped off Bette and pursued the interloper, both of them fleeing the edge of the video. Bette was left lying there, alone, her blood beginning to stain the ground underneath and around her body. The video cut off abruptly.

It was bizarre to watch. Stripped of any of the actual pain that had gone with the incident, it was like watching a silent movie without any captions. The movements of her assailant were so quick and unfeeling, as if he were opening a package with a box cutter. It had happened so fast, but it had taken Bette weeks to recover from the suffering captured in the video.

Bette felt clammy and her insides trembled. Her head spun and she thought she might vomit. It was so impersonal. It was so unsettling. The attack unfolded just like that, with no reason and no motive. It was chilling how senseless the violence was. Part of her felt like it had all been faked; she couldn't even remember most of what happened in that video. *But it had happened.* And now she was having a hard time reconciling what she saw, what she felt, and what she actually remembered. It was a strange out-of-body experience. She felt like she should be angry, but all she found in anger's place was confused bewilderment.

Roya scooted closer to put her hand on Bette's. "But . . . but David said they didn't know who did it. They *do* know who did it. He is right there. Why would they say that?" Bette mumbled, dumbfounded.

"Let's watch this other one really quick, and then get out of here, okay?" Roya said.

The next video opened onto a cinder-block room with a metal table bolted to the ground. Two men stood behind the table, their attention focused in front of them. The camera was filming in their direction, but they were not looking directly at it. Their eyes were trained just above it. Bette recognized one of the men from the first video and goose bumps erupted all over her. She could see him plainly now as the camera showed a close-up of her crazed attacker.

"So, is this some kind of trial?" Bette whispered to Roya.

"It looks like it," she whispered back.

The attacker was standing just out of arm's length of a well-groomed man with gray hair, and the attacker was screaming as loudly as he could. His filthy hands and bare feet were shackled. He shook where he stood, hair unkempt and wild, screaming a high-pitched shriek at the top of his lungs like a wild animal. The noise triggered a memory in Bette, and she gasped as adrenaline shot through her body. The clearly uncomfortable gray-haired gentleman shifted from one foot to the other. He tentatively took one step closer to the deranged man, as if to speak to him. Bette's assailant audibly snapped at him and the man jumped out of the video path. Two heavily armed men came into the frame to contain him. He stopped his screaming and began loudly yelling, "NO. NO. NO. NO. NO. NO." Shortly after this, he was removed from the room, scuffling and resisting the guards. The last thing he yelled as he was dragged from the cinder-block room was, "YOU DID THIS!" Throughout the several minutes of video that Bette had seen of the man, this was the only coherent sentence he'd uttered.

Bette blinked and turned to look at Roya, who gave a low whistle.

"Jesus," Bette breathed.

"You know what he is, don't you, Bette?" Roya asked.

"Fucking crazy," Bette said, still dazed.

"He is a Canner." It was not a question. It was a somber statement on something deeply disturbing. There were no words. There was no explanation. The room was heavy as they stared at the dark screen.

"Now, girls! We have to go!" Hector's hurried whisper brought reality rushing back. Roya began to tap and close the files with her free hand.

"Go, I'll get the rest of this," she whispered to Bette.

Bette darted back into the hall as she carefully kept her right eye obscured. Hector nervously crossed and then uncrossed his arms. "Roya!" he whisper-yelled into the office.

Roya appeared in the doorway, the door closing behind her. "I'm here, I'm here."

A loud clacking rang out at the other end of the hall. All three of them turned because the sound of those heels was unmistakable. Ms. Tyler was making her way quickly down the hallway and toward them. "Shit," Hector hissed under his breath. He turned and made his way up the ladder. "Roya, hand me a screwdriver. Bette, come over here and steady this side of the ladder."

The clicking shoes were nearly on top of them now.

"Hector, what is going on here?" Ms. Tyler asked suspiciously as she approached the three accomplices.

Hector turned from his spot on the ladder and smiled. "Good Morning, Director. Yeah, it seems like these cameras are cutting in and out. I wanted to get up here and see if it was a connection issue before I headed up to surveillance."

"How long has this cutting in and out been going on?"

"Oh, well, not sure. I noticed it a few hours ago," Hector calmly answered.

"Well, I need these cameras in working order," Ms. Tyler said.

"Oh, I know. What with the recent breach over at . . . "

Ms. Tyler's eyes widened. "Just get them fixed, Hector!" she snapped.

"Yes, ma'am," Hector said as he quickly pivoted his face back to the ceiling. From Bette's vantage point, she was the only person who saw the corners of his mouth indent.

56

Bette had never gotten a good look at a Canner. That detail remained conveniently absent in the news reports, alerts, and warnings. Maybe this was why.

Canners had been around for as long as Bette could remember, but they'd always been formless boogeymen who stalked the fringes of the civilized world. They had always been lumped in with Repatriates, as terrorists. Both marauded but Canners' notoriety came from their penchant for cannibalism. Tall, expansive barbed-wire fencing surrounded nearly every perimeter of public life. Daily life was scheduled around curfews implemented due to the threat posed by Canners. Bette had known to fear them her entire life, but now she was truly terrified.

Havoc had wrecked and beleaguered the nation. Droughts were long, floods were high, and winds were brutal. Citizens survived by strict rationing, resource stipends, and their own clever ingenuity. With a dropping fertility rate and skyrocketing self-euthanasia, humanity didn't have time for those with no regard for the society they were so desperately trying to preserve. There was no known deficiency that prompted their sick practice. No one understood why they were given to cannibalism. Some experts likened it to a religion, labeling them zealots driven by belief and ritual. After watching those videos, Bette realized that there was no higher doctrine guiding that person. Her attacker was crazed, unstable, and dangerous. He was not a person, not even in the broadest sense of the word. He had the silhouette of a human being but there was nothing human left in him. It was clear there was no reasoning with that man. There was no rehabilitation for him. He was no better than a rabid, wild animal.

But he looked like us.

It was disturbing having seen him up close like that. Bette was struck by the notion that he didn't look all that different from any other man she'd ever met. There was nothing extraordinary about his height or build. He was filthy and malnourished, but that alone wouldn't differentiate him from other normal citizens. The only thing that set him apart was his odd behavior, his constant involuntary writhing as if he couldn't stand the skin that held him in . . . and that shriek.

Where had he come from? Why was he like that?

Dazed, Bette followed Roya into the supply closet. Her mind reeling as she stacked boxes on the shelf in front of her. The insulated supply closet drowned out the sound of the ventilation system, making it possible to hear herself think. Roya stood steps away, unpacking the contents of a box.

"Is that what you thought we'd find?" Bette asked softly.

Roya stopped, placing her hands on her hips.

"More or less." She brought her right hand to her chin. "The videos were a surprise, though."

"What does it mean, Roya?"

Roya crossed her arms in front of her. Bette glanced over to see a scowl forming on her normally serene face.

"Nothing has changed," she said stroking her chin. "And if it hasn't gotten better, then it has probably gotten worse."

She bent over, tearing plastic packaging open, stretched and jagged edges quivering as she rifled through the box.

"Back at the beginning of the infertility epidemic, the newly formed Propagation Department was mass-vaccinating everyone against sexually transmitted diseases."

Between the rustle of packaging and the shuffle of boxes, Roya continued. "The vaccine had been fast-tracked past the time-consuming rigors of clinical trials. For the most part, it was a resounding success. But there was a small percentage of the population that suffered extreme side effects. Uncontrollable tics, extremely aggressive and irrational behavior, a regression of cognitive abilities."

Bette immediately thought of Melody.

"Their offspring were violent and emotionless, suffering from attachment disorders. They couldn't bond with other humans. The whole thing probably would have been scrapped but there was a trend scientists noticed . . . Everyone with the mutation, whether caused directly by the vaccination or passed down in later generations by the vaccinated, was fertile."

Bette wanted badly to look at Roya's face.

"Someone in some lab found that if they used mutated reproductive material with conventional reproductive material, the resulting offspring were less violent. They still struggled with attachment disorders and empathy, but a lot less violent and still fertile."

Fern?

"How do you know all this?" Bette asked, feeling more than a little suspicious.

Roya stopped digging in the boxes, staring at a spot on the wall in front of her.

"The first time I killed a Canner, I was fourteen," Roya said. "I looked into his incoherent, wild eyes as he writhed on the ground snapping at me, and I shot him in the head."

Bette's blood ran cold as she was reminded of the black-and-white footage of the shrieking man who attacked her. *To have been a child facing that . . .* But Roya's tone brought an added chill. Bette remembered the flash of her face when Melody had ambushed her in the hall. *She hadn't been afraid.* It hadn't been the first time Roya had stared down a threat.

"Is that how you knew . . . "

"Yep, I've had more than my fair share of encounters with them."

"Is Melody one?"

"I can't say for sure, but if it shrieks like a Canner, it probably is a Canner. Plus, I mean, she is white. How many Caucasian people do you see walking around these days? They must have found that DNA in a bunker somewhere. God only knows how long they have been editing and cloning from that—"

"And you are sure about this?" Bette interrupted. "It just seems a little crazy."

"Crazy? Yeah, it is crazy. The entire reason people left the United States was because of the unethical things the government was doing in the name of survival. And the Subs are no better. When Repatriates, as we're called, saw the effects of this mutation, they knew it was beyond the pale. They would rather leave everything they'd known than to continue on with a government capable of something like that. If they were willing to do that to their own citizens, I mean, where would it stop? Where would be too far? These Canners aren't some twisted doomsday cult. They aren't radicals cannibalizing their own race on principle. They are the ultraviolent mutations of that vaccine. They were bioengineered by the Department of Propagation."

Silence hung between them as Bette took a moment to fully comprehend what she was saying. *They did this.* The Department had injected people with a vaccine that turned them into monsters. And instead of stopping, they doubled down to make it worth it.

"That is what they do in here, Bette. This conveyor belt of production is not normal. And the beings they are creating aren't normal, either. That mutation is being melded with non-mutated DNA and pushed out as the population. This thing they have cobbled together is the future they are engineering for all of us."

Bette paused to think about that a moment. A future of Melodys and Ferns. A future of skeletal, hollow-eyed cannibals. Roya glanced at the door, slightly ajar, suddenly aware of how long they had been in there.

"But what do *they* have to do with me being here?" Bette asked, still unable to put all the pieces together.

"Pheromones. They can smell fertility on you. Even before any test can show it. The mutation gives them an extremely sophisticated sense of smell. And as you are a natural competitor, they become very territorial. They don't want you having your young in their space."

Did that Canner, outside the Center, know? Did I attract him? Is that why Ms. Tyler brought me here?

"Hey, grab that cart, would you?" Roya asked with a somewhat exaggerated volume. Bette blinked and then looked behind her for the cart. Roya leaned in, setting down a small box she'd been holding and pushed the cart out of the supply closet. The conversation was over, but Bette had more questions than she had before they'd visited the director's office. Bette stared after Roya, bewildered.

We are beyond the luxury of time and preference.

57

Bette looked around for Fern. The last time she'd seen her was at breakfast earlier in the morning. She scanned the room when her eyes were supposed to be closed, mumbling along half-heartedly while Ms. Tyler intoned. On the way out of the meditation room, she stopped one of the girls she'd seen Fern speak to.

"Hey, have you seen Fern?"

"I think she was being induced today," the girl said softly.

"Oh," Bette reeled. "Um, okay. Thanks."

Induced?

The thought banged around in Bette's head. Fern was about to give birth to a child, and she hadn't even said anything. Not as a heads-up, not a casual mention in passing, nothing.

"Well, you might not have put it together, but it was about time for Fern," Roya said later as they made their way down the hall the next afternoon to lunch.

"No, I believe you, it just seemed weird. I thought it would be a bigger deal. I thought she would've said something."

"She might not have known," Roya said as she shrugged her shoulders.

"I just think it is strange."

"It is wrong, Bette. All of it. What the Department is doing. What Fern has to go through next. That little baby . . . this is not what we want humanity to become. This is not the future we want." Roya shook her head, her gaze drifting to the floor. "If only people knew."

Without thinking, Bette harrumphed, "Like they'd care."

They strolled in silence passing the garden.

"You don't really believe that, do you, Bette?"

Avoiding eye contact with Roya, Bette moved to the edge of the garden and stopped to stare into the evergreen foliage. "You can only be bothered if you have time to think about it. Out there, trying to get by, clearing all the Department's hurdles, half-starved, choking on our own air, conscripted into indentured sex . . . it is exhausting. I understand why people self-euthanize the way they do."

Roya stepped up to Bette's right, also contemplating the garden. "I believe it can be better. I refuse to believe that there is no hope."

Bette's shoulders sagged. "Roya, I think we could expose every secret the Department has, stream it twenty-four hours a day, and I doubt a revolution would happen. The Department would just wash it away with censorship, misinformation, and spin. People are tired, Roya. Christ, I'm tired. They don't have the energy or fortitude to stand against the Department. They don't have any hope."

"And you? Do you not have any hope?" Roya implored.

The answer was no, of course; Bette didn't have any hope. Not out there, not as an infertile woman in a crumbling society. Her only hope had been this place. Her last hope had hinged on her very unlikely fertility. And now? After what Roya had told her . . . well, no, hope did not gush forth from her like a river. It was the sound in Roya's voice that made Bette hesitate before she answered. There was that incredulous lilt before disappointment was confirmed, that earnestness. Roya had been in this place for three years and she still had it. She was still hanging on to the hope that things *could* be better.

"We can't do anything from here," Bette sighed.

"Agree to disagree," Roya said.

Bette glanced at her, quizzical.

"Bette, that is the only reason I came to this horrible place."

"Came? What do you mean *came?*" Bette grappled with the thought. "I thought you were raided?"

"After my mother was killed, my father, determined to keep us safe, made my older brother and I train with our militia. Days before I turned eighteen, we got word of an imminent raid. My father asked me to do something very dangerous. He asked me to allow myself to be taken."

She'd gotten herself kidnapped, on purpose?

"Why would you do that, Roya?"

"To tear this place down from the inside out." Roya spoke in full voice, fervor rumbling from deep within her.

She stood, ramrod straight, eyes fixated on the false Eden in front of her; a woman of a different place, a different time. No one spoke like that anymore. No one believed in anything anymore. No one was risking their life for a cause. No one had hope. This was not who people were anymore. They were beat, content to lay down in the dust and be eroded away with the wind and rain.

"Sure, I didn't think it would take this long, but they are coming for me." Roya smiled as she whispered, "My brother, Cyrus, will make sure of it."

"You don't actually believe you can do that, do you? Go against the whole Department of Propagation?" Bette said, still stunned at Roya's audacity.

"I do. It has to be stopped."

"Well, that sounds almost impossible."

"Does it?" Roya turned and stared hard at Bette with those relentless eyes. They had the ferocity and the determination to persuade a denier. Bette felt herself wilt a little under their intensity.

"I sacrificed my freedom and my second child because I thought it was possible." Roya's voice was stern. "I sure hope I'm not wrong."

Bette brought her hand to her forehead, "Roya, I just meant, this is a massive undertaking for one person."

"And you would prefer to lose everything, submit mankind to some kind of genetic takeover because you feel . . . outmatched?"

Bette could feel Roya's eyes on her, so she turned to look into them, beseeching and challenging all at the same time. They rippled much the same way liquid metal does, so hot the surface glistening like water. Bette set her jaw. "Roya, there is outmatched and then there is what we are."

"Hmm." Roya nodded. "But fair fights don't spark revolutions. A list where the pros outweigh the cons is not why we fight. There are ideas, there are beliefs that course through our veins, inevitably pushing us toward the impossible." Roya paused, placing both her palms over the center of her chest. "It makes sense here. *This* is what sparks change."

58

Three days later, Bette walked into the suite after meditation to find Fern slumped on the couch. She was wrapped in a thin teal robe and wearing plastic slip-on sandals. The swell of her belly had disappeared. Her hands rested idly in her lap. She was pale, lacking the pink vibrancy normally in her complexion. Greenish shadows lingered under her puffy eyes, and the whites of her eyes were rimmed with redness. She didn't say anything as Bette entered the room, only watched her, half interested.

"Hey, Fern," Bette said, uneasy. "How are you feeling?"

It looked as though the life had been siphoned out of her and someone had dumped her on this couch when they were through.

"Fine."

"You sure? You look a little tired," Bette said.

"Yeah, it is always like this right after."

Bette was worried about how washed-out and toneless Fern was.

"Can I get you anything?"

"No, I'm going to take a nap . . . I just stopped to rest here a minute," Fern drowsily replied.

Bette cautiously stepped toward Fern. As she got closer, she noticed what looked like flecks of crust on the part of Fern's chest that was exposed. Her eyes were bloodshot as she sat there listlessly. "Why don't I help you to your room?" Bette offered, holding out her hand. After a moment Fern's arm rose to meet Bette's extended hand. As she did, Bette noticed blotches of fresh blood seeping through the robe.

"Um, Fern? I think you are bleeding." Bette feigned calm trying to cover her alarm.

Fern looked toward her right breast and sighed. "Yeah, sometimes that happens."

Bette gently pulled Fern to her feet, careful to keep her hand on her upper arm while Fern painfully shuffled to her bedroom. Wincing, Fern pulled back the covers as if it were a monumental task and slowly climbed in. Exhausted, Fern lay there looking frail and weak.

"Bette?"

"Yes?"

"Can you get me one of those pads on the counter in my bathroom?" Bette nodded and walked into the bathroom. There was a stack of round gauze pads there. Bette took two and returned to Fern. Fern reached for them slowly. She grimaced as she pulled the robe away from her chest with one hand. With the other, she situated one gauze pad over her right nipple and then patted the robe back into place.

"Thank you," Fern said, her voice barely above a whisper.

Bette shifted uncomfortably on her feet, afraid to leave her.

"You don't have to stay, Bette. I'm fine."

"Are you sure?"

Fern shook her head. "Someone will be here soon enough. Those guys in lactation are on a tight schedule."

Lactation. Visions of the lactation room flitted through Bette's mind.

So, this is what they did. Fern had just given birth. Didn't they give her a few days before they hooked her up to that awful machine? Fern looked like she could be knocked over with a breath. All the strength and energy had been sucked out of her, and still, the Center took.

"Just let me know if you need anything," Bette said as she carefully backed out of the room to let Fern rest. Fern merely nodded her head and closed her eyes. Bette's hands trembled as she shut Fern's door, anger and disbelief coursing through her.

We are beyond the luxury of time and preference.

59

Bette was nearly ten weeks pregnant. Maria kept using the phrase "nearing the end of the first trimester." Bette noticed new veins on her breasts. Her nausea had improved some, but she tired easily and was readily repulsed by certain smells. One of those smells was the yeasty tang of the lab maintenance area.

Hector arranged the plates designated for disposal in straight lines on the table. The large lined trash can waited. The smell of disinfectant wafted like cleansing incense over the whole task. Behind her mask, Bette tried to breathe through her mouth. She separated the "for disposal" lid from its mate and placed it in the compartmentalized rack. She gazed at the glistening agar but was unable to discern anything with her naked eye.

What phase of cell division had this one got to? Gripping her spatula, she ran it around the edge of the dish. She turned over the plate, and the circle slid out and wobbled into the trash can with a soft plop.

"You are awfully quiet over there," Hector said, breaking the silence they'd been working in. "Something on your mind?"

Bette pursed her lips as a chunk of dried-out agar broke off around the edge of the plate she was working on. "I was just remembering all those stupid Department of Propagation commercials. How they made this place look. How childbirth was made out to be this immaculate celestial process."

Hector laughed a little.

"Why are you laughing?" Bette asked.

"It's just funny to hear you say that."

The skin around his eyes crinkled as he smiled. Bette could see Hector was genuinely amused, not just making conversation with her. "The marketing worked on you, did it?" he said as he bent over to drop his empty dish in the rack.

"I guess it sort of did," Bette said, admitting she'd been duped.

Hector's gloves were creased with globs, his unwieldy mitts making it obvious why Roya and Bette were better suited for this work. "I don't know why I am surprised," Bette continued as she shrugged her shoulders. "I guess I didn't think this pregnancy stuff would be so . . . exacting."

"Well, perception is everything," Hector said as he placed an empty dish in the bin, "and you are not the first person to feel bamboozled by the Center."

"Well, I don't know if I am cut out for this."

"Being a mother is hard, Bette," Hector said, slowly lifting his eyes from his work. "No matter where you do it. In here, out there. It has always been exacting. It has always involved sacrifice."

Bette paused before starting another dish. Hector returned to his work, head down. "Think about your mother," Hector continued. "She raised you during a time when the government was separating women from their children. They were able to wedge themselves in like that because of how bad things were. You survived despite the monitoring, rationing, shortages.

How do you think that happened? As she looked into your face knowing it was her responsibility to keep you alive, what do you think it exacted from her?"

"Jesus, Hector. That is deep."

"There is more to it than just the Department's goals."

Bette was nearly the same age now as her mother was when Bette was born. Not only had her mother taken care of Bette, without the help of the Center or a Sub, she'd also taken care of Bette's grandma. Her mother had been rigid and dutiful, not unlike Fern. She had been tightly wound, often lashing out over minor things. But Bette remembered her mother's set jaw and the determination that flickered in her faded blue eyes. Her mind must've been constantly churning with responsibilities as she wondered how she could ever fulfill them all with so little. Bette had felt the same way with only herself to take care of.

Duty motivated her mother. Duty must have been what held her up as she faced the end of the world with a small child and an aging woman. Bette couldn't even remember a time when her mother seemed afraid. *Angry, yes. Afraid, never.* Duty backfilled all the dark places that trembled with fear.

We are beyond the luxury of time and preference.

Bette's mother lived it. She made sense now, more than she ever had when Bette was growing up. Bette yearned so badly to speak to her mother one more time. She thought of her mother, her grandmother, and Roya, immediately struck by the similarity of the women. Each had carried the weight of obligation; each had borne the commitment to protect. There was more to this pregnancy business than simply growing a baby to term. She looked down, surprised to see her palm over her sternum.

What about everything that comes after?

60

Melody came in late to dinner one night. Roya and Bette were carrying on polite small talk as she approached the table. She purposefully let her dinner tray smack Roya and Bette in the heads as she passed. After Melody sat down at the table, she picked up her roll, broke off a piece, and began to chomp loudly as she stared at Bette. Melody's chomping slowed. She swallowed.

"Do you have something to say to me?" she asked, smoldering.

Bette ignored the question and continued to eat.

"I said," Melody said, raising her voice, "do you have something to say to me?"

Bette looked up and responded in a calm, even-tempered manner. "No, Melody, I have nothing to say."

"Oh, I think you do." Melody smirked.

"Nope, I promise, I have nothing."

The robots began to whir around and busily clear plates. Roya pushed her chair away from the table and stood to leave. As Bette stood, Melody said, "Bette, I wouldn't leave yet if I were you."

Making direct eye contact, Bette held her gaze for a matter of seconds before turning to leave the dining room.

"Hey!" Melody yelled. "I'm talking to you!"

Bette continued walking beside Roya, refusing to acknowledge Melody's shouts in her direction.

"Bette!" Melody barked after her.

There was a loud *thwack* and Bette turned. Melody had knocked over her chair and was advancing quickly after them. Both Bette and Roya stopped. All the remaining residents in the dining room paused and turned their eyes to the drama about to unfold. As Melody drew closer, Bette took one step in front of Roya to shield her. Melody stopped inches from Bette's face; her eyes were ice cold and a sneer played on her lips.

"I said," she spat as she gave Bette's shoulder a shove, "that I was talking to you."

Bette took a half step backward as she absorbed the push and tried to create a bit of space between the two of them. She took a breath to collect her irritation, mindful this could escalate quickly if she chose her words incorrectly. "Okay, Melody," Bette said, lifting her arms in a gesture of surrender, "let's talk."

Melody paused; this was not the reaction she'd expected from Bette. Her brow creased as she considered Bette's motives. The air hung heavy between them as neither said a word.

"Melody," Bette finally spoke, "I'm going to go to meditation now."

Bette slowly turned her back to Melody and began moving cautiously through the dining room toward the exit. The other residents, somewhat disappointed, began to move around; the strain in the atmosphere slackened momentarily.

Roya and Bette were near the doorway when Melody screamed. The skin all over Bette's arms pricked in fear. She heard the scraping of chairs, a couple of thuds, and turned to see three residents who had been pushed to the floor in Melody's wake.

"Melody, what are you doing? Stop it!" Bette cried. "You are going to hurt somebody!"

A group of girls gathered outside the door in the hallway to watch the fray. Melody charged Bette. Bette stood still and braced for impact when Roya stepped in front of her. Melody crashed into Roya with such force, they all found themselves in a heap on the hard tile of the dining room floor. Rattled, Bette rose to her knees to find Roya on the floor underneath Melody, who had her hands laced around Roya's neck. Melody screamed as Roya clawed at her neck and made strained gasping noises. Her legs flopped wildly on the floor.

Bette came at Melody from the side, frantically pushing the crazed attacker to knock her off-balance or somehow break her grip on Roya. Melody's strength was unexpected. Her thumbs were shoved into Roya's neck; her nails were already piercing the skin. Blood flowed down the side of Melody's thumb.

"Stop it, Melody! Stop it! You are hurting her!" Bette yelled, desperately yanking at Melody's unrelenting arms.

Positioning herself squarely behind Melody, Bette wrapped her arms around Melody's torso to pull her away. Melody let out a growl as she released her left hand and formed a fist, which she landed on Bette's left temple. Bette was momentarily stunned, falling backward onto her rear end. As she shook the stars from her eyes, she watched Melody's head swoop down. To Bette's utter horror, Melody opened her mouth and clamped her jaw into the side of Roya's neck. Roya's eyes bulged with fear and her legs kicked violently.

"What the hell are you doing?" Bette yelled as she crab-walked over to save Roya. "Get off her, you crazy bitch! Get off her!"

Bette's hand landed squarely in a small pool of liquid, causing her to slip. She stared at the blood on the heel of her hand as her startled brain tried to figure out how it had gotten there. Suddenly, it seemed as if Center staff were all around them, yelling at each other and Melody. It took three of them to pry Melody off Roya. Melody was screeching incoherently; the pitch of the noise was deafening. Her arms swatted and punched at the staffers like a rabid, wild animal. Bette could see the bright red blood smeared around her mouth and on her right cheek.

From where Bette sat, she could see a needle in the fourth staffer's hand. Melody reared back, trying to shake the three staffers' hands and arms off her. A guttural noise rumbled from her core just before the needle was plunged into her thigh. Her mouth contorted almost in slow motion. The sedative went to work immediately and her screaming was reduced to groaning. Melody fought hard to stay conscious, but she was no match for it. Her clenched teeth relaxed, her head drooped, and her feet stopped kicking.

Bette, still stunned and on her hands and knees, moved closer to Roya. The nearer she got to her, the more blood there was to crawl through. Roya's neck was covered in it and with each beat of her heart, blood pulsed out from wounds on her neck.

"B-Bette . . . " the syllables hissed out of Roya's mouth.

"No . . . no . . . no . . . " Bette moaned. "Please, Roya, we have to get you home."

Icy fear overwhelmed Bette when she realized the seriousness of Roya's injury. She quickly pressed her hands over the wounds while warm blood seeped down the backs of her hands. Applying as much pressure as she could, Bette begged the bleeding to stop to keep any more of Roya's blood from spreading onto the floor. Bette's hands felt sticky as she resolutely willed her friend to stay alive. As a sick gurgling noise escaped her lips, Roya's eyes slowly closed.

As she stared into Roya's bloody and pale face, Bette heard Center staff yelling around her, but their alarmed voices seemed far away. She heard the clatter of equipment and the sound of gurney wheels. She inched even closer to Roya, careful to keep her hands in place. She didn't hear the wet gurgling noises anymore. Bette's stomach dropped.

"Bette, honey, you have to let go. We need to take her." White-gloved hands covered Bette's bloody hands and gently pulled them away from Roya's neck. Bette elbowed the hands out of the way, scooting in closer to Roya's side. Bette pulled Roya's blood-streaked face close to her chest. She was quiet and limp. Bette bent down near Roya's ear.

"Please, stay, Roya . . . please . . . " Roya's face blurred as hot, salty tears pooled in Bette's eyes and burned down her face.

"Bette, you have to let go now."

"No, please . . . don't take her away . . . please . . . " Bette stammered in between sobs.

Two gloved staffers slid their arms in between Bette and Roya, forcing Bette to let go. Another helped Bette up by her elbows. A small section of Roya's dark hair hung from the edge of the gurney while drops of blood dripped intermittently from the ends. The once-light tile floor was now painted a dark red.

"What should I do with her?" the staffer yelled as he helped Bette to her feet. Bette's legs shook as she tried to stabilize herself in the slick of Roya's blood.

"Christ, just get her out of here and cleaned up!" another staffer yelled back over his shoulder as he hurriedly pushed the gurney out of the dining room, leaving a trail of bloody footprints for Bette to follow out of the dining room.

I understand that there is violence all around me.

61

Bette stood in the bathroom of her suite, not quite sure how she'd gotten there, as the tech ran the bathwater. Bits and pieces of what had just happened flitted across her mind.

Roya is dead.

Roya is dead and Melody killed her.

Bette could still hear the disembodied gurgles from Roya's inert body. She could see Roya's blood oozing across the floor and encircling the grisly scene. Bette could remember the delighted grimace on Melody's face, the blood smeared around her mouth.

"Now don't sit on anything. Once I get this water drawn, I want you to hand me those clothes."

Bette winced as she flashed back to Melody's savage screams. *How could she do that? She sank her teeth into Roya's neck . . .*

"Bette . . . Bette?"

She looked up at the tech, lost.

"Bette, the water is ready."

Bette eyed the bathtub as if there were something in there that couldn't be trusted. She remained motionless.

"Bette, honey, please . . . let's get you cleaned up. You will feel better after." The woman's large dark eyes were sympathetic. "I promise."

Bette blinked and looked down at the front of her. There was blood spattered everywhere. The knees of her leggings were soaked dark, as were her sleeves. The blood had begun to crust on the backs on her hands, causing the skin to feel taut. Her nails were black from the blood that had settled under them.

How had it gone so wrong?

She was unnerved to be covered in death. *Roya's death.*

Bette finally obeyed the staffer and took off all her clothes; she quietly left them in a stained pile on the pristine white ceramic floor. She stepped in and lowered herself into the bathtub. As the water rose up around her, it quickly turned pink. She sat there, transfixed by the color. Pink, smoky swirls moved through the clear, warm water.

It must be heavier than water, Bette thought absentmindedly as she watched blood move just below the surface.

The tech gathered the soiled clothes and swiftly left the bathroom.

Bette saw Roya's blood-sprayed face. She saw her closed eyes.

Roya is dead. Melody killed her. It was the only thing she knew for sure had happened back there.

Roya is dead. Melody killed her.

Bette's eyes grew hot as they signaled impending tears. She squeezed them shut and pulled her knees to her chest while the water rippled around her. She wrapped her blood-flecked arms around her knees and trembled. A loud wail ricocheted off the tile bathroom, amplifying her grief. Bette put her blood-crusted fingers over her mouth when she realized the heart-wrenching sound was coming from her.

62

Two days had passed since it happened. Bette was sitting on the couch, not because she wanted to, but because she'd been told to. She'd spent the entirety of the previous day in her room with the door shut. She didn't want anyone to try and comfort her. She didn't want anyone to tell her to eat or exercise or meditate. She just wanted to be left alone. But, one day of grieving was about all the Center would tolerate, as evidenced this morning by the tech who rousted Bette from her bed with a reminder: "We must try to keep to our normal routine."

But it wasn't normal. Nothing was normal. The "incident" had happened in only a matter of minutes. It only felt longer for Bette because she had been in the middle of it. The Center staff swooped in quickly and sedated Melody before removing her from the dining room. She had been put in quarantine until further notice. All the girls had been cleared from the common areas and, until further notice, were to wait in their suites.

Bette grew bored sitting on the couch and found herself standing in Fern's doorway. Fern, restricted to bed rest when she wasn't in the lactation room, would intermittently break the silence with random sound bites about "the incident"; she sounded like some newscaster reading a script. Bette, too, saw the notifications as they came to her lens, but she refused to open them.

Fern struggled to sit up straight, the way she did when she got an incoming message. "Oh. There will be a meeting today in the meditation room after lunch." Bette saw the alert in the corner of her lens but said nothing. Fern stared as though hypnotized while she sent out her own messages to gossip on what the meeting would be about.

"Has this ever happened before?" Bette asked Fern, who looked startled since Bette hadn't said anything in forty-eight hours.

"Like a fight?" Fern asked, breathy.

"Is that what you would call that?" Bette's tone was acerbic.

"Look, Bette." Fern stopped to swallow. "Girls fight. They fight here, they fight in the Subs. I'm sure they fight on the outside."

"No, Fern. People don't use their teeth on another person's neck. That is not normal."

"Oh, well . . . then I don't know what you want me to say," she said, shrugging her shoulders and returning her attention to her display.

Her indifference to the situation made Bette's blood boil. It was astonishing that one pregnant girl had killed another inside the walls of the Center in such a ghastly way. That Fern was so ambivalent about it was beyond belief. Not once had she said anything that sounded like outrage or fear. Not once had she exhibited anything like real emotion.

Stable but still struggling with attachment issues.

"I want you to say this is terrible, Fern," Bette spat. "I want you to say you are appalled. I want you to show some fucking shred of emotion! I don't want you to shrug your fucking shoulders and tell me that *girls fight*! That was not a fight, Fern!"

She stared at Bette silently for a long uncomfortable moment. Her skin had taken on a gray waxy cast. Her eyes flicked to the side a few times. Fern looked wasted and empty, her dark bangs stuck to the sheen of her forehead. Her voice registered just above a murmur.

"I told you to ignore her, Bette."

The gravity of her accusation was like a sucker punch to Bette's gut. Bette could be as angry as she wanted with Fern's reaction, but Fern wasn't the one to blame. Fern hadn't even been there. She had indeed warned Bette about Melody. She had told her to ignore her. Had Bette only done so, Roya might still be alive. How could Bette have imagined that Melody would react so violently that day? How could she have guessed that Roya would insert herself into the middle of the confrontation? Bette remembered how Roya had taken that one step in front of her. *Why had she done that?*

The weight of Bette's own misstep punctured a hole in her indignation and she felt the anger fizzle out of her.

63

"There is a bit of unpleasantness that we need to address," Ms. Tyler said to those gathered in the meditation room. "It is true that we lost one of our residents two days ago as the result of an altercation." She scanned the room, making eye contact and nodding knowingly.

"And though this is, indeed, a terrible thing, there are some things we can all learn from this." She clasped her hands in front of her. "It is very important for us to continue to prioritize keeping our emotions in check. Until further notice, there will be mandatory meditation in the morning before breakfast *and* after dinner. I also want you to know that we have engaged the services of a highly recommended life coach who will work with Melody in quarantine through this time of introspection and self-improvement. We must all continue to strive to be the very best version of ourselves."

The room was silent save for some nervous shifting. Ms. Tyler let the somberness of the mood hang for several more seconds.

"I think," Ms. Tyler broke in, "that the best way to honor our friend is to not stop what we have come here to do. In life, there are often setbacks. The difference between good people and great people is how we deal with them."

She nodded comfortingly and looked from face to face. "You are all great women," Ms. Tyler continued, almost beseechingly, "and I know that we can bounce back from this, stronger."

Some of the residents nodded their heads.

"Now, what I'd like to do is work on a centering exercise." Ms. Tyler transitioned seamlessly into her guided meditation practice. Bette was dumbfounded. She wasn't exactly sure what she'd expected but this had not been it. Her stomach churned and she became keenly aware of her heartbeat in her ears. Her pulse quickened.

"And that's it?" Bette asked. She wasn't even aware that she had said it out loud until she noticed every head in the room had turned to look at her.

"I'm sorry?" Ms. Tyler said as if she had not heard the question.

Emboldened, Bette raised her voice a bit. "That is it? There is no punishment for killing someone here?"

All breathing stopped; the air was laden with suspense. Ms. Tyler smiled without warmth and held her hands clasped together at her heart. She was calm and deliberate as she spoke. "Bette, I acknowledge your grief. I also know that grief can sometimes cause us to act a little out of character . . . "

Bette became jittery with adrenaline as she stood up from her seated position on the floor, causing Ms. Tyler to trail off. "No, this is not grief, Dorothea," Bette said, her affront apparent. "This is outrage."

Bette could see the subtle clench of Ms. Tyler's jaw at this open defiance. Every resident was wide-eyed and looking to Ms. Tyler to see what she would do. Ms. Tyler took a deep breath in through her nose. "I understand it may appear that way to you, my dear. But I can assure you, we are all outraged by this incident. I would love to talk with you further about this, but here is not the forum for your personal emotions. Now," she said as she motioned toward the floor, "if you would retake your seat, I think you will find this centering exercise beneficial."

Bette knew that she should sit down. There was nothing that could be done at that moment, that could right the wrong or bring Roya back. On some level, she knew this standoff was futile, that decorum dictated she comply, but something in her would not let her sit. She could not sit down and allow the enormity of Roya's death to be diluted or normalized. So, Bette remained standing.

"Okay, staff? Would you mind removing Ms. Donovan?"

Two Center staffers walked to the row where Bette was standing and signaled for her to come with them. She hesitated, wondering how long she could stand there and glare at Ms. Tyler. As they made a movement to come down the row of seated girls, Bette decided to go with them. She didn't want to be in that sham of a meeting anymore.

64

Bette waited in Ms. Tyler's office, the one she and Roya had help breaking into not all that long ago. Suddenly, she heard the clacking of shoes down the hall followed by murmuring. As the shoes got closer, they stopped. Bette heard the director yell, "What kind of morons do we have in monitoring?! I want their badges! This is the Birthing Center for Christ's sake! How could they let this happen!"

The door opened, and Ms. Tyler stormed past Bette behind the white desk. "And you," Ms. Tyler blurted as she disgustedly rolled her eyes, "what do you have to say for yourself?" Ms. Tyler placed her fingertips on the barren desk and leaned forward, balancing her weight on the tips of her fingers.

"Well, speak up! You seemed to have no trouble earlier when you had an audience." Ms. Tyler stared angrily at Bette with her slightly discolored eye, daring her to say something.

"What Melody did was . . . sickening," Bette started in a low voice.

"Oh, that." Ms. Tyler nodded curtly, cutting her off. "Yes, Melody knows that what she did was wrong. She will be quarantined and rehabilitated before she returns." The director lowered herself into the chair behind her desk. Bette blinked in disbelief.

"You're going to put her back . . . with the rest of us?"

"Bette, in case you have forgotten, I run this center," Ms. Tyler snapped. "You seem to have also forgotten that the goal of the Birthing Center is to make babies."

"But, Dorothea, she killed a pregnant woman, with her . . . My God, she put her teeth into her . . . "

"Enough!" Ms. Tyler leaned forward, her silver hair glinting under the lights. "How I do my job is none of your business. I know what I am supposed to do and I'm good at it. The only reason you are here is because I brought you in. You would've died in that shithole complex if it hadn't been for me. Your only purpose is to deliver me a healthy fetus, do you understand? That's it. Do your job and spare me your whining."

Ms. Tyler sighed as her fingertips moved to her temples. "You don't really expect me to euthanize a fertile woman, do you?" Ms. Tyler broke into a chuckle. "Jesus, after the day I just had. Roya, while not the ideal resident, at least had a few more years in her. That loss hurts, but when you add in Fern." Ms. Tyler clenched her teeth as she shook her head. "Those dipshits in monitoring. She was a director's dream. I could set time by her."

"What do you mean? Did something happen to Fern?" Bette asked, confused.

"Oh, yes." Ms. Tyler glared. "While you were throwing your temper tantrum, Fern bled out unexpectedly."

"Is Fern . . . "

"Dead? Yes." Ms. Tyler snorted as she pinched the bridge of her nose. "A crap week for production."

Bette's heart sank. Fern was dead. Roya had been killed at the hands of Melody. And for Ms. Tyler, this was a problem. The problem wasn't that she'd grown attached to Fern and would miss her. The problem was that she was down a top-notch producer due to an unexpected hemorrhage. The problem wasn't that a killer was living in the Center, or that the killer was unstable and possibly a cannibal. The problem wasn't even that it might happen again. No, the problem was Ms. Tyler's numbers.

All of them were merely devices, vehicles for procreation.

Bette was already familiar with what it felt like to not matter. Years of being classed inconclusive would do that. But, with a new status, she had hoped to feel different; to be treated like she was special. She had expected things would be better in the Center. Now, as she sat there, pregnant, listening to Ms. Tyler bemoan her quota, Bette only felt hollow inside.

Ms. Tyler stood and slowly made her way to the front of the desk, leaning on its corner. "Right, wrong, justice . . . these are abstract concepts for a society with options. I don't know if you have noticed, Bette, but we aren't a society with a lot of options these days. There is no reflection in survival mode. There is no introspection. There is no moral high ground. There is only live or die." Ms. Tyler smiled her uniform seamless smile. "Women have always had the ability to save humanity, even if some are just too *stupid* to figure it out on their own."

Ms. Tyler's cold eyes pierced her. Bette winced as her right temple began to sting. The stinging quickly bloomed into a burning sensation. Bette reached up to touch her temple, and as her fingers grazed her skin, the pain intensified to the point that her vision flashed and blurred. She doubled over in the chair crying out.

She involuntarily seized, biting down on the inside of her mouth. Tasting blood, Bette felt alarm tear through every fiber in her spasming muscles. Her body tightened defensively against the waves of hot, stabbing pain. She gasped and gulped as she tried to catch her breath. Then the blinding pain stopped as suddenly as it had started. As the stabbing ebbed to a tingling sensation, her eyes were able to focus again. Ms. Tyler seemed pleased with Bette's reaction.

"See, Bette." She smiled, visibly relaxed. "This is how things get done. This entire system has been set up to save us. This Center is the reason humanity will survive. But it doesn't work if you don't follow the rules."

An involuntary tremor rippled through her. Bette tensed while she anticipated another attack. When the tremor subsided, relieved tears sprang to her eyes. Chastened, she brushed them from her cheeks.

"History will not remember the slack faces of these pregnant girls. It will not remember you. It will not remember Roya or Fern or Melody. It won't even remember me. It won't care what I did to get results. History will just be grateful someone had the backbone to do it."

As she spoke, Ms. Tyler crouched slightly to look Bette full in the face. "Do you want to get in my way, Bette?" Ms. Tyler asked in a deadly serious tone. "Do you want to get in the way of our survival? Go ahead. But I will break you," Ms. Tyler hissed through her icy composure. "I will have order in this Center. I will have compliance. And I will get results." Standing abruptly, Ms. Tyler raised her voice, presumably to someone she'd engaged through her lens. "Take her to quarantine!"

Then, glaring down her nose at Bette, she spat, "Get her out of my sight."

65

Bette was in her quarantine room when the lights flickered. Before she came to the Center, it wasn't uncommon for the power to go out once every couple of weeks. Any decent-sized storm could cause a blackout. Sometimes, they would last for weeks. That meant that nothing worked. The doors wouldn't lock, the air-conditioning stopped, the lights went out, and the Internet went down.

Flickering lights at the Center seemed strange since it hadn't happened once in the time that she'd been here.

Must be one hell of a storm, though, to make the Center's lights flicker.

Back in her complex, a storm like that would bring with it gale-force gusts of wind and flash flooding. It would pound and shake the windows in their tracks. The Birthing Center had been constructed to insulate from such warning signs. As if on cue, the lights flickered again.

If a storm could cause the lights to flicker within the Center, maybe it was not as impregnable as Bette once thought.

The sound woke Bette up. It sounded like a huge piece of machinery powering down. The window simulation of the moon and stars went out. The room was completely dark.

Bette lay patiently, waiting to see what would happen. When the room grew stuffy and her thin cotton pajamas began to stick to her, she got out of bed. The lights that normally illuminated the floor when her feet hit did not turn on. She moved to the left and to the right to see if the movement would trigger the lights in the floor. Nothing. She jumped up and down. Still nothing.

The power is out, I wonder if that means . . .

She ran to the door, placed her hands squarely on it, and tried pushing it to the left. Back in her apartment, if the power went out, the doors unlocked automatically to ensure no one would be trapped. She leaned in and strained a little harder, hoping the Center had set up its blackout protocols like in the complexes. Nothing. She threw even more effort into her next push, her sweaty palms squeaking as they slid on the metal door. This time she thought she felt it budge.

Damn, it's heavy.

She stepped back to regain a strong stance and stopped. If she could get the door open, she probably couldn't keep it open on her own. She needed something to prop open her progress if she was going to get out of there. Bette groped her way around the room until her hand landed on a chair. Smiling while letting a small sigh of relief escape her lips, she picked it up and lurched back toward the door. After many minutes of straining and grunting, she was able to shove part of the chair in the crack she'd managed to create. Given the lack of lighting, the only evidence she had of her progress was the faint red emergency light that glowed in the hall. With some more pushing, she was able to get the whole chair between the doorframe and the door. From there, she hopped over the chair and slapped down barefoot into the deserted hall.

The hallway was a murky red, growing darker in the recesses of the doors. At the end of the hallway, she could see white light in the med floor lobby. Bette jogged down the hallway into the round lobby, which was illuminated by emergency floodlights.

So, if these are on, there must be some type of backup generator?

The real question now was, would the elevator work?

Bette stopped in front of the elevator and pushed the button. Nothing. She pushed it again. No lights, no sounds, nothing. "Fuck," she swore under her breath. She turned and surveyed the lobby. With the harsh lighting, it had the eeriness of a desolated arena.

There has to be stairs around here somewhere.

Bette doubted power outages were a regular occurrence there. It was the middle of the night and most of the staff was gone. For the limited staff still there, it was probably chaos right now. How long would it take for someone to realize that girls were locked down in the quarantine ward with no electricity?

Would it be enough time? Can I actually get out of this place?

The mere hope of escape caused Bette's stomach to flutter. *Okay, think, think.* Maybe there was an emergency exit near the elevator. Bette couldn't remember an exit behind the med bay reception desk, so she started with the quarantine hallway she'd just come from. She moved back down the hallway, blindly groping along the walls, looking for a previously unnoticed door or door handle. The infernal sleek design of the wretched building left her with a lot of smooth doors powered by electricity, however.

Bette was halfway down the hall, her left shoulder dug in and straining to push a door, when she heard it. She stopped what she was doing and closed her eyes to focus on the sound. It sounded like footsteps but not the footsteps of someone in shoes. It was the unmistakable slapping sound of sweaty bare feet on tile. She opened her eyes and stood ramrod straight while her hands fell to her sides. Hot adrenaline spread through her body as her stomach lurched. Bette turned her head toward the weird unnatural light at the end of the hall, her breath coming in short, uneven bursts. From the side, a blob moved into the light, like when ink is dripped in water from a dropper. The darkness bobbed in the light and began fanning out to materialize. Bette gulped and her heart beat double time in her chest, but she couldn't take her eyes off the end of the hall. The ghoulish lighting haloed a woman's dark figure, the edges of the outline trembling as if they, too, were fearful to commit her to shape. She seemed to flutter as she moved; the ominous etched lines around her blur red. The shadow advanced toward Bette with the thwacking cadence of a beginning sprint.

No, no, no . . .

Petrified, Bette watched, holding her breath.

It has to be her. She must've been down here when the power went out. We were quarantined at the same time.

Melody screeched while picking up speed and hurtling toward Bette. She was close enough that Bette could hear the throaty rasping of her exertion and the whoosh of air as her arms pumped. The horrible guttural sound that framed Roya's final day in Bette's mind rumbled from within Melody. There was nowhere for Bette to hide in the corridor. It came to a dead end behind her. Even though she knew this, Bette frantically looked to her left and her right and hoped a way out would magically present itself.

If Melody wants to kill me, she most certainly will.

Bette was paralyzed. Even as her mind screamed at her, she could not make her legs move out of the path of the unstable woman tearing through the hall at breakneck speed. Bette squeezed her eyes shut and braced for impact. She heard the sticky smack of skin on skin. She heard the thud and squeak of flesh on tile as they both slid across the floor. She heard the grunt of someone who unexpectedly had the air knocked out of them. She felt a gust of impact breeze at her feet. It wasn't from her, though, because she was miraculously still standing. Then came the screech, that angry primal screech of a cornered wounded monster that put Bette's teeth on edge. The skin on the back of her neck contracted before all the hair stood on end. Bette's eyes snapped open and struggled to see in the low light.

Melody had stopped mere inches from her. She was on her knees in a defensive pose, blond hair swinging on her back as she faced the entrance of the hall, away from Bette. Melody let loose another piercing shriek. Bette winced, raising her hands to her ears. It didn't make any sense; Melody had barreled down the hallway to attack Bette. She was sure of it. Had she tripped? What was she looking at? Then, over Melody's ragged breathing, she again heard footsteps. Bette leaned back from the door she'd been trying to open, looking past Melody to get a glimpse of this new dread. Tremors flailed through Bette's body as she saw how close this second figure was to her. Whatever or whoever it was, it was nearly on top of Melody. She could also see that the screech was not coming from Melody.

The revelation turned Bette's blood to ice.

The new figure slammed into Melody, and Bette could hear the dense sound of flesh blunted against muscle. Melody was knocked back and landed at Bette's feet. Bette jumped back, and in the process, she was able to make out that the other figure was also a young woman with long hair. Melody growled and sprang to her feet, hurtling after the assailant with her head down like a battering ram. There was screeching and snarling as they met in combat. One of them undercut the other's legs and caused them both to tumble to the floor. One of the combatants broke free, scrambling to her feet with lightning speed. Catching sight of Bette, she came directly at her. Bette's eyes widened as she brought her hands up to shield her face.

The figure collided hard with Bette, knocking her off-balance, and she hit the cold, hard floor. Immediately the girl was on top of her, arms thrashing and clawing at Bette's neck. Bette kept her arms up around her face, trying to protect it, but she was only able to shove off the incoming fists.

Bette had landed on her left side. The girl sat unevenly on Bette's right hip. Bette wriggled and kicked her legs to throw her off. The girl proceeded to wrap her arms around Bette's chest, squeezing her with tremendous strength. Bette felt the air leave her and she struggled to inhale. Hot determined exhales garbled in Bette's ear like static as the girl tightened her rubber band of a body around her. Her feet tried to lock around Bette's legs. Bette elbowed the girl with renewed force and thrashed about as she tried to hit her anywhere to loosen her grip. Finally, Bette connected hard with her face and felt her recoil. Bette took the reprieve to pull herself away with her arms and crawl. The girl immediately grabbed for Bette's leg. Bette shook and stomped at her assailant with her free foot. The girl let go, emitting a frustrated grunt as she did. Bette quickly shot up but only made it a few steps before she felt the assailant launch into her. Again, Bette was on the floor, facedown with this unyielding, superstrong girl on her back. Bette tensed against the barrage of punches to her head, face, and neck.

I can't beat her.

Suddenly, Bette heard a commotion from above and behind their scuffle. It sounded like a door had been opened. Bette tried to look around and was hit hard in the back of the head. Cold hands closed around her neck, bringing back flashbacks of the last time this had happened to her in the med floor. Bette's hands instinctively clawed at her attacker's hands.

Then she felt the weight on top of her suddenly lighten, and then it completely dissipated. It felt as if the girl were being pulled off. Bette could hear her screaming and thrashing.

"Jesus Christ! Shut her up!" she heard a woman hiss.

A quick buzz and a thud followed.

"Fuck, don't kill her," the woman's voice scolded.

"I didn't," a man whispered loudly. "It is just set to stun."

Bette turned over to see what had happened. A flashlight pointed in her direction obscured everything but their booted feet.

"Please, don't hurt me," Bette strained hoarsely, raising her hands to shield her eyes. They were just a pair of black shadows, but Bette got a distinct impression that they were not Center staff.

"Who are you? What are you doing out here?" the woman asked gruffly. Bette couldn't tell which, but one of them used a booted toe to tap her leg. She withdrew it quickly and struggled to sit up.

"There was a power outage, I think, so I was looking for help," Bette said between quick bursts of breath. She pulled her knees to her chest.

"And them? That one kicking the shit out of you, was she looking for help, too?" The tone of the woman's question was slightly mocking as she shone her light on two immobile forms. Bette sucked in a breath when she saw they both had blond hair. She sat up on her knees to get a better look at their faces and her heart stopped.

There are two of them.

Stunned by what she was seeing, Bette's mouth fell open. They both looked like Melody. Bette leaned in and looked closer. The likeness was uncanny, but one appeared younger than the other. It was as if one version was just a little further along than the one that came after it.

"What, you never saw twins before?" the gruff woman asked sarcastically.

"Um, no," Bette said, unable to take her eyes off the pair, "but they aren't really twins, are they?"

The woman trained her harsh light back in Bette's face and caused her to pull back and squint.

"Fucking shit," Bette heard the man say under his breath.

"What?" the woman whispered to the man. "What is it?"

There was a slight pause. "Actually, we can make this work," he said. "This might be better. Get that light out of her eyes before you blind her," he instructed the woman. "Help me get her up, back to the stairwell."

66

The woman lowered the flashlight and Bette blinked as she watched spots dance in her line of sight. The man bent down and pulled Bette up from under her arms, then pushed her into the doorway through which they'd entered. The woman had the flashlight clenched in her teeth while they both pushed the door shut. Once it was closed, they turned to Bette. The woman held the light up slightly so that they could all see each other in the closeness of the maintenance stairwell.

"Oh my God . . . " Bette breathed when she saw his face. She took a step back, bumping the staircase. She sat down.

Why is he here?

He, too, was a bit addled but recovered quickly. He briefly brought his finger to his lips, indicating that they needed to be quiet.

Then Cabe began a whispered barrage of questions. "Bette, is that really you? I hardly recognized you. How did you get here?" He seemed genuinely surprised to have found her there.

"You *know* her?" the woman incredulously whispered out the side of her mouth. She was a small, powerful woman. She looked as though she had been lifting weights since birth. Her thick black hair was slicked back into the submission of a coarse ponytail.

This must be some kind of accident. The Cabe I know is . . .

He was a Subbite, right? God, what did she even know about him? They'd had sex dozens of times, but he always avoided specific information about himself. Hell, when she first got there, she thought it was because of him.

Who is this guy, anyway?

"Bette?" It was like she didn't even recognize his voice.

"Cabe?" Bette said, finally finding her voice. "You . . . you didn't know I was in here?" she asked haltingly. Clearly, he had no idea she'd been interned at the Center. The woman with the dark ponytail turned to Cabe and looked as if she was about to say something. He quickly held up his hand and avoided eye contact with her.

"What? No, I thought you were inconclusive. Why would you be here? One day you were there and then the next you were gone . . . " He trailed off as if remembering some encounter she was not privy to. "Look, Bette," he picked back up, "we don't have time to get into all of that. And, really, it doesn't matter. I need to know if you know of a girl named Roya."

Bette stared at him, dumbfounded. She felt as if time had slowed and everyone was speaking in an indecipherable language.

It was too much, the outage, two Melodys, Cabe?

"Bette?" Cabe gave her right shoulder a little shake.

"What?" Bette asked, confused, in her full voice.

He knelt so that they were eye level. "Do you know a girl named Roya?" he whispered. "They might call her by another name." He fumbled in his pocket and removed a small flat rectangle, no bigger than the palm of his hand. He made a few swipes before showing Bette the screen. It was jarring to see her out of context. But it was her; that smile struck Bette as bitter-sweet as she remembered what Melody had done to her friend.

"Why do you want to know?" Bette asked, obviously distrustful.

"It's our mission to locate her. I don't have a lot of time. Do you or do you not know her?" His voice rose with urgency.

Why does he have Roya's picture? Why is he looking for her? What kind of mission involves breaching a birthing center to find Roya? How did they even get in here?

"Do you know her?" he repeated, cutting through her swirling thoughts.

"How do you know her?" Bette was accusatory now.

"So, you know her?" he said as relief swept over his face. "She is here? Where is she? Where can I find her?" There was excitement in his voice. He nodded knowingly to his accomplice beside him. "See, I told you it was her. I don't know how she did it, but I'll be damned that she did."

They do not know.

They had broken in for Roya and they would not find her. They were too late. Roya had been right in believing someone would come for her. But it had not been her brother because Roya's brother's name was Cyrus, not Cabe.

Unless . . .

Either he knew Cyrus, or he was Cyrus. It was too much of a coincidence to not be somehow related to her brother.

What are the odds?

"You actually came for her." Bette was astonished. He said nothing in response to her statement. He only stared at her, his eyes begging her to answer him. It made sense now. Why the Mandate meant nothing to him, why he had kept coming back to her. He didn't live in a Sub. He had used her to be closer to the city. He was a spy, sent from the Repatriates to find one of their own.

"Please, Bette." His voice had softened. "This is very important."

"She's not here anymore," Bette said, looking down at the floor.

"Okay, that's something. Do you know anything about when or where she was moved?" His voice regained its momentum.

"Is your name Cyrus?" Bette asked, afraid to raise her gaze to meet his. This stopped his line of questioning. No one spoke. The hot, still air of the stairwell felt heavy on their shoulders.

"She said she had a brother, Cyrus," Bette finally said. "Are you Roya's brother?" She shut her eyes and turned her face to the floor, petrified that she already knew the answer.

"I am," he said.

The words crushed her soul. The air left her. A feeling much like jealousy specked with despair rose up inside her chest. She could feel the beginning of tears. They were for Roya. How gut-wrenching it was to know that Roya had believed in him, until the very end, and she still died in the Center.

He came for her. She had been right. What does it feel like to mean this much to another person?

Had Roya been disappointed lying there? Did she feel abandoned as she bled out in Bette's arms? Bette's tears were also for Cyrus, who had been too late. How awful that he had been looking for her but couldn't get to her in time.

They had been family. They were tied together by blood and bone. They were a part of each other. And now Bette had to tell him. It would be her that would break his heart. It would be Bette he would associate with his sister's death.

"Roya is dead," Bette said, tears trickling down her face. There was no way she could look at him. She heard the wind rush out of him. The woman who had been silent now spoke.

She pushed Cyrus out of the way. She took Bette's chin in her hand and forced her to meet her intimidating gaze.

"And you are sure of this?"

Bette nodded. The woman's eyes were like that of a hawk's. They bore through Bette and dared her to lie. "How sure are you?" she asked firmly.

"I . . . I was there when she died," Bette's voice trembled.

"Tell me what happened."

Bette closed her eyes. "That girl in the hallway—well, one of them, at least. She did it. Roya bled to death."

The room was oppressive.

"Cyrus, we need to leave." The woman was terse.

He didn't say anything. He stood to Bette's right, his back to both of them.

"Cyrus? Did you hear me? Now. We have to go, now."

"I heard you!" he snapped. "I'm thinking."

"There is nothing to think about. You knew this mission only had two outcomes. We had contingencies for both. We have our answer, and we need to go."

"So *she* says," he said, turning around and waving his hand toward Bette. "Are we just going to take her word for it? Sol, we have been looking for Roya for over three years! And now this woman says she was there when she died. We can't just leave . . . We have to take her with us." He crossed his arms to punctuate his decision.

"Are you out of your mind? Absolutely not!" the woman named Sol exclaimed.

"We bring her with us." He lifted his chin defiantly.

"That is not the mission."

The space was tense. *They are going to leave me here . . .*

Fear welled up inside Bette. Her stomach began to churn as panic engulfed her.

No . . . I can't stay here. They are my only chance.

"She was my friend, we worked together. She told me about you," Bette said abruptly. "I held her. I tried to stop the bleeding." They both looked at Bette. "I can tell you anything you want to know."

"She comes with us, Sol," Cyrus said, his mind made up.

Sol clenched her fists at her sides and pursed her lips. "Goddamn it, Cyrus!" she cursed at him. "We can't smuggle out a Center resident! What if she is lying? It's suicide! We didn't prepare for this! This wasn't the mission!"

"The mission has changed," he said, resolutely.

Sol looked over at Bette.

"I swear to you, I am not lying," Bette pleaded. "I will do whatever you say. Just . . . just don't leave me here."

"Christ, Cyrus." Sol closed her eyes and shook her head. "What is your father going to say? There are going to be consequences, you know that, right?"

"Sol, we can't leave her," he said.

"I know, damn it!" Sol sighed as she relented. "I know. Just . . . we have to be inconspicuous this time, you got it?"

Cyrus nodded.

"I mean it. You better not make me shoot my way out again," Sol said pointedly.

67

They climbed the maintenance stairwell and stopped at the top. The door had been pried open as evidenced by a gaping black void. Cyrus turned and whispered to Sol. "I'm going to go out first and make sure it's clear. On my signal, move, okay?"

Sol nodded and held her flashlight to illuminate the landing. Cyrus reached out and patted her shoulder. "No worries," he said, "just like before."

Cyrus paused in front of the open doorway before poking his head into the hall. He looked left and then right before slipping out. Sol and Bette stood side by side at the top of the stairwell. Bette was close enough to feel the heat radiating off Sol's body.

Sol perked up as her posture became more rigid. She turned her head a little as if she heard something. Bette heard it, too. Outside in the hallway, something metallic clattered across a tile floor. Then there was a strangled yell.

"Shit," Bette heard Sol whisper under her breath. Sol pressed herself flat against the wall next to the doorway and took a measured breath.

"Bette, when I leave, I need you to count to fifteen and then follow me." Her tone was low and measured. "Do you understand?"

"Yes," Bette said while nodding, "count to fifteen and follow you."

"Good." She gave one quick nod and turned off her flashlight. Then she, too, slipped into the hallway.

Bette began to count. She'd only gotten to eight when a strident alarm began to wail. Startled, Bette lost count. Panic welled up inside of her. Had something happened? Should she go out there and check on them?

But Sol said to count to fifteen.

The look of Sol's stern, intense eyes flashed through Bette's mind and triggered her to pick back up at eleven. She willed herself to make it to fifteen as she had been instructed. At fifteen, Bette tentatively stepped out into the dark hallway. The alarm continued to wail and red flashing lights blinked intermittently. She could tell someone was running in her direction. The strobing lights confirmed it was Sol; her lips were moving but any speaking was swallowed in the noise.

As Sol got closer, Bette could make out what she was yelling. "Back! Back!"

Bette wasn't sure if she meant back into the stairwell or down the hall, but something about the way Sol was yelling told Bette that this was no time for clarifying questions. Bette turned and started running down the hall as fast as she could. There was a loud explosion behind them. As the heat and percussion pushed them both to the floor, Bette heard a dull ringing in her ears. She pushed up on her hands and knees, feeling crumbled bits of the building under and around her palms.

"Up! Up!" Bette heard Sol yelling through the din. Turning her head, Bette could see Sol was up and motioning. "Let's go! Let's go! Let's go!" Bette pushed herself to her feet and followed

Sol through the smoke. Sol grabbed her arm and yanked Bette in front of her.

"Run like hell!" she yelled above the screaming alarms.

Bette couldn't see much of anything. There was a haze of smoke that obscured the already darkened hallway. The pulsing light looked like red lightning in a dust storm. Bette took a step forward, flinching as she found the way littered with debris underneath her bare feet. She tiptoed into the haze while Sol's hand rested on her back.

Bette stumbled over unseen, sharp obstacles. The air was smoggy, smelling of burnt plastic and charred metal, and it made Bette's eyes water. She squinted and pulled the neck of her shirt up over her nose. Her feet stung with each craggy shard she stepped on. In what seemed like a few short minutes, the shiny and clean Center had been turned into a smoky, hazy war zone. Even though she had lived there for months, had it not been for Sol pushing her forward, Bette would have had no idea what direction to go.

Bette reached the end of the hall where the smoke had cleared and the siren waned. She put her hand to her mouth and loudly coughed into it. Sol tugged on her sleeve and stalked cautiously down the darkened corridor. This floor was not familiar to Bette. They passed doors with skinny rectangular windows in them, and Bette had no idea what was on the other side. This was not a resident floor.

As they approached a nexus of converging hallways, Sol stopped short and slammed her hand protectively across Bette's chest to stop her. Sol stood at the corner of the hallway and slowly reached for the hilt on her back. As a figure rounded the corner, Sol spun her machete against the stranger's throat.

"Make one noise and I will cut your head off," Sol whispered menacingly. The figure threw up his hands.

"I can get you out of here," he murmured. There was some-thing familiar about the voice.

"Hector?" Bette whispered.

"Yes!" The tremble in Hector's voice receded.

Sol held her machete a second or two longer before drop-ping her hands to her sides. "You said you can get us out of here?"

"There is another guy with you, right?" Hector asked.

Sol waited to see if Hector would continue, refusing to give him any clues.

"Well, he is already in the loading zone. There was a trans-port truck preparing to leave before, well, everything went to hell. If you hurry, no one will know it's been taken until you are long gone."

"Lead the way." Sol nodded her terse acceptance of his proposal.

Hector scuttled back down the way he'd come, throwing instructions over his shoulder. "You'll have to exit the building to get to the loading zone."

"How far are we talking?" Sol demanded.

"Uh, not too bad. There is some tree cover and it's rain-ing. You'll have to go down a hill. At the bottom, the truck is waiting."

"And the other man, he is already there?" Sol confirmed.

"Yeah, he told me two others would be coming and to show you the way."

"And what about the staff? Security? How much time do we have?"

Hector laughed. "Lady, this has never happened before. I imagine it is one hell of a clusterfuck up there. It will probably take them at least thirty minutes to pull any kind of sweep team together."

Hector stopped at a set of large double doors. His eyes widened in recognition as he looked at Bette. Sol stopped and took an uncomfortable step into Hector's space. "I don't know what you are up to, old man, but I suggest you forget you saw us tonight."

"Oh, you don't have to worry about me. I never see anything around here." Hector pushed the door open to reveal thrashing rain and gusting winds.

"Remember, straight down the hill. He should be waiting with the truck."

Sol gave two bounces and bolted out the door. Bette smiled at him, mouthing, *Thank you.*

Hector put his hand on her arm. "Bette, do you really want to do this? Your sorrow will not be alleviated out there, either."

Bette stopped scrutinizing his face. "Hector, I . . . I can't stay here."

A pained smile twitched on his lips. "Remember what they did to Roya, then. To bear witness to violence leaves you with a choice. Will you look the other way or will you confront it?"

Standing there, backlit in smoky red light, Bette twisted over Hector's words. They stood a few seconds longer, their eyes locked. When she didn't move, Hector nodded and patted her on the shoulder. "Then go, and take care of yourself, okay?"

Bette nodded as she felt emotion squeeze her stomach. Turning toward the open door, she took a trembling gulp of air and followed Sol out into the lashing storm.

68

Bette jogged behind her, but Sol was much faster. Her black-clad form quickly became lost in the night. Drops hammered down from the dark night sky relentlessly and soaked Bette in a matter of seconds. New, louder sirens began to blare behind her. She could make out some distant yelling. Her heart was pounding in her head. Mostly, she could hear her breath and the sound of the rain. She forced herself to move as fast as she possibly could after Sol, terrified that she would be left behind. Bette heard what she thought was the report of a gun. She did not turn around. She was moving so fast she thought her legs might just run out from beneath her and leave her pregnant torso behind.

Bette ran down the slope. Losing her balance, she tumbled through the mud until she landed hard on her right elbow and came to a stop. She looked around in a daze. She could see lights shining at the bottom of the hill; closer inspection told her they were headlights. Bette strained to see; between torrents of rain, she could make out a waiting navy transport van.

She heaved up from her hands and knees, slipping as she tried to regain her balance. Bette could see Sol at the back of the van holding the doors open, waiting for her arrival. Bette quickened her pace despite the cries from her torn-up bare feet and bruised knees.

"In! In! In!" Sol motioned as Bette moved closer toward the open van doors.

Sol shoved Bette in, clambered in behind, and slammed the doors. Before the interior lights shut off, Bette noticed there were no seats in the back of the van, just racks and racks of gel-like bags with dark masses suspended in them. Cyrus gunned the engine, taking off before the doors were fully closed. When the doors slammed shut, the lights went out, and there were no windows except for the rear windshield. Bette sat on the floor in the makeshift walkway between the racks of bags to the front seat.

Out of breath, Sol climbed up front into the passenger seat next to Cyrus. "They were assembling," Bette heard her say. "I don't know how much time we have. Minutes, maybe."

The van bounced and groaned until it hit the smooth surface of a road. The plastic bags rubbed against each other as the metal hooks they were suspended from squeaked. The rain fell in heavy sheets across the windshield and hampered visibility. Bette gripped the bottom of one of the poles holding the bags.

Cyrus's jaw set as his eyes flicked back and forth between the rearview mirror and the road in front of him. "Do you know where we are?" he barked at Sol.

She had her small rectangular object out. "Yeah. We are close. Take the next right. I'm going to weave us around a bit first for more exposure."

He quickly turned onto a side street. Bette's eyebrows raised. *More exposure?*

They had taken a risk using a propagation vehicle. But, if they bobbed and weaved throughout the streets, she supposed it might take the police a while to reconcile all the street-cam footage. It all depended on where the cams were. In the wealthier areas, which were closer to the Center, it would be a mess assembling all the footage. A strategy of hitting conflicting cams would create a diversion.

The van's central console looked as though Cyrus had taken a hammer to it; the screen had been smashed and exposed wires were poking out. All vehicles were manufactured with mandatory monitoring. By destroying the console, Cyrus blocked Center security from tapping in and take over the steering of the van. They would be in a scramble to find it before it disappeared. The driving rain didn't hurt, either. This was one of the few times Bette was grateful for a torrential downpour. There would be no eyewitnesses to definitively say they knew what direction the van had been heading.

Sol instructed Cyrus to drive toward the edge of the city. "Left . . . left . . . right . . . left."

Soon they were in a run-down section of town, which would contain few street cams. "Take a right," Sol said. It looked as though she had directed them right into a brick wall. But as Cyrus approached the wall, a door began to open from the bottom.

It was cavernous and jet black as they entered. Cyrus drove for a moment in complete darkness before coming into a dimly lit, windowless concrete room. He parked the van next to a newer, much less conspicuous car.

"Out," Cyrus ordered.

69

Sol opened the doors on the back of the van, and the interior lights blinked on. Her eyes widened in shock as she gasped, "What the hell . . . "

Bette immediately looked up from her spot on the floor. Above her, in the light, they looked like pink-stained orbs with glob centers. The light slanted through them and created a crimson kaleidoscope. Thin, dark lines veined the interior of the bags, obscuring their contents. Bette stood to get a better look. Peering into a bag, she saw a floating mass as it bobbed within the solution. The shape that drifted past had five tiny fingers.

Bette jumped back, finding herself enveloped by more bags. She shook them off wildly like swarming gnats from her hair and jumped from the van. Turning to make sure nothing followed her out, she was able to put together what she saw. Each pole had four or five bags hooked in the holes along its length. There were at least six poles on each side of the tall transport van.

Cyrus joined Sol and stared with disgust at the van's cargo. "What are those?" Cyrus asked.

Bette gulped. "I think this is a transfer van." She was, in fact, sure it was a transfer van. The strangeness of the fact did not subside the longer she stared at it. In a different venue, these poles could be mistaken for decorations with marbled, translucent pink and bloodred ornaments.

"What is a *transfer*?" Sol asked as her nose crinkled.

"The . . . um . . . fetuses they sell to the Subs."

Stunned silence ensued before Sol whistled and uttered in dismay, "Jesus Christ."

Bette limped away from the grotesqueness of the van, wincing as her bare feet touched the dusty floor. She noticed a nasty gash on the top of her right foot, which was still oozing blood. She almost didn't want to see how the bottoms of her feet fared. Water dripped from her hair as she tugged at the wet pajamas now clinging to her.

Sol gestured to Cyrus and they walked to a corner of the cement room just out of earshot to speak in low tones. Sol did most of the talking, every so often glancing in Bette's direction. Bette shifted self-consciously in the stale air. She looked around the garage, which contained nothing except a nondescript gray sedan.

Cyrus brought a hand to his temple partway through the muted conversation; subdued nodding commenced between the two of them. When the discussion concluded, they approached Bette.

"We have a little bit of a problem," Cyrus began.

Dread washed over Bette with a shiver.

Oh God, please don't leave me here.

Bette swallowed hard, almost afraid to ask: "What is it?"

"Um, we have to do something about your corneal lens . . . "

Shit. Of course.

"And it is safe to assume you have numerous nanobots coursing through your blood."

She had been cataloged, tagged, and pinged. Bette was definitely a serial number in the Center's inventory. There were any number of ways the Center could track her down. "How will we do that?" Bette asked.

"Well," Cyrus said, "we have a Pulsor. We can pulse you here to, uh, deactivate them."

"Okay. Then what are we waiting for?" Bette asked, wondering why this was a problem.

Sol stepped in. "You see, Bette, the Pulsor uses a concentrated ray of energy to overload and fizzle bionic components. The nanobots could be anywhere. In order to get them, we will have to slightly damage *all* the cells to damage the ones we need."

She paused, watching Bette closely.

"Oh," Bette said, suddenly realizing what they were tiptoeing around. "All the cells? You mean even . . . " Bette trailed off mid-sentence.

"You are going to lose function of the corneal lens," Sol said. Her dark, hawklike eyes softened as she continued solemnly. "And you will more than likely lose the baby."

Bette visibly deflated as if a large pin had poked a hole in her skin. Sol lurched forward to put her hand under Bette's bruised elbow to steady her.

"I-I think I need to sit down," Bette stammered. There were no chairs in the room, so Sol helped Bette to the floor. Bette pulled her damp stained knees to her chest and wrapped her arms around them. For all the events that swirled around her, Bette's mind was blank. She stared at her mud-streaked feet.

Mud lined the free edge of her toenails. The blood had begun to coagulate on her scratches and gashes. The way the overhead light washed out her pigment, she silently remarked at how her feet looked like those of a dead person. This was what you should see under the unsympathetic lights in a morgue.

Or in a Collection truck.

Bette blinked, looking back and forth to Cyrus and Sol, suddenly feeling lost. Of course, she had heard what Sol had said, but this couldn't be it. Were there no other options?

Cyrus lowered his eyes to the floor. Sol crouched down, putting her hand on Bette's arm.

I begged them to take me with them.

Bette shrank at the thought. Now, here they were in some dark concrete garage, the minutes ticking down before the Center realized Bette was gone, if they hadn't already. They would try to detect her location. She was theirs, after all.

No, it is theirs.

"Bette." Sol's tone was comforting. "I know that this is an awful choice. If you don't want to do this, Cyrus and I can just leave you here."

She squeezed Bette's arm and continued. "But if you want to come with us, we have to neutralize the threat of being found."

Neutralize the threat . . .

This little baby wasn't a threat. But everything it had taken to conceive it was. The Center had pumped her full of technology and science to make this miracle possible, and now it was what stood in the way of her getting out. Bette shook her head at the cruel irony. All she'd ever wanted was to get pregnant. That was all they had ever said was important. Pregnancy was her ticket to a better life, her purpose, her duty. She had given everything to that end. Now she was cursing the fates it had ever happened. She wished the Center had never succeeded.

Bette scrutinized Sol's face. She was a brave woman, Bette had to give her that. She must have been the bearer of bad news many times before this. She took no joy in this conversation. Bette wished that she could be as strong as Sol.

"There is no other way? You are sure?" Bette hardly recognized the tiny voice that came out of her.

Bette could stay here, and the Center would find her. If this baby did make it to term, it would be yanked away and institutionalized by its country. The Department of Propagation viewed its life the way it did all the others, as part of the production line. The future for this child would be a bleak one, a life of instruction, training, and analysis. The anguish of another child becoming a numb cog in an inescapable cycle settled heavy inside of her.

Precisely what Roya had wanted to stop.

Knowing what Bette knew, could she go back? Could she be an incubator, aiding in the procreation of beings like Fern or worse? Bette's stomach lurched as she thought of Melody. Could she subject a child to that? Could she subject humanity to that? The obligation that drove Roya resonated now. The immensity of it was staggering. Roya was revolted at how the Center was dictating humanity's future. So appalled, she willingly submitted herself to it, hoping to dismantle it from the inside out. And she was dead, killed by what she was trying to stop.

It's not their decision to make.

The cold, hard truth was that Bette was not Roya. There was no way Bette could go back to the Center. There was no way she could go back to the place that killed Roya. There was no chance she would ever willingly put herself in Melody's way again. She could not watch Dorothea be so cavalier with the inputs and the efficiencies of life itself.

Bette looked down at her stomach and felt her eyes get hot. *But I must give this up.*

God, what she had put up with to get to this place. The way she'd been debased, the agency she'd given up. Everything she'd endured to be considered worthy. To have proved that she had earned her right to be. But it wasn't right, not for either of them.

Survival was not a pretty thing. Permanence had to have something hard to hang on to, like rock or bone. It was not rooted in the beauty of fragility; it was not fed by the abstractness of essence. Survival pierced through the soft, rich topsoil and anchored itself to a hot metallic core. It was a ruthless driving thing, this survival. Nothing any of them had done to get here had been noble or heroic; everything had been motivated by desperate, searing survival.

Neutralize the threat.

It wasn't a threat, but it embodied the threat. This tiny fetus, this small baby implanted by the Department of Propagation would have to pay the price of survival. The innocent always did.

"Bette?" Sol's voice intruded.

Bette could not move forward or go back until she made a decision and she was quickly running out of time. This abysmal decision was the culmination of a life where she made no real decisions. She would not find any consolation here, nor would she find any absolution or peace. Here, in this dusty, abandoned garage on the outskirts of a dying city, she would make that decision. And she would survive.

"Bette?"

"Fine," Bette whispered, "do it."

Cyrus returned from the van with a device and somberly handed it to Sol. "And you are sure?" Sol asked, giving Bette one last chance to turn back.

"Yes," Bette murmured.

"Please hold out your arms and stand with your feet apart," Sol instructed.

Bette squeezed her eyes shut as the device powered on. The tears slid like lead down Bette's face as Sol slowly wanded the device over her, its low, static-filled hum sounding like the ominous roar of water. The Pulsor pulled in places Bette didn't expect and made her feel woozy.

The purpose of nanos was to heal a person, to make them whole. Microscopic machines were printed in a lab that made spare human parts, which were injected to float in places unknown. Sol was trying to destroy them.

The Pulsor stopped. The cement room felt strangely somber. Bette felt like all the strength had been drained from her body. Her muscles ached and she was suddenly extremely thirsty, but she stood with her eyes closed. She wanted to sob or scream but didn't have the energy to do either.

"We have to go," Cyrus said. The deadpan command hung sedate in the air, hesitant anyone would follow it.

Bette opened her eyes and saw immediately that her right eye had gone dark, as if someone held a black board over that side of her face. She blinked. Her eyes were open, but she could only see out of her left eye. She rubbed the back of her hands across her face to wipe away a few tears that managed to hang on. Sol handed the Pulsor to Cyrus and assisted Bette into the back seat of the car.

"What about them?" Bette asked, gesturing toward the van, its doors closed to hide the otherworldly scene of the fetuses in transport bags.

"They were cursed before they were conceived," Sol answered, grim faced.

Cyrus started the car. Sol slammed the door as she got into the passenger side. They drove out the same way they'd come.

Life ended and began all within a matter of moments.

70

The car headed away from the underground garage in the opposite direction they had approached it. Cyrus drove cautiously, the most inconspicuous thing they'd done yet. He let out a low sigh as he moved back in the direction of street cam saturation.

"Sol, you did a great—" he started.

"Shut the fuck up," she snapped, cutting him off. Her scorching fury was evident even to Bette from the back seat. The occupants of the car stiffened.

"Do you have any idea what we just did, Cyrus? Do you? Do you have any fucking idea the shitstorm that we have started?"

Cyrus said nothing.

"Oh, now you have nothing to say?" Sol turned her head to look out her window. "It was supposed to be really simple, Cyrus. We were to go in and find Roya. If she wasn't there, we were to leave just as we came. Un-fucking detected."

Cyrus shifted uncomfortably in his seat.

"I told you I didn't want to shoot my way out of that place, didn't I? I asked you to be inconspicuous, didn't I? Careful.

Just be goddamned careful." Sol put her hands over her eyes and then let them slowly slide down her cheeks. She shook her head, hands still on her cheeks.

"But is that what happened?" Sol asked sarcastically. "Nope. Not even close. You blew a hole in the side of a birthing center as a distraction. You stole a van filled with Center fetuses. We kidnapped a Center resident, whom we just pulsed."

"I'm sorry, Sol," Cyrus said woodenly.

Sol laughed with a tinge of hysteria. She brought her hands from her face, clapping them in front of her.

"No shit!" she exclaimed, shaking her head in disbelief. "You are going to be sorry! Jesus, we are all going to be fucking sorry!"

"I know," Cyrus said, gravely.

"Cyrus, this will be considered an act of war! Soon, all of the fucking United States military will be after us!"

"I know," Cyrus said again.

"I know, I know," Sol mimicked him scornfully. "Is that all you have to say?"

She took a few shaky breaths. "And what is your father going to say?" Sol asked, "Have you even thought about him? What you are about to make him do? This is a real gem, Cy, a real goddamned gem."

Sol huffed loudly and leaned her head against the headrest. "I'm going to close my eyes now," she said. "Can you *try* not to bring down the apocalypse while I do that?"

Cyrus did not answer; his eyes did not deviate from the road.

71

Dawn broke over the flat arid land. The city had melted away behind them. Even though the sun had risen, the sky was still overcast. Nothing moved on the landscape. No wind, no bird, no branch. This was Canner Country.

Canners.

She had been damaged by their violence. Their existence was to blame for her last few days—hell, her last few months. She sat filthy and gutted, sticking to the back seat of a car, headed to nowhere because of Canners.

They were an accident, the unintended result of a measure to keep the species going. They hadn't asked to be here, but here they were; they had been turned out into the world to roam with no direction or compass, influencing the path and forcing perimeters on the population. And it wouldn't stop. The promise of fertility, ensuring the longevity of humanity, was too compelling to deny. There was no way to walk back the solution; they had to deal with the consequences that came with it. Humanity had to lean into the self-created horror, the Melodys and the Ferns, and grapple with the outcome. Was this the way to preserve the species? Was this what survival would look like?

Bette's eyes burned due to lack of sleep. A dull ache enveloped her from the top of her rumpled hair to the torn nail at the tip of her left toe. Her skin itched from the patches of dried mud she could not scrape off. There was precious little water in the car and Cyrus had advised to only use it for drinking since they had a long way to go. They had spent two stifling days in this car, only stopping to relieve themselves. Disoriented with the use of only one eye, edgeless nausea ebbed and flowed over Bette. Some moments it felt like she might throw up but, before she could, the feeling would subside. Her dry and tacky tongue stuck to the roof of her mouth. Leaning her head on the warm window, her hair crunching from the leftover mud, she closed her eyes; she felt like such a wretched thing sitting in the back seat. She shifted and felt the backs of her arms peel away from the polyurethane upholstery with a slight crinkle. The interior was humid with two days' worth of unbrushed exhales and unwashed bodies. Her only hope right now was that the car would stop moving soon so her stomach would stop rolling.

A cold metallic tap on her knee startled her. Opening her eyes, she turned her head to see Cyrus's arm extended from the front seat with a stainless-steel canteen. Sol had fallen asleep with her head propped against the passenger-side window.

"Here, drink this," he said.

Anytime any one of them moved, a wave of stale and reeking body odor rolled throughout the car. It had ceased to sting the nostrils, but it coated every surface, the entire inside of the car, with a film of moldy, rancid stink. Bette could taste it on the inside of her cheeks. The more you moved, the more the stink was disturbed. Bette had tried hard to keep as still as possible, as every putrid wave made her want to turn inside out in hopes of escaping it.

Taking the canteen, Bette unscrewed the lid and pressed the cold container to her dry lips. She swallowed, immediately grateful to feel her tongue dislodge from the roof of her mouth and the tang of decay wash away. But it could not get rid of the gritty tartar on the surface of her teeth.

"Thank you," she mumbled, offering the canteen back to him.

"You keep it, I've got another up here," he told her.

Bette pressed the cool metal to her hot forehead and felt temporarily relieved. She looked out the window of the car, scanning the dry-packed earth along the horizon with her good eye. This was the farthest she had ever traveled out of the city in her entire life. Bette's thoughts returned, unbidden, to the dark garage behind them. Sol was a woman who meant what she said. Sol had said they would have to take care of the corneal lens and, boy, did they. Dread began to knot in Bette's stomach as she waited for evidence of Sol's *other* prediction.

It had to be done.

A sharp, shooting pain stabbed Bette behind her eyes, punctuating every uneven bump in the road. "How much longer will we be in the car?" Bette groaned. "I don't feel so good."

"Um, it will probably be another few hours," Cyrus said.

It took the last bit of her strength to squelch the wail in her throat. The idea of another few hours in this rank and malodorous hotbox was unbearable. Bette crammed her palms into her temples to try and neutralize the stabbing pain behind her eyes.

"Where are we even going?" Bette snapped, unsatisfied by his answer.

"To the farm."

"What farm?" Bette asked, her teeth gritting in anticipation of a round of need-to-know riddles with no answers.

"My home," Cyrus said.

The word clattered woodenly on what was left of Bette's emotions, a word so banal it was easy to dismiss. But the word echoed in her mind the way a bell would as it lingered after the initial chime. What a bizarre concept, the idea of home, leaving Bette with a feeling of empty indifference. The word, "home," didn't mean anything to her. It did not define a clear destination. She was not comforted or propelled by it. A place where people of shared DNA lived was almost an alien idea. Bette had known it once, but that was so long ago. It was a language she used to speak but could now barely recall a single word.

Sweat began to bead on her upper lip. Wiping it away, she leaned her head on the headrest, interlaced her fingers in her lap, and squeezed her eyes shut. The air all around her smelled of decomposition. Everything was corroding around her; she was breaking down. This is what it wanted, what Decay had always been after—the prolonged demise of her flesh. All she wanted to do right now was die. To just give up, wither, disintegrate, and be swept outside. She felt the side effects of the Pulsor beginning to surface with a vengeance. Her heartbeat throbbed loudly in her head. Tears spilled out the side of her clenched eyes.

I deserve this.

Who was she to ever think she could escape the Department of Propagation? They had ruled her entire life. Why had she ever left her room that night when the power went out? How stupid was she to think that it could be that easy? And what? Just escape with the first pair of mutinous Repatriates she met? What were they even doing there! Bette's heart caught as she remembered the photo of Roya that Cyrus had shown her.

I just want to get home.

Roya had said that.

I just want to get home.

That was why they were there. Their mission had been to bring her home.

Home was an actual place. Home was where Bette was headed now, Roya's home, the place she had been taken from. The place she longed for. The place that she hung on to despite how the Center had tried to assimilate her. It shouldn't have been Bette in the car. It shouldn't have been Bette who was alive. It shouldn't have been Bette who was rescued by Roya's brother. It wasn't fair that Bette got to go to this place; this "home" was a place that meant nothing to her but everything to Roya.

72

Bette felt she would be sick. The undulating motion and the roughness of the road did not help. They'd been in the car for days. It was hot and stale. Bette was still wearing the pajamas she'd been wearing when they had broken out of the Birthing Center. Her bare feet were still crusted with streaks of mud. She'd done the best she could to scrape it off. They had not eaten. They had very little to drink. Cyrus and Sol had enough water for three people but were being extra careful, just in case.

Cyrus kept saying they were closer. But, what did close mean? Bette had been pulsed, the effects of which were coming to fruition. Bette was nauseous, and her head and back were beginning to ache. Cramping waxed and waned in intensity over the last few hours. Sweat soaked Bette's shirt. She tried to close her eyes, but it only made her more aware of the car's movement. She tried to keep them open, but fatigue made them burn and half sight made her irritable.

"Cyrus, can we stop?" Bette begged meekly. She felt the bile at the back of her throat and clenched her teeth.

"Cyrus," she said again, a little louder, "please."

Sol shifted in her seat. "Cyrus, stop now," Sol said urgently.

"Sol, if we stop now, I might not be able to get it started again. The charge is low."

Sol looked back at Bette to see if she could persuade her to wait just a little longer. "Cyrus, we have to stop."

"Sol?"

"If it won't start, we'll walk." Her tone was stern. Cyrus heaved a sigh of rebuttal.

The car slowed. Bette was not even sure if it had come to a complete stop as she grappled with the handle and spilled onto the ground. Not even three steps from the car she fell to her knees and threw up. Throw up may have been a generous term. It was mostly heaving with a dribble of yellowish-green liquid signaling there was nothing in her stomach. The thin, rank fluid pooled in the dust between her knees. Bette looked down and made sure it hadn't gotten on her clothes.

That was when she saw it. The fresh red blotch in the crevice of her light-colored pajama bottoms. Her stomach swelled. Her hands hit the ground in front of her, breaking her plummet. Her back arched but nothing happened; the spasm paralyzed her momentarily.

It is happening.

The ground crunched next to her. She glanced over to see Sol's shoes. "Bette, you have to get up." Her voice was guarded.

"I'm sorry," Bette whispered, swallowing hard.

"Don't be sorry, just get up." The slightly higher pitch in her voice made Bette look up. Sol stood tall as she surveyed the land around them. Her lips were tight and her body was tense. Something was wrong.

Bette willed herself to stand. Feeling simultaneously dizzy and guilty, she shakily stood next to Sol. Bette blinked to focus her one good eye and looked in the direction Sol was looking. She didn't see anything. A door slammed behind the two women. Bette looked over her right shoulder toward the dust-covered car. Cyrus held a shotgun in one hand and the Pulsor in the other as he stomped to the other side of Sol.

"How many do you think?" Bette heard him ask in a low voice.

"I don't know," Sol murmured. "I see two dust trails. Worst case? Six to eight."

"Shit," said Cyrus. "Which one do you want?"

"The shotgun."

Cyrus extended the shotgun to Sol.

"Extra ammunition?" she asked.

Cyrus paused before answering, "Uh, no. That's it."

"Fucking story of my life," Sol sighed.

"Tell me about it."

"Well, I also have this." Sol patted a handle on her back, a leather strap slung around her to hold the machete.

Bette squinted and finally saw what they were talking about. She could see thin wisps of dust coming off the scrub.

"What is it?" Bette asked. No one answered. Cyrus and Sol were primed for and dreading something, but what? Bette continued to stare in the same general direction.

"Um . . ." Bette tried again. "I don't understand. What are we looking at?"

Sol sighed heavily. "Canners."

It took Bette a split second to comprehend what she'd said. *Canners?*

"Wait, what?" Bette shook her head. "How?"

They were miles from anything remotely civilized.

There is nothing for them, why would they be all the way out here?

Bette looked around just to be sure.

"They must have caught wind of us somewhere," Cyrus said.

"But we drove straight through. We barely stopped. That is impossible." Bette began to panic.

"Well," Sol said, "there they are." She and Cyrus continued to stand and watch the dust trails get closer.

"Then we should go! Why are we standing here?" Bette asked, her voice tinged in agitation.

"We are too close," Cyrus said.

"Too close to what?" Bette demanded. "There is nothing fucking out here!"

Cyrus turned to look at her, his dark eyes glinting a warning. "We are too close to the farm," he explained, "and we can't lead Canners in. We will have to fight them here."

Bette's mouth dropped open. *He has lost his mind!* Bette turned to implore Sol.

"He is right," came her pat answer.

They had both lost their minds. They were close to nothing. And now Cyrus and Sol wanted to—what? Stand and fight, worst case, six to eight Canners?

"Are you crazy?" Bette breathed.

"Those are the rules, Bette," Sol said, "and since we've already broken a shit ton of them, we are at least going to follow this one. Cyrus and I can't knowingly lead Canners into the farm."

Both their faces were grim. "So, we are, uh, just going to fend them off? Is that the plan?" Bette was nearly beside herself with disbelief.

"Nope. We have to kill them," Sol said solemnly.

Bette barely survived an encounter with one Canner months ago. Her thoughts went to the scar on her back and then to the marks on her neck. Her eyes bulged from their sockets as she shook her head. "With what? A shotgun and a Pulsor? Are you kidding me? They are animals! They will kill us!"

Bette looked back to the dust trails. Shapes of figures were visible now. They were getting closer. Her heart beat faster and her palms grew clammy.

"Can't we just get back in the car? Try to outrun them?" Bette petitioned.

"The car won't start."

"Is there no way to get help? Is there no one we can call? You keep saying we are close; are we close enough for anyone to help us?" Bette pleaded.

"They'll see us," Sol said.

It was maddening playing the worst riddle game in the world. Bette couldn't keep her eyes off the dark figures heading their way. She was terrified. She wanted to run as fast and as far away from them as she possibly could. But her traveling companions, if you could call them that, were rooted by some mysterious and unspoken code, the rules of which were unyielding enough to keep them stolidly in place in the face of certain death.

"But how do we know if they even see us? If they can see us, don't they know we are in danger?" Bette's voice was hysterical now.

"Bette, they'll get here as fast as they can," Cyrus said. But she was not comforted.

The figures were now more defined. Bette could plainly see that there were five of them. Their hair wild, a few had pieces of tattered fabric that fluttered from their arms and legs as they ran.

Bette put her hand to her mouth and choked back a sob. She had never heard of this, let alone seen it with her own eyes. She'd only ever heard of episodic attacks by a lone Canner on the outskirts of town. It had never occurred to her that they would travel together in packs.

She had never seen one, not up close and in the flesh, not even when she'd been attacked from behind. She was unconscious moments after she'd hit the ground. The only reason she'd ever seen one was because of the secret video footage she and Roya had seen. Now, these five squalid, cannibalistic, feral men bore down upon them in the middle of nowhere. The three stood in a line holding two weapons between them. Bette could feel her teeth beginning to chatter.

The Canners started howling an all-too-familiar screeching wail. Goose bumps erupted all over Bette's skin; this was a sound she remembered. These were deeper and more masculine sounds, but she'd heard the wails before.

She had done it when they'd pulled her off Roya. He had done it on the video during his trial.

Their skin was almost gray. Their cheeks cut deep recessions in the sides of their faces; their skulls were sparsely padded with papery flesh. Brown scabs and scratches overlaid their chest and arms. They were so close, Bette and her fellow travelers could see the rotting teeth in their yowling mouths.

Sol primed her shotgun. Bette heard the stinging crackle from Cyrus's Pulsor. Her own hands sat empty and trembling.

"Bette, get in the car," Sol commanded.

"Lock yourself in," Cyrus instructed.

Bette nodded mutely and shuffled backward to the car. She was never again going to turn her back on advancing Canners. She bumped into the car. Her fingers trembled as she pulled on the handle, missing it a couple of times before finally getting it open. She climbed into the back seat and crouched on the floor, trying to make herself as small as possible.

She was still adjusting when she heard the explosive sound of the shotgun, which caused her to jump. Bette slammed her eyes shut.

Please, please, please, she silently pleaded. With whom or what? It didn't really matter. Bette only wanted to make it out of this desert alive.

There was incoherent shouting between Cyrus and Sol outside the car. Bette tried to make out what they were saying, but it was drowned out by wild screeching and yelling. Shots were fired intermittently. Bette detected the smell of burnt hair.

A thud hit the car so hard it rocked the vehicle from side to side. Bette heard something slap against the window, but she was too scared to look up. The deafening screeching was right above her head. The car rocked as it continued to be pounded. A shot went off that sounded like a bomb right under her feet.

Was Sol shooting at the car?

The screeching stopped. The car stopped shaking. All Bette could hear was her anxious breathing. The blood pulsed in her ears. She strained to hear over the adrenaline. Nothing.

I'll just wait for Sol or Cyrus. They will let me know when it is okay. They will get me.

But nothing happened. There was no more noise. Bette did not want to look outside for fear of what she might find.

Where are Sol and Cyrus?

That was the question that moved Bette. Surrounded by Canners, Cyrus and Sol stood their ground. These people had saved her, and she couldn't stay in the stuffy back seat indefinitely.

Jesus, what if they are dead?

No, no, they can't be dead. But they might be hurt.

Bette took a deep breath and unfurled from the tight ball she'd drawn up into. Hesitant to pop up and look out the window directly over her, she scooted across the bottom of the back seat to the other side of the car. Bette waited just a breath more near the door, straining to hear something, anything that would tell her if this was a good or bad idea. The eerie silence lingered. She swallowed hard, unlocked the door, and crept outside. Her bare feet molded around the small rocks and sand to insulate her footfalls. Hunched over and out of sight from the windows, she moved and stayed low, trying not to announce her presence.

There was no one on this far side of the car, the driver's side. Crouching by the trunk, she peeked around the backside of the car with uneasy anticipation. She sucked in a breath. In the foreground, closest to the back-passenger-side tire, she saw a dirty hand smeared with blood. The nails were long and yellow and jagged. The fingers, relaxed but still curving toward the ends, looked like bones shrink-wrapped in a cracked and scaly shroud.

It was a Canner.

Trembling, she stood up to look over the car. There were bodies scattered everywhere. Maybe eight to ten feet from the one at the end of the car were three more filthy Canners, two lying faceup, their bloody chests saturated nearly black. The other, mere feet from those two, was lying facedown on the dirt.

But that is only four . . .

Panic welled up inside of Bette's stomach with enough adrenaline to propel her feet around the car. As she came around, the hand of the Canner she initially saw was attached to its prone, outstretched owner. It looked as if it had been trying to flee before it fell. As Bette followed the direction of its skeletal legs, she saw Cyrus on the passenger side of the car. His back was leaned against the car and the Pulsor rested just inches from his left hand. A foot away from the Pulsor lay the last Canner who had come to rest on his side. Finding the fifth reassured her, but only a little.

Cyrus was unconscious. He was sporting a large gash across his nose, and his right eye was beginning to puff up. Bette knelt next to him and placed two fingers on his neck. She could hear him breathing and his pulse was strong. She surveyed the rest of him but was unable to make out any more noticeable wounds. She turned around to look for Sol. She found her off to the left and in between the duo and the facedown Canner, and almost directly across from the one felled by Cyrus's Pulsor. She, too, was lying facedown, the shotgun still clutched in her hand. Bette trudged over and put a hand on her back.

"Sol . . . Sol," she said as she gently shook her.

There was a movement in the dirt behind her. Bette whipped her head around in enough time to see the Canner on his side, near Cyrus, vault to his feet. It was like watching a marionette suddenly yanked into motion. It didn't look like he was in control of his own body, as if it were being directed from elsewhere, an unconscious vessel switched on as a result of a computer command. The dark veins bulged in his knobby feet, like roots steadying the wasted ashen tree of a man that shook before her, flecked with dirt and blood across his shirt-less torso. His black eyes smoldered with wolfish ferocity. The pallid skin on his emaciated arms flinched as his sinewy muscles contracted and flexed. All those little movements happened in a rapid-fire sequence as if whoever was directing him had pressed fast-forward. Bloodless lips parted within the scraggly, dreaded beard and a savage shriek tore the air as he raced toward her. Time slowed as Bette watched in horror as the Canner launched himself at her. As he sailed through the air, time sped back up and she did not have a chance to move before he was on top of her.

White lines of impact streaked across her good eye as he plowed into her. Caught in the urine and sweat-soaked mist of déjà vu, Bette was able to put her arms in front of her to defend herself, making certain to keep them close to her neck. He snapped and snarled at her, weaving up and back as he tried to strike her neck. His smell was a weapon unto itself, violently burning her nostrils and choking her, then distorting and muddling her senses. He was as lithe as he was vicious, looking like a corpse but moving like a mercenary. He took hold of one of her waving wrists, gnashed his stained canine teeth, and sunk them into her forearm.

Bette screamed as his teeth cut down into her flesh without remorse, and a burning, searing pain exploded from his vise-like jaw. She balled up her other fist and punched him in the side of the head, then again squarely in the nose. She heard a distinct crack and felt his teeth withdraw from her ulna. He rose up, reared back his head, and screeched into the sky. An object whirred past her, just over her head, and slammed into his chest. Fat drops of heavy splatter rained over Bette. The Canner quieted, mid-strike, while confusion spread over his pockmarked face. Bette looked up to see a machete handle sticking out of the middle of his chest. One of his hands grazed the handle before he slumped backward.

Bette turned to see Sol flop down on the ground. Blood pumped out of the Canner's chest and was immediately sucked up by the thirsty ground around him. Bette shunted his legs off her and scrambled over to Sol.

When Sol didn't respond, Bette tried pushing her onto her side. It took a couple of shoves before she managed to get Sol on her back. Her eyes were closed and her cheeks were scraped and red with blood. Alarmed, Bette looked over and around Sol to make sure she wasn't bleeding from somewhere else. It was hard to tell in her black clothes, but the dry ground gave her away. Blood was spattered on the ground and puddling next to her right leg. Bette delicately felt along the leg until she found the largest concentration of dampness. Sol moaned.

Bette put her hand, slick with blood and perspiration, to her forehead. Her manic thoughts were racing. She turned her neck and gripped the collar of her shirt with her teeth. Bracing, she tugged and yanked at her sleeve until the seam came apart. She jerked the sleeve off and tied it around Sol's leg. The light material was soon doused in Sol's blood. Bette worried it would not be enough.

She rose to her feet, wiping blood on her pants, and felt herself begin to tremble. Her quick, shallow breaths were the only sound she could hear. Her eyes darted from Canner to Canner, wondering if they were all really dead. Her gaze landed on the Pulsor. She was terrified to move or make a sound, engulfed in fear of another one charging at her. Cyrus was still slumped over by the car; Bette could see the blood around his wounds was beginning to coagulate. Sol's back barely rose up and down. The desert stretched into oblivion. An unexpected wind came up, spiriting dust over the desolate scene. Bette wrapped her arms around herself as she continued to shiver.

What the hell am I supposed to do?

73

The wind persisted, rushing and whistling all around her. If she relaxed her focus, she could almost make out patterns of sounds, like a deep rumble of a machine. She could not close her eyes, not with the carnage that lay around her. As she rubbed at the dirt that stuck in her eyelashes, she heard something. Not the hallucinations that the cacophonous wind brought with it, but a real sound, the first sound since the fighting had stopped. Straining to listen, making sure she hadn't imagined it, she leaned into the wind. It grew steadily louder and sounded like an engine, but the engine of something huge.

Bette cocked her head and furrowed her brow as she tried to figure out what it was and where it was coming from. Over a clay-colored fold in the land, a large yellow machine emerged. She blinked twice. It resembled a sort of tank, only higher and with more windows. As it rumbled toward her, realization struck her; it looked like farm equipment. Bewildered, she stood still as it approached.

It grumbled to a stop several feet from the front of the car. It was absolutely enormous. The engine continued to churn and cause bits of gravel to jump around her, then giant spotlights blazed from its front. Bette put her hands over her eyes, shielding them from the glare. The fumes from the hulking vehicle reminded Bette of boiled vegetables. The faint sound of a creaking door opened and closed. Bette lowered her hands, squinting for a clearer view. A tall, thin man dressed in a cowboy hat and work boots approached her hesitantly.

Pausing in the crunchy soil, he took a moment to survey the scene. As he drew closer to her, Bette heard him whistle and say to himself, "Damn, what the hell happened here?"

He walked right past Bette, like she were a broken, leafless tree and not the only conscious individual left standing. Baffled, she turned and watched him. The sun was beginning to set but she could see he was suntanned, with dark hair and eyes. He wore a long-sleeve khaki shirt and denim work pants. He squatted and flicked one of the Canners with his finger. Suddenly, the Canner's arm shot out and grabbed his wrist. The Canner bolted up, screeching. Bette jumped as every muscle in her body seized. The man wrenched his wrist from the Canner and jumped back. It barely had a second to advance before he withdrew a gun and shot the Canner in the head three times. Bette threw her hands over her ears, realizing only then that she was screaming. The screeching Canner toppled back to the ground. Unshaken, the man walked over to the three other Canners and shot each of them in the head. He then yanked the machete from the chest of the fourth Canner and shot him in the head once for good measure. Finally, the man turned to look at her. He looked like a crazed killer as he held the blood-smeared machete in a raised position in his hand.

"I reckon you are a friend and not a foe?"

Bette nodded; her eyes glued to the machete.

"Well, that is good," the man said as he lowered the machete. He stepped over to Cyrus and checked his pulse, nodding to himself. He moved over to Sol and assessed her injuries. His eyebrow rose slightly as he noticed the skinny, blood-soaked tourniquet. He turned to Bette, eyebrow still arched, and asked, "You do this?"

She nodded.

"Hmm," was all he said.

He peered out into the scrub, touching his left ear. "Home on the range, home on the range, this is Mic. I've got a five-pack out here in West Seven. I also have two sleepy-eyed rangers, a transport, and uh . . . " He hesitated, glancing at Bette. "And a neighbor, unknown. Please advise."

Bette swallowed. Grit scoured the edges of her teeth and sounded like steel against concrete in her tender, throbbing head. Her left knee buckled but she caught herself, swaying as she did so.

"You hurt?" he asked.

"Uh, um, no," Bette stammered.

"You got a lot of blood on you," he remarked in a no-nonsense way.

Bette looked down and the edges of her vision darkened. She blinked, her thirsty eyes puckering as she tried to focus. Dark blooms of semidried blood stained her one-sleeved shirt. Lighter swipes of blood feathered her outer thighs while darker globs of blood speckled the inner thighs. That was not something she wanted to get into right here, right now, with this guy. He seemed helpful enough, and while he did not appear to be affiliated with the Department of Propagation, she remained cautious.

"What's your name?"

"Bette," she said hoarsely.

"Can you help me get them in the combine?" The man's face softened as he asked for help. He sheathed the machete in a strap across his back like the one Sol had.

"Uh, yeah." Bette nodded. "Of course."

"Let's get her first." He nodded to Sol.

He picked her up under her arms while Bette mustered all her remaining strength to lift Sol's legs. Approaching the combine, he said, "Now, this will be a little tricky. We got to go up before we can get in." Bette's legs wobbled under the exertion as she held the brunt of Sol's weight while the man tugged her in and arranged her in the back seat. Once Sol was in, they went back for Cyrus.

"Do me a favor," the man in the hat said. "Grab that shotgun and electrocutor thing. I can hoist this guy over my shoulder." Bette retrieved the weapons as she was asked. As she leaned down to get the Pulsor, Bette heard the man murmur to Cyrus, "Jesus, buddy, what did you get yourself into this time?"

Bette stood outside the combine while the man arranged Cyrus. The sun was beginning to set. Her legs felt as though they would crumple beneath her at any moment. He hopped down, thoughtfully considering Bette again.

"Did you say it was Bette?"

"Yeah."

"Well, okay, Bette, get in."

Bette let out the breath she'd been holding and exhaled a sigh of relief. She had been half-afraid he might leave her out there. He swiveled toward the cab door with his hand extended, and said, "After you."

Bette climbed into the combine and situated herself with Cyrus on one side and the man in the hat at the wheel. She leaned into the headrest and felt herself go limp on a weighty exhale in the scratchy cloth seat. Her shoulders sagged and a slight buzz began in her ears. She had to blink twice to stop seeing double. The cab smelled like boiled cabbage, and Bette brought her hand to her nose.

Once the man was situated and they began moving, he said, "I'm Mic."

"Thank you, Mic."

His lip poked out as he considered something. "What are you doing all the way out here?" Mic asked.

Bette tensed as a sliver of alarm shot through her.

Oh God, these are the people who were supposed to come, right? This man has to be from a farm. There wouldn't be anyone else, would there?

"Yeah, that's kind of what I thought," Mic said when Bette said nothing. He whistled low and to himself. "This is gonna be a good one, I reckon."

The combine rolled toward no discernible destination. As the adrenaline from earlier wore off, a pulsing discomfort seeped through Bette. Nausea bobbed just below the lump in her throat. Clammy perspiration formed a delicate sheen over her. She swallowed hard and fought to keep her eyes open. Deep and heavy fatigue yanked at her consciousness.

The combine began to slow. Bette turned her head fully to sweep the horizon with her limited sight. In the twilight, there was not much to see, just the dark line of the horizon miles and miles in front of them. The landscape was made of hard-packed earth and clumps of anemic ground cover. But, as Bette watched, the scene before her began to stretch ever so lightly. The horizon line became a shadow and then bled into smoky horizontal gradations. The area in front of the combine moved like silk and turned chatoyant. It was like the land and sky began to smear together in such a way the light itself didn't quite know how to behave.

Then, almost as if a switch had been flipped, the vista before them morphed. Vivid details bounced back from the hazy smear with startling clarity. The combine was approaching an establishment. As Bette watched the scene with her good eye, a small city materialized out of uninhabited air. The air, the earth, the wind all seemed to be working in concert to hide this place, then, as if on cue, they revealed their secret to Bette and Mic. *This is it. This has to be it. This is the farm.* Sol and Cyrus had said it was nearby, and here it was. All of a sudden they were driving on a dirt roadway, flanked on either side by a dozen low, one-story cement buildings. In between two of the buildings sat a few large dark machines, smaller than the one Bette currently occupied. Multiple planters, each of varying size and shape, were stationed around the doorways. Sprigs, fronds, and leaves fluttered hello as they passed. The windows of the structures were all dark except for the last one ahead on the right. Bette's weary eyes gravitated to it. Emotion welled up inside her as a beleaguered sigh of relief left her. *We are not going to die today.* Warm light spilled out in a tapered stream onto the road, beckoning them inside. In the light loomed three or four shadows, and one of them looked to be waving.

"How-how did you do that?" she whispered in amazement.

"How, indeed?" Mic winked.

The very last shred of her vigilance collapsed. The contracted muscles keeping her upright finally relented. Awareness softened and Bette's eyes closed, her chin slumping to her chest.

Mic slowed to a stop in front of a low, flat building where a few people in medical scrubs waited for him. The door of the combine opened and slammed shut as they maneuvered Sol and Cyrus out. Amid the din of chatter and medical jargon, one of them yelled, "Mic, what is the deal with this one?"

Bette heard the stranger yell, but it sounded far away, as if he was facing the other direction and talking to someone else. Some part of her felt obligated to respond, but she was too tired. She couldn't make her lips move, she couldn't get her voice to raise, she couldn't get her eyes to open. She felt some-one gently shake her shoulder.

"Miss? Miss? Are you okay?"

"Her name is Bette!" Mic's voice shouted above the noise.

I'm miscarrying. It was the only thought that came to mind. Sol had been right again. She was miscarrying and none of these people knew it. They were pulling on her arms, trying to move her. Bette couldn't understand why there was so much yelling.

"Bette? She isn't responding! Get Lyle!"

Bette heard Mic again, this time as he spoke gently to her. "Bette, honey, you got to stay awake, you hear me? You gotta talk to them, do you understand me?"

Okay.

Bette tried to answer him, but her tongue remained still. He sounded worried. She didn't want Mic to worry.

I owe it to him.

He'd saved her. He'd saved them all. Plus, he was magic. Hadn't he made this town appear? She would have to thank him just as soon as she didn't feel so tired.

74

She woke in a strange room with multiple beds. Cyrus and Sol were sleeping in two of the beds near her. She had to shift to her side to see them due to the lack of periphery from her left eye. It took Bette a moment to remember what had happened.

Right. The combine. Mic. The doctors.

That explained how she'd gotten here, but she wasn't clear where "here" actually was. Pushing herself up to a sitting position, she felt a tug on her arm. Bette glanced over to find an IV in her arm. Looking down, she noticed that her bloody, dirty pajamas were gone, replaced with a blue-and-white-striped hospital gown.

So, a hospital of some kind.

The beds were set perpendicular from the wall. Sol and Cyrus were in the beds to Bette's right. Cyrus's nose had been stitched up. She couldn't tell how Sol's leg was, as she was covered with a blanket. It was amazing the three of them had come out alive. She remembered the despair as she stood there and stared out at emptiness; she'd been sure they would die in the desert.

Better shuddered involuntarily. She remembered their grizzled faces, dirty matted hair; she could still see their bony rib cages poking under their taut, ashen skin. She could smell the stale piss cloud that followed them and she could hear their screeching. It felt like it originated from inside her bones and radiated out, as if they could feed off the marrow. If she never heard that sound again, it would be too soon. Haunting, primal, but so desperate all at the same time. And the blood. There had been so much blood. The ricochets from the bullets resounded in Bette's mind as she remembered Mic shooting every one of them in the head.

Bette exhaled and rested her head back on the pillow to stare at the ceiling. It wasn't the worst place to end up, especially after everything that had happened. Her mind drifted back to the night they'd broken out of the Center and then to the garage. There was the van filled with biobags. There was the hum of the Pulsor. Unconsciously, her hands went to her stomach. Bette felt tears well up at the edge of her eye. She closed them and felt a tear slide down her cheek. She wiped it away quickly, as if brushing it away would negate its existence.

A short and solid man dressed in greenish-blue scrubs entered the doorway on Bette's left. His hair was dark but his temples and beard were flecked with gray. "Hello," he greeted warmly. "I'm glad to see you are awake. I've got a few questions for you."

Bette bit her lip. He held up his hands as if in surrender.

"Nothing to worry about," he said, noticing her apprehension. "Just trying to get an idea of what happened. That's all. Now, your name is Bette, correct?"

"Yes," she responded hoarsely.

He pulled a metal chair from behind him and sat down beside her. "Mic told me that he picked you guys up after you were attacked by some Canners."

Bette nodded gravely.

"Okay, so, them I know." He swung his chin in Cyrus and Sol's direction. "Where did *you* come from?"

Bette paused as she remembered Sol's angry tirade in the car. She kept alluding to Cyrus's father and the ramifications of what they'd just done. Bette didn't know what she should say. Sol and Cyrus risked their lives to get her out of the Center. She would not inadvertently betray them now, while they lay unconscious and recuperating from fighting off a pack of Canners.

The man in scrubs waited.

"I'm not sure," Bette said.

"All right." Content to leave it at that, he moved on. "Well, you were covered in blood and unconscious when you got here, not to mention extremely dehydrated. So, we have you on fluids. We did a full body scan to make sure that you didn't have any internal hemorrhaging or broken bones." He paused as he contemplated her and weighed his words carefully. "It did look as if you had sustained a low-level electro-magnetic pulse. There was cell damage in nearly every inch of your body."

Bette swallowed and blinked, waiting.

"It caused that modified eye to fritz. And," he started cautiously, "there has been some intermittent bleeding."

Bette held her breath.

"Bette, honey"—he sounded concerned—"did you know you were pregnant?"

His voice grew softer as he said the last word. Bette stared at him and then past him. The walls were painted a flat white, taking on a gray cast from the cloudy diffused light coming through the skylights overhead.

Were. Past tense. Like a thing of the past.

Bette regarded the edge of her blanket and nodded hesitantly.

"I am really sorry." He placed a consoling hand on hers. He sounded like he really meant it. The tears welled up fresh in her eyes and rolled onto the blanket. She hung her head, unable to look at him. He had confirmed what she thought to be true. He shifted in his chair as he got up. Bette fully expected him to leave now that her interview was over. Failure, regret, and loss swept over her in successive waves.

But then he did something she could've never expected. He moved to the edge of her bed, leaned in, and hugged her. She stiffened more in surprise than defensiveness. He folded her tighter in his strong, stout arms and an audible sob caught in her throat. He was not going to hurt her. He did not scold her. He didn't express disappointment in her. Her skeleton felt like little hollow bird bones in this man's embrace; he did not let go, and Bette felt safe. A safety that she had not remembered since her grandmother had been alive. The kind of safety that let a person drop their caution and rest their alertness. A place of unconditional protection and care. When was the last time someone had looked at her as more than what they could get from her? The walls that had cobbled together to defend her over the years crumbled. She sobbed into this stranger's chest for what seemed like forever. She cried for how much she missed her grandmother. She cried for her mother. She cried for Roya, who should be there now. She cried for all those fetuses, ready for sale, hanging abandoned in the back of that van. She cried for what she had lost—her eye, her own attached embryo, her chance at fertility. God it hurt, it all hurt so much.

When the sobs died down, the doctor held Bette just a moment or two longer before letting go. As he released his hug, he patted her on the shoulder and smiled. "Let's talk about your friends here. If this were a contest, it would be a real toss-up to see who was the most beat-up out of the three of you." His segue was seamless and merciful.

He stood up and made his way between Cyrus and Bette.

"This guy, broken nose and a cracked cheekbone. Not to mention all the bruises. He was lucky, no organs ruptured. I couldn't find any other laceration to sew up, but man, is he going to ache for days."

He looked back to Bette.

"And you," he began with a look of disbelief on his face. "I can't even believe you stayed standing long enough to get here. It is amazing any of you are alive."

He then pivoted his gaze to Sol and his voice softened. "I guess if there had to be a winner, it would probably be her." He tossed a look at Bette over his shoulder and winked. "I mean, I'm not surprised. Heart of a goddamn lion, that one. But she has always been like that. Missed her femoral artery by millimeters. She will recover, but lord, she is going to be irritable in the process."

He shook his head; this man had known Sol for a long time.

Bette wiped her nose on the back of her hand. "Is this . . . is this place the farm?"

"La granja." The doctor nodded.

The farm.

"Whose farm is it?"

Laugh lines rippled around his eyes and mouth. "Now, that's funny," he said. "It's your farm, it's my farm, it's our farm. It's *the* farm."

Bette smiled but still didn't get it.

"Bette, I'm going to let you get some rest. If you need anything, just press this button." He pointed to a button on the line of the IV that was in her arm. "The nurses are monitoring you from the station. Okay?"

She nodded her understanding, leaning back into her pillow. The doctor left the room. Bette glanced back over to Cyrus and Sol. They could lay down their defenses; they were home.

75

Bette felt him before she saw him. She looked over to the door leading into the infirmary. All she saw at first was a glossy head of black curls and wide, curious eyes that came to the middle of the doorframe. His miniature fingers curled around the edge of the doorjamb as he tentatively peeked into the room. A sound from outside in the hallway made him look behind him. Quickly darting into the room, he pressed himself flat against the wall to the right of the door he'd just been lurking in. Two people walked by murmuring to each other, deep in conversation.

The child locked eyes with Bette, examining her and waiting to see if she would turn him in. Bette held his gaze, curious to see what he might do next. He broke the stare and craned his neck to make sure the hallway was clear. Satisfied that there was no danger, he tiptoed over to Cyrus's bedside. The small boy paused, his huge, warm eyes surveying the sleeping injured man. At his full height, he only came just above the infirmary cot Cyrus lay upon. The child hesitated as he reached out to touch Cyrus's shoulder. Then, emboldened, he gave Cyrus a little shake.

"Uncle Cyrus," he whispered, shuffling in closer. "Uncle Cyrus."

Cyrus gave no response. The little shoulders sagged and his arm fell to his side when the wounded man would not wake. He put his small hand on the back of Cyrus's hand.

His attention drifted to the cot next to Cyrus. The child patted his uncle's hand and flitted to Sol's bedside. Bette could not see his interaction with Sol since his back was to her, but after a few moments, the child darted back to the doorway, looked to his left and his right, and vanished out into the hallway.

It was a strange sight to see a small child scurrying through the infirmary unaccompanied. He seemed completely at ease on a solo mission.

Where had he come from?

His nose favored Roya's, like in the photo Cyrus had shown Bette. She was in his bright, giant eyes. And again, in the brave, determined resolve of his mission. Stealthily, he came in under the radar to gather his intel. Watching him play spy, Bette knew who the child was. But unlike his mother, he had made it out unscathed.

I just want to go home.

That was what Roya had said. It finally dawned on Bette that it wasn't a *place* she wanted to get back to. Bette had gotten it wrong. She'd stupidly assumed it was a location . . . But that wasn't it. A place didn't inspire her brand of tenacious ambition. A patch of dirt wasn't what gave Roya hope. You didn't volunteer your life for a point on a map.

She did it for him. She'd held on for him.

Bette's stomach dropped as if the floor had suddenly given way, and tears stung the edges of her eyes. Her son was home and all she wanted was to get back to him. Home was the people she'd loved, a way of life she'd been committed to. The only reason she ever left was to try and make it better for them.

The Department of Propagation knew how to make people follow the rules, but they did not know how to knit them together. Not like this. They would never be able to manufacture a bond like that. The Center knew how to engineer people; they had mastered the process to create a product, their own variant of fertile humans. But at what cost? This entire initiative to keep the species viable had changed it. Was it worth it in the end if the result was but a shadow of the species that used to be?

In the process of trying to keep humans on Earth, had they lost what it meant to be human? That energy that sparks the heart and causes blood to pump and cells to divide; could it be found in their industrialized assembly line? Could consciousness ever be synthesized with efficiencies and algorithms? Could souls really be created in petri dishes? Would something so nebulous ever stand to be measured or distilled? Maybe the purpose of real creation was the blood and the chaos and the pain.

76

The gray daylight filtered through the skylights. It was weird, natural lighting. Lighting had always been simulated for Bette, in her home, at the Center, everywhere. But here, these were real skylights, actual windows to the outside. Today was overcast just like yesterday and the day before. Bette couldn't tell if it was the diffused sunlight or the intermittent bleeding that made her feel puny and wanting to curl up and go back to sleep. Still in the infirmary, she stared at the ceiling and listened to Sol breathe while she slept. The cot next to her was empty. Cyrus must've been discharged sometime during the night.

The doctor came into the room, pushing a wheelchair.

"Oh good, you are awake," he said. "Darius has asked to meet with you."

"Darius?"

"He is kind of in charge around here."

"Oh," Bette said, arranging herself in the wheelchair.

The doctor wheeled her down the hall and into what resembled a cafeteria. The linoleum, while dated with its wide light-blue diamond design, had been well maintained. There were boards with handwritten menus and reminders on the faded cerulean walls: *Wash your hands. Check your rotation for kitchen duty. All food scraps HERE!* The yellowed tables were the kind that came with seats attached and folded in the middle. A dozen or so were stored by the door Bette had entered. Two tables were set up on the other side of the room where half a dozen people sat and faced a speaker whose back was to Bette. There were no windows, not even skylights. Recessed bulbs in the ceiling gave off cool fluorescent light. Everyone glanced over as the doctor pushed Bette into the room. The speaker stopped and turned his head. Cyrus's jaw stiffened when he saw Bette, indicating he was not at all pleased to see her.

The doctor left Bette just inside the entryway. Leaning in, he spoke softly to not interrupt the meeting. "Darius will be ready for you when he is finished here." He patted Bette on the shoulder and took his leave.

"I made a judgment call, sir," Cyrus continued resolutely. "This woman was a known asset to me and had been in the Center for months. She knew Roya. I believe she could be valuable to us."

From a seat in the middle of the long cafeteria table rose a mountain of a man. He had medium-length gray hair that looked as though it had been blown into place by the gods themselves. Dressed in khaki work clothes and boots, he looked like the janitor. The way he spoke, however, made it clear he was in charge.

"Cyrus," Darius rumbled, "you have endangered the entire community by bringing her here."

His bottomless slate eyes gave no hint as to what he was thinking. He continued. "You went off script, deviated from the mission, and exposed us. You blew up the genetics hub of the Department of Propagation and kidnapped a resident. You nearly got yourself and your cousin killed in a standoff with

Canners only mere miles from the farm, the place you swore to protect. Cyrus, you . . . you pulsed a pregnant woman." The unseen lines in his square face deepened with his grimace.

Cyrus looked down at the ground. Bette heard a shocked intake of breath from the members at the table. Cyrus's shoulders drooped at the weight of the charges piled on him.

He must not know about the transfer van.

"You have put me, this council, the whole farm, all Repatriates, in a terrible position. And this poor woman." Darius raised his hand in Bette's direction. "You have dragged her right into the middle of all of it. I can't in good conscience keep her here, but at the same time, I can't send her back undetected. She isn't safe here, but she won't be safe there. This woman has no home now."

The silence in the room was suffocating. Bette expected the Department of Propagation's Enforcement Unit to storm the doors and arrest them all.

"How long do you think we have before they retaliate?" Darius's foreboding voice boomed. It was a rhetorical question that made everyone in the room shift uneasily. Darius let out a heavy sigh.

"You can go, Cyrus," Darius said as he once again took his seat. "We are going to need to talk about this." Darius showed no emotion as he dismissed Cyrus, who brushed past Bette, his face stormy. Bette stood with somewhat of a wobble to speak to Cyrus.

"Bette," Darius said, noticing her movement, "would you please stay?" Bette's eyes widened, taken off guard that this man had specifically addressed her. Somewhat awestruck, she nodded and sat back down in her wheelchair. Darius looked around at the grim faces at his table.

"We need to implement the anti-raid measures. I want all security doubled. I want curfews in place. I do not want any unnecessary personnel out during the day. Reinforce the shields, secure the lenses, double-check their camouflage. I want everything that can be moved moved to the subbasements. Anything close to harvest, take it."

He leaned forward, taking care to make eye contact with the handful of people at the table. "I want to know where every single person is at every moment of the day. I want all our fertile men and women out of sight, along with all the children. No one leaves the farm. This is a lockdown, folks. Any questions?"

There were a few questions about things Bette didn't understand. Once they were answered, Darius concluded the meeting and the members vacated the room.

Bette nervously shifted in her chair. Only she and Darius remained in the room. "Come over here, Bette." Darius patted the top of the table.

She stood steadier this time and moved over to where he still sat. She seated herself opposite him, the tabletop between them.

Power radiated off this man like a force field, yet his face was clouded and his eyes were weary. The folds of skin between his eyes remained in a constant furrow. But there was something else to his eyes, something familiar to Bette. She noticed a curious intelligence the moment she sat down at the table, clear and comprehending.

Roya had his eyes.

This was Roya's father. Bette could see Roya in his concern, his calm demeanor, and the deliberate way in which he spoke. Bette could not hide from this man; his sharp unrelenting watch saw everything just like Roya's had. Bette could not lie to this man, for like Roya, he would know. She swallowed nervously.

"Bette, I want you to know that I have nothing against you, personally. You seem nice enough. This whole situation with Roya is a real point of contention between Cyrus and me." He folded his bear paws in front of him and gazed past Bette. Age flecked him like mica; with one turn of the head, he looked weathered, but with another, reflective and fresh. Now, his hard somber face was chiseled with misgiving. "I shouldn't have let him go, but at the same time, I knew he was the only one who would risk everything to bring her back."

Bette clasped and unclasped her hands in her lap in the hush of his contemplation.

"But this, you . . . I didn't think he would go this far. I've been around a long time. I've dealt with skirmishes from your government and I am familiar with its brand of backlash. And what my son did will have terrible repercussions." He shook his craggy head as he said it.

"You and I both know what the Department of Propagation is capable of."

Bette nodded.

"So, you understand the dilemma I have?"

"Yes, I do," Bette said.

"What would you do, if you were me?"

Bette looked down at the table acutely aware of the liability she was to these people. It would be selfish of her to ask to stay. What could she add to this community that could justify them using their precious resources on her? They had saved her life, and she couldn't ask them for more.

"I appreciate what you have done for me, but there is no reason for me to stay indefinitely. Take me to another city. I'll figure it out."

Darius rested his clefted chin on the heel of his hand, his mouth faintly turning up at the corners. "Tell me how she was in those last days. Don't tell me about how she died, just tell me about her."

Bette leaned back in her chair. Snippets of Roya's last gory moments flitted through Bette's mind. Then there was a break. What came together was a memory. Of the two of them cleaning the sponsor room. Of Roya, glancing at her and laughing. The chirpiness of her laughter, the endless depth of her brown eyes, the ease at which they became friends.

"It was like she knew me before we ever spoke. She saw everything, every piece. Then she was able to sum up all of the parts. I was drawn to her the first moment she winked at me. Which was *something* in that place, to wink, to laugh, to connect with another person. Even with what she was trying to do . . . even though it was daunting, she was determined but good natured. She had a fortitude of granite. Purposeful and graceful . . . "

Darius's eyes glistened. "It's good to hear that she was still Roya, even after all those years in that place."

He straightened as he folded his massive hands on the table in front of him. "It is no good, you know, this idea of dropping you in another city. They will find you if you try to live a conventional life. And if you grift, well, a Canner will get you. I know you mean well, but it is no good. Maybe Cyrus is right. Maybe you will prove valuable to us."

Bette tried not to squirm under his level stare.

"You are welcome to stay here, Bette," Darius said as he leaned forward, his eyes inescapable. "But know that they will come for you. We will do our best, but they will come."

DECEMBER 8, 2112 | RECEIVED BY THE DEPT.
OF JUSTICE

RE: HQ Breach/Missing Resident

The central genetic processing lab was badly damaged in the
breach at HQ. No new production can move forward for
at least the next six weeks as repairs are made and dishes are
re-cultured. A full accounting of the destruction is attached. It
is the opinion of this center that this was an act of terrorism.
We expect the Dept. of Justice to act accordingly. An attack of
this type and severity is unprecedented and only points to an
increasingly hostile enemy.

Upon a thorough search of the facility, it has been determined that one resident is missing after the HQ breach. The
resident was ten-and-a-half-weeks pregnant at the time of her
disappearance. We are requesting the Dept. of Justice's help
in recovering the resident. Attached, please find the resident's
information and last known GPS coordinates.

Appreciatively,
Dorothea Tyler
Director
Birthing Center HQ

ACKNOWLEDGEMENTS

Thank you, Inkshares. This is not a big operation, so it is a testament to them how many authors they support and how many books they publish. They do not hire hacks, which is both intimidating and reassuring. They made me a writer.

To my family, friends, friends of friends, and people I have never actually met during the crowd-funding portion of this process - Thank you. You gave me oxygen, exposure, momentum, and accountability. I hope you are proud of what we accomplished here. It would not have been possible without you.

Gaven Watkins - My god, did you ever think we would stop talking about this book? I hope you will forgive me for all the angst and insecurity and moronic things I've said. And that I stole your phrases and borrowed your likeness in order to write this. I think we both know I have always been a bit shameless.

Jessica Trow - My reader extraordinaire, thank you again and again and again. Whenever people say, "imagine your ideal reader" it is always you.

Sara Sikkelee-Bair - Everyone should have a friend this smart and supportive in their corner. I swear all my decisions got better after meeting her.

As an older sibling we are constantly admonished "to share," and it doesn't go away when you grow up. Because it is so much fun to see your name in print, for my sisters and brothers - Heather, Trystan, Jesse, Adam, Malachi, Marcus, Jacob, Becca, Lizzie, Isaac, Janae, Ethan, Jonah (you are missed), Christopher, and Micah.

To my Grandmas, Nettie, Betty, Shirley; my mother, Kim; and my stepmother, Anne - You have shown me that being a woman and a mother is part heartache and part grace. The ratio differs in each season of life. Sometimes we even get it right.

To Gordon Woods, who only knows how to work hard - Thank you for your example.

Ron McMillian - A pre-order friend who unfortunately passed before this was published. And to Janiece who loves and misses him.

Shout outs to - Joseph Wallace, Matt Bueltel, Martin Trow, Misty Woods, Melinda Guillemette, Misha Kazi, Hip Dad, Rylee Godwin, and Mande Horne.

Jonathan Godwin, "thank you" doesn't quite cut it. I guess I'll just have to spend the rest of my life making it up to you.

It is our connections and relationships that keep us human. We nurture and inspire each other. We brace and steady each other. We lend to and we help each other. We prod and we cajole each other. And when we are unsure, scared, or anxious, we hold, we hold up, and we hold on.

Gratefully,
Meghan Godwin

GRAND PATRONS

INKSHARES

INKSHARES is a reader-driven publisher and producer based in Oakland, California. Our books are selected not by a group of editors, but by readers worldwide.

While we've published books by established writers like *Big Fish* author Daniel Wallace and *Star Wars: Rogue One* scribe Gary Whitta, our aim remains surfacing and developing the new-author voices of tomorrow.

Previously unknown Inkshares authors have received starred reviews and been featured in *The New York Times*. Their books are on the front tables of Barnes & Noble and hundreds of independents nationwide, and many have been licensed by publishers in other major markets. They are also being adapted by Oscar-winning screenwriters at the biggest studios and networks.

Interested in making your own story a reality? Visit Inkshares.com to start your own project or find other great books.